"You're out of your mind, Carrera. Insane! I forbid it. You can't see her! I won't even hear of it. Not one word!"

Carrera, standing at ease in front of Parilla's desk merely said, "Explain it to the president, would you, Fernandez?"

Unlike Carrera, Fernandez couldn't stand. A bullet had shattered his spine years ago. He, instead, sat in what was probably the best wheelchair in the Republic. "Unfortunately, Mr. President," he said, "this is not just any girl. In the first place, as a spy she is a pearl beyond price. In the second, our main enemy, the Earthpigs' high admiral, seems to love her like a daughter. But in the third case . . ."

Parilla, now aged beyond his years with stress and worry, used one arm of his chair and the opposite hand on his desk to help himself to stand. But then the hand clutched at his chest. He began to sink to the tiled concrete floor.

Carrera almost knocked Fernandez over in his rush to support his political chief. "Medic!"

"They say he'll make it," Carrera told Fernandez shortly afterward. "But he's going to be out of commission for anywhere from about ten days to three weeks."

"Then," said Fernandez, "do we forge a paper in his name to appoint you dictator for six months, per the national constitution?"

"'If nominated I will not run. If elected I will not serve,'" Carrera quoted. "Trust me, here; I know my limitations. Anyway, if Raul is going to make it, let's not borrow trouble. Things will continue on for a bit without his hand at the tiller. On the other hand . . ."

"On the other hand," Fernandez continued, "you can now visit our mole. Even though we both know it's box of rocks stupid."

"Yeah; set it up, would you?"

"Sure. Now what do we do about rumors?"

"Rumors?" Carrera replied slyly. "We stoke them."

A PILLAR OF FIRE BY NIGHT

TOM KRATMAN

A PILLAR OF FIRE BY NIGHT

A Baen Books Original

Baen Publishing Enterprises
P.O. Box 1403
Riverdale, NY 10471
www.baen.com

ISBN: 978-1-9821-2426-7

Cover art by Kurt Miller
Maps by Randy Asplund

First printing, November 2018
First mass market printing, December 2019

Library of Congress Control Number: 2018032982

Distributed by Simon & Schuster
1230 Avenue of the Americas
New York, NY 10020

Printed in the United States of America

10 9 8 7 6 5 4 3 2 1

CONTENTS

DEDICATION

For Major (Retired) Donald B. Walton, 1956–2014, Lt Col (Retired) Walter E. Bjorneby, 1931–2016; Captain Dan Kostyshak, 1958–2012; Alfredo E. Figueredo, archeologist, teacher, writer, and poet, 1949–2013; SSG Mike Sayer, 1959–2016; MSG Ray Krivacka, 1939–2016, CSM Blagoe Paul, 1928–2015; and Kevin O'Brien, Special Forces, aka Weaponsman.com, 1958–2017. Damn it.

ACKNOWLEDGEMENTS

In no particular order:

Yoli and Toni who, in their different ways, put up with me, Steve Saintonge, TBR (the Kriegsmarine contingent of the bar), Ori Pomerantz, James Lane, Jack Withrow, Tom Wallis, Thomas Mandell, Krenn, Jasper Paulsen, Matt Pethybridge, Conrad Chu, John Becker, Patrick Horne, Sam Swindell, Tom Brophy, ARRSE (even if they don't know it), Bill Crenshaw, Andy and Fehrenbach at old Cambrai-Fritsch Kaserne, Dan Neely, T2M, Henrik Kiertzner, Greg Dougherty, Keith Glass, Leonid Panfil, Ernest Paxton, Chris Bagnall, Jean-louis Beaufils, Chadd Newman, Jeremy Levitt, Bruce Cook, Sheinkin, Jasper Paulson, Keith Wilds, Charles Krin, Mark Bjertnes, Alex Shishkin, Larry Fry, Robert Hofrichter, Ned Brickley, Joel Salomon, John Biltz, Seamus Curran, Tommie Williams, Emeye, DanielRH, Tom Lindell, Arun Prabhu, Jacob Tito, Nigel the Kiwi, Joseph Turner, Dan Kemp, Robespierre, Jon LaForce, John Prigent, Phillip "Doc" Wohlrab, Chris Nuttall, Brian Carbin, Joseph Capdepon II, Mike Watson, Michal Swierczek, Harry Russell, James Gemind, Mike May, Guy Wheelock, Paul Arnold, Andrew Stocker, Nomad the Turk, Paul 11, Geoff Withnell, Joe Bond, Rod Graves, Mike Sayer, Jeff Wilkes, Bob Allaband, John Jordan, Wade Harlow, Michele Chini, Jason Hobbs, Jim Curtis, Bob Oberlender, Darwin Concon, and by no means least, Justin Watson.

If I've forgotten anyone, chalk it up to premature senility.

Oh, and everybody else who buys my books? Yeah, I know it's been a while. The next one will be much quicker, and that will be it for the series. Thanks for your patience.

—Tom

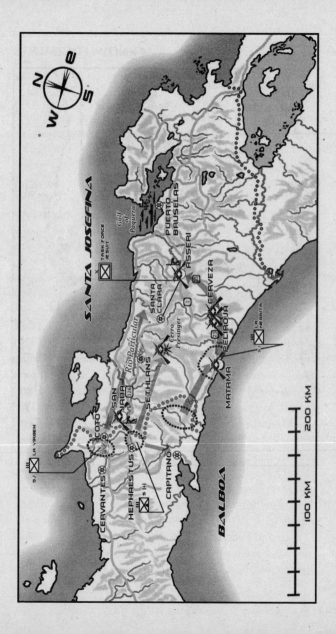

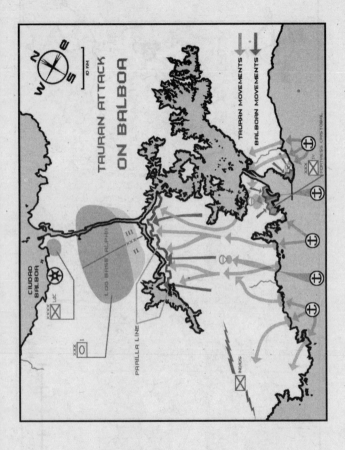

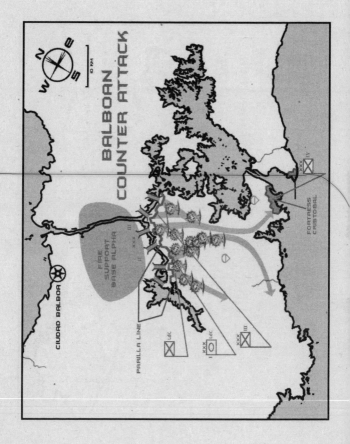

BALBOAN
COUNTER ATTACK

N
W E
S

10 KM

CIUDAD BALBOA

FIRE
SUPPORT
BASE ALPHA

FORTRESS
CRISTOBAL

PARILLA LINE

I adc.

I adc.

III

A PILLAR OF FIRE BY NIGHT

WHAT HAS GONE BEFORE

(5,000,000 BC through Anno Condita [AC] 476):

Long before the appearance of man, there came to Earth the aliens known to us only as the "Noahs." About them, as a species, nothing is known, least of all what they called themselves. Their existence is surmised by the project they left behind. Somewhat like the biblical Noah, these aliens transported from Earth to another planet samples of virtually every species existing in the time period approximately five hundred thousand to five million years ago. They also appear to have modified the surface of the planet to create a weather pattern and general ecology suitable to the life-forms they had brought there.

Having transported these species, and having left behind various other, genengineered species, apparently to inhibit the development of intelligent life on the new world, the Noahs disappeared, leaving no other trace beyond a few incomprehensible and inert artifacts, and possibly the rift through which they moved from the Earth to the new world. No other such rift has ever been found, suggesting, though not proving, that the Noahs can create and eliminate them at need.

It was through that rift that, in the year 2037 AD, a robotic interstellar probe, the *Cristobal Colon*, disappeared en route to Alpha Centauri. Three years later it returned, under automated guidance, through the same rift. The *Colon* brought with it wonderful news of another Earthlike planet, orbiting another star. (Note, here, that not only is the other star *not* Alpha Centauri, it's not so far been proved that it is even in the same galaxy, or universe for that matter, as ours.) Here, finally, was a relatively cheap means to colonize another planet.

The first colonization effort failed due to ethnic and religious strife. Thereafter, rather than risk further bloodshed by mixing colonies, the colonization effort would be run by regional supranationals such as NAFTA, the European Union, the Organization of African Unity, MERCOSUR, the Russian Empire and the Chinese Hegemony. Each of these groups were given colonization rights to specific areas on the new world, which was named—with a stunning lack of originality—"Terra Nova" or something in another tongue that meant the same thing. Most groups elected to establish national colonies within their respective mandates, some of them under United Nations' "guidance."

With the removal from Earth of substantial numbers of the most difficult and unprogressive people, the power and influence of supranational organizations such as the UN and EU increased dramatically. With the increase of supranational power, often enough expressed in corruption, more of Earth's more ethnocentric and traditionalist population volunteered to leave. Still others were deported forcibly. Within not much more than a century and a quarter, and much less in many cases, nations had ceased to have much meaning or importance on Earth. On the other hand, and over about the same time scale, nations had become pre-eminent on Terra Nova. Moreover, because of the way the surface of the new world had been created by the Noahs and divided by the supranationals, these nations tended to reflect—if only generally—the nations of Old Earth.

Warfare was endemic, beginning with the wars of liberation by many of the weaker colonies to throw off the yoke of Earth's United Nations.

Into this environment Patrick Hennessey was born, grew to manhood, and was a soldier for many years. Some years after leaving service, Hennessey's wife, Linda, a native of the Republic of Balboa, along with their three children, was killed in a massive terrorist attack on Hennessey's native land, the Federated States of Columbia, said attack having been aided by the United Earth Peace Fleet, or UEPF, in orbit over Terra Nova. The same attack likewise killed Hennessey's uncle, the head of his extended and rather wealthy family. As his dying testament, Uncle Bob changed his will to leave Hennessey with control over the entire corpus of his estate.

Half mad with grief, Hennessey, living in Balboa, ruthlessly provoked and then mercilessly gunned down six local supporters of the terrorists. One who survived being gut shot Hennessey pistol-whipped to death in retaliation, and with astonishingly bad judgment, the terrorist organization, the Salafi *Ikhwan*, attacked Balboa, killing hundreds of innocent civilians, including many children.

With Balboa now enraged, and money from his uncle's rather impressive estate, Hennessey built a small army within the Republic. For reasons of internal politics, Hennessey assumed his late wife's maiden name, Carrera. It was as Carrera that he became well-known to the world of Terra Nova.

Against some expectations, the *Legion del Cid* performed quite well as auxiliaries of the Federated States. Equally against expectations, its greatest battle in the campaign was against a Sumeri infantry brigade led by a first-rate officer, Adnan Sada, who not only fought well but stayed within the customs, rules, and laws of war.

Impressed with the Legion's performance (even while loathing the openly brutal ways it had of enforcing the laws of war), and needing foreign troops badly, the War Department of the Federated States offered Carrera a long-term employment contract. Carrera likewise offered to not only hire, but substantially increase, Sada's military force. Accepting the offer, and loyal to his salt, Sada revealed seven nuclear weapons to Carrera, three of which were functional and the rest restorable. These Carrera quietly had removed, telling no one except a very few, *very* close subordinates.

Insurgency blossomed across Sumer. In Carrera's area of responsibility, this insurgency, while bloody, was contained through the help of Sada's men and Carrera's ruthlessness. In the rest of the country it grew to nearly unmanageable levels. Eventually, Carrera's area of responsibility was changed and he was forced to undertake a difficult campaign against a city, Pumbadeta, held by the rebels. He surrounded and starved the city, letting none leave it until he was certain that every dog, cat, and rat had been eaten. Only then did he let the women and children out.

After the departure of the noncombatants, Carrera's Legion continued the blockade until the civilians within the town rebelled against the rebels. Having a rare change of heart, Carrera aided those rebels to liberate their town. Thereafter, nearly every insurgent found within Pumbadeta was executed, along with several members of the press sympathetic to the them. The few insurgents that he—temporarily—spared were sent to a surface ship for *rigorous* interrogation.

With the war in Sumer winding down, Carrera and his legions were—as it turned out, unwisely—let go. When the Federated states needed them again, Carrera exacted an exorbitant price before agreeing to commit to the war in Pashtia. That price being paid, however, and in gold, he didn't stint but waged a major—and typically ruthless—campaign to restore the situation, which had deteriorated badly under Tauran Union interference and faint support.

Ultimately, Carrera's intelligence service got wind of a major meeting taking place across the nearby border with Kashmir between the chief of the United Earth Peace Fleet and the emir of the terrorists, the Salafi *Ikhwan*. Carrera attacked, killing thousands, capturing hundreds, and seizing a dozen more nuclear weapons, intended gifts of the UEPF to their terrorist allies. One he used against the capital of the major terrorist-supporting state of Yithrab. When detonated, this weapon not only killed the entire clan of the chief of the Salafi *Ikhwan*, but also at *least* a million citizens of that city. In the process, he framed the Salafis for the detonation. This ended the anti-terrorist war . . . at least for the nonce.

Among the captures were High Admiral Robinson, of the United Earth Peace Fleet. His position was taken over by Marguerite Wallenstein, who had actually helped Carrera to remove her former chief from the playing board.

The price to Carrera was also heavy; he collapsed, physically, mentally, and emotionally, going into seclusion until persuaded back to active duty by Legate Jimenez and Sergeant Major McNamara. There followed a vicious no-holds-barred, and little-quarter given war with the quasi-sovereign drug cartels of Santander, along with an attempted *coup d'état* by the treacherous Legate Pigna. In the same coup, the rump of the old, oligarchic Balboan state was reabsorbed into the rest of the country, the oligarchs and their lackeys being driven from the country or killed. The Transitway, however, the canal linking the Shimmering Sea and Mar Furioso, remained in Tauran hands.

An easily winnable war against Balboa on the part of the Tauran Union was precisely what High Admiral Wallenstein wanted, on the not indefensible theory that such a war would serve as a catalyst to turn the Tauran Union into a real country and a great power, which would serve to stymie the other great powers of Terra Nova. That war came to pass, though not by the high admiral's doing and not to the result she wanted. Instead of defeating Balboa and changing its regime, the Tauran forces went for high-value targets that turned out to be bait for a countrywide ambush. When the smoke had cleared, thousands were dead, and almost twenty thousand Tauran troops were prisoners of the Balboans.

All was not obviously well for Balboa, however. In the course of the battle one of its double handful of stealthy coastal defense submarines managed to sink an aircraft carrier of the Navy of *Xing Zhong Guo*, New Middle Kingdom. This would have been fine, had the carrier actually been involved in the attack on Balboa. Unfortunately, it was not; it was evacuating Zhong non-combatants from the fighting. No one knew how many thousands of innocents—men, women, and children—burned or drowned in the attack. Interestingly, Carrera didn't appear to care about rising Zhong anger. One might almost have thought he wanted them to join a continued war.

Whatever he wanted, though, Carrera needed time. He'd been preparing Balboa for war for about a decade but, of necessity, many of those preparations were out of sight or not quite complete or both. He bought time for that completion by returning a trickle of TU prisoners.

There had to be a peace conference, of course, and so there was. Carrera and the President of Balboa, Raul Parilla, sent to the peace conference Carrera's second wife, Lourdes, with a small contingent. It was an unusual peace conference insofar as almost no one present had any particular interest in peace. Still, a false peace prevailed while the conference wore on. In that false peace, all the more desperately clutched for its very fragility, Carrera and his legions completed their final preparations. From all over the world, contingents of troops from allies and well-wishers large and small poured in to help defend Balboa. Next door, with the introduction of Tauran troops to defend a neighbor from Carrera, an insurgency sprang up, which insurgency Carrera fed. In the Tauran Union, the very lists of dead and captured were perverted and twisted to undermine the governments. Best of all was the thing Carrera had never anticipated or planned for— he acquired a spy well placed in the highest enemy camp. It was a very nice complement to a lesser, localized spy.

Conversely, Carrera's fleet, the *classis*, first engaged a Zhong submarine flotilla, then sailed under orders to Santa Josefina, to the east, and voluntarily interned itself. This gave a much-needed shot in the arm to both the morale and the various propaganda ministries of Carrera's and Balboa's enemies. Interned, the *classis* was able to catch up on quite a bit of deferred maintenance.

With Carrera's naval power thus disposed of, the Zhong made a forced landing against the island fortress dominating the northern terminus of the Balboa Transitway. It was a move as obvious as it was necessary; without the island, the Transitway could not be cleared; without the island, no landing near the capital, *Ciudad* Balboa, could be supported. Because it was so obvious, the defenses were immense. Between those and a few secrets, the Zhong were unable to do more than seize a part of the island, and that the most easily contained and least useful part. A substantial portion—some claimed a majority—of the Zhong fleet was sunk in the attempt. What remained, with the troops not committed to the island, bounced off but then effected a landing along the essentially undefended coast east of the capital.

Meanwhile, in the city of First Landing, in the Federated States of Columbia, before the World League, Carrera's wife, Lourdes, had thrown down the gauntlet to the Tauran Union and the United Earth Peace fleet, her speech ending with the words:

"Come on, then, you fat and lazy tyrants. Come on, then, you tools of terror and of a murderous alien whore. Come on you political harlots. Cowards. Filth. Swine. We, the free people of Balboa, are waiting for you, side by side with our faithful and gallant allies and under the just God who stands above us all, but who stands on our side, not yours!"

DRAMATIS PERSONAE

In order of appearance:

Patricio Carrera. Dux Bellorum, or Duque. Born Patrick Hennessey. Former officer in the Federated States Army, retired, moved to his late wife's—Linda Carrera de Hennessey's—native country of Balboa, raised an army to avenge the death of her and their children at the hands of Salafi terrorists. Currently commander, or Dux Bellorum, Legion del Cid, a former private military corporation, now the armed forces of the Timocratic Republic of Balboa

Juan Sais. Sergeant, Fourteenth *Cazador* Tercio, (Top Secret, Special Compartmentalized Information) Maniple. In charge of a small team tasked with arming a Volcano FAE following an enemy landing.

Virgil Rojas. Sergeant, Deep Recon Maniple, Fourteenth Cazador Tercio. Leads a small team of stay-behind scouts, in Cristobal Province, consisting of himself and *Cazadores* Domingo and Flores.

Xavier Jimenez. Senior legate commanding Fourth Corps, charged with the defense of Cristobal and the Shimmering Sea side, near it.

Sarita Asilos. Corporal, Headquarters, Fourth Corps. A rather beautiful junior non-com, a signaler, with a more than casual interest in Jimenez.

Jan Campbell. Major, intelligence officer from the Anglian Army, seconded to the Tauran Union Defense Agency. Female, highly decorated, and "more deadly than the male." Prior to her capture, Campbell authored a report, the Campbell Report, which advised, correctly, that the legion was dangerously tough and large. Ignored then, her star had risen, along with her rank, upon sudden and shocking discovery that her report was, if anything, conservative. Released, after capture, for reasons not entirely understood.

Jamey Soult. Warrant officer, Carrera's driver, confidant, and friend.

Bertrand Janier. Commander, Tauran Union Expeditionary Force, Balboa. Effective commander, Tauran Union Defense Agency. Former chief of staff, Tauran Union Combined Staff. Former commander, Tauran Union Security Force-Balboa. Janier was once rather overbearing and arrogant. Events have muted those defects, leaving a superior general officer in their wake. He has, though, in light of a couple of sharp and unpleasant lessons, become something like paranoid on all matters Balboan, Legionary, or Carrera-related.

Denis Malcoeur. Major. Aide de Camp to Janier.

Omar Fernandez. Legate in the Legion del Cid. Chief of Intelligence, which includes counterintelligence. Crippled and wheelchair bound by a would-be assassin's bullet. A widower, Fernandez's only child, a daughter, was killed in a terrorist attack. Utterly ruthless and utterly loyal to his country and its war chief.

Achmed al Mahamda. Warrant officer, Legion del Cid, Fernandez's chief interrogator. A Sumeri immigrant to Balboa.

Alfonso Ramirez. Tribune. A battery commander of a light, eighty-five-millimeter, artillery battery.

Avilar. Centurion. One of the better centurions of Ramirez's battery.

Werner Verboom. Sergeant. Thirteenth Company, Royal Haarlem *Commandotroepen*.

Van der Wege. Reluctant private, Thirteenth Company, Royal Haarlem *Commandotroepen*.

Nadja Felton. *Hauptmann* (captain), Sachsen *Luftstreitkräfte*. Pilot and recalled reservist, would just as soon be back in Sachsen with her husband and family.

Marguerite Wallenstein. High admiral of the United Earth Peace Fleet, a fleet of observation in orbit above the Planet of Terra Nova. She acquired her position largely through the actions and intervention of Patricio Carrera. The high admiral is of the Reformed Druidic Faith, repentant for her previous ("and they were many, oh, many") sins. Still, she has a duty to her home planet to keep the barbarians of Terra Nova from breaking into space and trashing her system of government, even though she detests that system. She has a plan for Terra Nova, too, though that has proven, to date, somewhat problematic of execution. Lover of Xingzhen, the Empress of Ming Zhong Guo

Xingzhen. Of indeterminate age but painfully beautiful. Empress of Xing Zhong Guo, or New Middle Kingdom. Real ruler of the Kingdom. Rather despises most men.

The Khans. Referred to as Khan, the husband, and Khan, the wife. They are members of Wallenstein's staff, highly valued, very capable. They have some rather odd views of marriage and sex, by Terra Novan lights, but are still quite within the mainstream culture of Old Earth,

Ricardo Cruz. Sergeant major, Second Cohort, Second Tercio. Highly decorated. Battle hardened. Rather young for his job, in years, anyway.

Francois D'Espérey. Major General, Gallic Army, Chief of Staff to Janier.

Wanyan Liang. Fleet admiral, Zhong Empire,

commanding the Zhong invasion force. Defeated in his bid to grab the Isla Real from Balboa, Wanyan has done the best thing remaining; he has succeeded in effecting a landing on the coast east of Balboa's capital.

Digna Miranda. Former restauranteur in Ciudad Balboa. Quite aged. Volunteered, along with two of her great-great granddaughters, to cook for Ramirez's battery.

Blue-eyed Rodriguez. A gunner in Ramirez's battery.

Khalid. Druze assassin and spy working for Fernandez, on assignment to the Tauran Union. Like Druze, generally, Khalid is loyal to his adopted homeland of Balboa. Pretends to be a Moslem, most of the time. Good friend of Ricardo Cruz and Rafael Montoya.

Anton Pavlov. Medically retired Volgan sergeant, formerly of the Twenty-second Tercio, now working for Fernandez in Volga.

Vera Dzhugashvili. Sergeant. Long Range Bombardment Group. Currently in Volga.

Esmeralda Miranda. Ensign, United Earth Peace Fleet. A former slave girl, slated for human sacrifice and cannibalism before being rescued from a slave pen by High Admiral Wallenstein. Now effectively Wallenstein's aide de camp and quasi-daughter. Also, a very distant Old Earth relative of, and dead ringer for, Carrera's late first wife, Linda.

Jesus Villalobos. Legate, commander, Tercio la Virgen, seconded to the Santa Josefinan Liberation Army.

Claudio Marciano. Tuscan general officer, retired but called back to duty as a compromise candidate to command the Tauran Union Security Force in Santa Josefina. Capable and cynical, he detests most things about demilitarized Santa Josefina and rather admires his official enemy, Balboa. Much loved by the soldiers of the multinational TUSF-SJ, his task is a forlorn one.

Ernesto Aguilar. Tribune, *Escuela de Cazadores*, seconded to Fernandez for a special project.

Martin Robinson. Former high admiral of the United Earth Peace Fleet, now prisoner, along with the Marchioness of Amnesty, of the legions.

Stefano del Collea. Operations officer, Task Force Jesuit.

Friedrich Rall. Executive officer, Task Force Jesuit.

Esteban Sanchez. Corporal, Second Cohort, Tercio la Virgen, serving as a guerilla in the Task Force Jesuit rear area.

Richard, Earl of Care. Captain of the UEPF *Spirit of Peace*. Foisted on Wallenstein as a sop to the ruling class of Old Earth. Fairly competent but advanced too young and knows it. In love with the ex-slave girl, Esmeralda. Much cared for by Wallenstein, because fundamentally decent despite the class that bore him and raised him.

Cass Aragon. Warrant officer, intelligence, assigned to Santa Josefina. Female, tall, slender, and light skinned, she blends in perfectly with the Santa Josefinan norm.

Rafael Montoya. Flight warrant officer, though former infantry. Marginal graduate of Cazador School, hence selected for flying rather than leadership. Fine, but very unlucky, pilot.

Alena Cano, AKA "Alena the Witch." First Pashtian of her tribe to recognize Hamilcar as Iskandr. Married into the Legion at a young age. Husband is Tribune David Cano. No one, least of all she, knows if she's a witch or just supremely insightful. Dedicated to her Iskandr.

Johannes Litten. Left-wing lawyer prosecuting, along with his firm, the legal action to persuade the Global Court of Justice to grant an injunction against Tauran Forces damaging the rain forest in both Santa Josefina and Balboa, as well as to order to release of guerillas being held by Task Force Jesuit. Believed in some circles to have been hired by Carrera or his staff judge advocate.

Ignacio Macera. Tribune, commanding an almost tercio-sized cohort of the *Tercio la Negrita*, waging a mostly guerilla campaign in southwestern Santa Josefina.

William Ruiz-Jones. Centurion, 94th Engineer Tercio. Inventor of the Diana, a form of camouflage for anti-personnel land mines.

Roderigo Fosa. Legate and admiral, commanding the *classis*, or fleet, of the legion, currently interned in Santa Josefina.

Alfredo Ramirez. Sergeant Major, BdL *Dos Lindas.* Brother of the artilleryman.

Antonio de Lagazpi. Legate, commanding, initially, Fifth Mountain Tercio, and then the Santa Josefina Liberation Army.

Moya, no first name, no last name, just "Moya." Indian corporal, doing piece work for the legions.

Pablo Carrasco. Legate, commanding Tenth Artillery Legion, "Terremoto."

Paul Cheatham. Sergeant and squad leader, Fifth Mountain Tercio.

Richard Halpence. Squadron commander, Royal Anglian Air Force. Seconded to Task Force Jesuit and, later, moved to Cienfuegos.

Marqueli Mendoza. Wife of Warrant Officer Jorge
   Mendoza. Ph.D. Author and philosopher in her own
   right, and, with her husband, one of the two main
   intellectual architects of the Timocratic Republic.
   Seconded to the propaganda ministry for some
   educational work in support of the war effort. The
   essence of pure feminine charm in a very compact
   package.

Juan Ordoñez. Tribune. Mosaic-D Fighter Pilot with
   Legion Jan Sobieski.

Conrad Chu. Captain (Warrant Officer), Coast Defense
   Submarine (SSK) *Megalodon*.

Achmed Qabaash. Sumeri, brigadier, Army of Sumer.
   Legate, Pro Tem, Legion del Cid. Qabaash commands
   a brigade in the Presidential Guard of the Republic
   of Sumer, which brigade, sent to help Sumer's ally,
   Balboa, was appointed Forty-third Tercio, Legion del
   Cid. Most Balboans who know him would agree,
   "Qabaash . . . mean motherfucker . . . glad he's on
   our side."

Aaron Brown, AKA "Sancho Panzer." Legate.
   Formerly of the Federated States Army, Sancho
   commands the Legion's heavy corps, First Corps.

Alexander Constantinescu. Dacian senior non-com.
   POW camp guard force.

CHAPTER ONE

The blood-dimmed tide is loosed, and everywhere
The ceremony of innocence is drowned.
The best lack all conviction, while the worst
Are full of passionate intensity.
　　　　　　　—W.B. Yeats, *The Second Coming*

Near the Trans Balboa Highway Bridge, *Rio* Gamboa, North of the "Parilla Line," Balboa

From near silence the air was suddenly filled with the rising sound of sirens. At the sound Carrera's heart leapt into his throat. *Being emulsified by a Tauran bomber that doesn't even know I'm here is not my preferred way to go out.*

He forced himself to remain calm, then began following the signs to the nearest bomb shelter. That was also from where the sound of the nearest sirens emanated. This was a bunker in what the president, Raul Parilla, refused to hear referred to as anything but the "Gamboa Line," but which everyone out of earshot called the "Parilla Line," anyway.

I wish, he thought, *we'd come up with some method to*

modulate the sirens to give some idea of how far out the attacks were. I wish we'd even thought of it. Or . . . then again . . . maybe not. There are only so many secrets that can be kept. Our having the ability might have gotten out. That might have started people wondering why it might matter to us. And that . . . no, let's not even go there.

Since his return from the *Isla Real*—a return in every way less eventful than the near fatal trip out—Carrera had come under aerial attack; *Let me think . . . must be thirty-five or forty times.* For the most part, the bombing had shifted from the city and the island fortress out in the *Mar Furioso*, to the area in and around, especially to the north of, Cristobal. It didn't take a genius to understand that that was the Taurans' logical point of attack. It would have been obvious enough even without the bombing. The logistic needs of a modern army, on the planet of Terra Nova, *demanded* a major port. Cristobal, on the Shimmering Sea, was the only one available of any size, and the only one that was also connected to the road and rail net.

Walking the well-worn trail to the bunker, Carrera half raised one hand. Looking down at it, he noticed once again a slight tremor of the hand and of the fingers that ran from it. *That wasn't there six months ago. And if I'm doing that, what of the troops that have endured twice as much and don't have the benefit of even knowing why they have to endure it?*

He clenched the hand, opened it, clenched it, and opened it again. By the second opening the tremor had gone. Whether that was a physical thing or the result of the routine, he didn't know.

Just imagine if we hadn't taught the Taurans a sharp

lesson about "air supremacy" and the value of a high tech-low tech mix, coupled with unusual ruthlessness and an aviation branch that thought of itself more as flying infantry than as ever so precious knights of the air. Just imagine being under attack—oh, sure, a less intense level of attack—more or less continuously, rather than two or three or four times a day.

We'd all be trembling wrecks that no amount of routine or exercise would fix.

Course, buying us those breaks was hard on the Legion Jan Sobieski.

"Jan Sobieski," the Sixteenth Legion, was the air force for Balboa, and completely subordinate to the ground forces.

At the end of the trail, at the entrance to a concrete bunker, a noncom of the Legion, an elderly corporal, stood directing troops to seats along benches or on the floor. There was a semicircular concrete overhang sheltering the entrance.

Between the overhang and the deep jungle shade, the corporal didn't at first recognize Carrera. Putting a hand on his chief's shoulder, the corporal said, "Keep calm. Take a seat along the right-side bench."

Carrera removed the hand gently and said, "Any place will do, Corporal. As a matter of fact, let's make sure we get everyone else seated before we join them."

At seeing Carrera, his country's *Dux Bellorum*, the corporal stiffened.

"And relax," Carrera chided. "I can see you're doing a fine job. But it wouldn't do for the men to see either of us act nervous now, would it?"

"No, sir," agreed the corporal. "But you being out here still makes me distinctly nervous."

"I can go look for another bunker," offered Carrera. "I don't know if . . ."

As it turned out, there wouldn't be time for that. The first Tauran bombs landed—*Quarter tonners, would be my guess*, thought the corporal, gulping nervously—at about the same time Carrera reached, "if."

"Don't think that will be necessary, sir," said the corporal. His voice cracked once from nerves as he said it. "Don't think it would be . . . shit!"

The near burst—well, "near" for a five hundred and fifty pounder—sent a shockwave-borne blizzard of leaves and twigs and dirt to pelt both men, even as the concussion induced a nauseating rippling in their internal organs.

"In, in, get inside!" shouted the corporal.

Always do what the man who seems to know what he's doing says, agreed Carrera, silently, holding down his bile. He grabbed the older man and sprinted the few feet to the inside, half pulling the corporal after him. Once almost surrounded by the concrete the corporal turned back and looked out in both directions. Seeing no one, he slammed shut a heavy steel door, such as one might find on a major warship, then began turning the steel wheel that locked the door in place.

Which is precisely where that one came from, mused Carrera, *though I can't say which of the Volgan cruisers we scrapped provided it.*

Turning back to the inside of the crowded bunker, the corporal announced, "Everybody get your canteen cups out. My tercio's policy is to issue an extra rum ration with each bombing. So we do. Now me, I think we're all well on the way to becoming alcoholic, but what the fuck do I know?"

Note to self, thought Carrera, as he reached behind to pull out his canteen and cup, *find out whose idea that really is, the corporal's or his tercio commander, or someone in between, and commend them . . . maybe . . . because note to self number two for the day; we're getting the shit bombed out of us; figure out where the hell all that rum's coming from.*

Not too long after that point Carrera noticed something odd. Rather, he noticed two linked oddities. The sirens were still going. And he could still feel the bombs dropping.

One of the downsides, Carrera thought, *to setting things up so that the enemy has to use pricey and rare precision-guided bombs if he's going to bomb one particular area, is that he's going to bomb other areas a lot harder, since he can. Oh, well.*

Some distance to the north of Carrera's temporary shelter, a group of construction engineers came out of their own shelter and, almost as a single man, cursed the enemy roundly.

In their view, a substantial bridge over the Gamboa River sagged at one end. "Motherfuckers," said a corporal. "We just got that son of a bitch fixed, too."

"Then we'll get to fix it again," announced the centurion in command of the detail. "Get your tools and the trucks and let's get to it."

"What I don't understand, Centurion," said the

corporal, "is why we even bother. I mean, it's not like we actually need these bridges, considering . . ."

"Shut the fuck up right now," said the centurion. "What we need and don't need isn't your concern." He raised his voice quite a bit, adding for the entire platoon's benefit, "and the next man I see pretending to be walking on water, on his feet or on his hands, I'll shoot him on the spot."

Volcano Number Nine,
south of the Parilla Line, Balboa

Number Nine was located in a recently abandoned legion housing area, not far from where the twin highways connecting the capital and the port of Cristobal crossed. No one but Carrera really knew if the housing area had been built to hide the Volcano, or the Volcano had been placed there to take advantage of the fact that a housing area was being built.

If Carrera and the corporal were nervous under the bombing, that was as nothing compared to the crew of the Volcanos.

The Volcanos? Think of a—well, "large" is hardly an adequate description so—think of a *ginormous* fuel air explosive bomb, hidden, often under fairly recent construction though sometimes buried just out in the jungle near a suitable access road, big and powerful enough to be a fair equal to a very small nuke. Indeed, they were more powerful than some nuclear weapons and had the additional benefit that, where a volcano went off, there would be no free oxygen in the area for a significant period of time.

The basic shells had been laid long since, years since in some cases. This was starter explosive, an oxygen booster, incendiaries, and some additives. The rest of the mixture, the fuel, had only recently been added, by tankers, during the lull that accompanied the now ever-so-*obviously* failed peace talks. Thus, even though each crew for a Volcano had a decent shelter, once the tank of their Volcano was filled, survival of a premature detonation was *most* unlikely.

That said, a premature detonation was, itself, just as unlikely. The things had been designed for considerable stability. They had two mechanisms for detonation, radio command—which nobody expected to work, really—and seismic. The former took a special code and an extant antenna while the latter took the kind of shaking that only a near miss from a large bomb or shell could provide. Even then, there was a timer that had to be set and had to run to allow either to work, and, at that, only at certain times after it ran. They were intended to be emplaced, and then set to arm themselves at a later time or times, and to be detonated on command when expedient.

"None of which," muttered Sergeant Juan Sais, himself from a maniple of the Fourteenth *Cazador Tercio* sufficiently secret that even its number was secret, "cheers me up in the slightest. If this thing goes . . ."

A nearby private fed a small morsel from his rations to a trixie, an archaeopteryx, that had adopted the team, or at least its food, over the past several weeks. Nobody minded having trixies about; they helped keep down the population of the never sufficiently to be damned antaniae, the septic-mouthed moonbats, that infested the planet.

The trixie was actually rather a beautiful creature. This

one, a juvenile, most likely, was brightly feathered, and maybe two and a half feet long, including tail feathers. It had probably been a semi-domesticated mascot for the housing area, before its abandonment.

"What was that, Sergeant?" asked the private of Sais. With his boss, the boy sheltered in the earth-covered bunker.

"Nothing, Espinal," said Sais. "Just cursing the enemy."

"Curse them for me then, too, Sergeant." He opened his can of chorley tortillas fully, and showed it to the Trixie, which squawked its disappointment. "See, told you, birdie; that there was only so much."

Indignant, the Trixie took off for a higher and safer plane.

Sais did curse the enemy, then, which didn't seem much to bother a low flying Tauran fighter bomber as it laid a carpet of bomblets all across the area, driving the team deeper into their earthen hole.

That's one good thing, thought Sais, raising his head and brushing dirt from his hair, after the storm of steel had passed. *If they had clue one about what we were, it wouldn't be useless bomblets they were dropping, but heavier ordnance to shake up, wreck, or prematurely detonate the Volcano. Thank God for small favors.*

Hide Position Sierra Two-Nine, Cristobal Province, Balboa

The Fourteenth *Cazadors* was actually a rather diverse *tercio*. Besides the men for the Volcanos, a limited number of what might be called "shock troops," foreign internal defense teams, a hostage rescue maniple, maniples for deep recon, strategic recon, nation building, and this and that and whatnot, it also included some small numbers, no more than a couple of hundred, of stay-behind reconnaissance troops.

Some of the latter were on islands out in the *Mar Furioso*. Still others monitored the expanding lodgment of the Zhong, after their mostly failed attempt at capturing the *Isla Real*. There were also a few teams along the coast of the Shimmering Sea, just in case.

The majority of the stay-behinds, though, were in Cristobal Province, north of the city of Cristobal, and well south of the Parilla Line. They were emplaced in hides both carefully and cleverly designed, but also put in places that no one in their right minds would want to be stationed or to station troops.

Cleverly? There were subtle sumps dug that were fed by the thinnest excavations practical, to provide water and flush away waste. This wasn't that hard in a place with over twenty feet of rain a year, one where even the dry season could be pretty wet. There were pipes that led down to substantial bodies of water, usually stinking swamp water, so that the wastes would not be noticed. Sound and seismic proofing framed the shelters, even as the radar scattering metalicized strips in the trees above could be expected to foil ground-penetrating radar. Food was stored in both the main shelters and various caches. Cooking by flame was right out, but they each had a small, fuel-cell-powered cooking unit, expected to be sufficient to heat one meal every other day for . . . well, for long enough, if they didn't overdo it on the light that also ran from the fuel cell. Air was let in via a bamboo pipe system, with a pump that ran off the fuel cell, as well. There was also a backup hand pump, but nobody wanted to depend on that. Carbon dioxide was, somewhat like the waste, removed by gravity, though spread out, where possible.

Carefully? Some hides were sited in the middle of dense clumps of the black palm the Noahs had so negligently or maliciously transferred from old Earth, for example. Others sat in excavations near swamps with the entrances under water. One was up in a hollowed-out crevice in the jungle-shrouded face of a seemingly unscalable cliff. Indeed, of the twenty-two three- and four-man teams scattered about the area, not so much as one team was anyplace where they might have been expected to gather any information more important than the number of mosquito bites on Sergeant So-and-So's posterior or the number of lice on the carrier pigeons they kept in cages.

"And that's the beauty of it, boys," said Sergeant So and So, more commonly known as Sergeant Virgil Rojas. "Here we don't get bombed. Here, when the enemy comes, we don't—well, we probably don't—get hunted for."

"I still don't see the point of it, Sergeant," said *Cazador* Domingo, who was, any way you looked at it, too big to be a comfortable fit in the cramped bunker and practically had to be hauled out the entrance bodily, even when the hinged tree stump covering the entrance was tilted out of the way.

"Well," said the sergeant, "try this, Domingo. As long

as the enemy is not here, which higher will know as long as we keep sending in reports when asked for, then they must be somewhere else. Isn't that clear?"

"No, Sergeant. Sorry, Sergeant."

"Then try this: Knowing where he isn't gives a very good idea of where he probably is."

Domingo glanced around the walls of the hide. His gaze seemed to go past them to the miserable and inhospitable swamp outside. "We don't need to be here, Sergeant, to know nobody else is stupid enough to be here."

"Point," agreed Rojas, with a shrug. "Still, you never know."

"Okay," said Domingo. "Do you mind if I go topside for a bit while I can?"

"Nah," Rojas shrugged, "go ahead. One of us, even one of us your size, isn't suspicious enough to compromise the position, provided we don't go up too much. There's too many other people doing too much other stuff in places a lot more important. Go on; we'll be stuck in here almost all the time soon enough."

As Domingo slithered out the narrow passage to the tilting tree, the third man of the team, *Cazador* Flores, breathed a sigh of relief. Domingo simply took up too much space.

Rojas feigned to ignore that, and looked over the stacks of packaged rations for the hundredth time. The hide held enough for three men for right at sixty-six days, which is to say, a pile about four feet, by five feet, by four, containing six hundred meals, or between thirteen and fourteen of each of the Legion's forty-five menus. Legion rations tended to be bulkier and heavier, both, than rations from places like the Tauran Union and the Federated States. On the other hand, they contained cigarettes and rum, both canned, which had made them highly prized trade goods wherever the legions had deployed with allies. They also tended to be calorically pretty dense, even beyond the rum. The sixty-six days of rations would probably do for twice that time, given the sedentary life they were facing for the nonce.

"Unless, of course, the supply rats fucked us," murmured Rojas, "in which case we'll be ready to kill each other out of . . ."

He stopped the murmuring as Domingo, scrambling like a frightened rat, emerged from the tunnel. The *Cazador* slithered onto the floor then lay still for several moments, panting with exertion or with something else. After he flipped over on his back, Rojas could see that Domingo had gone unusually pale, even by the dim artificial light in the shelter.

"Listen!" insisted the *Cazador*.

"Wha . . . ?"

"*Listen*, Sergeant!"

Rojas made a motion at the other man in the hide, Flores, for him to be quiet, to shush. Then he listened carefully for several long moments.

"What is it?"

"Helicopters," answered Domingo. "Not ours. Not our type. Troop carriers. Big ones. Little ones. Gunships. They're *everywhere*."

"The invasion's on," said Rojas, heart sinking. "We knew they were in range, but . . . I'd hoped . . . oh, well."

IV Corps Headquarters, Magdalena, Cristobal Province, Balboa

The bombing-induced pall of smoke hanging over the area did nothing to disguise the invasion coming in to hem it in on three sides. Though the Taurans made a fair effort to disguise their intent with a mix of false directions on the part of their helicopter streams, false insertions to the east, west, and north, and liberal blasting of likely spots for observation posts, it just wasn't that big an area, hence just couldn't provide all that much in the way of options. The only real question had been, "Will they try to seize it directly, by a *coup de main*, or surround it for a more formal siege?"

There was never really a chance of the former, thought Legate Xavier Jimenez, watching for glimpses of the naval aerial assault from the safety of a small bunker outside his concrete headquarters, itself under a fairly new apartment building in the old gringo town of Magdalena. *More's the pity; I could have beaten that handily.*

From the town itself, as well as from the city of Cristobal and all the other towns in the area, most civilians had been evacuated to the refugee area on the *Mar Furioso* side. That refugee area had fallen under Zhong occupation. Jimenez had reports of a vicious guerilla war that had broken out all over that part of the country, as well as east and west of it, the guerilla movement being fueled by Carrera's *Tercio Amazona*, reinforced by a slice of the *Cazadors* and a sprinkling of retired legionaries, along with a few contract specialists in guerilla warfare, and the heavily reinforced Fifth Mountain *Tercio,* all under the broad direction of Sixth Corps, which was mainly composed of citizens of the Republic.

Legate Xavier Jimenez had long since given up the immense Cristobal brownstone that had served as his corps' headquarters since formation. This was just as well, since the brownstone was a ruin, and anyone who had been caught inside it during the bombings was either dead or wounded or, at best, twitching badly. He didn't even know how many Tauran bombs had hit the place; there had been that many.

The bunker holding Jimenez and his key staff had been put into the basement of the apartment complex, outside the city, built as part of a Legion program, about seven years before. The intent had from the beginning been less about providing housing and more about hiding the contingency headquarters.

There was an alternate staff of about equal size in another location, under Jimenez's executive officer. They did routine work to keep things functioning but could take over command if the main command post were destroyed or cut off.

Almost none of the fortifications in and near Cristobal matched or even came close to matching those built on the *Isla Real*. In the city, itself, the water table was just too high. Instead of bunkers and trenches, most positions in the town were sangars erected inside the ground floors of buildings. Tunneling, except from building to building, was right out, though some prefabricated steel arches, made to fit together, connected certain positions. These, too, where possible, were sheltered under pre-existing construction.

Outside the town the fortifications were better; bunkers, shelters, trenches, and a fairly complex obstacle system. There were even a couple of strongpoints built on key terrain, plus a number of very strong positions inherited from the Federated States, both in the town and flanking it. Some of the latter, however, had already been blasted pretty badly on the surface, though their underground components still served as excellent shelters for headquarters, medical facilities, and supply.

A flurry of shockwaves assaulted Jimenez, as he stood half covered, watching the busy air. *They've got their artillery in, I see, or, at least, some of it. I mark those as One-fifty-fives. Ouch. Still, no big surprise there, except how quickly the Taurans can move when they decide to take something seriously. Interesting, though, that they're putting their guns in out of range of most of the things I have to hit them with, my 160mm mortars. And my relatively few guns and rocket launchers I cannot yet risk.*

With a thin smile, Jimenez thought, *I suppose we should be flattered they've decided to take us seriously.*

A new sound entered the battle space and Jimenez's consciousness. *Multi-engined propeller-driven transports . . . and there they are.*

To the northeast of where he stood, the legate caught sight of a stream of lumbering, fat-bellied aircraft, from the foremost of which poured a stream of parachutists. They jumped frightfully low.

Ballsy fucks, the Sachsens, thought Jimenez. *Got to be them, at least in the main, since the Gauls' para brigade died at Herrera International and the Anglians were smashed at Lago Sombrero. The Sachsens are the only major country in the Tauran Union that still has an airborne capability of any size. Yeah . . . got to be them, maybe with some augmentations from lesser states.*

Also, an interesting way to reinforce quickly, provided the drop zone is secure. I suppose security was Job One for the people who came in by helicopter.

A uniformed radio-telephone operator, an intensely beautiful and very young black female corporal named Asilos, from Cristobal, emerged from the bunker, carrying a field phone in one hand, and the phone's handset in the other. The phone trailed a wire across the concrete floor.

"Sir," she said, interrupting Jimenez's thoughts even as she proffered the phone. "Sir, Ninth Legion is asking for permission to retire on the city and assume their defensive positions. Their commander says it's now or never, at least for his more exposed units."

"Thanks, Sarita," answered Jimenez, taking the phone. The legions tended to informality, after all, and if there was any senior officer Carrera trusted not to be screwing the female staff, nor showing favoritism, it was certainly Jimenez.

"Jimenez," said the legate into the phone. ". . . no, not yet . . . you can fight to keep the lines of withdrawal open . . . yes, I am fully aware that means blood . . . yes, I know you don't want to waste the lives of your boys and girls on a losing endeavor . . . tough shit, Legate; we can't let them just walk in and take over. Fight, damn you!"

CHAPTER TWO

"I just want you to feel you're doing well. I hate
for people to die embarrassed."
— Fezzik in *The Princess Bride*

**Tauran Defense Agency Headquarters,
Lumiere, Gaul, Terra Nova**

To be striking back, finally, was the sovereign cure for
most of the humiliations inflicted by upstart Balboa on
Tauran arms, over the last several months. The men and
women of the headquarters, once utterly downcast and
demoralized, walked now with a spring in their step, their
chins high, and something of a pirate's gleam in their eyes.

This was a new building for the headquarters or, rather,
an old one repurposed. The foundations were thick, the
walls essentially soundproof. A former palace, the building
had stood abandoned but for a guard for thirty years
before being repurposed as a replacement for the old
TDA headquarters, burned to the ground by a Balboan
aerial attack using a large, but stealthy, drone carrying a
"five-minute bomb."

While some good people had been killed in that attack, it was generally agreed among the survivors that those deaths in no way harmed the cause quite so much as the death of the former agency chief, Lady Elisabeth Ashworth, had helped it.

General Janier pretty much summed up the sentiment of nearly everyone concerned who wore a uniform: "Good riddance to the ignorant bitch."

Still, the sentiment wasn't entirely universal. There were those who missed Lady Ashworth. Among these was a certain Anglian Royal Signals officer, a major by the name of Jonathan Houston.

It was dark outside, but everyone still was working with something like joy. Overhead, in distant space, the Smilodon stalked the Leaping Maiden, as the Beer Glass Galaxy poured from the Tap.

Far below those constellations, and below the first floor of the headquarters, Jan Campbell also stalked. Her prey was not a maiden, though it was not impossible that Major Houston was a virgin.

Short, blonde, shapely to the point of extravagance, and more than a tad pretty, Jan wore mufti, and only mufti, around the headquarters. This served primarily to disguise her rank in a headquarters where majors counted as "mere." Given her easy and immediate access to the military head of the Tauran Defense Agency, the Gallic general Bertrand Janier, it was widely assumed she was quite a bit senior to that, and civil rather than military. This wasn't in the least hurt by her having been a late-entry officer, hence rather older than the norm for a major.

But, major or sergeant major or colonel or well-connected bureaucrat, everyone simply assumed clout. This, too, wasn't in the least hurt by the fact that she acted like she had clout, possibly even beyond the not insubstantial clout she did pack.

That clout *was* real, deriving partially from direct access to Janier and partly by direct access to Lieutenant General (Retired) Sidney Stuart-Mansfield, the head of Anglian Intelligence, which organization was also known as "Pimlico Hex." That clout had enabled her to do three key things.

The first of these was to set up a sacrificial intelligence organization composed of nine hangers-on to the exiled Balboan, Belisario Endara-Rocaberti. These had taken a short course run by the Anglian intelligence apparatus, and were then reintroduced into their homeland, Balboa, to try to reconnect with certain intelligence assets with whom communications had been lost as a result of the previous Tauran defeat and expulsion from the country. Of those, three were still at large, to no one's surprise more than Jan's. And one of those had even managed to establish contact with a former asset, a machinist in the arms works at Arraijan, in Balboa, who wondered why no use had been made of an earlier report he'd submitted.

If this first organization had produced nothing except a flurry of activity and a lot of smug satisfaction on the part of Balboa's chief of intelligence, Omar Fernandez, that would have suited Jan well enough. After all, its primary purpose was to provide cover for the second organization.

That second organization was smaller and considerably

more elite, for certain values of "elite," and was certainly
not intended to be sacrificed. It consisted of three assets,
with Jan serving as handler, personally, aided by a close-
mouthed secretary, a cryptologist, and a communications
specialist.

This first of these was a diplomat from La Plata,
assigned to their embassy in Balboa, and in dread fear that
the Balboan revolution would come to his country and
displace his class. Young *Señor* Avellaneda, handsome,
with his Anglian education, posh accent, and ten thousand
Tauro suits, had gone home to La Plata for consultations
and promptly offered his services via the Anglian embassy
there. That his country had sent a brigade of marines—
now enrolled in the Legion as the Thirty-ninth *Tercio*, and
serving in Jiménez's corps—made his offer something
very like treason. This would have set Jan's suspicion
circuits to tingling madly if she hadn't known that, in La
Plata, treason to fatherland was far less of a crime than
treason to class. And that was true of *all* classes there.

Sadly, Avellaneda had yet to produce anything of real
value.

The second operative, a Volgan, Jan trusted more
readily. He, a newsman, was assigned by his bureau to
cover the Twenty-second *Tercio*. This unit had begun life
as the Tsarist-Marxist 351st Guards Airborne Regiment,
before signing on, en masse, with Carrera. The regiment,
the *tercio*, was mostly Balboan, now, but still retained the
traditions and customs that it had brought with it to
Balboa. There was also, among the old hands, some
emotional connection to the Volgan Republic.

Jan trusted the newsman, not least because she

understood and trusted his motivations. Pyotr Simonov simply wanted money.

"Ideologues and idealists," she had said to her secretary, in French, "cannot be trusted. Trust money. Trust greed." While Jan's English always carried an accent, light or heavy depending on many factors, her French, courtesy of the Anglian Army, was about as good as that of the crown prince of Anglia.

That trust in Simonov had been well-placed, since the Volgan, before departing his homeland for Balboa, had managed to acquire quite a bit of information on some of what the Volgans had supplied to Carrera, and just how much of an interest Carrera held in certain Volgan defense companies.

"Holy shit!" had pretty well summed up Jan's thoughts on that.

The third active member of her elite, non-sacrificial organization, however, had proven the most disappointing. Sister Mary Magdalene, of the international pacifist organization, Pax Vobiscum, had been recruited on what the nun thought were ideological and idealistic grounds. Jan had a better measure of the woman; the short-skirted, thin-shirted "nun" wanted payment, sure enough, but in perks and prestige, rather than in money. Unfortunately, and to Jan's mind most shockingly, when Pax Vobiscum had shown up on the figurative Balboan doorstep, offering to become human shields, they'd all been put on trial for treason . . . to Balboa's enemies. Sentenced to death, the group had instead been deported to neighboring Santa Josefina, where a guerilla war raged. It was made very clear to them that the full penalty would be exacted if they returned.

Who would have expected one of my primary intelligence assets to be booted for something like that? had thought Campbell. *These people are too insane to predict. Maybe Kris was right, and they're too insane to leave in peace. Or maybe they pegged the group for having spies within it, and decided this was a useful way to get them out of the way. If so, damned clever of them.*

Hmmm . . . Maybe I can get the bitch infiltrated with the guerillas. But do I want to?

The third leg of Jan's little unofficial and carefully hidden organization was a direct-action team, seconded to her via the influence of Stuart-Mansfield. Two of these now accompanied her—Sergeant Greene and Corporal Dawes—as she stalked the halls of the newly repurposed Tauran Defense Agency Headquarters, looking for the basement office of the aforementioned Jonathan Houston, seconded from Anglia's Royal Signals Regiment, and flying a desk formerly devoted to intelligence on Balboa but now rather underused.

Corporal Dawes, short himself, had a much taller Gaul in hand, the Gaul's arm twisted up behind his back, wrist painfully bent, walking on the balls of his feet to keep from having his arm or wrist broken, and just barely audibly whining on the way. Since the good corporal had already demonstrated that whining loudly would cause him to twist the wrist enough to elicit a scream, the Gaul had to content himself with no more than that subdued whine.

Another Gaul, a not unattractive but rather cold-faced woman, Captain Turenge, followed along purposefully. She was Campbell's liaison with Janier or, rather, his office, when Jan couldn't meet directly. Somewhat to her surprise, the Anglian had found the Gaul most *sympathique*, indeed, almost a sister in wickedness and sin.

How fortunate, thought Campbell, *that these basement rooms are soundproofed, in the main. How lucky, too, that almost no one is down here.*

Someone, nationality indeterminate, did look out from an office, alerted by the whimpering of the Gaul. A quick, infinitely wicked smile from Jan sent that someone reeling back into their office, slamming the door behind him.

Houston, as short as Jan, chubby, and with an anemic caterpillar of a blond mustache, showed no alarm when Jan entered his basement office uninvited and, smiling sweetly, took a seat. He didn't know anything much about her but, like most of the rest assumed she was a highly connected bureaucrat. And he'd seen and noticed her physical charms, of course, as had every man—including the gays—in the headquarters.

On the other hand, when the bruiser pushing the Gaul entered, with tears running down the Gaul's face, Houston took some notice. When the other bruiser and the other woman entered, and the former closed the office door and took a station behind Houston's own chair, the signaler really began to feel distinctly uncomfortable. And when Jan Campbell, holding two rolled up pieces of paper in her left hand, stood and slapped him across the face with her right, he was so shocked he couldn't speak initially. And then, of course, bruiser number one, Sergeant Greene, made sure he couldn't speak at all, at least for the nonce, pulling the desk jockey's head back by his hair and wrapping a thickly corded forearm across his mouth, almost covering his nose.

Campbell held one piece of paper before Houston's wide eyes.

"Dae ye nae ken this?" she asked. When she was furious, as she was now, and speaking English, she tended to revert to the thick Scots of her girlhood.

When the signaler's eyes, wide over Sergeant Greene's burly crooked arm, showed nothing but incomprehension, Campbell placed a dainty finger on the address block, repeating, "Dae ye nae ken this?"

Houston's eyes flicked down the page. It was a report originating with a machinist in the enemy's main armaments complex, detailing the special milling of something over a thousand arrow shells, in 122mm, and the fitting of same with sabots in 180mm, along with the dimensions and threading particulars for the fuse wells.

"DO YOU NAE KEN THIS?"

The eyes only widened further.

"Sairgant Greene, scomfisht him." The perfect calm with which she said it, after the shouted query, set Houston to emitting a high-pitched squeal—all that he could get through Greene's gagging arm.

"Bide a wee, Sairgant," she commanded, then again asked Houston, "Dae ye nae ken this?"

The latter managed the most constrained of nods.

"A see," said Campbell, then turned her attention to Corporal Dawes's captive. "Now *why*, Monsieur," she asked, switching to French, "did you not inform Houston of the purchase by Balboa of a large number of laser guidance packages and emitters for artillery shells, with the fuse well requirements for the fuses? You had the information."

The Gaul gave Campbell a pitying look, as if she were an idiot child. That caused Campbell to shoot a glance at Dawes, who promptly lifted the Gaul by his bent wrist, eliciting thereby a most sincere scream of pain, while also illustrating in a very clear way why contemptuous glances were not to be directed at Miss Campbell.

Yes, it is fortunate, indeed, *that the walls are thick and soundproof.*

When Dawes let the now sobbing Gaul down enough to put his weight on his own feet, Jan asked, rhetorically, "It was the old political game, wasn't it? The keep all information close hold game? The give away nothing for free game, not even to one's allies?"

"Yes . . . yes . . . yes," the Gaul admitted, in a series of sobs.

"And ye," she accused, turning her attention back to Houston and the language back to something approaching English, "war thay the sel an same games for ye? Or were ye wirkin for the fae's chief o' intelligence?"

Houston's eyes, if possible, grew wider still. The Tauran Union, like all civilized polities, had long since done away with capital punishment even for treason. That did not necessarily mean that death could not be meted out, even on mere suspicion, if the suspicious were ruthless enough.

He gave off another "girl in a horror film" shriek, mostly muffled by his captor's arm.

"Nae workin' for Fernandez, then?" Jan enquired, with a dubious moue, her blonde head shaking just as dubiously. "But how can A be certaint? How can A be certaint whan vital intelligence is nae passed on, vital coordination nae done?"

"Shall I kill him now, Miss?" asked Sergeant Greene, on cue. "It won't take long."

This time Houston's scream almost escaped the knotted muscles of the sergeant's forearm.

She knew that, working in the TU Defense Agency, Houston spoke good French. She switched back to that so that both Gauls present could understand her words, as well.

"The unnecessary dead we're going to have suffered because the Zhong got hammered by the Balboan artillery, firing these shells from their island fortress, thereby releasing Balboan legions to face our own invasion, almost demands the deaths of these two," Jan agreed. "Still, we are civilized folk." She turned to the Gallic captain. "What do you think, Turenge?"

"I think the general would not miss these two," said the female Gaul, her lip curling in a contemptuous sneer. "I think there would be no serious investigation, even if they were found, each with 'is knife in the other's chest, especially after I testify that we were involved in a sordid love triangle. We Gauls understand these things 'appen, you see."

"I think I do see," Jan agreed, with the faintest hint of reluctance in her voice. At her words the other Gaul promptly voided his bladder, much to the worsening of Corporal Dawes' shoes.

"Bastard," said the corporal, giving the Gaul's wrist a vicious, scream-extracting twist. "Tha filt'y fuck."

"Still, don't you think something else could be done, Captain? I mean, if these two agree to place themselves under our modest little organization, and to work diligently and honestly for it, to devote their funds to our purposes . . ."

"We don't, after all, have proof that this chubby pig, Houston, was working for the enemy, do we?"

"Sadly not," Turenge admitted, then offered, "but a stint with the general's interrogator . . ."

"But people are *so* ruined after something like that," objected Campbell. "Why, no one would get any use out of them then."

"But, then again, I would personally be inconsolable, just *inconsolable*, if these two were to fail to cooperate or coordinate in the future, in any way that brought harm to our men at arms or their cause . . ."

Dawes used his right hand to grasp the Gaul's hair, then bent his captive backwards until his ear was about at a level with Dawes' own mouth.

"'Inconsolable,'" Corporal Dawes explained softly, into the captive Gaul's ear, in an accent not dissimilar to Old Earth's Tyke, "is Anglian code for I rip thy fuckin' 'ead off and shi' down t'ole."

Landing Zone / Drop Zone Trixie,
Cristobal Province, Balboa

Ammunition was still highly limited, for the batteries of the *Fallschirm-artillerie Batallion*, so the half dozen Sachsen-manned 105mm guns, from their position at the southern end of the drop zone, were having to be rather circumspect in their allocation of fire. Their flailing away at the Balboan defenders was, therefore, somewhat fitful. When they did have the wherewithal to fire, the trees over which they hurled their shells shuddered and shed leaves to the point of barrenness.

North of the battery, Sachsen *Fallschirmjaeger* continued to pour in from the lumbering transports passing overhead. Those mainly infantry sorts didn't stick around, but moved off smartly into the surrounding jungle expanding the airhead, and providing security by, in the main, sending the Balboans nearby reeling for shelter.

They were normally half mobile, that battery, with one truck for every other gun, another for ammunition, a smaller one for battery headquarters, and one for the FDC. With one vehicle having streamered in—ouch!— they were down to five sets of wheels, one of them light. The FDC was sitting in the dirt, ear glued to a radio handset, while the two junior men in that section furiously scooped out a shelter; the battery commander was standing on his own feet, while those five trucks scoured the drop zone for the pallets of ammunition that had been dropped just before the troops and guns came down.

Every now and again one of the trucks would return to the firing position. Then there would be a mad scramble to get the ammunition off and to the guns. For a while thereafter, the pace of the supporting fire would increase, before tapering off until the next batch of shells showed up.

The battery had one serious problem. It was a problem that plagued the Taurans any time any substantial numbers of different nationalities worked together. This was that its primary mission was to support the Anglian Marines cutting out a beachhead to the east of Cristobal, at Pernambuco Beach, a sandy, shoal- and reefless stretch of white sand, east of the mouth of the Rio Gamboa. Of course, the Anglian Marines spoke English—though there were well-educated Sachsens who disputed this—while the Sachsens spoke something quite recognizably German.

There had already been one unfortunate incident that had caused the commander of the Marines to enquire of the Sachsens, by radio, "Have we offended you in some way?" Understanding of the radio transmission had not actually been improved by the fact that the speaker on the other end was having to shout to be heard over the sound of incoming Sachsen 105s.

Both the Anglians at Pernambuco and the larger but mixed Gallic and Tuscan Marine brigade to the west, storming ashore at Puerto Lindo and points east of that, were dependent on the Sachsens for artillery support until the shore was cleared enough for their own batteries to set up for business. And with both, as was only to be expected, there were language issues.

Though the Anglian landing was necessary fully to invest the town, the Gallic and Tuscan assault was the more important. This was because, until Cristobal surrendered or fell, the only practical route of supply would be aerial drop (always limited), helicopter (often even more problematic), over the shore (and the Taurans didn't have the kind of capability for that that, say, the Federated States Navy and Marine Corps did), air landing (except that they'd either have to capture or build a decent airfield, which was in the plan, but not for today), and through a port.

Puerto Lindo, though—as the name suggested—a beautiful port, was quite small and not fully developed. Indeed, the port served mainly as a naval and maritime scrapyard, although it was also the factory for the Megalodon Class Coastal Defense Submarines. The town hosted the Military Academy Sergeant Juan Malvegui, though the school was abandoned.

In any event, the Taurans needed a port. Hence, even before the Gauls and Tuscans brought in their own batteries, they would be offloading a mixed port construction battalion.

Both landings were too far away for most of Jimenez's heavy mortars to do much about. He had a limited artillery pack, but that he'd been told to preserve as long as possible. Some of the nearer mortar platoons and batteries had tried, on their own, but the Tauran air forces had soon put paid to their pitiful efforts.

HAMS *Typhoon*, South of Cristobal, Shimmering Sea

The thrum of helicopters refueling topside seemed to reach down deep into the ship, punctuated by the hydraulic whine and metallic clang of one of the lifts, bringing supplies up on deck.

There, deep in those steel nautical bowels, General Janier fumed. It grated on him, though he tried not to let it show, that the only ship suitable for a command vessel for the invasion was Anglian. Oh, Gaul's fleet had more surface combatants, to be sure, accounting by sheer numbers. But the experience, the balance, the intuitive grasp? Those were all in Anglia's corner. Even outnumbered, no English-speaking people had ever lost a naval war except to another English-speaking people. Their officers, ships, and crews, on average, simply turned out better suited for their tasks, that being driven by an institutional memory that spanned two worlds.

The *Typhoon*, an assault helicopter carrier, was also fully equipped to serve as the headquarters for even a multi-corps landing. Indeed, though it carried a fair complement of medium and heavy helicopters, this voyage, almost none of the lift had been used for the troops carried. Instead, other than a small headquarters cell Janier had launched in behind the mixed Gallic-Tuscan brigade of marines, the other seven hundred and fifty or so ground troops carried by the ship would stay there until Janier, himself, went ashore to take charge. The helicopters, conversely, returned to the ship only for fuel, as they ferried combat troops in from other ships, to include impressed merchantmen with hastily designed and erected helicopter platforms.

"You look concerned, General," said the Anglian admiral commanding the combined fleet, in the Gaul's bowel-deep command center.

That raised a scowl from the Gaul, though the scowl didn't seem to be directed at the speaker.

Admiral Pellew had descended to Janier's command center to inform the Gaul in person that, with the reinforcing paras dropping in from Cienfuegos and Santa Josefina, there was now more combat power ashore than at sea. This, by present agreement backed up by at least one interpretation of longstanding doctrine, marked the point at which the naval commander became de jure subordinate to the ground commander.

"Pity they didn't take the bait," observed Pellew. The bait, in this case, had been the invasion fleet demonstrating near the port of Capitano, very far to the east, near the border with Santa Josefina, coupled with the landing of about a brigade of mixed troops, mostly second line.

"I am concerned," the Gaul admitted, somewhat nervously chewing at his lip.

"But everything's going well, is it not?" asked the Anglian.

"*Et dona ferentes*," answered the Gaul.

"Ah."

"I have seen things start well before here," Janier elaborated. "It was always a ruse. When things are going well now? I have to assume that it at least *might* be a ruse."

"You know what his best weapon is, this Carrera person?" the Anglian asked.

The Gaul answered, "That he started ahead of us and is so far ahead of us in the decision cycle we've never had a chance to catch up . . . .at least until now . . . at least *maybe* until now."

"That's something," the Anglian agreed, "if one buys into decision-cycle theory. But that's not his best weapon or chief advantage."

"Which is?" asked Janier.

"He's free to fight a war, without having to restrict himself only to those actions which can be justified even to the most militarily ignorant mommy in the land."

"Point," conceded the Gaul.

Janier was about to say something further when an enlisted man handed him an annotated map, of the old-fashioned variety, covered with old-fashioned acetate. *The staff*, he thought, *simply assumes that using a paper map, rather than a computer screen, is just one of my personal quirks. It is that, of course, but it is also a better and less obvious way for me to record the intelligence I get passed on from the High Admiral, from the Peace Fleet overhead. Makes me look brilliant . . . to everybody but me.*

"I'll be in my quarters briefly," the general announced.

CHAPTER THREE

"All the business of war, and indeed all the business of life, is to endeavour to find out what you don't know by what you do; that's what I called 'guessing what was at the other side of the hill.'"
—Arthur Wellesley, 1st Duke of Wellington

IV Corps Headquarters, Magdalena, Cristobal Province, Balboa

The irregular *crump-crump-crumb* of bombs—filtering through the earth and then to and through the thick-walled concrete shelter—was frequent enough now that nobody really paid it much mind. The people in the shelter knew, too, that they'd never hear the one that came for them, so why worry about it? They went about their chores and duties, thus, with fairly light hearts . . . or, at least, they were able to put on a good enough show of it, even though, however carefully they hid it, they *did* worry.

Fourth Corps was something of an ethnic mishmash. In and around the city of Cristobal, the bulk of the populace was more or less black; "more or less" because, after centuries of crossbreeding on Old Earth, followed by more centuries of crossbreeding on Terra Nova, *nobody* was pure. The most that could really be said was that someone tended black or white or brown or yellow or red. Thus, for example, Legate Arocha, Jimenez's Ia, or operations officer, was black, like Jimenez, himself. Conversely, his Ic, or Intelligence Officer, was almost pale and bore the surname of Standish, even though almost no one in the area with an English-sounding name was white.

The two glared across the map at each other.

Other armies used most advanced computers for this, but Balboa not only didn't have money to waste on such luxuries, it had an active prejudice against anything that could be hacked. As such, Jimenez's operations and intelligence staff plotted known and suspected enemy positions on a huge map, set up on moveable tables at the center of the ops room. Those positions looked like a series of spreading stains on the map. Some of them already leaked tendrils toward each other. In places, the stains had merged into ominous blobs.

The corps logistician, the Ib, black and named Harris, didn't plot anything, but took notes for places and units of the IVth Corps he thought might need a tad of logistic succor, as well as trying to pierce the enemy's logistic plan, the knowledge of which would be the surest possible guide to his intentions. That was one of the reasons for the staff arrangements in the legions, actually, with operations, logistics, and intel all in the same section, that intelligence types were not usually as good at analyzing logistics as logisticians were, while nothing was quite as good a predictor of enemy actions as were logistic realities.

The Ia, Arocha, looked at a several recent plots on the map, then announced in a loud voice, "It's not fucking possible; somebody's full of shit." His accusing glare was directed at the intelligence officer.

"What's not possible?" asked Jimenez.

"Sir," said Intelligence, "Operations has a point. We know what the Taurans had for airborne forces. We know—we know beyond the slightest shadow of a doubt—that we destroyed two of the four brigades they had, the Gauls' and the Anglians'. We are certain that the defection of Colonel Muñoz-Infantes is keeping Castile, which has one of the two remaining brigades, out of the war in any serious way. I am seeing, *we* are seeing, impossible numbers of paratroopers, coming into the airheads established by their helicopter-borne troops. I can't tell you where they're coming from. They ought not exist, not in the numbers we're seeing."

"Show me," ordered Jimenez.

The Ic grabbed a wooden pointer from an underling. Moving it from east to west, tapping the map as he went, he explained, "The Tauran paras all came in on airheads previously grabbed by airmobile forces. They are reinforcing by parachute, not doing parachute assaults."

"That's a lot safer," Jimenez observed.

"Yes, sir," Standish agreed. "Also, much more reliable, certain, practical . . . sir, we need to adjust our opinion of Tauran arms upward . . . way the fuck upward.

"Reports are that the Sachsens—they have a very distinctive field uniform so we are quite certain who they are—came in here"—the pointer went *tap*—"and here"—*tap*; the taps indicating drop zones northeast of Cristobal and northwest of Puerto Lindo.

"That's all perfectly understandable," the Ic continued, "Sachsens reinforcing the perimeter and supporting the marine forces while the latter clear their beachheads. It's working for them, too."

Jimenez scowled but then said, "I follow so far. Continue."

The pointer went *tap, tap, tap* across the map in rapid succession. "But we are seeing more than that. Each of those places has something like a brigade or a short brigade landed or landing. That's not counting the reports of smaller teams coming in outside the area of their major drops.

"There seems to be a brigade of Gauls, another of Anglians, and a mixed group of I don't know what, but they're probably Tuscans, Haarlemers, and maybe Leopolders. They might be Hordalanders and Cimbrians in there, too, since the Cimbrians have two companies, and only one is in Santa Josefina.

"That last group is predictable but . . . well, sir . . . where did the Anglians and Gauls come up with more?"

"I don't know how they did," Jimenez said, "but I can tell you how I would have. I'd have called up reservists, especially if I had a formed unit. I'd have used my special operations people as cadres for new battalions. And I'd have raped the school system as completely as possible for more cadres. In all, if you tally it up, that may account for both the Anglians and the Gauls' newfound airborne capability.

"We may find, too, if we ever manage to get a prisoner, that for some of those jumpers it's their first jump.

"Note, too, gentlemen, that we didn't, in principle, do anything much different in using the training brigade cadres to form forty-sixth through fifty-first *tercios*."

Standish still looked a little skeptical. "Yes, sir . . . maybe, sir, but we didn't use any of those to parachute into a hot drop zone, either."

"Is it working for them?" Jimenez asked.

"Well . . . yes, sir."

"If it looks stupid but works then it isn't stupid."

"All right, sir," Standish agreed. "But I can't help but wonder why Fernandez's organization didn't warn us of this. It's his job, after all. But, yeah, sure; we'll assume that those paras are not figments of our imagination, but were reconstituted somehow." Grimly, the operations officer nodded agreement.

"Do that," Jimenez said, "and make a mental note that, as they're reconstituted, which is to say, kind of new, those formations may also be kind of fragile . . . .hmmm . . . speaking of which . . ."

Jimenez turned away and walked to the artillery desk, where his chief of artillery, Legate Arosamena, looked ready to weep. Arosamena had once been acting chief of staff for the entire Legion. Fired by Carrera for incompetence in that role, Jimenez had taken him on as, first, an artillery *tercio* commander, and later as chief of IVth Corps Artillery.

"Every time I allow somebody to fire," Arosamena told

Jimenez, "that firing battery's life is measurable in minutes. I never saw or anticipated what that kind of air superiority could do. I'm sorry . . ."

"Not your fault," Jimenez assured the gunner, adding a hearty slap on the back. "You would be doing better, Legate, if we were allowed to use our air defense and if we could use everything at once. Since we're not, and we can't, you just have to mark time and wait for a target that's worth losing a battery or platoon over."

"I don't know that I've seen anything worth losing a battery over," Arosamena said.

Jimenez shook his head. "It's not really the damage to the target we care about, but the overall threat and the friction we inflict on the enemy by making that threat credible."

"Yes, sir. That's what doctrine says, sir." Arosamena didn't sound like he had a lot of faith in doctrine.

I'm not too sanguine about doctrine, either, Jimenez thought. *And, just like Standish, I wonder why Fernandez didn't find out and let us know about the reconstituted para brigades. And I wonder what else he's let us down on.*

Estado Mayor, Sub camp C, Ciudad Balboa, Balboa

The General Staff building, *Estado Mayor* in Spanish, was, if anything, even more thoroughly wrecked than Jimenez's brownstone headquarters in Cristobal. That was to be anticipated. Moreover, it *had* been anticipated, with widely scattered concrete fortified camps having been constructed long since, to hold and shelter evacuees from the main building. Sub-camp C held about half of Legate Omar Fernandez's organization, to include the *hard* interrogation section headed up by Chief Warrant Officer Achmed al Mahamda. He was a Sumeri immigrant to Balboa, expressly recruited for his peculiar expertise more than a decade prior, and sheltered from paying for his crimes on behalf of the old Sumeri regime ever since. It was said of Mahamda that he could make a rock weep and, given two rocks, could extract the ultimate truth from both.

If this was an exaggeration, it was not much of one.

The screams coming from a chamber to the south of Mahamda's office seemed to make the underground, concrete lined tunnels reverberate. Fernandez shuddered with sympathy. Not that he didn't detest the men undergoing interrogation; he did, just as he'd detest any native-born Balboan caught spying for the enemy. This detestation, though, was coupled with a measure of admiration for how long this particular set of captives had held out.

Even at that, Mahamda hadn't gotten everything. Fernandez knew, and took considerable personal satisfaction in knowing, that between seven and twelve spies from the Rocaberti camp had been reintroduced to Balboa. He'd be more sure of the numbers except that the prisoners were still lying about them. He knew some of the methods of reintroduction, ranging from parachute drop, to submarine, to simply walking across the border or, in one case, coming in via a Castilian diplomatic passport and, in another, as a notional member of a news organization. He also knew their mission hadn't been either espionage or direct action, but to re-establish contact with sundry spies already in country.

But I don't know who is still at large. With names, real names, I could come up with pictures. With pictures we'd have the last of them rounded up within the week. But those miserable bastards simply won't give up the same stories on the names. Fucking . . .

Fernandez let the thought die. *Best I remember that just because I think somebody is wicked, wrong, evil, a traitor, a swine . . . that doesn't mean he thinks he's any of those things, or is any less dedicated to his cause than I am to mine. If there weren't . . .*

The thought was interrupted by a long and heartrending shriek of utter agony.

Ah, that sounds like the young captive.

Fernandez turned his wheelchair toward the interrogation chamber, using the small stick on the right arm to direct it forward. *What I can order Mahamda to do I can make myself watch.*

The boy—and he *was* just a boy, no more than eighteen—hung by his wrists from a rope running through a hook overhead. His wrists were behind him. His shoulders strained near to dislocating. Mere inches below his outstretched toes, his feet twitched and danced to find purchase on the floor. Tears ran down his face, while snot poured from his nose. The three streams joined somewhere below his lower lip, the mix dripping from his chin onto the floor.

The thing is, boy, thought Mahamda, *that this is the*

light stuff. It can get a lot worse, and will, unless your story and the stories of the others come to match.

Mahamda barely glanced over as Fernandez silently rolled in on his powered chair. The chief didn't often come to watch and, when he did, Mahamda was fairly sure it was to punish himself for the punishment he had inflicted.

Reaching out one hand to grasp the boy by the hair, Mahamda visually signaled an assistant to let the rope down a bit, enough for the boy's toes and the balls of his feet to rest on the floor. It wasn't entirely unprecedented when the boy's sobbing increased at even that much relief from the pain.

Pulling back on the prisoner's hair, thus raising his face, Mahamda said, not ungently, "It can only get worse from here, Sancho. You've had the tour. You know what awaits you. Why don't you tell me the truth? You know you will eventually."

Mahamda, naturally, had no particular moral issues with lying to the people he tortured, especially if the lie might reduce the amount of torture he had to apply, which reduced the risk one of them might die before spilling his guts.

"The others," he said, "have broken, boy. Whether from having their nuts squeezed in a vise or a blowtorch applied to their feet; whether from the dental drilling or the rack or Skevington's Daughter; they've all broken. Still their pain goes on because you won't tell me the truth." The warrant seemed most distressed at this, for all one could tell from his voice.

"You *want* their pain to stop, don't you, Sancho? Sure,

you're young and healthy, you can take it for a while longer. But old Pedrarias? He's just this side of death from the pain."

In fact, Emilio Pedrarias had died under interrogation, but no sense letting the boy know that.

Mahamda let the boy's hair go, then signaled with his chin for his assistant to turn the wheel to raise him off the floor again. The screaming resumed, with new intensity.

"We'll leave Sancho here to think a while, especially to think on what his comrades are enduring because he refuses to speak the truth."

As Mahamda left the chamber to confer with Fernandez, he said to his assistant, "Don't pull on his legs yet or start the raise and drop routine."

Outside the torture chamber, shaking his head, the Sumeri warrant said, "*Sayyidi*, I've been in this business a long time. I honestly don't think the poor shit knows anything beyond what he's said."

"So why are you continuing?" Fernandez asked. "Piping the sounds into someone else's cell?"

"Yes, sir, with a ten-second delay. Sometimes it helps. And, besides, I could be wrong; he just might know something significant."

"Any insights from the others?"

The Sumeri shook his head, saying, "Nothing beyond what I've already sent you."

"Any chance it's all a fake," asked Fernandez, "or a mere distraction?"

"No way for me to be sure," admitted the warrant officer, "but I am sure that *they* don't think so. People do not put up . . . well . . . unless their name is Layla Arguello, of course . . . anyway, people do not put up with what these men have put up with unless they believe it's for a purpose they consider among the highest. I think we have to take them at face value, as the enemy's main effort in trying to restore their old intelligence network here.

"And if it's obvious and we crippled it quickly? Well . . . sir . . . it's not like the Tauran Union has proven to be all that competent to date."

"They're invading pretty competently," Fernandez countered.

"That's operations," the warrant said, "not intel. In intelligence matters they've been pretty poor so far."

"Point," conceded the crippled legate. "Unless we don't catch the somewhere between none and five infiltrators still at large. In that case, they may prove competent enough."

"Point," agreed the Sumeri.

South of the Parilla Line

The battery commander decided to walk point himself. He had no one more qualified, at hand, in any case. It was a function of having a largely citizen-soldier army—technical expertise tended to be thin and narrowly focused at the top.

Tribune Alfonso Ramirez had only two officers in his battery, himself and his exec, the latter back with the rest in so-called "Log Base Alpha." All but one of the centurions were back there, too, with the sixteen shipping containers and eight guns the battery had dug in under the jungle canopy.

The other three guns, the three the battery had held before the first Tauran invasion, were out here, likewise dug in, along with just enough men to minimally man them, a tiny cell from the fire direction center, and a quantity of ammunition well over what they were likely to need. The ammunition was actually dug in better than the guns were, with the fuses stored separately and dug in better still.

Unlike back at Log Base Alpha, there was no overhead cover for the guns here. All they had were the radar scattering camouflage screens, simple pits, a few fighting positions, and some crawl trenches. Even the fire direction center wasn't properly built, though the logs overhead might be adequate to shrug off cluster munitions and their small bomblets. And there were some small personnel scrapings in the sides of the gun pits, which might or might not have served well enough to the same purpose.

The detachment's greatest and best defense, though, as the battery commander ruefully admitted, was that they hadn't fired a round, simply because no one had asked.

And now, with reports of Tauran fingers closing in around the detachment, it was time to go, without even that one shot of defiance having been fired.

"Sucks, boys," Ramirez admitted to the one junior centurion and eighteen enlisted men with him, "but there you have it. I've asked permission already, which was granted. It's time to go. Or will be in an hour, when Second Infantry is in position.

"Centurion Avilar?"

"Sir." The junior centurion was on the tall side, taller than his commander, in any case, and of a medium brown complexion. A nose broader and lips fuller than the national norm for mestizos told of somewhat more mixed ancestry than most. He was probably the second-best centurion in the battery, after Top, which was why Ramirez had him along on this detached mission.

"I'll take point. You take tail. Make sure to take the sights with you and to bury the breechblocks."

The centurion nodded, sadly, then called off three names. "You rats will leave last, in order of march, with me. Get the shovels and dig out a small pit, fifty meters west of gun three, half a meter deep."

"*Si, Centurio.*"

Turning back to his commander, Avilar asked, "What about the radio the Fifty-second *Tercio* left with us, sir? I know what they said, but . . ."

"They said 'leave it,' so leave it," answered Ramirez.

Avilar was inclined to argue, but it might be one of those close-hold, hush-hush, dumb-assed officer things, so, *Maybe better not. The tribune usually knows what he's talking about.*

Avilar gave a thumbs up to Ramirez. From a civilian or a private it would have meant little. From a centurion it meant, "All personnel present or accounted for. All weapons accounted for. All personal gear packed and on the troops' backs. All non-firearm serial number items present and accounted for and on the troops' backs. All radios but one are on the troops backs. Field phones and their wire is collected and on the troops' backs. I have the sights. The men have sufficient food and water for the trip, and are healthy enough for it. They're camouflaged to standard. Loads are more or less evenly distributed, allowing for different levels of fitness. The gas is drained from the tanks for the auxiliary propulsion units of the guns. Etc. Etc. Yes, that, too. Etc. And that. Etc. Trust me on this, Boss; I took care of it. We can go on your order."

Saves so much time, thought the tribune, *when you can just count on the routine shit getting done routinely.*

He raised the flaps of his *lorica,* his legionary issue silk and liquid metal body armor, and ran the zipper down the bottom without quite undoing it. The thing was miserably hot just sitting there; doing any kind of labor in one was right out. *But we'll have to, just to get home.*

Then he turned north, consulted his compass, and said, over his left shoulder, "Follow me."

All around, a rising noise in the jungle gave Ramirez the sense—correct, as it turned out—that most or all of the detachments that had been posted forward of the Parilla Line were likewise pulling out and heading north to shelter.

Then came the warning shout from Avilar, the ferocious scream of the incoming Tauran jet, and the pummeling impact of rockets on the old position.

"Twelve o'clock!" the tribune shouted. "Two hundred meters."

As Ramirez turned his eyes forward and began to sprint, he saw that Avilar and three gunners had already passed him by.

***

Within the first mile, every eye in Ramirez's small detachment was scanning through the small gaps in the thickly interwoven jungle canopy overhead, every ear straining to hear through the muffling tree cover the harpy's shriek of incoming bombers. A mile after that they found the smoking, cooked remains of what was probably an infantry squad, dismembered, burned, with a naked, blackened, armless torso impaled on the ragged stump of a tree branch, overhead. The torso dripped blood down the stout, bomb-sharpened stump of the tree branch on which it hung. Half a mile further, the party went to ground at a crescendo of small-arms fire, coming from ahead.

Even the normally phlegmatic Avilar exclaimed, "Fuck!" at that.

CHAPTER FOUR

"War is a natural condition of the State, which was organized in order to be an effective instrument of violence on behalf of society. Wars are like deaths, which, while they can be postponed, will come when they will come and cannot be finally avoided."
—Philip Bobbett,
The Shield of Achilles: War, Peace and the Course of History

Above Landing Zone/Drop Zone Pandion, Cristobal Province, Balboa

". . . .three thousand . . . four thousand . . . oompf!"

The opening shock wasn't bad, actually, as such things go. *At least my balls weren't busted*, thought Sergeant Werner Verboom of Thirteenth Company, Royal Haarlem *Commandotroepen*, as he looked up to check his parachute. *That's sort of the definition of not-bad, at least when we have a fully deployed chute, like this one*.

Above, the fourth of the six thundering Hacienda-121

transport aircraft that had brought in Thirteenth Company began disgorging its two dozen jumpers, the men more or less pouring off the load ramp in a human flood. Yes, it was more dangerous to jump that way, but not as dangerous as it would have been to be caught in the aircraft if intelligence had proven wrong and the Balboans able to engage it with something moderately heavy.

Distantly seen and completely unheard, four miles away, another half dozen of the two-engine, propeller-driven aircraft were in the process of dropping Verboom's sister company, the Fourteenth, plus battalion headquarters, to LZ / DZ Teratorn.

A smoke pot burned at one end of the drop zone, set up by the pathfinders or maybe the airmobile brigade, as an aid to the reinforcing jumpers. Verboom, floating down from about four hundred and fifty feet up, with a fully deployed parachute, saw the smoke rising. He knew from the twisting of the smoke trail that there were erratic ground winds down below. He could live with that, since the rising of the smoke said they weren't especially strong winds.

The tracers, however, skipping madly across the drop zone, had come as something of a surprise to the sergeant. Between them, trying—not entirely successfully—to control the oscillation of his parachute, and twisting his head to try to keep eyes on his men, however little good that might do, the beefy non-com was too busy to be afraid. He did take time to release his rucksack to hang on a strap below, then did the same with his weapons case, which slid down the same strap to rest on the rucksack.

This cut down on the weight he had to land with even as it tended to stabilize a bit against oscillation. There was more in the weapons case that just his own rifle.

Silly of me to be surprised, really, thought Verboom, drifting down just that much faster than most of the men of the company. *I mean, I've seen tracers in the day. I've seen them lots of times, hundreds of times. Can't see them from the side, of course, but they're obvious enough when you're behind a machine gun firing four by one.*

That it may have been silly didn't stop the sergeant's lungs from acting like bellows. He wasn't terrified—nothing like that, of course; the Haarlemer Commandos were, like the Marines and unlike the rest of the Haarlemer Army—quite elite, with perhaps the odd and occasional individual exception. Still, even a very elite body has its own ways of preparing for danger. Among those is stocking up on oxygen.

Verboom didn't see any tracers as a long flurry of machine-gun fire passed him by. He didn't think the gunner down below had been aiming for him; the area through which the bullets passed had remained steady as Verboom fell. He suspected that the gunner had simply fired below a paratrooper and waited for his target to descend into his cone of fire. This suspicion was confirmed with a scream, quickly cut short, that arose over the *crackcrackcracking* of a long burst of machine-gun fire.

The sergeant twisted his head again and saw a limp body, hanging from a chute, toes pointed down and arms swaying low and free. The body wasn't close enough to see blood, but the way it hung so limp said to the sergeant, *Dead. Never saw that before. Never . . .*

Never mind. Business first.

With the ground closing fast, Verboom automatically tugged at the toggles to try to face into the wind. His parachute, however, was not really very steerable, no matter what the advertising said. Moreover, the unpredictability of the breeze worked against him. In short, his efforts did him little good. Then again, as he got closer to the ground and the tracers, they tended to occupy more and more of his thoughts.

But I never saw them on a jump before. No one ever thought to have somebody shoot across the drop zone as we came in.

Let's hope the men take it well, what with not being mentally prepared for it. Of course, hope is not a plan.

And . . . oh, shit . . . left rear . . . ooof.

The commando hit the ground, chin tucked and knees bent, about as well as could be expected. This is to say, he hit a lot harder than he wanted to and a lot more awkwardly that he'd hoped to.

"But any one you can walk away from," the sergeant muttered, after he took mental inventory of his aches, sprains, and bruises.

Rolling to his back, Verboom slapped the release on his chest, freeing himself from the 'chute. A bullet cracked loud overhead.

Not all that much overhead, either. They told us this DZ was secure, the lying fucks.

Around him, the rest of the company began to assemble on the woodline to the west, the men sprinting as soon as they doffed their parachute harnesses. Not all sprinted, however; the two commandos, hit while descending, hit the ground like the sacks full of dead meat they were.

What really bothers me here is that these guys were our allies. Surely someone could have found a way to let us and the Balboans get together in peace, love, and harmony to kill somebody else. What else do we pay the bureaucrats of the Tauran Union for, anyway?

Moving toward the rally point, Verboom came upon one of the company's lesser lights, Private van der Wege, hiding in the low depression, weeping and shivering. Even elite units sometimes acquire the odd shithead.

Reaching down, Verboom grabbed van der Wege by the back of his harness and bodily lifted him to his feet. Then, with a kick and a curse—"Move, you fucking coward!"—Verboom drove the boy bodily forward.

Above Landing Zone / Drop Zone Teratorn, Cristobal Province, Balboa

Hauptmann Nadja Felton, Sachsen *Luftstreitkräfte*, turned her Hacienda-121 to the southeast, even as she pulled back on the yoke to bring the plane up to dropping altitude. Behind her, in their turn, five other planes of her squadron followed, one after the other.

Tall, slender, blonde, and with a seriousness that even her bright smile and healthy looks didn't quite hide, Felton was a recalled reservist. She wasn't especially happy about the recall, since it involved a massive cut in pay from what she was used to in her normal job, which was piloting for a civilian cargo aviation firm.

As such, Felton was used to flying much bigger and more ungainly aircraft. Unlike those, with the Hacienda she could actually feel the stomping of the cargo as they stood up, hooked up, and shuffled to the ramp.

Not that she was a stranger to the Hacienda, no; she'd flown them during her own military service, a dozen years prior.

And qualified to drop Fallschirmtruppen, *too,* she self-congratulated. *Wish I'd had a couple of more practice runs after they mobilized me, though. Still . . . what I had . . . it should be sufficient. Some things one doesn't really forget.*

And I, at least, am not a slave of the global locating system.

That was a military problem, generally, for the Tauran Union, as it was for any highly technologically advanced state on Terra Nova. It seemed that the legion, being not nearly as dependent on high technology as its foes, had developed a means—or several means; opinions were mixed—to interfere locally with even encoded signals from the satellites that emitted the GLS time stamps. The United Earth Peace Fleet could also send a signal, though it hadn't, as yet, for this. There was no principled reason anyone could think of for the signal that the UEPF could send to be immune to Balboan sabotage. Hence, no one up above wanted to risk the potential damage to the Peace Fleet's public image.

Among the reasons Hauptmann Felton—her married name, and married to an *Auslaender*, at that—had left service before retirement were certain unwise personnel management decisions on the part of the Sachsen defense ministry. Those same decisions had left younger pilots frankly wretchedly trained in comparison to those assessed into the LSK in earlier generations.

All of which explained why Hauptmann Felton, though a reservist, was in the lead bird; she was from the last generation of aviators on Terra Nova that could still do the job without the aid of the GLS.

There was a river below—*Ah, there it is*—that was Felton's marker for when to begin the drop. *Well . . . the river plus twelve seconds.* The drop zone itself was reportedly cleared of the enemy. *Which is appreciated.* But the reports also made no warranty about the ground within a kilometer of the DZ. *Which is distinctly troublesome.*

A buzzer in Nadja's headphones told her she'd reached drop altitude, some two hundred and sixty meters above ground. She leveled off and made a fine adjustment to her heading, to take the troops right down the longest part of the oval drop zone. Normally she'd have offset to allow for wind drift but, in this case, *No way to tell, too damned erratic. So, the jumpers are on their own.*

Normally, too, she'd have preferred to drop from about one hundred and twenty meters above ground, to limit the airplane's exposure, as well as that of the men, and also to get them on the ground tight enough for rapid reassembly. She wasn't quite sure what had nixed that, though it may have been the presumed presence of the helicopter gunships she could see through the window as they patrolled the perimeter of the drop zone.

That's one downside of the Gauls' ever-so-clever planning. Yes, the airmobile operation rapidly reinforced with paratroopers may get more combat power on the ground, quicker, than the other way around, but it is not without its—

She sensed rather than saw the blizzard of machine gun fire that arose from the jungle below, as she neared her release point; in full, her Computed Air Release Point, or CARP.

—downsides.

Speaking into the boom mike in front of her mouth, Nadja transmitted by radio to the other aircraft that she was slowing to dropping speed, about one hundred and twenty-two knots. She hoped, but had no real confidence, that this might throw off the aim of the enemy gunners below.

The lack of confidence was well founded. The tremors she'd felt from the troops' movements back in the cargo bay were as nothing to what she felt when a dozen or so machine gun bullets perforated her aircraft. The screaming and shouting coming from the rear told her that not all the damage done had been to unfeeling metal.

God help them, she thought, as she pushed the button for the green light that would send the troops out into the air and down to the battle zone. Wounded men in the back or not, the time span could hardly be measured between her pushing the button and then feeling her plane shudder and balloon; the Haarlem men were springing off the cargo ramp.

With notice of the last jumper gone who could jump, Nadja applied full throttle. Any damage to her plane apparently was not to its engines; it spurted ahead, even as she pulled back on her yoke to bring it above machine-gun range.

HAMS *Typhoon*, South of Cristobal, Shimmering Sea

Alone in his suite—spacious by shipboard standards, and prettified a bit, but still gray paint over cold steel—where he could expect not to be disturbed, Janier took the communications device and pressed the button to contact the commander of the space fleet, far, far, overhead.

The voice from the communicator's small speaker—husky, but very, very female—seemed positively buoyant. "Marguerite speaking, Bertrand. Things seem to be going swimmingly from up here. How can I help you?"

She was always fairly easy for me to deal with, thought Janier, *but, I confess, she's gotten to be a real joy to work with since she took up with Her Imperial Fragrant Cuntedness.*

That last thought, perhaps a little unkind, referred to the High Admiral of the United Earth Peace Fleet's lover, Xingzhen, the Empress of Ming Zhong Guo. Of indeterminate age, the Empress was, Janier admitted, almost painfully beautiful. *And steeped in sin and vice. I hope she is sincere with Marguerite; the woman deserves some happiness in life.*

With an audible sigh, Janier began, "How many times before have things seemed to be going 'swimmingly,' my dear High Admiral? Yes, it's working. Yes, inverting the normal procedure from airborne followed by airmobile to air assault, rapidly reinforced by airborne, may yet get me into the history books, it's working so well. Why, I am practically Napoleon reborn."

That last was spoken sardonically; Janier had long ere now decided that he was *not* Napoleon, nor even too very great. He'd been finding for a while that a touch of humility worked somewhat better for him than had arrogance.

"I don't trust it," he blurted out, "not in the slightest."

"Because it's going too well?" asked the disembodied voice.

"Precisely."

"Well, Bertrand," Marguerite stated, "this is your area of expertise, not mine. But I can tell you, as I often have, what I can see from up here.

"The enemy is retreating into his works as quickly as his legs and wheels—where he has wheels—will carry him. We've intercepted—I am sure your own people have, too—any number of panic-stricken radio transmissions. Via recon skimmer I can see some dozens of artillery positions, abandoned or destroyed or both. There are a fair number of bodies and, if no one's told you, your forces are capturing prisoners, in some numbers. A few hundred, anyway.

"He's fighting hard where he has a chance; that much I agree on. But, Bertrand, is that not itself an indicator that he was taken by surprise?"

The Gaul mulled that. He knew that he was reluctant, genuinely and sincerely reluctant, to expect any tremendous success from his generalship. But, *maybe . . . just maybe, the disasters of recent times were flukes. It is not necessary for me to think I am Napoleon for me to have confidence in what abilities I do have. Is it?*

"It could be so, High Admiral," Janier conceded. "Very

well . . . we'll proceed as we have been. But I would like a couple of things cleared up, if you can, that my staff is unable to."

"Go ahead, Bertrand; ask . . ."

UEPF *Spirit of Peace*, in orbit over Terra Nova

Wallenstein didn't need a communicator; Janier's voice came through the ship's comm system, emerging from a speaker built into her quarters' wall.

Like Janier, Wallenstein preferred to take messages from her opposite, in this case ground-bound, number in the privacy of her own quarters. This, formerly somewhat spare, she'd taken a woman's touch to decorating. It now held various decorations both from back home and from down below. Unwilling to be even partly responsible for the death of a beautiful flying creature, she had, instead, a wonderfully carved Trixie, made of silverwood, but with brightly painted indented lines. It was, perhaps, her favorite piece. The air filtration, purification, and refreshment system didn't like dealing with smoke, but she still had a couple of candelabra which held a trio each of fragrant tranzitree wax candles. Her desk, like the carved bird, was also of silverwood, though unpainted. On one wall hung a saber-tooth's skin, complete to head and long, wickedly curved, fangs.

Though she took some messages in her own quarters, Wallenstein didn't feel the need to be completely alone. Both Xingzhen, her lover and the Empress of Ming Zhong Guo, and Esmeralda, her sometimes cabin girl, rapidly evolving to aide de camp, were present, as was Khan, the husband half of the pair, and Khan, the wife, who was somewhere behind Xingzhen, hidden by covers, on the bed. The ivory-skinned empress lounged in an embroidered green silk robe on her left side. Esma, on the other hand, sat on the edge of a well-padded swivel chair, permanently affixed to the deck through the carpet. Khan sat at the admiral's desk, typing data into her computer, which data was reflected on the wall screen.

That screen, mounted at one corner so all could see it, was large. It was not nearly so large as the locally manufactured Kurosawa filling an entire wall in the main conference room. On the screen was a map of Balboa and Santa Josefina, along with their surrounding waters.

"Go ahead, Bertrand; ask. If we can see it, I'll tell you."

"Have they moved any of their armor," Janier asked, "either against us or against the Zhong landing?"

Marguerite scowled at the screen as she answered the air. "I can't tell you where it is, Bertrand, but I can tell you nothing's moved. Hmmm . . . let me clarify. It's got to be mostly in their log base or in the city. Those are the only two places where they could be hiding the, we estimate"—she cast a glance at Khan who held up two fingers and mouthed, *legions*—"two legions of armor, based on"—again, she looked Khan-ward, then gestured in the direction of the speaker.

"General Janier, this is Commander Khan. We counted some hundreds of tanks, and over a thousand infantry fighting vehicles coming off the ships. At least that many. Plus, something over a hundred self-propelled guns, again, at least. That, with what they already had on hand, tells me that they have the equivalent of two of your mechanized or armored divisions . . ."

"I already knew that, Commander." Janier's tone, despite his interruption, was much more deferential to the spaceborne field grade than he was likely to have been with one of his own. "I have some sources of my own, after all."

"Yes, General, I'm sure of both." Khan's tone was, likewise, much more deferential to the groundling barbarian than was his wont. That could be attributed to the value the high admiral placed on said barbarian groundling. "I mention it so you can be certain; we counted those things off the ships, such as we could, and followed them as far as we could.

"Unfortunately, they played a shell game with us, so we lost most of them in transit. It shouldn't be a surprise; we were trying to keep track of over twenty thousand pieces of equipment and containers.

"How the hell do you play a shell game with a forty-ton tank?" Janier demanded.

"Among other methods, airships," Khan answered. "We can't see through them and when they're over a ship we can't see what comes off the ship. Same when they get over a parking lot. And then we don't know what they unload, when they unload, especially when they might make a dozen or twenty stops on the way. If we'd had eyes on the ground, or on the ships, of course . . ."

Khan let the thought trail off. *No use in reminding the general just why we no longer have any eyes on the ground.*

He continued, "The ones we didn't lose are

suspiciously ill-placed, so I can't say what they mean exactly, except I am inclined to think they mean nothing, that we were *allowed* to track them to delude us into thinking we were doing well."

"You mean," asked Janier, "whatever we think the ones you've been able to track portray, they certainly portray no such thing?"

"Yes, General, that's what I mean. On the other hand, we've done considerably better in identifying which of the protected points the Balboans gave out hold your soldiers they're keeping prisoner, which are medical facilities, and which are nothing at all."

Janier snorted. "No clue about which ones are covering up those tanks and guns you lost?"

"No, General," Khan said, "except that we don't think Carrera's used any of them for an illegal purpose."

"No, he's just hiding those tanks and tracks you can't find among them."

"No, General, we don't think so. Really, we don't. We can't get any magnetic or heat signature consistent with a major piece of equipment from anything within two hundred meters of the protected points the Balboans announced. That does allow you to bomb. Except . . ."

"Except," supplied the Gaul, "we would need to use precision-guided munitions to bomb so close, small ones and a lot of them. Worse, we'd have to use PGMs that don't use the global locating system, since the Balboans can apparently sabotage that. And we don't have them to use. Or not enough of them, anyway. And laser guidance is almost useless in the jungle, while television guidance isn't all that great either.

"Anything on their air defense umbrella and the aerial fleet they used to humiliate us?"

"Sorry, General," said Khan. "Those are even deeper hidden than their tanks."

"We do have some better intelligence for you, Bertrand," Marguerite said.

"You could hardly have less," Janier sneered, then said, with apparent sincerity, "I'm sorry, that was uncalled for."

Hmmm . . . I suppose I haven't quite eliminated the old me.

"What is it you have?" he asked.

"Santa Josefina," Wallenstein said, ignoring the previous sally, because, after all, *The bloody Gaul really is trying.*

"I can pinpoint the locations of anything above a platoon-sized organization from the second regiment of Santa Josefinans, the one that used to be glaring at Marciano over the minefields east of Ciudad Cervantes."

"Why there and not here?" Janier asked.

Khan took the question, answering, "It was a case of preparation, control, planning, and time. They were able to prepare in Balboa to screw with our sensing, because they had control of the ground, the time to do it, and the means to do it. Santa Josefina . . . they didn't. Santa Josefina's always struck me as a sideshow, true, but they also just didn't have the means to do any serious preparation, either."

"Okay," Janier agreed, "that's useful. Can you get it to Marciano directly, or do you want to funnel it through me?"

Wallenstein didn't answer right away, thinking hard for

a short moment. Eyes roamed the corners of her quarters until falling, at last, on Esmeralda.

"We'll send it down to Marciano, Bertrand," she said. "You have enough to do."

"Thanks," Janier agreed. "Marciano might find it insulting to get the information from me. He's an independent campaign, after all. And besides, he has time in grade on me.

"And then, too . . ."

"Yes, General?" Wallenstein asked.

"In thinking about it . . . well . . . frankly, this is the part where we were vulnerable. If they moved their armor now, they could catch us scattered, in poor positions, under-supported, in an absolutely crappy supply situation, with no defenses prepared. Yes, even in the jungle. I've already learned that tanks can still be useful in the jungle.

"But, in any case, I mean that the knowledge they are not committing their armor is as valuable, not least to my piece of mind, as anything else you could have told me.

"And it means one other thing."

"What's that?" Wallenstein asked.

"I suspect that Carrera made a mistake." Janier gave a tentative laugh, followed by a much fuller one. "Even if he'd intended to put on a mere show of resistance around Cristobal, once he had us here and vulnerable he should have struck. So maybe, finally, *finally*, the son of a bitch made a mistake."

CHAPTER FIVE

"In all the trade of war, no feat
Is nobler than a brave retreat."
—Samuel Butler, *Hudibras*

***Estado Mayor*, Sub camp C, Ciudad Balboa, Balboa**

Carrera sat on a camp stool set up on a low dais, one that was still high enough to see the large map and its movable troop markers. His head hung. Hands folded, forearms resting on thighs, the slumped shoulders told of a man in the pits of despair from an unaccustomed defeat.

That image, their never-conquered commander in a blue funk, infected every member of the staff who saw it, which infection—"defeatism," it was called—was passed on to everyone they came in contact with. Unlike normal, biological diseases, this one could be transmitted by radio and landline.

Moreover, he'd maintained something much like that posture during a just finished meeting with the ambassador from the Federated States, Tom Wallis, on the reasoning that, *Wallis will have to report my demeanor and there are enough Kosmos and Taurophiles in his organization that they'll get the word to where it needs to go.*

Whatever visual image he presented, Carrera still listened carefully to reports from both Second Corps and Fourth Corps as their subordinate units, such as were exposed, escaped from the area of the Tauran incursion to either the safe area on and behind the Parilla Line or into Fortress Cristobal. As he listened, he watched the map being updated. He watched it discreetly, eyes hidden under brows, unwilling to show anything to anyone.

He almost blew his feigned disinterest when the first Tauran units bumped into the Parilla Line, and loudspeaker-borne reports of the action, punctuated with rifle and machine-gun fire, were broadcast into the operations room.

Really have to watch that, he cautioned himself. *Really have to make sure that any transmissions coming out of here and intercepted tell of nothing but despair.*

Ambassador Tom Wallis was just about to leave the compound to return to his staff car, thence to his not-yet-bombed embassy, when Fernandez stopped him for a brief word.

"I won't insult you with an offer of either women or money, Ambassador," Fernandez said, "but you've always seemed to be a true friend to us and even to our little political experiment."

"I am," Wallis answered. "I always have been."

"Ah, very good. I was wondering if you might, then,

manage to leave certain intelligence items where, say, somebody on both our payrolls could see them."

Wallis barely kept from laughing. *Well, of fucking course Fernandez has people in my embassy. Silly not to have.*

Instead, with his face the essence of diplomatic neutrality, he asked, "What, specifically, do you want, Legate?"

"Satellite imagery, actually, of the Tauran air bases in Cienfuegos. Do they send you that kind of thing?"

"Not usually," Wallis answered carefully. "When we get sent something like that it's generally to put us in high dudgeon so we don't have to just *act* angry or sympathetic in negotiations."

Fernandez considered that, then asked, "Well . . . what if you asked for them to give you conviction enough to show us the hopelessness of our position, the better to restart the peace negotiations?"

"You have an evil mind, legate. But, you know, that might work."

South of the Parilla Line

Foliage was scarce at ground level in the deep, dark jungle. Only with the death and rotting of an old tree, or the lightning-blasted sundering of a major branch, had enough light leaked through to allow anything much to grow, those places, and in the few Carrera had cleared allegedly for housing and farming purposes.

Of course, now, what with the war and the bombing,

there were a lot more places where sufficient light to feed life could leak through. A LOT more places. And, in some few spots, there was already the beginning of what might turn out to be substantial growth. Or might not, bombing schedule depending.

Tribune Ramirez lay in the dirt, the detachment from his battery strung out in the damp draw behind him. The tribune's dirt-camouflaged face lurked behind a patch of thick grass, raised where the sun peeked through the canopy, caressing the spot on which the grass grew for a portion of an hour a day.

Ramirez stuck his fingers into a grass clump then spread them, forcing the grass apart just enough to peer through, as one might peer through a keyhole. It was not enough to be seen by someone distant on the far side. What he saw was a firefight. Rather, he saw the enemy side of it, their machine guns pounding, providing cover, chipping bark off trees and sending clods of dirt into the air, while riflemen and grenadiers lunged forward in short leaps and bounds. He didn't recognize the uniforms, but the shouted orders sounded distinctly Teutonic to him. Worse, though the Balboan F-26 rifle and M-26 light machine gun put out rounds at a much higher rate than anything the Taurans had, he heard little of that rate of fire being slung toward the enemy.

He slowly moved his head left and right, making a few tiny changes to the sheltering grass as he did so. Eyes darted back and forth, engraving a replicable picture on the brain. Then he slithered back, with the mud forcing itself up under his uniform jacket and lorica as he did.

With curt whispers and a finger drawing in the muck,

Ramirez illustrated what he wanted done. "Some of our guys are in trouble ahead . . ."—scratch, scratch—"the enemy is here"—point, circle—"We're already on line, here"—point, scratch—"and about well-enough oriented."

Avilar raised one eyebrow. *You sure about this, Boss?*

"They're our guys, we can't just abandon them."

The eyebrow dropped. Avilar, reluctantly at first, and then with determination, gave several curt nods. "All right."

"Walk the line to the far end," Ramirez said, pointing in the direction from which they'd come. "Tell the boys, fix bayonets . . . *quietly*. Full auto, not burst. I'll lead. You follow, kicking any stragglers in the ass. We'll charge. Screaming like maniacs, we'll charge."

Again, Avilar gave a couple of curt nods, then arose to a crouch and began walking the line down the draw, giving whispered orders even more curt than his commander's had been.

Ramirez watched for a second, then took up his own rifle. Normally, being a tribune, he bore only a pistol, but he'd figured this mission might call for something heavier when he'd been ordered out, so had drawn a spare from his unit's arms room. Everyone carried the same model bayonet cum wire cutters, so he hadn't had to borrow one of those.

With one thumb, the tribune unsnapped the clasp, his hand covering the thing to muffle sound. Unnecessary? Who could say? But few if any soldiers in human history had lost their lives for being too *quiet*.

Not untypically, his heartbeat became much more

rapid as his fingers closed around the bayonet's plastic handle. The pounding came faster and harder as he maneuvered the blade onto the muzzle, seated it, and checked that it was firmly affixed.

Glancing down the line, Ramirez saw that Avilar had beaten him to the draw, despite having to walk and give orders as he did. *How the fuck does he do that?*

Oddly, the tribune's heart rate slowed considerably after that. It went up again as soon as the centurion gave him the thumbs up.

Ramirez rolled to get on one knee, his left, with his right foot planted firmly in the muck. He took a final deep breath—*and it might be final, at that*—then launched himself up and over the lip of the draw.

His brother, the senior non-com of the aircraft carrier *Dos Lindas*, now interned in Santa Josefina, had taught him a battle cry once. The tribune used it now. Firing from the hip at a machine-gun crew about one hundred meters to his front, his men joining in almost immediately, Ramirez screamed, "BANZAI, MOTHERFUCKERS!"

Sergeant Major Ricardo Cruz prayed silently. At least when he was conscious, he did. When he prayed, it wasn't for his life; he thought that was lost anyway. At least, the amount of blood he'd been coughing up suggested very strongly that this was pretty much it. Rather, he commended his soul to God and asked of his God that He should look to the welfare of his wife and children.

For doesn't the song the cadets sing insist that God in His Heaven loves His faithful soldiers?

How the fuck did we end up like this?

Cruz asked the question, but he already had the answer. *We never really trained for this. A little lip service, sure, but really, we trained for attack, attack, and attack some more. And we never lost while doing that. So, when it was the enemy on the attack, and we had no ambush ready, we fell apart a little. At least . . .*

At least that was what happened when the maniple Cruz was accompanying was hit from the flank by a unit—*hell, was it even a platoon?*—of Tauran paras. The maniple commander went down quickly, followed by the first platoon leader. The exec had gone ahead and the first centurion was still waiting back at camp, to the north. And the platoons had simply broken and scattered, demoralized in advance by the unaccustomed retreat.

Cruz had managed to round up ten men, forcing them by sheer force of personality—well, that and a credible rumor that the cohort sergeant major wasn't above shooting a coward—to hold a line to cover the rout of the rest, hoping that enough of them would get through to reform the unit under the exec. And they had bought some time for the rest, though all but two were dead or wounded now. And Cruz . . . Cruz . . .

"Sergeant Major," asked the private, his voice filled with fear and desperation. He was a young kid, fairly new to the maniple. As he shook the bleeding Cruz to something like alertness, he asked, "Sergeant Major, what do we do now? I'm just about out of ammunition. So's Salazar. And that's after looting the dead and wounded. What do we do now?"

"Fix bayonets," said Cruz, though he was hardly aware of having said it.

"Yes, Sergeant Major," said the private, and was just about to click his bayonet home when he heard, coming from his front, a flurry of fire such as he hadn't heard since the Mad Minute in basic training. The fire shocked him, which shock became deeper still when it was followed by *"Banzai*, motherfuckers!" in turn followed by a less distinct bellow of pure rage, coming from a mass of animals or maniacs, somewhere to his right front.

Ramirez's first burst, not unpredictably, missed the machine-gun crew. It hit close enough, though, to make the gunner and ammo bearer nearly soil themselves, and to stop their continued firing on whoever or whatever it was that had been in the gunner's sights. The assistant gunner took a shot at Ramirez, no better aimed than had been the tribune's. Ramirez raised his F-26 rifle to his shoulder for a better aimed burst, but even as he lined the sights up, someone or someones in his crew bowled over the machine-gun team in a red misty haze. He dropped the rifle back to a lower position.

The tribune charged on, still screaming wildly and firing from the hip. If he'd been thinking he'd have, rightly, doubted he'd hit anything. Thinking, though, was quite beyond his capabilities at the moment.

Passing a thick tree, Ramirez sensed a hulking presence. He was just turning when said presence launched himself forward, his unbayoneted rifle raised with the stock forward, for a butt smash.

Ramirez ducked, which was a lot easier for his being

so much shorter than his assailant. The butt smash went right over his head, leaving the Tauran tottering forward from the overbalance.

Instinctively, as the hulking Tauran tottered, Ramirez lunged with the bayonet. He cursed at having the point fail to find any purchase on the Tauran's body armor. The bayonet slid off, sliding further under the Tauran's load carrying equipment, the harness holding ammunition, canteens, and first aid pouch. Instinctively—"Attack! Attack! Attack!"—Ramirez pushed forward on his rifle, twisting the falling Tauran around and causing his legs to entangle. The Tauran went down, losing control of his rifle as he did. However, with hands firmly—nay, desperately—holding onto his own F-26, Ramirez was pulled down with him.

And came up to hands and knees just in time to take a ferocious punch to the jaw from a Tauran who recovered his senses just a fraction of a second faster than Ramirez did. The tribune flew sideways, spun by the blow. His helmet flew off in a different direction.

Landing on his back, the wind knocked from him, and stunned besides, Ramirez's swimming eyes saw the Tauran stand and draw a knife. Inanely, the tribune thought, *What kind of moronic army issues a knife that can't be fixed to a rifle, when they could issue a bayonet that can always serve as a knife?*

Somewhat less inanely, realizing what the advancing Tauran intended for the knife, Ramirez's right hand scrambled to his left side for the legionary issue, large bore pistol, held in the underarm holster there. He pulled out the firearm, aiming it at the Tauran with one unsteady hand, pulled the trigger and—

BLAM! *Shit! Missed!* BLAM!

The second shot did hit but the bullet, not yet having travelled enough for the spin to stabilize it, hit at an off angle, and thus merely staggered the Tauran, lurching him back a couple of feet, and probably hurting like hell.

BLAM! BLAM! BLAM! Two misses and a hit; the Tauran coughed from the blow, and seemed stunned, but definitely did not go down. Instead, he shook his head, tightened the grip on his knife, and came on.

"Die, goddammit, die!" Ramirez exclaimed. Still on his back, he took his non-firing hand, his left hand, and placed it under the magazine well to steady it. Wincing a little in advance at what he expected to happen, he took a more careful aim—the care coming from his desperation—and with equal care, squeezed the trigger at the Tauran who was now no more than ten feet away.

A hole, about half an inch across, appeared in the Tauran's face, about an inch to the left of his narrow nose. His head snapped back at the same time as the hole appeared, then, pulled by the head, the body arched backwards and collapsed.

Stifling a sob, Ramirez likewise folded into the dirt, exhausted beyond care by his ordeal, by the close call, and by the feeling of having committed murder.

He actually came to his senses while being led by Avilar to a place with several bodies, and some thousands of spent stubs from their 6.5mm rifles.

"I'm okay, Centurion; I can walk now."

"If you say so, sir," Avilar agreed. "The leader here"— Avilar pointed down at someone bloody, still breathing, and unconscious—"is Sergeant Major Cruz from Second *Tercio*. He's hurt bad—sucking chest wound, both front and rear—but our medic reset the bandages and resealed the plastic, and gave him a blood expander. This group didn't have a medic so it was just what a private remembered from basic training. At least his lungs have stopped collapsing and he's got a fair chance of not drowning in his own blood if we can get him out of here. There are also two unhurt ones, two walking wounded, plus two more of ours. And five dead of the sergeant major's along with two dead of ours.

"I'm having litters prepared from ponchos but we can't carry all of them, not if we try to take the corpses out. And sir? There's absolutely no time to bury the bodies."

Ramirez winced, nodded, then said, "Sometimes I hate my fucking job. Leave the bodies. Load the litters as soon as you can. We move out in fifteen minutes."

"Yes, sir."

"We're going to switch, too. You take point, head north. I'll need whatever can be spared from the litters for a rear guard."

Avilar nodded. "I'll set it up sir. Now sit and rest, why don't you?"

Ramirez sat. He was shocked, then, when the wounded sergeant major opened his eyes, looked at him, and said, "Ramirez? What are you doing here? I thought you were on a boat."

"Ship, Sergeant Major," Tribune Ramirez corrected. "My elder brother, the squid, would insist on calling it a 'ship.' We look a lot alike."

"Elder brother? Oh . . . oh, okay. Tell him I said 'hi.'"

Then Cruz closed his eyes, letting unconsciousness take him once more.

Parilla Line, Balboa

As they had gotten closer to the line, Centurion Avilar had aimed for wherever he didn't hear firing ahead. Passage of lines was a stone bitch under almost any circumstances. Trying to do it where a battle was in process approached the suicidal.

He tried the recognition signal over the radio and got nothing. He tried shouting out the approved code phrase and got a blizzard of bullets in return. The bullets that thunked into the tree behind which he sheltered were "friendly," he thought, based on the rate of fire. What worked, however, was simple. In their own accent he said, "This is Centurion Avilar, Sixty-Second Field Artillery, with a party of twenty-one. If you motherfuckers shoot at me again I am going to come forward, take your fucking rifles, and shove them up your asses."

"Cease fire! Cease fire!" passed along the line ahead. A voice called out, "Come forward, centurion, with your party of twenty-one. You've got to be friendly because nobody but an Anglian or a legionary centurion talks like that, and you don't sound Anglian."

"Fine," Avilar shouted back. "We need an ambulance or three, and a landline to graves registration."

"The command post can give you the landline. I'll call for the ambulance or, if I can get them, ambulances. Come on in and welcome back."

Log Base Alpha, so-called, Balboa Province, Balboa

Avilar was still away, taking care of some details with graves registration and seeing to the men put in hospital. *He'll be along within an hour or so*, Tribune Ramirez thought.

Exhausted as he hadn't been since *Cazador* School, Ramirez dumped his lorica and load-bearing equipment, leaned his rifle on a stump, sat down on a short stack of ration boxes, and then leaned his back against the corrugated metal of the repurposed shipping container that, buried and sandbagged, served for his battery headquarters. The chill metal was almost a shock against the commander's sweaty back. After a few moments of reveling in the sweet cool of the shelter, he asked of his small battery headquarters staff, "Where's Top? Where's the Exec?"

The company clerk's eyes rolled. The supply sergeant cleared his throat. Commo began to whistle. The battery chief of smoke started to say something, then clammed up.

"It was a simple question," said Ramirez. "I want an answer. I . . ."

"They're under arrest and on charges," said the chief of smoke, *Optio* Rosario.

"WHAT?"

"Charges, sir. They put up a sign saying who and what we were. A big sign. 'Morale,'" the XO said.

"Within two hours of the sign going up, some of Legate

Fernandez's people had shown up." Everyone, including Ramirez, felt a little shiver at that name. "Next thing I knew the XO and Top were in cuffs, being marched off, and the sign was being taken down. We've still got it, hidden away. Then the *tercio* commander came by and chewed my ass on general principle. He said he'd try to get them out and get the charges dropped, but he wasn't sure he could."

"Shit."

At the word, as if on cue, the sirens began blaring.

"Shit," cursed the chief of smoke, "another goddamned air raid."

Estado Mayor, Sub camp C, Ciudad Balboa, Balboa

"They don't know anything," was Warrant Officer Mahamda's judgment. "They don't even understand what they did wrong. That's good, isn't it?"

Fernandez began chewing his lip, let his chin drop nearly to his chest, and thought about that question before answering. *Do I take Mahamda's judgment on this? I think so; he's probably—no, certainly—the best interrogator we've got, for any level of interrogation. As for those two ninnies and their fucking sign . . . it's . . . not actually their fault. Any instructions to avoid advertising what's in the "Log Base" would themselves be advertisements that something's in the "Log Base." Besides logistics, that is.*

I suppose I was asking too much when I told my people to go out of their way to make sure no paint went in there?

It was a silly cover, anyway, like someone was going to be able to paint a sign that could be seen from the air, through triple canopy jungle. And, anyway, who would have predicted that, in the absence of paint, someone would sit an artistically inclined private down, with a one-by two-meter piece of clear plastic and a shitload of alcohol pens, and have that private spend two weeks drawing a sign . . . with pens? Jesus. Just Jesus.

And what do I do about it if someone, say, one of those spies I haven't been able to catch the trail of, saw it? I suppose there's nothing I can do.

Maybe a little disinformation? Provide enough paint for everyone to make a sign, but have them all advertise themselves as something very rear echelon? No . . . that's suspicious in itself.

Ignore it, let them go with an ass chewing, and hope for the best? That might actually be best.

"You didn't . . ."

Mahamda shook his head vigorously. "No, sir. With people you think might be innocent and are your own? Terrible idea to put them to the question. Ruins them forever and makes even the most loyal men turn.

"No, I just interrogated them separately. Didn't even give them the guided tour of the instruments and techniques. Well . . . really didn't need to; just about every custodial interrogation has torture somewhere in the background, working on the mind of the man to be interrogated. It's only the really dumb ones who actually need the tour; them, and the ones who believe the propaganda about, 'Who? Us? We *never* use torture.'"

"Good . . . good. You did right, Achmed."

The Sumeri immigrant beamed. "Thank you, sir. Every now and then even *my* job allows a little charity."

Fernandez nodded, as if he mostly agreed. "Send them to my office in half an hour. I'll put the fear of God in them and send them on their way."

"Yes, sir. Half an hour."

Fortress Cristobal, Passage Point #2

At this portion of the perimeter, there were three gaps in the wire and mines. Other sections had other gaps, some more than three, some less. There wasn't a lot that could be done about the wire, though more wire was stockpiled nearby, along with caltrop projectors. Scatterable mine packs were emplaced to close the gaps in the minefield.

At two of the gaps, shells were falling with whistles and shrieks. At or above the ground, they blossomed into flowers of fire and smoke and whizzing shards of razor sharp steel. The third gap, covered by smoke, the enemy seemed not to have discovered yet.

By that third gap, half sheltered in a trench, Xavier Jimenez took his chances. Ashamed to take cover in one of the concrete bunkers, while men of his command tried to get to safety, Jimenez had to, just had to, share the risk. With him were a couple of secondary members of his staff and, for a radio bearer, the female signaler, Sarita Asilos.

Hmmmph, thought the Fourth Corps commander, *I can take the risk by my own choice, but the people with me didn't get a lot of choice, did they.*

He turned to the female soldier carrying his radio,

Sarita Asilos, saying, "Leave the radio with me, Sarita. You get back to the bunker."

"No, sir," she answered. "You're out here; it's my job and my duty to be out here, too."

Jimenez took a deep breath, preparatory to emitting a bellow. Then he looked at the plea written on the girl's face: *I may not be an officer but I'm as good a human being as you are, so don't shame me by sending me to shelter.*

Sighing, Jimenez nodded. The thought of that beautiful face being mashed into so much strawberry jam was difficult, but . . .

"Okay . . . okay, you can stay. Just keep low, will you?"

"Thank you, sir," the woman answered. "I will."

Jimenez alternated between shouting out encouragement to the men entering the fortress and talking over the field phone to his artillery commander, Arosamena, the latter struggling to keep a smoke screen up while preserving his command.

The men trying to get in also had to try to squeeze their way between the incoming shells, the churned-up ground, and the bullets, only one in five a tracer, that scored the air overhead. This crew were La Platans, part of the newly designated Thirty-ninth *Tercio*, Marines, hence somewhat elite. At least they were doing about as well as could be expected in dealing with something—artillery shells—that they had no hope of fighting.

Jimenez suddenly became aware of a pale soldier, young, and about as tall as himself, standing in the open trench with him. In the cover of the trench, the soldier saluted. Jimenez returned it.

"Sir," the newcomer said, speaking in that La Platan Spanish that might as well have been Old Earth Italian, "Lieute . . . I mean Tribune Pereyra, reporting, sir. These are my compa . . . .maniple's men coming in."

"Are you the commander?" Jimenez asked, suspicious that a commander might seek shelter before his men.

He relaxed when the La Platan answered, "No, sir; I'm the exec. My commander's out with them. He'll be the last in, I think . . . assuming . . ."

Estado Mayor, Sub camp C, Ciudad Balboa, Balboa

Carrera stood up from his camp stool, took the couple of steps off the dais, and exited the operations room. Warrant Officer Jamey Soult, his driver, was waiting, not far from the entrance to the thick-walled concrete shelter.

"Need a lift, Boss?" Soult asked.

"Yeah, Jamey," Carrera answered, climbing into the unremarkable staff car. "Take me to Fifty-second Deception *Tercio*, in Subcamp D."

"Wilco," Soult replied, starting the vehicle and easing out from under the camouflage and radar scattering screen overhead. "What, if it's okay to ask, is your business with the Fifty-second?"

"Nothing specific," Carrera replied. "I just want to get a general feel for how much bait the enemy might be taking."

CHAPTER SIX

"Therefore, the best warfare strategy is to attack
the enemy's plans, next is to attack alliances, next
is to attack the army, and the worst is to attack a
walled city.

Laying siege to a city is only done when other
options are not available."   —Sun Tzu

Academia *Sergento* Juan Malvegui,
Puerto Lindo, Cristobal Province, Balboa

The general's helicopter came skipping in, just above the
waves. Sure, the locals hadn't been using their air defense
much, but they'd already demonstrated that they could at
any time, and that when they did it could be in devastating
mass.

So why take the chance? thought Janier. *What profit
to it? The pilot of this crate can try to nab a fish with his
skids; it's all fine by me. Well . . . unless it's a meg he tries
for. Hmmm . . .*

A meg, or megalodon, was one of the species

transported by the Noahs to Terra Nova. To say they resembled great whites on steroids would be a serious understatement; the largest great white ever recorded on Old Earth wouldn't have fed a meg for much past a day. At the thought of a meg, Janier unconsciously leaned out to check the water. He felt foolish as he did so. Then he thought about it a bit more and looked again, feeling not at all foolish.

At nearly the last second, the pilot pulled pitch, lifting his bird over the stone wall surrounding the old fort's terreplein, then reversing that motion to come in fairly hard on the grass. Janier's stomach tried to crawl out his anus, first, then out of his mouth.

Beats taking a missile up the ass.

With the chopper firmly on the ground, vibrating with the turn of the motor and the rotors it drove, Janier took off his soft cap and stuffed it into the same pocket into which he'd stashed the communicator given to him by High Admiral Wallenstein.

Would never do to get it sucked into the engine.

Janier's Aide de camp, Malcoeur, toted his chief's helmet in a nylon bag, thereby allowing Janier to look ever-so-casual and unconcerned, while having at least that much measure of safety, safely hidden, nearby.

Head ducked perhaps a little lower than strictly necessary to avoid the blades churning overhead, Janier stepped to the ground and strode out to where his chief of staff, the newly promoted, rather short, stout, and fiercely intelligent looking Major General Francois D'Espérey, awaited. Breaking with custom and policy, Janier, which is to say the new and improved Janier, had reached down all the way to the, in his opinion, mostly no account-colonels of the Gallic Army to find a chief of staff he could have confidence in. D'Espérey was that man.

"The command post is all set," announced the chief, as soon as Janier got close enough. Even at that, he had to lean in and shout to be heard over the helicopter's steady beat. "Care for the tour, sir? It's an interesting facility here, where Carrera trained some of the children he surprised us with."

"Not yet," Janier shouted back, also having to lean in to be heard. "Show me the port; that's more important than any map or battery of radios and phones."

"Yes, sir," agreed the chief, leading the way across the terreplein to the gate that led out from the school. Malcoeur followed at a respectful distance.

D'Espérey continued, "We've got it pretty much intact. Even captured the facility where they built . . . maybe better said, molded . . . their coastal subs. And the scrapyard where they've been cutting up old warships."

"Learn anything useful?" the general asked.

"Not much," the chief admitted. "We came on too fast for them to destroy the facilities, but they had burn barrels running full steam to destroy the paper. Well, there was one thing."

"That being?"

"If the Anglians prove difficult, the machine on which they molded the sections of their acrylic submarines has 'Made in Anglia' written all over it. And I mean *really* written, not figuratively."

Janier laughed, then grew sober. *You know, it just might be a useful stick to beat the Anglians with.*

"There is one other thing, sir . . . . but . . ."

"Yes, D'Espérey?"

D'Espérey took a deep breath, then continued, "But, sir, this is just a big damned trap. Or, at least, it's intended to be."

"Your reasoning?"

"It's too easy," the chief said. "It's been impossibly easy. The army that ran us out of the country with our tails between our legs doesn't neglect the danger we posed. I mean, they had to have known we were out there, with a base on Cienfuegos, another one in Santa Josefina, and an invasion fleet. The army that defeated the Zhong invasion fleet doesn't forget about the threat elsewhere. The air force that dictated to us that we shall not send in our fighter-bombers in little penny packets does not forget to keep tabs. The navy that trashed the Zhong nuclear submarine fleet—and did no little damage to us, either— does not simply retire and get itself interned."

"No chance they took the bait we set by the secondary effort at the port of Capitano?" Janier asked.

"A chance, sir? Maybe a chance. But I don't believe it. As for bait, 'Under fragrant bait,' as the Zhong might say, 'there is certain to be a hooked fish.' We've been presented with just too much fragrant bait!"

Janier looked around and spotted a great stone slab, half sunk into the earth. He made a beeline for it, directing D'Espérey to follow. "Sit," he ordered, when they reached the slab. "Sit, and I shall join you."

"I go round and round on this myself, Francois," Janier admitted. "When I talk to"—he pointed a finger skyward—"they can usually convince me that this is all just good generalship on my part, with maybe a little luck, and a lot of mistake on the part of the enemy. When I am alone with my thoughts, though, I tremble."

"Me, too," D'Espérey admitted. "Especially when I look at the logistic situation. Sir, we have to get Cristobal. I think that's not just the key to the campaign, but the key to the enemy's thinking.

"Fragrant bait, yes; that's here. But he is probably assuming we can't go anywhere much, or do anything much, until we take the port, the big port. It's a fair assumption, too," D'Espérey continued, "because to take the big port we need a lot of firepower and a lot of infantry. Which we cannot support—"

"—because," Janier interrupted, "we can't supply a big enough force to take Cristobal quickly through this little bay, however pretty and well-shaped it is." Janier raised an eyebrow, saying sardonically. "Yes, all that I've figured out on my own."

"And taking the other ports further west," said the chief, ignoring the eyebrow and the tone, both, "doesn't really help because they add more to our defense problems than they solve for our offensive problems. And they're tiny and primitive, to boot."

Janier's eyes rolled. "Yes, D'Espérey, I figured *that* one out on my own, too."

The chief ignored that, too, saying, "But we don't need them anyway. I think the mistake the enemy made was in not figuring out how quickly we can turn this little bay, which, at more than half a square kilometer is not so little as all that, into a big port. And we needn't necessarily go to those far western ports, anyway."

D'Espérey gestured expansively. "The sheer beauty and convenience of this port stymied the development of at least two more sheltered deep-water anchorages. One, the smaller one, is about a kilometer and a half northeast of here. It will do, with a little work, for lighters and landing craft. The other is barely connected to civilization by a remarkably shitty road, about eight kilometers southwest of here. We can improve that road, and we can make that bay a useful port. There's a civilian marina there, already, though it's abandoned for now. And there are about five more little bays that just might do with some work.

"As to how we're going to do that, sir, let me show you the port as you've said, and then let me lead you to the engineer. He's shown me how."

"Anglian, right?"

"Yes, sir, but they're very good engineers, you know. Different from us, yes. Less elegant? Yes, that too. But quite good in their simple-minded and inelegant way."

"What's all this do to our security requirements?" Janier asked.

"Maybe need a brigade patrolling to the west, sir. Just a brigade. We'd need a lot more if we tried to use the port at Nicuesa, which is maybe eighty kilometers out and completely indefensible at any distance from the port."

"Fine," said Janier. "But instead of showing me the port and then bringing me to the engineer, have the engineer meet us at the port."

"Sir? But all his charts and plans are down below, where I've set up the command post."

"No matter," said Janier. "With these Anglians you

have to show them right away who's boss or there'll never be a moment's peace or cooperation."

And I say that, even in my newer, kinder, and gentler self, because it's true. Of course, it's true of both of us in about equal measure.

Isla Santa Catalina, Mar Furioso, off the coast of Balboa

Somehow, the island exuded a sense of despair that the overwhelming scent of flowers did nothing to dissipate. Why that should be so the Zhong commander, Fleet Admiral Wanyan Liang, didn't know. But it was so, everyone seemed to feel it. Perhaps it came, subconsciously, from the knowledge that this was a former prison island, reputed to have been an absolute hell.

Maybe, though, thought Wanyan, *it's left over from the whipping we received from their Isla Real.*

That whipping had been administered not only by the well-entrenched defenders on the ground, facing Zhong Marines across the surf, but also by a massive hidden park of heavy artillery, previously not even hinted at, firing very long-range laser-guided shells, that had gutted the Zhong fleet. In the wake of it, to save what he could, and to at least try to save face and perhaps even contribute to the war, Wanyan had led the remnants of his fleet, and the two corps of infantry it still carried, to this place, here to establish a base to support a ground invasion of the mainland. That mainland, already being occupied by Wanyan's two army corps, was only about ten miles away from this island. The locals hadn't even tried to defend it. The Zhong had also grabbed a smaller, equally undefended, island about fifteen miles to the west, *Isla Montijo*, for its proximity to a good hard surfaced road on the mainland.

And I don't understand why these two islands, nor any of the islands, nor the coasts, failed to put up even a symbolic defense. Well . . . there were those few platoons of commandos that went to contest some of the first helicopter insertions, but those hardly even arose to the level of a symbol. Did they expect to utterly destroy us at the big island? If so, I am ever so pleased they failed.

Are they just being sensible, not trying to defend everything? Do they have a different plan, one I am not seeing? I think the former is true . . . but I need to be on guard against the latter. Then, too, they can calculate logistic needs, too, and maybe better than we can, since they can know if they're going to do something that will drive up our requirements. So maybe they just know already that we can't do a damned thing except occupy a chunk of their country, and sit there, while feeding those half million refugees they put in our way.

Bastards, Wanyan scowled at the mainland. *Ruthless bastards.*

Looking out to sea, where engineers and divers in their hundreds and thousands worked, supplemented by impressed laborers—*Oh, may as well be honest with myself and call them what they are, namely "slaves"*— Wanyan scowled even more deeply. He thought, *This better frigging work or the empress is going to have my balls for earrings.*

The "this" in question was an ad hoc, emergency, *oh, we are so screwed otherwise*, plan to support the landing of the still substantial Zhong Expeditionary Force against the Balboan mainland, east of the capital. In other words, "this" was going to be an attempt to create a port, on the fly, ad hoc, where none had been before.

The problem was that there were no ports that mattered in the area. The seas here were too shallow for any ship of any size to even get close to shore. And there were, so reconnaissance insisted, something like half a million civilians in the area, who would have to be fed and cared for. *Or the bleeding-heart fucking Taurans will cut off our financial support and air support which, again, leads to my balls dangling from Her Imperial Majesty's earlobes.*

Zhong logistic needs were, on a per capita basis, much less than the needs of Tauran or Federated States forces, but they weren't nonexistent, nor even trivial. Fuel, parts, food, ammunition, not necessarily in that order. Nine kilograms per man per day was what Wanyan's chief logistician considered the minimum to be landed. That worked out to sixteen hundred tons per day, minimum.

And even that's only a guess and only for fuel, parts, ammunition, food, and a small increment for things like medical care. It also doesn't account for the roughly seven hundred and fifty tons per day of humanitarian supplies for the civilians the Balboans thoughtfully left in the way, nearly none of them in a remotely convenient location.

That was also not much more than mere occupation and survival. And it was also near the beaches over which the supplies would have to come. Inland, demand would go up. They would also go up if there were resistance or sabotage. And that also didn't include the need to build up a substantial stockpile of ammunition in case the Balboans sortied one or more of their heavy formations at the Zhong lodgment.

It would be *much* worse if Balboa couldn't be expected to provide the water on its own. It would be worse if they couldn't base a fair amount of the effort at sea, where supply wasn't such a problem. Almost all medical facilities and higher headquarters were going to remain at sea, though the calculation for how much shipping space was best devoted to that, and how much needed to be freed up to continue to ferry in supplies was a complex one.

And I'm not sure we calculated it all that well, either. How could we when we really can't predict what the enemy will do?

Thank the gods, thought Wanyan, *that airships can take up some of the slack, even though I can't risk them past the islands. Speaking—well, thinking—of which . . .*

Wanyan consulted his wristwatch and looked to sea. Pretty much on cue, a brace of heavy cargo lifting airships, on loan, with their crews, from the Tauran Union, appeared on the horizon. The Taurans had lent the Zhong four airships, to supplement Zhong National Airlines, but that really meant about five sorties every week, with Zhong and Tauran both, what with an eighteen-thousand-mile round trip, a speed of about seventy knots, and the need to load and unload, plus downtime for maintenance. The Tauran loaners weren't of the best or most capable, either.

We'll be lucky if we can get a thousand tons a week in that way, maybe fifteen hundred if we don't cube out before we weight out, though that would be unlikely.

Helps, sure, but not decisively. Decisive is ships and ports.
And the domestic cost of taking our airships out of service
isn't small or even, long-term sustainable.

With three small moons, Hecate, Eris, and Bellona,
tides were generally lesser on Terra Nova than on Old
Earth. There were odd exceptions, as when all three
moons were in position to pull together, but on a normal
day this coast of Balboa experienced tides of nine to ten
feet. With heavy silt covering the bedrock, out to a
distance of nearly eighty kilometers, this made bringing a
ship in to unload a very problematic issue. At high tide,
for example, a standard Zhong replenishment ship of the
309 Class, coming from the west, would ground out about
eight miles from the island.

But there were a couple of oddities that worked in the
Zhong's favor. The eastern coast of Santa Catalina, for
example, was actually quite deep for a few hundred meters
eastward. Thus, a ship that could be gotten into it during
high tide could stay there to unload, even during low tide,
without risk of grounding. It would have to be turned
around by something else; Wanyan's staff was planning on
cables and winches until some tugs could be ferried in.
Moreover, because just outside of that trench in the sea
bottom things returned to the more normal depth for this
part of the world, the Zhong engineers believed they could
ground two freighters, with their own integral cranes, and
link them by a mix of floating bridge and barges that had
been filled with rock and concrete and then sunk. Already
there were pilings pounded in, to hold both bridge and
barges in place and a set of anchored floating docks, as well.

That was all well and good, but the real trick was still to get their cargo ships to the trench to be unloaded, that, and getting the freighters with their cranes in, in the first place.

"The engineers report they're ready for the first stretch, sir," Wanyan's aide reported. The aide, the *new* aide, the old one being food for the fishes, was a marine, selected from among the unwounded who had still never made it to shore on the Isla Real for lack of transports to get them there. Though a lieutenant colonel, the aide, Ma Chu, carried a radio on his back. The radio was in communication with the party at work out at sea.

Letting his hand holding the hand mike drop, Ma Chu announced, "They say the tide will be fully in in a few minutes."

"They've accounted for every diver and all the slaves?" the admiral asked. Wanyan was perhaps ruthless, but no more, not a bit more, than the job required. When this was over he fully intended to release all the impressed workers and pay them standard Zhong rates for their pains. Not that that was overly generous.

Best I can do, though.

"They insist so, yes."

"Very well. Tell them to proceed."

Wanyan's engineer's trick was actually threefold.

The first part was that, in fact, there was bedrock under the silt. They knew it because they'd drilled down to it. Moreover, though there were a few projections upward from the bedrock, there were only that few, and they could be blown.

Secondly, silt could be removed explosively. At the moment there were explosive charges, hundreds of explosive charges, placed atop the bedrock sufficient to clear away the silt, over an area of forty-five meters—easily sufficient, if properly marked, for one-way nautical traffic—by eight hundred. The channel they intended to cut was oriented perpendicular to the tides, which could be expected to carry off silt suspended in the water before it could settle again.

The third trick involved shipping containers, filled with rock, sitting atop barges at a safe distance from the underwater blasting area. The containers had their walls perforated to sink, but not so quickly that they couldn't be guided into position.

For a blasting project of this size, a simple "fire in the hole" just wouldn't do. Instead, the Zhong began to sound sirens, not all that dissimilar really to the ones that announced air raids to the Balboan enemy. Everywhere people began to bolt for cover.

"Sir?" asked the aide, meaning, *Are we going to take shelter or what?*

"You go," said the admiral. "This, I really want to see."

"If it's all the same with you, sir . . ."

"Then stay, son, and acquire a memory to tell your grandchildren about. This is going to—"

The blast was like nothing ever in Wanyan's experience. The sound wasn't as much as he'd expected, but from placid seas, suddenly, the surface rose in a sort of boil, followed by a wall of water lurching essentially straight upward. The wall was clear above, but brown as mud below. Up it sailed, and up some more, before reaching apogee in a spray and then settling back with vast but reluctant majesty.

"Hmmmm . . . I wonder if the messes won't be serving fish tonight," the admiral said aloud.

"Wouldn't surprise me a bit, sir," said Lieutenant Colonel Ma, in a tone still replete with *wow*.

And, indeed, as soon as the water settled, small launches and rubber boats began to sortie, collecting up the blasted harvest. Among those lesser craft, tugs and landing craft began guiding in the barges to dump their loads, to seal off the edge of the trench just cut from a return of the silt.

Ma pointed his finger at something that had just popped to the surface. "Admiral, you know, it might not be just regular fish tonight."

"What?" the admiral asked, as he turned to follow Ma's finger.

There, out in the still roiling sea, bobbed a twenty-meter long megalodon.

"Meg tastes like shit, Ma," the admiral said. "Find the supply weasels and tell them that under no circumstances are my men, nor even the prisoners, to be fed megalodon. Yes, despite the poetic justice of it. Though, you know, it's sad, too. They're magnificent creatures, the Megs, much like the people we are here to subjugate or destroy."

Parilla Line, Balboa

The fire from the previously unsuspected trench line was nothing short of awesome. It was, if anything, the more so for the discipline the enemy had shown, to hold their fire until the Haarlemer Commandos were out in full view. A dozen men were bowled over in an instant, while the rest dove for the sparse cover on the jungle floor, the sparser for what had probably been a deliberate and careful clearing of fields of fire.

Somebody made a bad goddamned mistake, thought Sergeant Werner Verboom, heart doing the mambo as he slithered backwards, dragging his rifle behind him as he did. *"It's the rear of a fortified line," they said. What bullshit. "There'll be nothing there to stop you," headquarters insisted. Horseshit. "Cakewalk," they told us. My ass.*

He felt the solid *thunk* of one of those overpowered Balboan six-point-fives slam into his ruck, which was still perched on his back. *Shit. Too close. Well . . . at least it didn't feel like it hit my bottle of jenever. If they had, I'd have to start taking this personally rather than as an unfortunate professional matter.*

As soon as he sensed a change in the ground, a dropping of it, that had him more or less safely below the arc of enemy bullets—*And, Jesus, isn't that damned Zioni-Balboan rifle one fucking bullet hose? Or maybe a bullet firehose*—Verboom halted, and began scanning for other retreating troops from Thirteenth Company. These he began ordering back into a line under the cover provided by the fold in the ground in which they found themselves. Then he took his entrenching tool, the infantryman's standard "wretched little shovel," and held it up to show it to the men he had with him.

The message was clear: We've pulled back far enough; dig in.

CHAPTER SEVEN

"In the first assault on Vicksburg, Grant's theory
(when an enemy is disorganized an assault will
overwhelm him) broke down, because he failed
to realize that a mob of men entering an
entrenched line is automatically reorganized by
the actual trench they occupy. They are no longer
a mob. In place they are a line of men, nearly as
well organized, and far more securely protected,
than when they were in line in the open field.
There is no possibility of manoeuvre, their tactics
are reduced to the very simplest form; for all the
men have to do is to turn about, and open fire on
the advancing attacker."

—J.F.C. Fuller,
The Generalship of Ulysses S. Grant

South of Parilla Line, Balboa

*I have got to get back and report in that the Volcano is
ready*, thought Sergeant Juan Sais, sheltering with Espinal

in one of those rare patches of thick growth that happened sometimes when the fall of a tree left a light-permitting hole in the jungle canopy overhead. The fallen trunk, half rotten and more than half buried, had new plant life—the beginnings of a sickly gray-green progressivine colony— growing from and feeding on its mass. It provided a modicum of cover to go along with the concealment of the copse. That said, it was rotten enough that Sais had his doubts about just how much cover it might provide, were they to be spotted by the enemy.

And it stinks like a corpse.

It had been a long, hot, and miserable crawl just to get to the concealing plant life, with Tauran patrols thick on the ground. Sais' and Espinal's lungs still heaved with the effort, which made talking difficult. Sais could still think, though, and did.

The fucking Taurans are too many. That asshole Carrera has fucked this up right properly. Still, must report in. But, I don't know; can we get through to report in?

There was a flurry of firing ahead, the surprise of which made the sergeant shudder. The shots were a mix of the Balboans' distinctive F-26 rifles, distinctive mostly for having such a high rate of fire, when set to auto or burst, and the deeper sound of weapons that had to be Tauran, for lack of anything else they could have been. The sound was muffled and distorted, partly by the trees and partly by the undulating, almost bare surface of the ground. And, fortunately, given the state of the tree behind which they sheltered, the fire was directed in some other direction; all they heard were muzzle reports, not the crack of bullets passing close by.

From the little copse in which he and Private Espinal sheltered, Sais watched as a group of Taurans—Sais figured them to be a squad or so, sheltering down in a draw— looked up from heating their rations. The Taurans glanced in the direction of the firing, then shrugged it off, turning their attention back to whatever they'd been doing. Sais couldn't tell what that was until a minor shift in the wind brought with it the aroma of some kind of hearty stew.

Jesus, has it really been two days since we've eaten anything?

Concerned with the more immediately important task of getting something to eat, the Taurans didn't notice Sais licking his lips and giving some serious thought to trying to take on the Tauran squad to steal their food.

Nah . . . can't. Maybe if I still had the other half of the team.

Three days ago had been when a Tauran thousand pounder—well aimed or just lucky, Sais couldn't say—had killed the other two men in the team and obliterated their shelter, most of their equipment, notably the radio, *and* their stockpile of rations. He and Espinal had had their one carried ration, but that had stretched only a day.

Sais still didn't understand how the thing hadn't cracked the Volcano it had been his job, his and his team's, to fill and arm.

Fact that I'm still here suggests it didn't. Doesn't prove it, though, and slow leaks are possible. We need to get back to let higher know that the bomb might be defective . . . or might be defective now, after the near miss. And we need to avoid capture, too, because we can't risk the enemy finding out about the Volcanos.

I wish I could be sure . . .

Sergeant Sais was sure of only a few things at the moment. He was sure he'd set his team's Volcano properly, both the timer and the digital code. *Or, as least, that the test set said it was all fine and functional. Best I could do.* He knew half of his team was dead. *Fortunately, they were not captured, but then half-tonners don't take prisoners.* He was pretty sure he and his remaining man, Espinal, were going to be dead, too, pretty soon.

Sais was also sure that, if the Tauran troops he could see between himself and safety noticed him or Espinal, there'd be no getting away from them.

Espinal, able to see everything Sais could, leaned toward Sais' ear and whispered, "I don't . . . think we can . . . get through . . . Sergeant. I really . . . don't."

Not trusting his own straining lungs to make a soft enough answer, Sais shushed the boy with a finger to his lips. Then, in agreement, he shook his head. A couple of deep breaths further and the sergeant said, "We'll . . . hole up here . . . for now . . . behind this tree. Tonight . . . we try . . . to get through."

"Mines?" asked Espinal.

Sais shook his head and shrugged. *Sometimes you just have to take your chances.*

Log Base Alpha, so called, Balboa Province, Balboa

What are the odds? thought Tribune Ramirez, staring down at the hole where the battery kitchen used to be. A Tauran thousand pounder had done for that, along with the battery's cooks. They hadn't even found enough of them to bury. Deformed pots and ruined kitchen utensils, being stronger than flesh, had survived well enough to dot the landscape.

The tribune, standing on the crater's lip, was flanked by his much-chastened executive officer and first centurion. Of whatever treatment they'd gotten at the hands of Fernandez's department, neither one would say a word.

Eight guns I've got, thought Ramirez, *and sixteen barrels for them, plus in effect two headquarters bunkers, mine and FDC, plus three for supply. So they manage to hit the one thing I only have one of? There is no justice. If the troops didn't get a couple of days training in cooking for themselves in basic, we'd be screwed. As is, though, since cooking for oneself is pretty damned inefficient, and, since we're not infantry, tanks, or combat engineers, we get unit rations a lot more than combat rations . . .*

"Excuse me, Señor," queried a voice from behind the tribune, "but is this Ramirez's battery?"

The voice was an interesting combination of old, weak, and thin, and decidedly female, but with a curiously firm edge to it, as if the speaker was quite used to having her own way. Ramirez turned in surprise, as did Top and the exec. There, standing before them, was a tiny woman, *really* tiny. How old she was he couldn't tell. Wrinkles and steel gray hair suggested she was quite old, but bright blue eyes, a thin teenaged girl's general shape, and an unbowed back suggested she might be younger than she looked. The old woman was accompanied by two much younger ones, likely in their middle teens. Good looking kids, they were, too. Those stood well behind her, dragging a small cart behind them.

"I'm Digna Miranda," the old woman announced, "and I am a lot older than you think. These two"—Mrs. Miranda's head flicked once each, left and right—"are my great-*great*-granddaughters."

"Ah, yes, madam," Ramirez said, recovering from the surprise. "What can I or my battery do for you?"

"Nothing," she replied, "we're here to do for you."

The tribune cocked his head to one side, quizzically. The legions had had field brothels for the troops overseas, but none here at home that he knew of. Of course, the old woman could be a madam and the two young girls . . . but, *No, they just don't look the type.*

"Huh?" he asked, unintelligently.

"The call came out for people who could cook. We can; we ran a small restaurant in the city. We'd been taken over by the government anyway, catering to a couple of the bomb shelters. That was hot, miserable, and boring. Worse, with most of my male descendants out defending the island, it was too damned hard. So, hearing the call, we volunteered."

"Do you have orders?" asked Ramirez.

"No time," Mrs. Miranda replied. "'They'll be along,' said the man who took our oaths of enlistment."

"No basic training . . . never mind, silly question."

The old woman smiled. "I don't need basic to cook. Neither do the girls. So, tell me where the kitchen is."

Pointing at the hole, Ramirez, grimaced, answering, "Well . . . it used to be there. My exec"—Ramirez's head inclined toward the junior tribune—"has requested new pots and such but . . ." He shrugged, apologetically.

"Never mind," answered the old woman, firmly. "They

told us enough of the details. We emptied out the restaurant, plus grabbed a few things from home. We'll make do. But we need a place. And a stove; *that* we couldn't move. And we'll need fuel for the stove. Wood will do if you can come up with some."

"I'll get somebody right on that," the tribune answered. "Top?"

"All the natural wood is pretty wet, sir," the battery's first centurion answered, "but we've still got some of the lumber that came in the containers."

"Will that do?" Ramirez asked the old woman.

"I hate the waste," she said, "but it should do."

The XO added in, "And we're supposed to be getting a new set of burners in the next couple of days, those, or a kitchen trailer. But . . ."

"Don't worry about it. You get us food and something to cook on and we'll cook. Clear enough?"

Both the exec and Top cringed, bracing for a verbal explosion. Ramirez only smiled, answering, "Why, yes, Madam, it is very clear. And we still have some food, canned rations."

"Good. They'll do. And if you could get us a twenty-liter can of water, and the wood I mentioned, we can start on some stew."

"I'll . . . ummm . . . get right on that, ma'am."

"Excellent," said the old woman. "Oh, and one other thing. We ran into a priest on the way here. He's doing a funeral for another group but he said he'll be along later today, along with some people . . . what was it he called them? Oh, yes, I remember; he said 'graves registration.'"

Ramirez nodded, thinking, *I'd better set someone to finding the cooks' helmets. They should have survived even if nothing else did.*

To one side, just above the lip of the crater, the chaplain's assistant played a pedal-powered field organ. The assembled battery, loosely formed around the hole marking the former cooks' shack, sang in accompaniment:

"Yo soy el pan de vida.
El que viene a mí no tendrá hambre.
El que cree en mí no tendrá sed . . ."

Two makeshift crosses had been erected in the hole where the cooks' shack had once been. The crosses were adorned with helmets, one fairly whole and the other nearly flattened. The flattened one, on closer inspection, had proven to have some bloodstains, along with a bit of flesh that was probably brain matter. Even though the other was clean, both helmets would be placed in body bags and buried in marked plots in one of the field cemeteries. At least it would give the next of kin a place to visit after the war.

"Nadie viene a mí . . ."

The voices all died to uncertainty as the sirens began afresh. The chaplain's assistant looked at his boss, eyes querying, *What now, Father?* The gunners' eyes all seemed to hold much the same question.

With the first organ-rippling gift from above shaking the trees, the chaplain made a quick sign of the cross at the assembly, shouting, "In the name of the Father, the

Son, and the Holy Spirit, for God's sake get under cover!"

Sometimes the raids came and went quickly. Sometimes they lasted quite a while. Sometimes—well, just that once—they seemed to target the battery. Other times, more usually, they struck elsewhere.

But the problem, thought a tall, broad-shouldered, slender, and olive-toned gunner known to the battery as "Blue-eyed Rodriguez," *is that as long as the sirens haven't blown "all clear," and as long as you can feel the earth rumbling under your feet, through the soles of your boots, you're still scared shitless. It wears . . . God knows, it wears.*

Since he'd brought his guitar along when mobilized, Rodriguez was the battery's unofficial musician and ad hoc entertainment center. At least he'd play and sing something someone might want to listen to, rather than the official radio's hourly rendition of *Todo por la Patria* with *O Campo, Mi Campo* on the half.

Rodriguez cast blue eyes up at the bunker's little AM radio, sitting precariously on a shelf, and shaking from the bombs. The radio was, fortunately, silent. Indeed, nobody had turned the thing on in weeks.

We need a new song, the guitar-playing gunner thought. *Or a bunch of them. But maybe I can come up with just one. Now let's see; we were singing* "Pan de Vida." *Okay, as far as it goes. Nice tune. Maybe it could use some new words.*

Aloud he tried, "We are the cannon of death . . . Under our feet you are roaches . . ."

Yeah, maybe something like that. Needs some work, though.

IV Corps Headquarters, Fortress Cristobal, Balboa

The sun long down, this late at night the headquarters was comparatively quiet. Across the bay, to the east, tracers crisscrossed through the sky, leaving green and red streaks burned on the retinae of any who looked. That was Arturo Killum's *tercio*, the Eighth, hanging onto Tecumseh by their fingernails.

Occasionally, a brighter flash told of an incoming shell exploding over the bunkers and trenches of the defenders. As background, somewhere off in the distance, air pumps pulled the carbon dioxide from the shelter—it and many others—and spread it out on the surface so that no telltale trace would mark what mattered to friend or foe.

And I can't even let them surrender. Not ever, thought Legate Xavier Jimenez, watching over the indicia of the fight from the relative safety of the zigzag entrance into the shelter. *They're better off taking the pounding now, where they're sheltered, than a worse pounding later, without that shelter.*

"Hang on boys," he said to the air. "It's for a reason." Turning, Jimenez walked down the damp ramp and then passed through the double curtain that kept the light from escaping. He didn't have to count steps, so often had he made the same short trek. Each turn he took through the twisted corridor he took automatically, until, passing a

couple of other thick canvas curtains, he entered into the
dimly lit space set up for operations.

The first person he saw—no different this night than
any other—was Corporal Sarita Asilos, manning the
communications desk, lovely face lit by the various radio
dials.

Does she ever rest? Jimenez wondered.

"What's the word, Sarita?" he asked of the corporal,
walking to her desk after entering the mold-smelling, dank
and damp, concrete-enshrouded headquarters. The
beautiful young corporal caught her breath, as she did
pretty much every time her legate showed up. Corporal
Sarita Asilos had a serious crush, all the worse for being
so plainly unrequited. It was funny, too, because she had
much the same effect on every other male in the
headquarters—she being tall, slender, smooth of skin, fair
of face, and *most* delightfully curved—that Jimenez had
on her.

"No good words, sir," Asilos said. "The *Duque* refused
our request to abandon the outpost on the other side of the
bay." The woman sneered in the direction of the radio—
same legionary issue model as graced the shelf in Blue-eyed
Rodriguez's bunker, adding, "And the enemy propaganda
says that Carrera's abandoned us over here because we're
mostly black and he's white." Her eyes turned sad, soft,
plaintive, and perhaps a little moist. "It's not true, is it, sir?
The *Duque* wouldn't do that, would he?"

"Truth is always the first casualty, Sarita," Jimenez
answered. "I know Patricio probably better than anyone
does, to include either of his wives. For certain
constrained values of 'know,'" Jimenez hastened to add.

"He's got flaws in plenty, but neither racism nor disloyalty are among them.

"And if you consider the viciousness of the propaganda we've laid on the Tauran Union, well . . . our people aren't rioting in the streets over what they say about us. Over in Taurus, though . . ."

Wickedly and cynically, Jimenez snickered. "Now, is he using us? Well, duh. But we all volunteered to be used for a higher purpose, so we can hardly complain about that."

"I guess you're right, sir. But those men on the other side are taking a hard pounding."

Jimenez nodded. "Yeah, I know. I'm a little surprised the enemy came up with the logistic wherewithal to put in as heavy an attack as they have over there. But it's unlikely, even if Carrera had agreed, that we'd have gotten the men out safely, not with them having to cross the bay since the road to *Fuerte* Tecumseh was cut."

"There's one other thing," Asilos said, hesitantly. Her fingers began hunting for a written message, even as she relayed the gist of the thing. "The chief medico over at Tecumseh has asked permission to put some of the worst wounded out of their misery. He says he's running low on painkillers, and leaving them screaming will undermine morale in the other wounded badly enough to be life threatening.

"Sir, I've checked with the chief surgeon here," Sarita added. "We've got plenty of painkillers, if we could get it over to them. It would be suicide but I also checked on that. Every medic in the corps medical regiment volunteered to try. Every one."

"You're a treasure, Sarita," said the legate, which added

about a zillion percent to the woman's morale. "So are the medics. Let me mull that a bit, though. Tell the doctor over at Tecumseh I said, 'Not just no, but hell no.'"

Still mulling, Jimenez walked off to check on his artillery. Halfway there he changed direction, walking briskly to his intelligence section's desk.

"Do we have a frequency we can use to communicate with the enemy? In the plain, I mean, since our encryption gear and his aren't compatible."

The senior tribune manning that post answered, "Legate, we could get a message through if we had to—a couple of their logistic units seem to be having trouble with their frequency hopping system and have reverted to speaking in the plain—but do we want to? We're getting some good info through that leak; I'd hate to waste it for nothing. And using it to communicate might do just that."

"Yeah," Jimenez agreed, "No 'might' about it. It would. Okay, so do we have another route?"

"Well," the tribune spoke hesitatingly, "there's their chaplain nets, sir."

"Huh?"

"They've got radios, too, but never seem to have been given encryption gear. We haven't got a lot of intelligence that way, yet, but we will once units settle down for the longer haul."

"Any advantage to chaplains and not log?" Jimenez asked. Intelligence wasn't, after all, his specialty.

"They could fix log easily," the intel tribune answered, "if they found out about the leaks. It's only a couple of stations, after all. But there are scores of chaplains floating around, maybe as many as a hundred and fifty or so, most of which we've been able to identify by name, rank, and nationality, by this point. It would be harder for the Taurans to fix, and probably couldn't be fixed quickly without creating much worse leaks."

"Couldn't they just clip their chaplains' wings?" Jimenez asked.

"I sense their chaplaincy has more political pull than that," said the tribune. "To my mind, that's the only thing that explains why the largely—actually, almost entirely— atheist Tauran Union ruling class still funds a chaplaincy."

"Okay," Jimenez said, "I need the name and call sign of the senior Gallic chaplain, and a frequency to get ahold of him."

"Why a Gaul, sir?"

"Because, in effect, they're running the show?"

"Well . . . yeah, but what is it you want to *do*, sir?"

Jimenez thought about it, turning an instinct into something resembling a plan. He said, "I want a very local, very temporary truce. I want to send a small flotilla of rubber boats over to Tecumseh with medical supplies, and evacuate some of the worst wounded from there to here, where they can get better treatment. I want to do it plainly and openly, and I don't want them shot up, either coming or going."

The tribune shook his head slightly, answering, "Oh. Then you wouldn't want the senior Gallic chaplain, sir, you would want the Anglian. They're the bastards that have been giving Tecumseh such a hard time, the same bastards who cut the road and can see into the bay.

"Moreover, sir, while we aren't getting much from the enemy chaplaincy now, that leaky chaplain's net still might pay big dividends later on. I'd rather we left it alone."

"Well, how do we—how do I—contact them?"

The tribune thought for a moment, then suggested, "International maritime or aviation distress channel, might work, sir. Worth a shot, rather than compromising a source. That, or maybe we could dial every landline number in the area we know the Anglians have overrun. Some of the lines might still be up. Or we could try to jump into their satellite communications ability, though I'd rather not let them know we can do that."

"I want to keep it low key," said Jimenez. "Try landline first. And let me talk to them, personally."

"Do you speak English, sir?"

"Yes," Jimenez said, "and pretty well, actually."

"Okay, sir. This has some intel value, too, so give me a couple of hours . . . or maybe until dawn, if you can. Oh, and I'll get our corps chaplain to intercede, too. I'll set it up."

"No more than a couple of hours," Jimenez insisted. "We have friends and brothers in pain over there."

South of the Parilla Line, Balboa

Sais clapped a hand across his soldier's mouth, then whispered, "Get up, Espinal; it's time."

The boy's eyes fluttered open, unseen and unseeing. At the jungle floor's starless and moonless night, even the whites of the boy's eyes were invisible. He nodded, to let Sais know he was awake and unlikely to shout anything out. Once the sergeant had removed his muffling hand, Espinal softly said, "I'm ready, Sergeant."

***

The pair travelled light, carrying only their rifles, a red-filtered flashlight to signal to the friendlies to the north, if that ever became practical, a set of night vision goggles with some spare batteries, and a canteen each. Everything else was left behind, covered by some brush, some dirt, and a bit of the rotting tree trunk. The Taurans would find the packs eventually, but Sais had made sure while it was still approximately light out that nothing was left in them that would be of any intelligence value.

In the impenetrable gloom, and because of that gloom, Sais had tied a strong but light cord between them. It was a course of action not normally used but, in this case, he thought it was wise.

Even through the canopy overhead, a flash of lightning was visible. The crack of the lightning was muffled by the vegetation, but the flash was followed almost immediately by the sound of heavy rain falling on the leaves and branches above. That grew in seconds to a crescendo.

Sais breathed a sigh of relief. Not only would the rain drive the Taurans to shelter, even if it was only the shelter of putting on their headgear and mentally retreating under the brims, but the racket would cover their footsteps and then some.

Now we can move, by God or, rather, we can once the rain gets through. In the interim, though . . .

He held up a fist by sheer force of habit; but Espinal couldn't see it. Hell, without his goggles Sais couldn't have seen it either. Espinal bumped into his sergeant from behind, and came to a stop.

Sais turned around and whispered, "For now, it's just sound. In about fifteen or twenty minutes, though, the rain will get through the canopy. Then the Taurans are going to go half catatonic. That's when we'll move."

"Roger, Sergeant."

Feeling the first drop hit his soft, brimmed cap, Sais thought, *About time. First time I've ever wanted the rain to come down, I think.* The drop quickly became a deluge, as the leaves and branches above began to shed their excess water. It came down cold, causing the sergeant to shiver for a moment.

Once satisfied that the rain getting through was heavy enough to have the desired effects, Sais gave a double tug to the connecting cord and took off at a quick pace. *Got to make hay while the sun shines. Got to take advantage of the downpour while it lasts.*

Not unexpectedly, the spray of the falling drops began to cover the lens of the goggles, making them worse than useless. Sais persisted for a while, but after coming close to a heart attack when the distortion caused a hanging vine to look like a snake, and with a silent curse, Sais stopped and took them off his face. He left the goggles to hang from his neck by the head straps. Blinking against the purple haze the green light of the goggles brought about in human eyes, he rotated his eyes around, trying to cut the time until he could hope to see something again. Again, Espinal bumped into him from behind.

"Sergeant?"

"Never mind, it's going to be a little slower going than I'd hoped."

CHAPTER EIGHT

"How ridiculous and how strange to be
surprised at anything which happens in life."
—Marcus Aurelius, *Meditations*

**Tauran Union Expeditionary Force Headquarters,
Academia Sergento Juan Malvegui (Under New
Management), Puerto Lindo, Balboa**

Even when the academy, the shipyard, the scrapyard, and
the submarine factory had all been going concerns, the
port had never seen activity like this. It fairly hummed,
except when it screamed, whined, and roared. It wasn't a
smooth enough operation yet to call it a logistics
symphony, but things were clearly headed in a very
Mozartesque direction. Cranes whined continuously.
Some of these were ship mounted and newly arrived,
while others were integral to the port and which the
Balboans apparently hadn't had time to sabotage.
Helicopters *whop-whopped* in, bringing a steady stream
of men and equipment from freighters stationed over the

141

horizon. Lighters, too, chugged into the port, or split off to go to one of the two lesser ports framing this main one. The air was filled with a constant roar of big diesels, punctuated with the shriek of air brakes.

Teeth on edge from the brakes, Janier cursed the designer, long dead on Old Earth. *God, I fucking* hate *the sound of those things.*

But, on the other hand, I love *the smell of diesel in the morning.*

Janier stood atop old stone battlements, overlooking the terreplein, the town, and the asphalt surfaced road along which rumbled a steady stream of trucks, heading east to the building logistic base north of besieged Cristobal. He had a short brigade of engineers, two battalions and a headquarters, over fifteen hundred men working full time at keeping the road from crumbling completely away under the abuse. That was barely enough, as demonstrated by the frequent traffic jams where the two-lane highway had crumbled from the edges inward, turning it into a one-lane road, if that. A demi-battalion of military police was engaged along the same route, doing little but directing traffic along the stretches where that crumbling was worst.

Did they make the road deliberately so that it would crumble under heavy military use, Janier wondered, *or was it a case of corruption in construction they never got around to shooting someone over and fixing? Or did they maybe notice the road was poorly made, because of corruption, and decide to leave it that way, in expectation of us?*

Maybe I should call the high admiral; get another

morale-building session . . . No! No, she means well, but she is warping my senses and dulling my carefully nurtured paranoia. That paranoia was a gift from Carrera and I think I've come to treasure it.

Not too far from where Janier stood, below him out on the fort's old glacis, an Anglian soldier stood atop a captured Balboan cannon. He was recognizable, as indeed, were all Janier's national troops, by the pattern of his camouflage. The cannon was, the general saw, one of the Balboan' light eighty-five millimeter auxiliary propelled jobs.

The cannon had been rigged for sling loading, with steel shackles holding thick webbing, basically nylon straps, that ran from the axles at each side, and from the joined tubular trails. The three slings were joined by a "donut," a multi-thickness roll of the same kind of webbing, held together by a steel connector.

The soldier balanced himself precariously, with one foot on the recoil cylinder and tube, and the other at right angles to the first, balanced on the scalloped gunner's shield. He held in one hand the "donut," and in the other a screwdriver from which wire ran down to the ground. Janier couldn't see but presumed that the wire was attached to another screwdriver, or some kind of metal prod, stuck into the ground.

It was then that Janier noticed an Anglian helicopter coming in low and slow, and another soldier in the same uniform as the first, guiding the helicopter in.

I suppose I should put a stop to that, the general thought. *It's a waste of fuel, of parts, and of maintenance time, to say nothing of an unnecessary risk, to have my units looting souvenirs. Then again, what was it that Old Earth poet wrote? Something about, "Loot, loot, loot that makes the boys get up and shoot."*

How does one measure the morale value of letting men set up monuments to the future, especially when they're avenging a humiliation like we suffered here? How does one measure the value of the Emperor pinching a grognard's ear? How does one measure the morale value of a pickle and a loaf of bread?

So . . . I'll let them have their trophies, as long as it doesn't get out of hand.

Janier watched with interest as, under the control of the ground guide, the Anglian chopper assumed a low hover. It was low enough, in fact, that the donut holder had to duck. He tapped the metal hook under the helicopter with the screwdriver, then tapped it again.

From his perch, Janier couldn't tell if the helicopter's hook sparked when touched. Even so, he thought, *Good; I approve of making sure, son. And I learned that the hard way.*

Dropping the screwdriver to the ground, the soldier took the donut in both hands, and slammed it decisively into the hook, a sprung latch closing behind it. He then tried to pull it back the same way it had gone in. It stayed put.

At that point the soldier jumped off the gun to the ground, and trotted off briskly. The ground guide spun his hand over head, and pointed into the wind. With an increase in pitch, the chopper took off, the trophy gun swaying underneath. The helicopter was actually seriously undertasked, lifting a gun that weighed under two tons.

"Note to self," muttered Janier, "and to G4, and to

subordinate commanders, for next command and staff meeting: Burning up fuel and wearing out equipment for reasons of morale is one thing, but for God's sake put the damned business on an efficient footing. Three units could have absconded with a trophy each for the price of that one."

And the cannon are good choices; we captured something like fifty of the things, plus a couple of hundred rocket launchers and mortars. Most of it we got before their crews could shove thermite up the breaches or down the tubes.

Hmmm; that's another note for the staff. The Balboans hardly got a shot off, we hit them so fast, and there are some pretty large stockpiles of shells sitting out there. I'd like to know how long before we can collect the stuff someplace safe and destroy it. I suppose, for now, we have better things to do.

Isla Santa Catalina, Mar Furioso, off the coast of Balboa

Fleet Admiral Wanyan Liang paid no attention to the sounds of construction behind him, a battalion of engineers erecting earthen air defense towers for the guns and missiles already coming off the artificial docks, below. Though called "towers," in fact, they were more solid pyramid than anything else, albeit pyramids with softened corners and roads winding around their sides. A half dozen of the ninety to one hundred and twenty-foot high pyramids were done. To another ten spots long lines of groaning slave laborers carried baskets of stone and dirt from a quarry to put into the towers. Since the pyramids were located on high ground, that upward trudge added to the groaning.

Still others—impressed laborers—pounded the material poured into the rising structures into something approaching the strength of concrete.

The reasons for expending all the effort on pyramids included raising radars, cameras, launchers, and guns above the trees, and to extend their coverage by increasing their horizon. So far, the preparations hadn't been tested. Wanyan thought though that, maybe, just maybe, the Balboans hadn't figured out yet he was putting in a serious port where none had been before. When they did figure it out, the other benefit of raising the air defenses was that it changed their geometry as a target, mandating that only a direct hit would be effective, since shrapnel and shards would have no straight line to gun or gunner without that direct hit.

A serious port? Well, if Janier had cause for satisfaction at the logistic performance of his command, and he did, Fleet Admiral Wanyan Liang had still more. Wanyan had started with less, had no port to hand, had little in the way of heavy equipment, and far less in the way of modern engineering expertise.

"But through sheer bullheaded weight of effort, it's working! By the empress' fragrant cunt, it *is* working!"

"Admiral?" asked Wanyan's aide, Lieutenant Colonel Ma of the Zhong Marines.

"Huh? What? Was I thinking aloud again?"

"You must have been, sir. And you were right, sir, it *is*

working. Though I confess, I have no idea about Her Imperial Majesty's reproductive organs, nor of any alleged aroma thereto. I'm afraid I'll have to take your word on that matter, sir."

"Well," said Wanyan, "I heard it from . . . oh, never mind." The admiral glared at Ma Chu through narrowed eyes. "Say, are you trying to get me an appointment with the *Juntong*?"

At the name Ma Chu blanched. The *Juntong* was one of three branches of the Imperial Secret Police, all of which had overlapping jurisdictions, hence all of which unreservedly hated each other, and all of which were above the law as well as totally ruthless.

Ma said, with more calm than he felt, "Hardly, Admiral, since they'd eviscerate me on general principle even were I not your aide de camp."

"True enough," said Wanyan, mollified. He turned and signaled for his driver to pick up him and the lieutenant colonel up. Since the admiral's own vehicle had been landed, Ma Chu had not had to hump a radio around continuously.

"The engineers say they're ready to blow the last trench, Admiral," announced he driver. Unlike the aide de camp, the driver was a navy man, and enlisted.

"Tell me that, at this point, they're not still waiting for my order," said Wanyan.

The driver shook his head, emphatically. "Oh, no, Admiral, they just thought you might want to watch."

"Nah, I trust them. Well . . ."

"Yes, sir, they said they've accounted for all the drivers and workers."

"Okay, then." After Ma swung into the back seat, and he'd taken his own, Wanyan directed the driver, "Take me to the southern shore." Sirens began to sound loudly as people rushed either to shelter or to a good vantage point for the show, however the spirit moved them. To the north, behind Wanyan's party, unseen—for the briefest nonce unheard, too—a band of water half a mile long and a couple of hundred feet wide seemed suddenly to come to a boil.

That had been practiced enough, nineteen times in the last ten days, that Wanyan didn't worry overmuch about it. He was more concerned that the suction dredger he'd asked for might not make it to the island to keep the undersea canal they'd blasted through the silt open. He was *much* more concerned with air drop—the first of its kind, here—arranged with the Tauran Union for some heavy equipment needed on the *Isla* Santa Catalina that it was still some ways from being able to unload. The actual coordination for the drop hadn't been too hard, taking little more than a request to the Empress, her to the High Admiral, and the High Admiral to Wanyan's opposite number, Janier. It had still taken over a week *after that* to get the equipment off-loaded at *Puerto Bruselas*, moved to Julio Asunción Airport, near the Santa Josefinan capital of Aserri, and prepared for a drop.

Puerto Bruselas, Santa Josefina

Hauptmann Nadja Felton glanced down at the port as she veered to starboard, to assume her course for the island of Santa Catalina, nominally Balboan but currently under

Zhong occupation. She'd known, at a purely intellectual level, that the port was filled to bursting with interned Balboan warships. Still, knowing and seeing were two different . . .

Son of a bitch, she thought, *that aircraft carrier is tracking me with their lasers! Is that legal? Can anything be done about it if not?*

If anyone had asked her, Felton would have happily admitted that nothing, absolutely nothing, made sense to her in the Republic of Santa Josefina, anyway, so, *Why shouldn't ships theoretically interned be continuing to train to engage targets?*

Hauptmann Felton checked her position on the map, then again on the Global Locating System. It wasn't a surprise that they matched; in this part of the theater the Balboans either couldn't mess with the GLS or, for reasons of their own, refrained from doing so. That was just as well, she believed, since she was now flying a much bigger target, and one that would make for a very hard landing in case of a crash.

Felton was just as happy at having been pulled out of flying Hacienda 121s and put back on heavy lift in T16s. The "16" was for the tonnage. In other respects, they were twin engine, prop-driven aircraft, with relatively wide bodies and a tail ramp for ease of loading and unloading. In this case, unloading involved dropping by parachute. Part of her joy was that she'd seen the inside of the cargo bay after the drop on Balboa, and before the maintenance people had hosed out the blood and body parts. It had been a sobering experience and one she really didn't want to be reminded of.

Not ever again.

Back in the cargo hold of this plane she had six pieces of equipment, all unusually lightweight. These were two small bulldozers, manufactured by Wu Can Machinery Corporation (five and a half tons between them), a backhoe (Bright Day Industries, three tons), two towable backhoes (Model KB512, under a ton, between them) and a coral and rock crusher (Tiger Mining Machinery, Ltd., two-point-eight tons).

It wasn't an ideal mix, she suspected, for any purpose, but likely a compromise between what the Zhong needed and the weight and cube of the aircraft that would be delivering. Even with the weight, her T16 had cubed out before it had weighted out.

Or, more technically, squared out because there was lots of unused cube left, even after the square area of the deck was all taken.

What I'm carrying should be enough for the Zhong to start work, Felton thought. *And I saw enough other kind of equipment waiting for pickup that I'm not going to worry for a minute about whether the Zhong engineers have thought it through.*

Isla Santa Catalina, Mar Furioso, off the coast of Balboa

"There, Admiral," Ma Chu said, pointing at the approaching T16.

"Will they drop it all in one spot, or lay it on line?" Wanyan asked, while thinking, *You know, I really should have asked my staff.*

Ma shook his head. "I don't know, sir. I was a marine, not a parachutist. But . . ."

"But?"

"I'm guessing here, but my guess is that they won't want to risk dropping one heavy piece on another, and that they'd have to come around a bunch of times to get them all to land close together, even if they wanted to. No enemy is shooting now, but that's just fortune . . . and you train for bad fortune, not good. So, I think they'll do it on line, maybe come around once if there's not enough room, but otherwise drop and scoot."

"Makes sense," Wanyan said. "Let's see."

With the marked drop zone coming up fast, Hauptmann Felton's hands shook for no reason she could put a calm and objective, or even a trembling subjective, finger on.

Maybe that laser back at Puerto Bruselas *has me spooked,* she thought. *Or maybe it's the memory of my last drop. Or the flesh and blood or . . .*

Never mind, she reminded herself. *This is a secure drop zone. So they tell me, anyway. May it remain so.*

Wanyan snapped his fingers at his driver, who immediately produced a set of binoculars.

Putting them to his eyes, he zeroed in on the tail of the oncoming Tauran—*No, those colors say "Sachsen," don't they?*—transport. The admiral held his breath as first a small bundle appeared just behind the aircraft. It blossomed into a green streamer, a parachute, which filled with air then turned into four of them. Those four then seemed to stand still, once opened, while the plane continued onward. Indeed, from Wanyan's point of view, it seemed that the first item dropped suddenly materialized in the air where the plane had been when the parachute first opened. The heavy load, a small bulldozer, it seemed, swung down and around the four parachutes like a pendulum, except not so well-controlled.

Satisfied with that one, the admiral dropped the binoculars, visually reacquired the T16, and then slapped the field glasses back to his eyes. This time, he didn't see the small bundle of chutes appear. Instead he saw two open, and another vehicle appear. Unfortunately—and it was unfortunate enough to bring a curse from Wanyan's lips—the two chutes were not enough to do more than drag the load out. One chute tore, then fluttered into a streamer, while the other seemed to just disintegrate under the load. The load, a backhoe, spun end over end before smashing into the ground, creating a great geyser of rock, dirt, and vegetation, all nicely punctuated with shards of yellow painted steel.

"Fuck!"

"God-fucking-dammit!" exclaimed Felton, when her loadmaster informed her of the mishap. The anger lasted about as long as the curse did. Then she took to asking herself the serious question, *Did I screw something up*?

Mentally running over the sequence just past, she decided she had not, that it had to have been either a procedural or a material error back at the airport. She continued on.

***

The next drop went as smoothly as had the first, as did the next three. With a flutter of wings the Sachsen transport turned and made for home.

"Five out of six? That's not that bad. But, damn, we needed all of it."

Saint Nicholasberg, Volgan Republic

The diesel fumes and rumble of heavy traffic were a high price to pay, thought Jan Campbell, just to have a place to meet someone.

Though meeting an old . . . well . . . no, "friend" didn't quite cover it . . . was the ostensible reason for her subjecting herself to Volga, Jan Campbell wasn't entirely sure what had really brought her here to Saint Nicholasberg. Certainly, it wasn't the vodka, although that stood far above the generally poor food and unsanitary hotels. She looked at some trash blowing down the street next to the outdoor café in which she sat, thinking, *Someday the trash is all going to be picked up, the cleanliness of the restaurants will improve radically, the hotels will have fresh linen, and people will flock to the barricades because then they'll know that the Red Tsar is back.*

She took a sip of her ice-cold vodka, served in a glass that would have done for a beer, and reminded herself, *Oh, yes, I am here because Janier, at the bequest of the Gaul-dominated* Renseignements Generaux, *added some specifics to their intelligence requirements, and I happened to have a couple of personal connections for that. I still wouldn't be here if Sidney hadn't asked personally.*

"Sidney," AKA Sidney Stuart-Mansfield, lieutenant general (retired) and currently head of Pimlico Hex, which was to say, Anglian Intelligence, was the one who had arranged her secondment to the TU, her most-welcome promotion, and the independence in action she'd always craved.

So, I suppose I owed the bastard, she thought, taking another healthy slug from her glass.

At least the vodka's not bad, though the best of it is still horse piss next to a good twelve-year-old Kinclaith. Then again, I could still be in the POW camp in Balboa, so I'm not going to bitch too much about being here. Hell, it's something of a fluke that I'm not dead, so I really can't complain at all, can I?

Placing the vodka back on the table, Jan used her fingers to pick up a *pelmen*, a kind of thin-doughed, stuffed dumpling, from a bowl, dip it in sour cream, and pop it into her mouth. The dough of the pelmen was yellowish, since the flour that went into it came from chorley, a grain that grew on a sunflowerlike plant, the seeds of which, prior to grinding, resembled tiny kernels of corn. Where chorley came from, native to Terra Nova or imported long ago by the Noahs, none could say.

Yeah, not bad. So, yeah, it could have been a lot worse than this.

A hand snaked down to grab one of the *pelmeni*. She swatted at it instinctively but missed.

"You never *were* quick enough to catch me," said a plump and balding Volgan, speaking French and smiling broadly as he took a seat. He made the *pelmen* disappear as he did. A briefcase he carried was set down by his left foot.

"I never really tried, Vladimir Yefimovich," she retorted. At his sceptically raised eyebrow, she modified that to, "Well, I never tried that *hard.*"

The eyebrow dropped, replaced by an equally sceptical smile. "So what can I and the Volgan Republic do for you, my lovely *ecossaise*?"

"I need to know everything that you, that is to say, your country has sold to Balboa." In fact, Jan already had a good deal of that information. She concealed this the better to be able to judge the truthfulness of what she hoped the Volgans would give her.

"Only that?" the Volgan asked. "Just that little bit?"

"Exactly."

"Exactly? Nobody knows *exactly*. Well, nobody in this country. I am sure the Balboans know, some of them."

"How is that even possible?" she asked.

Vladimir sighed, whether at fate, at human iniquity, or both, Jan couldn't be sure.

"The short version," he said, "is that about the time the Balboans went on contract to the Federated States, we were still in a state of moral, emotional, economic, and accountability collapse. The difference between 'socialist principles of accounting' and 'generally accepted accounting principles' being several decades of gross domestic product.

"It was possible—hell, it was *easy*—for someone with cash in hand to go straight to, say, the Thirty-second Guards –that's right, *Guards*—Armored Division with a satchel of money and drive off with not just some of their equipment, but all of it. Yes, that included the secret material. Moreover, provided that the colonel or general or colonel general making the deal sent some of the money upward, and used some more of it to support his troops so that the government didn't have to, he'd be commended for his business sense."

"The Balboans didn't do that," she countered, "or at least not much."

Vladimir held up defensive hands. "No, they didn't," he admitted. "My example was just that, an example. Instead, they contracted directly with factories—they *bought* a controlling interest in some of those—for what they wanted.

"Now tell me, Major Campbell"—the Volgan laughed at seeing her startled—"well, of *course* we know about that . . . and congratulations. In any case, tell me how to tell if a factory that supposedly produced forty White Eagle tanks actually produced one hundred, but recorded only forty. Or if the factory from which that factory bought the one hundred engines didn't hide sixty or six hundred of those. Or took a hundred burned out engines and transferred them to that same Guards Armored I mentioned, with a little cash to their commander to accept the scrap as new. We spent *decades* under the Red Tsars, fudging production figures to prove this or disprove that in order to support some piece of propaganda. And we were, and still are, good at it.

"Let me give you another example, those eighteen-centimeter guns they used to so discomfort the Zhong recently. I can tell you where they came from. *Those* I can tell you *exactly* where. I got curious because the use to which they were put I found quite clever. They were in a depot-level storage yard in the frozen south. They were allegedly demilitarized, as part of the treaty regime on force reduction. Demilitarization, in this case, consisted of boring out the lands. And, surely you will agree, boring out the lands of a rifled artillery piece does make it unserviceable."

"Not," Jan said, somewhat bitterly, "if the shells they're going to fire are laser-guided, fin-stabilized arrow shells, with simply amazing range." Bitterly? Well, she hadn't a single fuck to give about Zhong losses, but the Zhong's losses meant Balboans freed up to fight Anglians and that meant *her* losses.

"Correct," Vladimir agreed. "They were bought by someone in Cochin, as scrap, for a fraction of their previous worth as arms. And then . . ."

"And then they were sent onward," she finished, "fully functional for their intended purpose."

"Yes," Vladimir nodded. "Sent onward, disassembled, stored in shipping containers, and then—so it would seem—reassembled. By the way, though we cannot prove it, we think Carrera had a hand in the method chosen to 'demilitarize' those guns.

"Some were bought openly, because your enemy needed some to train with. Most, however, went under the table. Aircraft? Those Mosaic Ds they used recently to give you so much trouble? Same story, or only slightly different, anyway. The one difference is that I think I can tell you how many of those they have."

Jan tilted her head with interest. That was one of the

intelligence requirements the Gauls had laid on her. "How many?"

"We think eight hundred and fifty-seven. From that you must subtract training and combat losses on your own."

Those, based on the training I saw, are unlikely to be small, she thought.

Jan felt something bump her right leg. It felt hard and sharp cornered and . . .

"In that briefcase," said Vladimir, "which is my personal gift to you, is enough information to get your bosses off your back. It is neither everything you want nor everything we know. We do, after all, have an interest still in selling our arms, and the more TU soldiers the Balboans can kill with those arms, the more profit we can make. But, for an old friend, why not?"

"How much of it is lies?" Campbell asked.

"Why none," he answered. "Though do be careful of half-truths that can be wholly misleading. And watch out for some oddities I, personally, cannot explain."

"Why give this to me at all then?" Jan asked.

"Longstanding affection?" he offered, a broad and insincere smile beaming on his face. At her scoffing snort, he said, "Not buying that, eh? How about so you'll owe me a favor when the time comes? How about because we don't think it, for the most part, matters? That we think in this case the material aspects of the war are the least important?"

"Not very Volgan of you." It wasn't clear whether she was speaking of the favor or the claim of irrelevance.

Vladimir shook his head. "No; no, it isn't." He didn't

make it clear either. Indeed, he found the whole idea uncomfortable enough that he decided it was time to end the meeting. Before he took his leave, however, he passed Jan a business card with an email address, and a written password. "If you need to get hold of me, sign in to that and leave the message in the draft folder. I'll get it."

IV Corps Headquarters, Fortress Cristobal, Balboa

The air, for a change, wasn't shaking with the impact of enemy ordnance. This was unusual enough to be remarkable, and some had remarked on it. Still, the assault could recommence at any time, so the sensitive communications equipment stayed mostly in the stifling command bunker. Hence it was there that Jimenez spoke calmly into a military field telephone that someone had spliced into the remnants of the landline system. Sarita Asilos, seated at her usual workplace, watched adoringly as he did.

"No," he said, "no, I know this isn't a small thing. It's a big one. And I'm not prepared to offer anything like what it's worth to me personally. You know I can't surrender Fort Tecumseh. And I can't and won't surrender Cristobal. All I can offer is a truce for both of us to evacuate our wounded and for me to put in medical supplies . . . .why don't we have enough there already? That's a good question, Chaplain, and someone is possibly going to lose a good chunk of his ass over the answer. I *can* trade some medical material, because apparently, we have plenty here, and I'll toss in a can of legionary rum if that will seal the deal . . . six cans? You don't need medical supplies but six cans and you'll arrange it . . . oh, you can only try. All right, Chaplain, but obviously if I can't get the truce I can't deliver the rum."

I know it's a joke, but I will, by God, get him the rum if he can get me the ceasefire. If necessary. I'll float it to their side in a balloon. Oops . . . not supposed to even think about those, am I?

"Yeah, sure . . . I'll be standing by here. Just let me know. But hurry, Padre; there are good men on both sides in needless pain . . . Yes . . . I know you know that. Jimenez out."

"Will it work, sir?" asked Asilos.

"Fifty-fifty," the legate answered. "But I believe the Anglian minister when he said if it fell through it wouldn't be for lack of trying.

"I'm going outside for some fresh air. Call me when the phone rings."

"Yes, sir," Sarita answered.

Nice girl, Jimenez mused, idly, as he turned and began to walk the twisting, turning half aboveground tunnel to the shell of a building that covered the tunnel's exit. A trench through the former floor of the building led from the opening to the ripped-up asphalt of the street. There, more trenches had been cut, a mix of torn-up asphalt, gravel, dirt, and sand being piled to either side to allow safe enough movement when half bent over.

Jimenez followed the trench to a sangar that faced north, one of a half dozen expressly sited to let him—or, should it come to that, his replacement—see and sense the battlefield.

It didn't seem like much of a battlefield at the moment. To the east, piece by piece, the pounding was lifting from Fort Tecumseh. *Quick work, if that's the Anglian chaplain's doing. And, if it is, I'll make it twelve cans.*

To the north, few aircraft flew, no bombs exploded, and the Tauran artillery had gone unaccountably silent. Even the aircraft sounded to be helicopters, perhaps under a bit more strain than usual.

Jimenez heard a small sound behind him. He turned to see a familiar shape or, rather, two of them. The larger shape was Asilos, who had apparently tracked him down. The smaller was a roll of wire she reeled out behind her.

"It's the Anglian chaplain," she announced, handing over the handset of a phone she'd hung from a strap across her back. It was then that Jimenez saw she'd pulled an operator's headset on. Into the boom mike she said, in pretty fair English, which he hadn't known she could speak, "Legate Jimenez will speak to you now."

"Jimenez, Padre."

Sarita heard the Anglian say, "Well, I've got you your truce. And you can come by small boats to bring over medical supplies and pick up your wounded. But we're having some communications trouble on this end so it will be some hours before I can be certain everyone here is on board with it. If you don't hear from me otherwise, sunrise is when it kicks in and it will last four hours."

"That will be fine, Chaplain," Jimenez answered. "Now, where can I deliver your booze?"

"I'm going to take a small boat out into the middle of the bay," the Anglian said. "I'll be the only one wearing a clerical collar. You can give it to me there . . . if you insist."

The chaplain couldn't see Jimenez's confirming nod. He did hear, "I do, and I'll send someone trustworthy. Oh, and good work on getting the artillery lifted off Tecumseh. I'll order ceasefire except in point self-defense on our end as soon as we finish here."

"That wasn't my doing," the Anglian said. "That was . . . well . . . you'll see in just a bi—"

Indeed, Jimenez saw it before he heard or felt it. Suddenly the night sky was lit up from dozens of locations, as if by strobe lights. He immediately dove into the bottom of the sangar, pushing Sarita down with him, eliciting from her a shocked scream. The sound followed along about a minute later, distant enough and from enough guns—*Artillery, it must be artillery*—that it was more a rumble than a blast.

But not aimed at us; the noise of the shells would have arrived before the muzzle blast. So what is . . .

That question was cut off by the scream of jets, both overhead and to west and east. Interspersed with the shriek of the jets was another sound, crisper than the first wave, but more distant.

In that moment Jimenez understood two things. One was that an attack was ongoing, probably aimed at what the president refused to call the "Parilla Line." About that he couldn't do much. The other was that he was lying atop Corporal Sarita Asilos. *Must have shielded her with my body automatically; dumb ass.*

Closely related were the facts that the breasts her uniform hid fairly well were, in fact, unfairly impressive under the material, and that this was all most irregular indeed.

"There's no one else here," she whispered into his ear.

Jimenez hesitated a moment before answering, "Just my conscience." He then sighed, before using his arms to push himself backwards, off of her, to his knees, and then onto his booted feet.

He bent to give her a hand up, saying, "Some different time and place, maybe, we can continue this . . . conversation."

CHAPTER NINE

"The best reconnaissance will always be the attack."
—Adolph von Schell, *Battle Leadership*

Bella Vista, Balboa

There was a small headquarters set up in the shell of a burned-out home, a couple of hundred meters away. For the nonce, though, Janier left it to his staff while he, alone, tried to get some sense of the looming battle from out in the open air.

He shuddered and almost cringed from the blast of jets moving fast and at low level, just overhead. They passed, this wave of them, in a fraction of a second, yet their roar stayed behind for much longer, reverberating from the ground, the rocky outcroppings, still-standing buildings, and from the very trees. Leaves fell from those trees, too, under the sonic assault. Janier saw the leaves fall but didn't notice that some few birds likewise fell dead, perhaps frightened into cardiac arrest by the sound. He'd have understood the cause completely if he'd seen them flutter to the ground.

Along with the jets, there was a steady freight train of artillery shells heading north as well. Coordinating those so that the jets and shells didn't try to occupy the same space at the same time had been a major job for his staff. At this range both cannon and shells were distant and weak, but every now and again the blast of a thousand or two-thousand pounder—*Anglian attack aircraft, Anglian measures*—rocked Janier back on his heels.

Poor bastards, he thought, in contemplation of the effect of the bombing and shelling on the Balboan defenders. He thought, too, of the troops he was going to launch into and attack on the ridge south of the river. The sentiment was almost exactly the same; *Poor bastards, but I have to know.*

Mentally, for the umpteenth time, Janier went over in his mind the indicia on offer. *We captured over fifty of their regimental guns. At the scale they were issued, previously, three guns per battery, that's enough for—oh, call it—six regiments, or two divisions. Or a corps, which we know was here. We also have enough heavier guns and rocket launchers in the capture pool to make it a corps that we seem to have caught flat-footed, and all oriented to the north, as if anticipating the Zhong eventually landing from the* Mar Furioso, *if they'd taken the Isla Real.*

Once the island was obviously not going to fall, nor the Zhong to land anywhere near Balboa City, they should have faced south, to contest our landing. Why didn't they? They could have hurt us badly if they had, maybe even defeated our landing. That's grounds for suspicion number one. Yes, yes, the deployment of the artillery, lighter and shorter ranged nearer the north and heavier and longer ranged to the south, was completely consistent with a focus on the Zhong. And it's plausible, as the staff insists, that they simply lacked the transportation to shift them around, so they were still in that configuration when we hit them. Yes, it's plausible. But I still don't believe it.

The artillery fire to the west slackened and then stopped. He shuddered inwardly again, as another wave of jets shot by overhead. He couldn't see them but following their progress by sound wasn't hard. This set peeled off to his right, or west, to lay their bombs along the ridgeline, using the airspace temporarily freed up by the halt in artillery fire.

I told the staff that the regimental guns, at least, the Volgan eighty-five millimeter, were auxiliary propelled and could have moved if their formations had wanted them to. Of course, the staff weenies had a good answer for that; "the guns may move themselves, yes, mon general, but the ammunition may not. No sense in moving them until you can move that as well."

And that's still plausible, but I still don't quite believe it. Call that one a "neutral indicator."

Every private, non-com, and officer we've captured also tells us the same story; that higher headquarters, in this case Carrera, himself, didn't seem to believe we'd actually have the balls to land. That's more than plausible; up until the first helicopters took off to secure the drop zones, I had my doubts we'd be allowed to land on the ground, too. I wonder if it was the death of one of the high Kosmos, Lady Ashworth—or, as our limey friends called her, Ashworthless—that persuaded the TU and our national governments to support the attack. After all, "people so insane as to kill important colleagues of the cosmopolitan progressive movement must be put down like the mad dogs they are" . . . or so I imagine the conversation to have gone.

So, okay, maybe that accounts for the lack of proper focus and direction on the ground. Best evidence we have, actually. Call that one point for the proposition that this is not a huge fucking trap. That's not a lot to risk an army on, indeed, to risk several armies on.

The artillery picked up again to the west, to be matched by a diminution in the east. This time Janier got hands over his ears in time for the gut-rattling passage of the jets.

So, it hinges on this; in which direction does that line the prisoners call "the Parilla Line" actually face. If it faces, even mostly, towards the Mar Furioso, I'm sold, we continue the buildup, clear out Cristobal, and eventually attack north. If it faces mostly south then it's not a misoriented defense line; it's a sally port cum bridgehead for something I don't want to deal with. In that case, I'm going to ask to pull out while we can. Well . . . at least I'll think about asking. I might just do it, instead, on my own hook.

But I must know which it is. And for that, we must attack—at least a local and limited attack—to see what kind of reception we get and what is actually there.

Assembly Area, Thirteenth Company,
Royal Haarlem *Commandotroepen*

Sergeant Werner Verboom felt mildly encouraged by the artillery and air preparation going in before the attack. Rehearsals for the attack were done, and the men were waiting in loose little knots for the order to move out. He took the opportunity to talk things up to the troops, though, perhaps a very little bit more than circumstances called for.

"There's not going to be much left there," Werner reminded the men of his squad, "and those will be shaking from the shelling. That doesn't mean we can slack off. There's going to be a period of time—and the trees will make it longer than it might otherwise be—when the artillery will lift and we'll be on our own; us, the machine guns and anti-tank weapons, and the company heavy weapons. Though don't expect sixty-millimeter mortars to do much.

"So, speed is going to be the thing. When we get to within four hundred meters the guns will, half of them, shift off and change from high explosive shell to white phosphorus. The others will stay on target, but they'll be firing pure delay fuse until we get within a hundred and fifty meters when they'll—"

"Sergeant Verboom?" came the bellow from the platoon sergeant.

"Ready."

"Move 'em out."

"Roger."

Werner turned to his senior corporal, Coevorden, making a forward slash with his left hand, in the direction of advance. The corporal, a little paler than normal, said not a word but began to move, his fire team falling in to either side of him. Werner, himself, followed behind the fire team leader at a distance of perhaps ten meters. The other team leader, short a man, formed a wedge on himself and followed Verboom. That team would have been even shorter, had not the corporal in charge dragged van der Wege out from the bushes in which he'd hidden himself and forced the slimy rat into formation.

The platoon leader, Lieutenant Kranz, along with one radio telephone operator and one of the machine gun crews, took position behind Verboom's second team. The rest of the platoon followed along from there with the platoon sergeant taking up the rear. The other two rifle platoons of Thirteenth Company formed up further back, so that the point of each defined a company wedge. Further to the rear came the other two companies of the battalion, along with the headquarters and the various support platoons. Only the heavy mortars were staying where they were, since they could already range about four kilometers past the objective.

The mortars weren't firing yet, either. It had proven much tougher to get a load of ammunition to them than it had to the artillery, further back. They'd save what they had until it was needed.

Some, apparently, was needed pretty quickly; Werner heard the distinct sound of one hundred and twenty-millimeter mortars opening up to the right and behind, maybe fifteen hundred meters in each direction. Small arms fire had kicked in, too, but only to the right. It was distant and faint, but he could make out the very distinctive cloth-ripping sound of Balboan F- and M-26 rifles and light machine guns.

About a kilometer and a half to the other side, another company of Haarlemers likewise walked forward, likewise with the rest of their battalion following along.

As a reconnaissance in force goes, this seems sufficiently heavy on the "force" part.

The rumble of artillery grew steadily, not only because they were closing on the objective, but, so Verboom thought, also because the artillery seemed to have picked up the pace, delivery of shell-wise. However, the sound of the explosions changed, too.

We must be within about four hundred meters, he thought. *Those shells are on delay.* Indeed, to prove the point Verboom saw through a recently created break in the vegetation overhead—*jets, I suppose*—and to the south a great plume of dirt and rocks rising to the sky. In seeming response, the trees about two hundred meters to the left were suddenly denuded of foliage as a Balboan bombardment—Werner thought he could count a dozen or so distinct explosions—detonated among them, rather than bursting through.

"Haul ass!" shouted Lieutenant Kranz. "Two hundred and fifty meters, then take up a support position!"

Bella Vista, Balboa

And there's an indicator to mark down on the side of the

"we out-thought the enemy" ledger, Janier mused. *If the artillery we captured were only a show, a bit of bait, they'd be pounding the shit out of our men all the way up to the Parilla Line. They're not; the little bit of indirect fire they're throwing out is scattered, thin, and not very effective. Moreover, the counterbattery people are not only silencing it quickly, but they tell me it's only mortars. So maybe, just maybe . . .*

Janier had a sudden thought. Pulling his communicator from a side packet, he called Wallenstein. She answered immediately, "Yes, Bertrand?"

Does the blonde bitch never sleep or is this as important to her as it is to me?

"Marguerite, I won't ask what you're still doing awake, but since you are awake what are you seeing on the ground?"

"Nothing much," she replied. "We've had to pull our skimmers back to protect them from your attack. But where they are, they can see in a few places increased medical activity, ambulances and such."

"No holes appearing suddenly in the jungle canopy?" Janier asked.

"Only the ones we watched your jets and artillery make."

"Troop movements? Armored vehicles?"

"We couldn't hope to pick up soldiers on foot," she replied. "The whole area is practically a beacon of refined metal and electronic activity. But none of the serious metal is moving, no. We'd pick that up, we think, for all the deception Carrera has put in front of us."

"You mean you can't tell the difference between forty

tons of warmed-up scrap metal and forty tons of tank until one of them moves?"

"Yes. And, tell you the truth, we probably can't always tell then. But if we got enough metal moving, a thousand tons or so, say, we'd see and know that. And there isn't any."

"Any electronic intercepts?" he asked. "We've been getting nothing that made any sense, other than a request for a short truce on humanitarian grounds. My staff thinks it's because they're using nothing but landline."

"Same and same."

"It's not suspicious, is it, Marguerite? Everything is exactly as it should appear? And I am just being paranoid?"

"I don't think actual paranoia is possible when dealing with the Balboans," the High Admiral returned, *or, at least, when dealing with their commander*. "But, yes, this time it still looks like you outfoxed them."

"It *is* looking that way; even I am forced to agree. Let's see what our reconnaissance shows up."

Parilla Line

Verboom's point man, Corporal Coevorden, found the first wire the hard way. Running at a breakneck pace, his left shin hit it about 12 inches above the left foot. He tripped and went flying forward, landing on a crisscrossed patch of single strand wire and bolshiberries that held him, a bit torn and bleeding, about a foot over the ground.

"Tanglefoot," Verboom shouted. "Alpha Team, cut

through to your corporal and recover him. Bravo Team, bayonets as wire cutters and follow me!"

While Verboom was doing the only thing there was to do, clear the obstacle to his front and recover his man, Lieutenant Kranz moved to the edge of the wire, directing the other two squads of the platoon to the left and right to provide overwatch to the breaching party. With the platoon leader came the forward observer. Kranz put him to artillery work. Looking between the trees he saw the beginning of a rise about a hundred and fifty meters to the front.

Pointing to the rise, he said, "I need smoke between us and that." The FO went prone, looked up, and immediately got to work on his digital device, punching in the shell and fuse combination he wanted and the to and from grids for the screen.

"Hurry the hell up," Kranz demanded.

"The mission's in, sir," the observer said, "but lots of people are calling for fire right now we got a few . . . oh, wait . . . we've got a 'shot, out,' sir, and a splash in twenty-eight seconds."

"Twenty-eight seconds is a long time to . . ."

Kranz never finished his sentence. His head simply exploded from the impact of one or more bullets in a very short space of time. The cloth-ripping *crackcrackcrack* that followed suggested it was more than one that hit him.

Kranz's brains and blood scattered over the observer, dotting his uniform, face, hands, and digital fire-control device with little bits of sticky red organic matter. The FO screamed like a little girl confronted with ultimate horror, before beginning an uncontrollable bodily tremor. The scream was loud enough for the point of the platoon to hear it.

Even with the FO out of commission, hopefully temporarily, the smoke shells began to fall and blossom, white phosphorus at first, followed by shells containing a mix of hexachloroethane and zinc oxide. Somewhere ahead an enemy soldier screamed more horribly than had the observer, a long, continuous shriek that never lost its volume for longer than it would take a man to suck in another breath. A fragment or several of white phosphorus, the fire that is almost impossible to put out, had probably landed on his skin. The scream went on and on.

Jesus, thought Verboom, leading the way through the wire one strand of tanglefoot or one bolshiberry vine at a time, *would somebody put that poor, sorry bastard out of his misery?* He also had to remind himself that only the fruit of the bolshiberries—*green on the outside, red on the inside*—was poisonous.

Snip, *twang,* snip, *twang,* and then, suddenly and unexpectedly, Verboom realized there was no more tanglefoot, or none he could see, ahead of him. Separating them, he resheathed his bayonet into its scabbard, then slid the whole into the oval of nylon webbing that held it to his belt. His next thought was *mines. Maybe mines.* The thought was pushed aside as another small salvo of Balboan mortar shells impacted in the trees behind him.

"There *might* be mines," he muttered, "but I know the indirect fire is there and getting closer. I'll go with the threat I know about."

Still, there were mines and then there were mines. The

most dangerous—whether fixed directional or bouncing—were likely to be on trip wires. From a cargo pocket Verboom grabbed a can of aerosol string and aimed it directly to his front. A short burst of the stuff shot out maybe ten feet, but then hung on the grass well above where a tripwire was likely to be found.

What the fuck was I thinking? Of course, it's not likely to do much good there.

Resigned to the risk, Werner cradled his rifle in the crook of both elbows and then began a very slow and deliberate crawl forward. The occasional Balboan shell landing behind tended to force him to speed up, unwisely. It took a major act of will to keep his advance to something that allowed him at least a fighting chance to see and sense mines, tripwires, and other kinds of traps. The fact that he didn't run into any made this harder still.

Crawling in the tropic heat was hard and sweaty work. While taking a reluctant break to catch his breath, Verboom looked behind him. One fire team seemed close on his tail, but he couldn't see the other one. He risked a shout out, "Where the hell is Alpha Team?"

"They dragged Corporal Coevorden to the rear. My crawling shit van der Wege joined them."

Dumb shits; he couldn't have been that badly hurt. Deal with them later, because I can't deal with them now.

"Okay; let's move out again."

Ahead, the formerly screaming Balboan seemed to have settled on a heart-wrenching, "Por favor . . . por favor . . . por favor . . ." It sounded to Verboom to be just what it was, *please . . . .please . . . please . . .*

Poor bastard, he thought once again. For reasons he

wasn't even aware of he aimed himself at the repetitive plea, half his squad, he assumed, still following. Ahead, the artillery had stopped landing. Whether this was because the FO was in control of himself again, or the guns had bigger and better tasks, or because they'd simply run out of ammunition, Verboom couldn't guess. It didn't really matter anyway, since the smoke hung around still, blocking unaided sight between Verboom and the ridge that was the day's objective. Occasional burst of fire lanced out from the dense cloud, but whether it was aimed via a thermal sight or just random shooting, Verboom couldn't tell.

Slithering forward, still, Verboom came to his first shell hole. Though it hadn't rained in the last twelve hours or so, the bottom of the crater was rapidly turning to mud. He decided to wait there briefly—*it's as safe as anywhere*—and let his squad, what there was of it, join him.

The hole was large enough to accommodate Verboom and his short fireteam in fair safety. However, Coevorden and his entire team also showed up and began to slither into the muck.

"I thought they carried you to the rear," Verboom said.

"Maybe a hundred yards," Coevorden replied. His eyes seemed to lack a degree of focus. "That's how long it took me to recover from hitting my head—well, recover *enough*; it's still ringing and swimming—and get them to turn around. It took a little longer to get that piece of dog shit, van der Wege, moving forward again."

Another Balboan shell, probably in the eighty-two-millimeter range, buried itself in the dirt fifty or sixty meters away. The resultant plume of flying rocks and dirt not only pelted the squad but reminded Verboom of why they had to keep pushing on.

"Please . . . please . . . please . . ."

Balboan fire again lashed out: *Crackcrackcrack-crackcrackcrack.*

Another body appeared at the edge of the crater. The platoon sergeant, van Beek, peered down at them. "Lieutenant Kranz bought it," van Beek announced. "Must have been instantaneous. The FO's gone sort of catatonic; he was looking right at the lieutenant when his head exploded. The radio operator for the observer is handling our calls for fire. You have no idea how lucky you are, by the way. The radioman stopped the artillery from dropping a package of white phosphorus approximately on your heads."

Van Beek looked directly at Verboom. "I've got the rest of the platoon behind me. Company commander is somewhere back there, too. Move due south by bounds. I'll keep as tight on your tail as I can. Got it?"

"Yes, Sergeant," Verboom said.

"Good. Now move out."

"Right. Coevorden, overwatch. Bravo Team, let's go."

Moving from prone to a low crouch, Verboom could see that there were likely enough craters, at least as far as the still-hanging curtain of smoke, for them to leap from one to the next with minimal exposure to fire.

"Come on!"

Bravo Team followed close on Verboom's heels, and still bunched in a tight little knot. Doctrine—anyone's doctrine—often overlooked practicalities. In this case, as a practical matter, spread out would have taken time and risked greater exposure, while sticking together got them to the next hole rather quickly. All dived in.

"Get up on the lip," Verboom ordered. "Overwatch." He turned to direct his voice in the direction from which they'd come, shouting, "Coevorden! Go!"

Crackcrackcrackcrackcrackcrackcrackcrackcrack.

Estado Mayor, Sub camp C, Ciudad Balboa, Balboa

"No fucking artillery," Carrera insisted, waving a glass of whiskey with his left hand.

"Those men are being butchered up there, Duque," the chief of staff insisted. "They need something to get the Tauran guns off their backs."

"No. Fucking. Artillery. They've got mortars; they can use those."

"Mortars won't reach for the counterbattery work they need."

"End of discussion; no fucking artillery support."

"But . . ."

Carrera's eyes flashed in a fair imitation of psychosis. "MPs? Military Police! Put this man under arrest and bring him to Legate Fernandez."

The cell went deathly quiet, half at Carrera's outburst and half at the mention of the dreaded name. MPs—it was their job, along with the main band, to guard the headquarters—came in and led an apparently shocked chief of staff out to an awaiting vehicle. Just about everyone else tried to pretend they'd heard nothing and tried very hard to look like they were totally rapt in the work in front of them. It was especially shocking in that the arrested chief of staff was Dan Kuralski, who had been with the legions since the beginning and was known to be one of Carrera's oldest and dearest friends.

One boy, though, a young signal corps signifer, maybe nineteen or twenty, had the guts to ask, "Well, how do they stop the Taurans, then, Duque?"

"With guts and bayoneted rifles," he answered, striding off to his own quarters, whiskey still in hand.

Jamey Soult, Carrera's driver, bit his lower lip and shook his head. His boss wasn't supposed to be like this.

North of the Parilla line, Balboa

Verboom looked down in infinite pity at the Balboan soldier, still smoking and with the better part of his face and both his eyes burned away. Unconsciously, he shook his head at the waste of it all. The kid—*well, maybe he's an old man, he's too badly burned to tell*—kept alternatively keening and mouthing, *"Por favor . . . ayudame . . . por favor . . ."* but lacked the energy and wind to shout anymore. His legs spasmed and hands fluttered without any control, splashing mud for a short distance around.

Taking one knee, Verboom thought, *I'd hope, if our positions were reversed, someone would do as much for me.* Then he placed the rifle's butt to his shoulder, took extremely careful aim, and squeezed off a single shot. The bullet entered the victim's face just to the left side of what had probably been a nose. A two-inch plate of skull detached from the head, flying upward and sideways for several feet, before spinning back down to the muck.

"*God zegene,*" Verboom whispered, taking the rifle from his shoulder. "God bless."

"Was that necessary, Verboom?" asked van Beek.

"I think it was," the former replied. "Even if he could have been saved by our side or his, saved for what? To be a blind, one-man freak show. I follow the golden rule; that rule demanded this."

Van Beek looked into the shell crater with its now still and silent body. "Maybe so. We'll let it go for now. Orders are to set up a hasty defense and look into what defenses we've found."

"Already doing the first part." Verboom inclined his head to his left rear, saying, "For the other . . . well . . . over there there's a small wooden crate that's been buried open side out to look like the firing port for a bunker. But it's just a wooden crate. There are some shallow scrapings behind us; but you probably saw those. There are some bumps that are nothing more than shipping containers covered with sandbags, rocks, loose dirt, and grass. I haven't seen anything else."

There was a sudden burst of that distinctively fast Balboan rifle and machine gun fire, followed by a long, blood-curdling scream of naked aggression. Van Beek and Verboom looked up to see shadowy figures emerging through the smoke, charging while firing from the hip. Both dived into the hole containing the remains of the late Balboan burn casualty.

"Fix bayonets!" shouted van Beek. "Fix bayonets!"

Bella Vista, Balboa

In the temporary command post, Janier watched as an enlisted man updated the map. He also listened very attentively to the reports as they rolled in from across the front. The Balboans were using mortars, but there was no artillery. They were meeting his thrusts head on, hand to hand and bayonet to bayonet. They were also beginning to infiltrate to the sides of his probes, indicating, *It's just about time to start pulling the troops back before they get cut off.*

Most importantly, he'd been forced to the conclusion that, after all, the Parilla Line faced north, not south. *No mines, limited wire, very few positions sited to fire toward us, and those, by reports, of relatively recent and somewhat shoddy construction.*

So . . . okay, I'll stifle my doubts. And continue bringing the rest of the armies ashore. And continue preparing for a push to the capital.

Shaking his head, Janier muttered, "You've disappointed me, Patricio, you really have."

Pointing to some graphics on the map, he told his operations officer, "Begin the pullback to what we want to keep as jumpoff positions. Don't try to control it from here, just give control of a slice of the artillery to the subordinate commanders and let them extract themselves as best they can, while they can."

CHAPTER TEN

"It is courage, courage, courage, that raises the blood of life to crimson splendor. Live bravely and present a brave front to adversity."
—Quintus Horatius Flaccus (Horace)

Parilla Line, Balboa

The Balboans were pressing tightly, probably on the sound theory that the Taurans wouldn't use artillery close enough to risk having to have to explain to somebody's mommy why her little precious bundle of joy had been killed by friendly fire.

Never mind if we're killed by enemy fire, sneered Verboom, *so long as the generals and politicians, to the extent those differ, don't have to explain anything . . . impolitic.*

If the Taurans were, by and large, bigger men, the locals seemed to have made something of a fetish out of the bayonet. At least whichever unit this crew came from apparently had.

Bastards.

Verboom no sooner finished the thought than he heard a shout of panic from Coevorden, off to his left. He turned in time to see three Balboans, one still in the process of rising, charging from that flank. Van Beek, the platoon sergeant, was the first one to react positively. He put a bullet into the throat of the nearest man among the charging enemy. However, it was the tiniest fraction of a second before another from among the Balboans fired a short burst into van Beek's lower abdomen, laying him out like a sack of fruit that could bleed red. Coevorden, on the other hand, still not entirely himself from his fall, reacted slowly as the Balboans neared to club range. Faced with a thrusting Balboan bayonet, his parry was too slow. The bayonet entered his throat just under his Adam's apple, and was then brutally ripped out the left side of his neck. Blood, thick and stinking, spurted out in four directions.

It was only as Coevorden's dying body fell that the way was clear for Verboom to get a shot off. His first shot, spinning away as it left the muzzle, was also, naturally, yawing like mad. It hit the Balboan's glassy metal and silk vest at an angle, denting metal without penetrating. The Balboan was knocked back half a pace.

The sergeant being frightened half witless, two of his next three shots went wild, while one again impacted the vest. Forcing calmness on himself, barely enough calm for the purpose, Verboom took careful aim at the Balboan's head, firing a single shot that connected.

The last Balboan, seeing his two comrades fall, dropped his rifle and put up his hands. No sooner had he, though, than a bullet launched from somewhere behind Verboom took him in the face.

Werner's instincts were to carefully avoid looking around to ensure he couldn't see who had done it. After all, it wasn't the time nor the circumstances for too close an adherence to the finer points of the law of war. Unfortunately, his instincts were overcome by his sense of justice. He looked and saw van der Wege, lowering his rifle and looking self-satisfied.

Men with their blood up, or half crazed with terror are not entirely accountable for their actions. But that private is still a worthless piece of shit.

So, Van Beek's down as well as Corporal Coevorden. The way that bayonet ripped his throat out, he never had half a chance.

He spared the body a quick glance. *Yeah, he's certainly dead.*

The arterial bleeding had stopped, not through either treatment or coagulation, but through simple lack of any more blood to squirt.

Looking over at van Beek, he saw the platoon medic working frantically. *On the other hand, van Beek's got half a chance if we can get him out to where we can get an aerial evacuation.*

But I don't know if we can, thought Verboom. *Considering the whole shitty situation, I really don't think we can. Fortunately, they're not coming right at us anymore.*

That whole shitty situation under consideration included not only the loss through hysteria of the forward observer, now being led by the hand by an *hors de combat* private, but the loss to a lucky mortar shell of the observer's radio operator. This meant no possibility of responsive fire support to cover their withdrawal. The digital fire-control device survived the shell that killed the operator, but, *I don't know how to use that fucking thing. What the hell were they thinking, taking people out of the artillery loop?*

His own platoon's radio operator was trying desperately to get through to the company, where the commander's observer might be able to serve as a link between the platoon, in desperate need of fire, and the guns who could provide it.

Crackcrackcrackcrackcrackcrackcrackcrackcrack.

Little brown fuckers aren't letting up either. I think they're . . . oh, shit.

That mental *"oh, shit"* was the sudden realization that the Balboan infantry—*tough little bastards; you've got to hand them that*—were working around the flanks to trap the platoon, or maybe the entire company, in a double envelopment.

"Goddammit, can you get through to company or not?"

"Just did, Sergeant. Here; the exec is on the other end."

Werner pressed the talk button and waited for the beeps and blurts of synchronized, encrypted speech. "Verboom here. I am in charge of the platoon now. We're almost trapped and need some fire support if we're going to get out of here. Can the FO help?"

"Lieutenant Jansen here." With the combination of encryption and known voices and persons it wasn't strictly needed to use complex call signs. "CO's hit; not dead and he'll probably make it but he left me in command. I think you've been taking most of the pressure, Verboom, because we got back to our hold line fairly easily and with light casualties. Even the CO's wound was mostly a result of him insisting on being the last man back. He'd still be out waiting for you and yours if he could be."

"Yes, sir, I am sure the CO is just wonderful, a credit to every officer corps since officer corps began, but that doesn't help me at the moment. Can you have the company forward observer translate my requests into calls for fire?"

Crackcrackcrackcrackcrackcrackcrackcrackcrack.

"Like, in a fucking hurry?"

Crackcrackcrackcrackcrackcrackcrackcrackcrack.

The exec didn't answer. Instead, after a few seconds' delay, came a voice Verboom didn't recognize. "Lieutenant de Groot, sergeant. A word of warning before we begin; we don't actually train on the old-style call for fire anymore, so I am going to have to ask you questions and punch the answers into my fire-control device.

"Now, first off, can you give me your *exact* location?"

It had taken a while, and some false starts and dangerously off impacts, but shells were now falling along three sides of a box. Only the southern side of the box wasn't being pounded, barring the odd, fitful, Balboan mortar salvo.

The shelling was thin, really. It probably wouldn't have stopped men determined enough. *But,* Verboom figured, *they're probably as ready to see the last of us as we are to see the last of them. From their point of view, they won, so why get killed to turn a victory into a rout. I think.*

Crackcrackcrackcrackcrackcrackcrackcrackcrack.

That, however, didn't stop the Balboans from firing into the area they could no longer attack bodily.

Crack. Crackcrack. Crack.

Crackcrackcrackcrackcrackcrackcrackcrackcrack.

This shit's getting old, too, Verboom thought. He looked behind the thin line composed of the remnants of his squad and one fire team from another squad. The remainder of the platoon, including the walking wounded, were formed up to the north. Some served as litter bearers for such as Sergeant van Beek. One of the walking wounded still had the FO by the hand. Some, holding bandages that dripped red as often as not, crouched on their own for the command to go. Verboom gave it, then turned his attention back to the front.

Crackcrackcrackcrackcrackcrackcrackcrackcrack.

"Yeah, this is getting old."

He had two fire teams with him. One was five men, a little larger than normal, from his own squad. The other was composed of four from third squad. He thought it would be less confusing to keep their normal nomenclature, even though they were much reduced. Hence, after waiting about fifteen minutes for the wounded to make their escape, his first order was, "Third squad, bound back seventy-five to one hundred meters. Go!"

Crackcrackcrackcrackcrackcrackcrackcrackcrack.

Werner got back with all but two of his rear-guard men whole and sound. One, he'd had to leave the body behind, what there was of it. The other he'd carried slung over his back.

The worst part is that he was alive when I draped him across my shoulder, but died while up there. I felt it happen. Horrible feeling. Horrible knowing. And for what?

Puerto Lindo, Balboa

Though he didn't know it, and might not have cared if he had, Janier stood on precisely the same spot from which Patricio Carrera had watched the *Megalodon*, the first of its class of highly stealthy coastal defense submarines, or SSKs, begin its maiden test voyage. However, where Carrera had been quite nervous and troubled about the former, as well as disgusted at its late arrival, Janier was positively jubilant about the activity he was watching. Moreover, it was happening sooner than he felt he had a right to expect.

At the harbor's new edge, a quay rapidly put in by his engineers, rode a mid-sized Roll On-Roll Off civilian transport, chartered to the Tauran Union. The RO-RO, somewhat lightly loaded due to the still relatively shallow draft of the bay, was currently disgorging forty-two armored vehicles, from tanks (eleven) to infantry fighting vehicles (seventeen) to armored personnel carriers (nine) to self-propelled artillery (four plus a fire direction center vehicle). There was also a mix of wheeled transport waiting for their big brothers to clear the way before getting in the queue. It was his first increment of armor other than the useful but small and weak Ermine class light armored vehicles of the Sachsen paratroopers, plus the half company or so of equally light, wheeled armor the Anglians had brought by helicopter in lieu of proper assault guns.

Ah, yes, thought Janier, *those things are just like* real *armored fighting vehicles, only with fetal alcohol syndrome. I confess, while I was still worried that this was all a trap, one of my major worries involved the idea of two brigades or even a full division of Balboan armor coming charging out of the jungle to toss us into the sea. It's still something to be concerned about; after all, desperate men and desperate measures, but less so. And I'll soon be able to handle anything less than a corps-sized armored thrust. This package, alone, can buy enough time for the air forces to get here, come to that.*

The RO-RO was a big improvement, but logistics, as much as politics, is the art of the possible. What had once been all that was possible was still, even now, in operation. Out in the bay, in the deepest part, rocked a larger crane ship, the *Hermóðr*. This was a semi-submersible catamaran-styled freighter with its own integral high-capacity cranes and stabilizing columns that could be lowered into the water. This vessel carefully raised other heavy vehicles from its hold, swinging them over the side and then lowering them to waiting landing craft and lighters. Its tandem cranes, at the stern, did similarly for two smaller vessels tied up alongside. The cranes were overkill, really; capable of lifting as much as nine *thousand* tons, using the rear ones in tandem, they'd never in this mission been called upon to lift as much as two percent of that.

Overkill or not, three cranes or not, several dozen

landing craft and lighters or not, this was still a slow process, not least because some of the cargos were not self-propelled, but had to be manually moved from the landing craft and lighters to waiting trucks ashore.

Further to the east, by the tiny speck of land called "Isla Pato," a fuel transport pumped its load into the floating terminus of a short, ship-to-shore pipeline. Still more trucks were awaiting at the landside terminus, filling up and moving off to either the logistics base building between Cristobal and the Parilla Line, or going directly to units to top off their tanks.

We need this little port so badly. And the enemy still has an air force. I wonder . . .

"Malcoeur?" Janier asked, in a tone far friendlier, perhaps even paternal, than those he'd formerly used with this particular officer.

"Mon General?"

"What's our air defense status here, now?"

The aide de camp didn't even need to consult notes. "There are three pair of interceptors—well, fighters with pure air-to-air ordnance aboard—plus an early-warning aircraft on station continuously. A battery of short-range air defense, missile-armed, is stationed around three sides of the port. That battery has been supplemented with twenty-four teams of man-portable missiles. Also, half at the old Balboan military school and half on a hill to the north, are a heavier, Sachsen-provided battery of self-propelled air defense, some missiles, some thirty-five-millimeter guns. Also at the school is a single battery, though only half unloaded so far, of heavy air-defense missiles."

"Hmmmm," mused Janier, "you know, Malcoeur, the reason they call them 'missiles' rather than 'hittiles,' is that they miss a lot more often than they hit. How long before we can get another battery of guns in place? No, don't answer unless you actually *have* the answer. What I want, rather, is that priority be moved up to get another gun battery ashore and set up quickly."

"I'll see to it, sir."

"Also, see if there isn't some way for us to get some air defense balloons airborne. Yes, yes, I know; all balloons are being used around the cities of the Tauran Union, lest the ever so-evil Balboans bombard us with money again."

Malcoeur had to grin at that one. In retaliation for Tauran bombing of their homeland, the Balboans had struck back with very hard to detect, low speed drones. One of these, slamming through a window at headquarters, had done for Elizabeth Ashworth, the worse than useless TU defense minister. Another had dumped several million in mixed real and counterfeit currency on a well-attended soccer game, the resulting riot having caused the death of about as many Tauran civilians, soccer hooligans in the main, as the Tauran bombing had in Balboan. The Tauran Union's various militaries had thought extremely well of both events, and one Anglian regiment had officially added to its list of mess night toasts, "the missile that had rid us of 'she's-no-Lady Ashworthless'."

Almost everyone military and not directly impacted by the drone attack grinned about the soccer game. Janier was one of a very few exceptions. *They're not just hitting back and making us look and feel stupid; they're also demonstrating the ability to hit a target in the TU with considerable precision. In itself, this would hardly matter, but there is a strong suspicion in the intelligence community that the Balboans have nuclear weapons. I don't know where they'd have gotten them, but the world is a wicked place. So maybe they're also letting us know, in somewhat uncertain terms, that we cannot nuke them without being nuked in return.*

"There is one other thing, sir, but I don't know what to make of it. We've received a report, whether from one of Major Campbell's people or more routine channels, that Duque Carrera is beginning to lose his composure, his judgment, and the respect of his subordinates."

Janier sighed. "A lot of things, son, that I once thought impossible seem to be coming true."

South of the Parilla Line, Balboa

No rest for the wicked, thought Werner Verboom. At the moment, the sergeant was overlooking a mostly dry draw—*that's not going to last long*—with his reconstituted squad stretched to either side of him in a V. Verboom laid down the device he'd been holding in his right hand and flicked fingers to shoo away a mosquito, persistently buzzing by his ear. Although they were most annoying, and even potentially dangerous, his views on his unwelcome buzzing company could be summed up as, *Still beats the shit out of trying to fight our way into their lines without anything like enough preparation again. And it's miles better than trying to fight our way out again.*

Verboom automatically recovered the device as soon as the mosquito had moved off. He held the device's twin, a small, cheap, disposable detonator for a directional anti-personnel mine, in his left hand. He really didn't think that the spot his acting commander had chosen for him was a very good spot for an ambush. On the other hand, as Lieutenant Jansen had pointed out, "No place that the enemy is unlikely to show up is a good place for an ambush. Anyplace the enemy is likely to show up is a good place for an ambush. That draw will channelize people trying to escape from our lodgment or patrolling from their lines. That makes it a good spot. So quit sniveling, Sergeant, and go."

I suppose he had a point, thought Verboom, *and if they'd given me the five mines and the det cord I'd asked for . . .*

Mentally, the sergeant sighed.

Well, I suppose that they're still having trouble getting supplies ashore. Or maybe it's trouble sorting out what they've brought in. Whatever it might be, two is not enough to cover this draw very well. Five maybe wouldn't be enough. Needs must, though. And it still beats trying another attack before they've unloaded enough artillery ammunition to rearrange this part of the country.

Thinking of the attack, the "reconnaissance in force" in which Thirteenth Company, Royal Haarlem *Commandotroepen*, had participated, Verboom still couldn't figure out the whys of it. Sure, it had been costly for Balboa, but probably not as costly, as a fraction of available force, as it had been for the TU.

It had been a bit of a shock, really, after the easy initial landing and fairly easy initial assault. But then they'd stymied, after which, *the enemy infantry, too, had seemed to come from almost everywhere. It's almost as if the bastards let us get in just as much as they wanted us in. We might have whipped them when they were on a not very well-planned defensive, but give the fuckers their due, when they attack you* know *you're under attack.*

Verboom gave a little unwilling shiver in remembrance. Maybe they'd gotten more Balboans than the Balboans had gotten Haarlemers—*And maybe not, either*—but there was no doubt who'd ended up in possession of the contested turf.

No doubt who's still in muddy scraping, either. Got to give them credit, too, though, for sending someone to arrange to give us our bodies back . . . and the worst of our wounded.

The thought of the dead gave Verboom another involuntary shiver.

Completely unbothered by his shivering, the mosquitoes still landed for their feast on Verboom. They also quite ignored the insect repellent with which he'd doused himself. The repellent was some new stuff, without much smell to it to a human's sense of smell. If the bugs smelled it at all it was tolerably hard to notice.

Again dropping his clacker and flicking his fingers at one particularly bothersome pest, Verboom noticed the smell of explosive, a very distinctive solvent-like aroma, clinging to his fingers from handling the two directional mines he'd set out.

Hmmm . . . I wonder if they're attracted by that? Something's got them riled up, sure as hell. I wonder if the

Balboans—he cast his eyes northward, in the general direction of the enemy defensive line—*have figured out some way to make them worse, too. Wouldn't surprise me a bit.*

Lying in the mostly quiet ambush position, course *du jour* at Chez Buggy, and with the cry of the antaniae—*mnnbt, mnnbt, mnnbt*—sounding in the distance, Verboom thought, *It's a defensive line, a deep and strong defensive line. Okay, we always knew that. But who the hell puts a defensive line on the wrong side of the river, and why? Makes no sense. Makes as much sense, anyway, as laying out in the . . . oh, oh . . .*

Sergeant Sais wasn't aware of the first warning, the absence of close animal sounds, until he got the second, a brief whiff in the shifting breeze of something like solvent. It couldn't have been natural, but it still took half a second for him to recognize what it came from.

Automatically, Sais began to raise his F-26 rifle. "Fuck . . ."

If he were going to say anything else, the words were lost in the twin explosions that shattered the evening stillness. In that instant, time seemed to slow down to a crawl.

Sais felt a half dozen or so small impacts on his unarmored legs, two more on his left arm, and one in his neck. Some numbers, too, seemed to hit the plates of his *lorica*, the Legion's silk and liquid metal armor, while still others he thought he felt burying themselves in the silk.

Pain wasn't instantaneous, neither after seeing the explosions nor even feeling the impact of those fifteen or so pellets. Before pain came shock, then rage. Only after that, did Sais begin to feel the burning of the hot bits of metal buried in his flesh. He never really did notice the blood that began to leak from his wounds.

The rifle's safety was already off. Indeed, it hadn't been on since about the time they heard the first word of enemy parachutists. At the first stroke of the trigger, it began to spit out 6.5 mm full metal jacket. That fire was answered by at least one machine gun and seven or eight rifles.

As he had been trained, Sais' first instinct was to charge the ambush, screaming and firing like a maniac. He could scream, and did. He could fire, and the F-26 spat out its nearly two thousand rounds a minute. Charge he could not do. When he turned to assault the fire-spitting line to his left, his legs simply gave way under him, tumbling him into the moist earth below. It was that fall that, at least for the nonce, spared his life by dropping him below the enemy's line of sight. Something tore his night vision goggles from his face as he fell.

Espinal, on the other hand, had been saved from major perforation by the fact that his sergeant's body had stopped all the pellets that might have hit him. He'd been trained, too, to assault the near ambush. He did so, unintentionally leaving Sais behind. He was out of the kill zone, unhit, in a matter of about two seconds or perhaps a bit less. If he'd hit any of the ambushers in his wild firing charge, he didn't know about it.

But where's my sergeant? the boy wondered, once he'd gone about seventy meters past the ambush and found a tree to hide behind. In a lull in the firing, Espinal heard foreign voices, Taurans, shouting something harsh and guttural. Then he heard his own name, weak and indistinct, but clearly in Sais' voice, followed by a few bursts of fire, accompanied by one of the Taurans screaming.

For a few moments—long moments, to be sure—Sais lay stunned, face down in the dirt, while tracers streaked just barely overhead, impacting the banks of the draw to either side of him. He was far more emotionally aware of them, of their flashing and cracking and dull thudding into the dirt, than he was intellectually.

It was the pain, especially the pain from the wound in his neck, that brought him around to a more acutely intellectual sense of, *Jesus Christ; they're trying to kill me!*

"Espinal!" shouted the sergeant, as he took what passed for aim in the night. His point of aim was a series of flashes, about seventy meters to the front. He pressed the trigger twice in rapid succession, causing the rifle to spit out at least nine or maybe as many as a dozen bullets. He must have hit something, because one of them screamed.

"I'm here, Sergeant," the boy shouted back. "I'm coming back for you. Hold on!"

"NO!" That was distinct and didn't sound especially weak. Neither did the ripped-cloth bursts that followed. "Just shut up, boy, and run for it. Let them know we accomplished our mission, and the issues with that. Now go."

"But . . ."

"Goddammit, private, *go!*"

Estado Mayor, Sub camp C, Ciudad Balboa, Balboa

A profoundly nervous Jamey Soult knocked on the door to Carrera's suite in the sub-camp.

"Come in," came the answer.

This was a relief. *Given his mood, I wasn't sure he'd be willing to see his wife, let alone me.*

"You okay, Boss?" Soult asked, padding in on quiet feet and shutting the door behind him. Carrera sat in a comfortable reading chair, staring at an old-fashioned paper map and a clipboard with some papers—*reports, I suppose*—attached to it. He looked up at Soult, directly, a questioning expression on his face.

I expected him to be half drunk but . . . well . . . if he's had anything to drink it's tolerably hard to tell. Soult looked down at a table sitting just to the right of the entrance. A full glass of whiskey sat there, still. *He didn't drink any of it, as far as I can tell.*

"No, Jamey, I didn't have any more than a sip to cover my breath in case anyone got close enough."

"But the glass, Legate Kuralski, the refusal of artillery support. Boss, you and I both know we've got more guns dug in and ready than . . ."

"Don't say that out of this room. Don't even think it. In fact, when you leave here I want you to look like a mix of disgusted and hopeless."

"But . . . why? I don't understand."

"It's Fernandez's idea. He says there are still enemy informers, spies, in plain language, among us. He insists there's no way he got them all, even though he thinks he's rounded up the bulk of them. So we're making use of them, or him, or her, or however many. Movement is tightly controlled, so no one is likely to see what Logistics Base Alpha really is. Rumors, though, somehow always pass unimpeded. I've been setting up a rumor mill that I am demoralized, lost, depressed, and rapidly climbing into a bottle. Fair chance—no, a better than fair chance—that my opposite number on the other side will hear of this within, oh, call it two days, at the outside."

Carrera passed Soult the clipboard. "Only four people in the world I ever trusted completely, Jamey; my late wife, Linda, Lourdes, Mitchell, and you. Read it."

Soult read. It was a compendium of reports from stay-behinds in the occupied area. Fully a third of them said, "Last report for a while." Another third said "negative report."

"Why, 'last report,' Boss? And where did they come from, and how?"

"In some cases, because a group of Taurans are sitting on top of their hideouts so they couldn't risk coming out. Some came by directional radio, rather, radio with a directional antenna. Some came by radio lifted by a balloon and floating, this time of year, out to sea. A few came by carrier pigeon, too. Yes, really.

"Turn the page."

Soult complied, then asked, "And this is?"

"It's a report of estimated tonnage landed at Puerto Lindo." Carrera smiled broadly then. "They're sending not everything they can spare, but everything they *have*. Fernandez's tame Druze, Khalid, along with the other men we have there, is going to have a fine time in the TU, very, very soon."

CHAPTER ELEVEN

"We are the worm in the wood!
"We are the rot at the root!
"We are the taint in the blood!
"We are the thorn in the foot!"
—Kipling, *A Pict Song*

Moseal *Fluss*, near Treverorum, Sachsen

The Tauran Union, Khalid the Druze decided, *has two big problems stemming from one bigger one. The two problems are that it not only has no defense in depth, but it has no defense on its extremities, either. That, of course, is because of the bigger problem, the people running the place.*

What spurred the thought were the dozen packages of rifles and rocket launchers, mines and machine guns, grenades and demolitions, plus a fair load of ammunition, that he and two of his devout Moslem assistants, Maytham and Bandar, had brought up the river network without anything resembling hindrance, to a place near this city located near the border between Sachsen and Gaul. Where the arms had actually come from, Khalid didn't know and didn't want to know. He suspected a factory somewhere in the Volgan Republic was turning out lower receivers without serial numbers at Fernandez's or Carrera's behest. *For that matter, who knows; maybe our side owns the factory. Though I don't know why we would, since we developed our own family of small arms. Maybe Carrera and Fernandez think that far ahead. I'll have to ask someday, Allah permitting.*

Under the declining sun, their boat, a small yacht, passed picturesque towns, banks covered with vines, church towers, and centuries-old ivy-encrusted stone fortifications. Nobody stopped them. Nobody questioned them.

I suppose they're afraid that if they were stopping boats and questioning people, they'd find out how many illegal immigrants were coming in. Worse, they might actually find some illegal immigrants and then have to escort them to the nearest refugee acceptance center. That, of course, would never do. And turning them away? Unthinkable!

Ordinarily, the Druze were pretty much a live and let live people and faith. Moreover, they tended to a fierce loyalty to their homelands. That loyalty, however, was not likely to survive damage done to the Druze in those homelands. Moreover, since Islam considered the Druze to be irredeemable heretics, that kind of eventual damage was a given. To combat that, the Druze tended to hide who and what they were except among their own.

Khalid didn't let even the mildest trace of these

thoughts appear on his face. Rather, he kept them off the
face he currently wore. He'd had so much reconstructive
work done in the legion medical facilities that he wasn't
quite sure what he used to look like, anymore.

The plastic surgery, though, wasn't the reason for
the blank face. Rather, he, as a good Druze who had
had a goodly chunk of his family murdered by a
Moslem-planted terrorist bomb, many years before, in
Sumer, thoroughly detested Moslems and Islam, even
while manipulating them to do the will of his adopted
country.

*Oh, sure, I'll make exceptions for the odd decent one,
but I wouldn't lift a finger to save those few if by not lifting
it I could get rid of all the rest. And these two fanatical
minions I'll use like cheap whores and toss aside when and
if they become inconvenient.*

Savoring that happy thought for a while, Khalid almost
missed the lighthouse that was his checkpoint for a turn
into a tributary of the Moseal, the Konzer *Fluss.* Bandar
had to point it out to him, even while Maytham was
already bringing the wheel over in that direction.

Khalid made a hand motion, the universal palm down
and parallel to the ground or water pumping that said,
"lower the volume" or "slow it down," context depending.
Maytham immediately grasped and pulled back on the
boat's throttle.

From a pocket Khalid pulled out a small notebook
containing the calculations that would put him in precisely
the right spot, at precisely the right levels of darkness, to
dump his cargo overboard to where some of the more
devout members of a local mosque would recover it.

He turned to the last fading embers of sun, checked position against the lighthouse and decided, *Should be just about right on time*.

To Bandar, he said, "Start inflating the floats for the first four packages. Stand by to help me with the tank after that."

Less than half a minute later, there came the sound of rushing air as Bandar filled the first of eight flotation devices for the first two packages for this delivery. When he was done he informed Khalid, who simply nodded in the gathering gloom.

Looking ahead off the starboard bow, Khalid saw a van parked by a small civil park with boat ramp, a half dozen men and a couple of women in burkas standing around. They were the only ones there; any Sachsens who might have wanted to enjoy the park in the evening having scurried off to avoid the Moslem presence and the implied, and usually overstated, threat. Khalid put on a set of night vision goggles, turned them on, and then pulled out a throwaway cell phone. He lifted the goggles, fiddled a bit, then dialed a pre-set number. Pulling the goggles back into position he was gratified to see someone ashore answer his call. He couldn't see it, but he could hear that the van had coughed to life. He could also see a couple of the men waiting there stripped to their shorts and dive into the water, one of them with a rope wrapped round his waist.

Khalid ordered Maytham to close on the park, then said to Bandar, "Okay, let's get the cargo over the side."

Taking opposite sides of a large package, two crates, tied together and the whole assembly wrapped up in a plastic tarp, sealed with duct tape, Khalid and Bandar lifted it and began to carry it to the side. The two dozen firearms inside, one sniper rifle, one general-purpose machine gun, two light machine guns and twenty rifles, weighed a bit over two hundred and forty pounds. There wasn't enough air trapped inside to float that much weight, which is where the four flotation devices, each of about six cubic feet, came in.

Waddling sideways, Khalid and Bandar got the package to the boat's gunwales. With an effort they heaved it over, a thin but strong line running out from the ship behind it.

"Okay, ammunition now," Khalid said. When they went to that package, it could be seen that the line ran from it to the previous package.

With four connected packages in the water, the swimmers had no hope of actually moving the things by their own power. Instead, while the boat still dragged the packages behind it, they got their own stout rope around the one nearest the boat.

"We've got it," a swimmer called to Khalid, as loudly as he dared.

"Cut the line, Bandar."

Two more drops, two more armed mosques, and we're done with this section of Sachsen.

Though I wonder still what part this plays in the grand plan. That there is a grand plan, of course, and that all this is part of it, I have no doubt.

"Ahead slow, Maytham," Khalid said. "I don't trust the waters of any river."

MV ALTA (Cochinese Registry), Puerto Rodil, Bolognesia del Sol

The smell of the sea, which is to say the smell of rotting vegetation, fish, and the occasional dead bird, where sea met land, was strong here.

The interior of the ship was hot, dull, and a generally unenviable place to live. Music was mostly forbidden. Competitive team physical games were forbidden. And time on deck was tightly rationed for everybody except Hamilcar, who wasn't allowed on deck at all.

"No, Ham," Terry the Torch Johnson had insisted, "You look enough like a mix of your father and mother, who are both rather well-known faces, these days, that we can't risk someone getting a shot of your face and doing computer analysis of it. So, you, my boy, will stay below, even at sea."

It was especially galling insofar as his best wife, Pililak, or Ant, was back home in Balboa. Everyone had been a little surprised that she, who had crossed the country at considerable risk to find her Hamilcar, had allowed herself to be left behind. Alena the witch explained it perfectly, "She would surely prefer to be here with her god, Iskandr, but her duty is to give birth to Iskandr's firstborn. And Pililak the Chosen is a girl of staunch duty."

I imagine that, hot as this ship is, with Ant here I'd be roasting in bed with her. Can you give yourself heatstroke from screwing? Maybe best not to have the chance of finding out.

The ship's heat came from the problem of dumping

excess heat without being noticed. They didn't know what the United Earth Peace Fleet could sense, hence had to presume that it could possibly see a trail of unusual temperature left behind a ship, either in the air or in the water, if that ship were dumping an unusual level of excess heat. Pushing two thousand men was likely to create that much, the more so if it were pumped into the air and water. Music, games, and anything noisy had to be curtailed lest somebody's submarines or surface sonar or permanent underwater battery of microphones pick up the sound and get suspicious. There was a small area that had been specially soundproofed at the Cochin naval yard where the ship had been converted, but that area was only twenty by twenty feet, and two decks deep. Eight hundred square feet of recreation area worked out to something less than one half of a square foot per man aboard. Subtract for the books and the recreation center was preposterously tiny. On the other hand, it was just peachy for a command post to plan an attack.

The heat was less oppressive when at sea, when certain vents could be opened to allow at least a fresh breeze to circulate through the ship. Even then, though, the passengers and crew had to be quiet as church mice when outside of the rec center. And the breeze wasn't generally enough to make up for the lack of air conditioning; it merely turned Hell into Purgatory.

Though he couldn't go on deck, Ham did cheat a bit. He was allowed up on the deck below the bridge and there, standing at a porthole, he fiddled with the venetian blind, a cheap plastic thing, to watch what was going on topside.

What he saw was what he had seen at the previous ports visited, young men—well, boys, really—unloading humanitarian supplies for hundreds of thousands of Balboa's displaced children from the ship to waiting trucks on the long pier. He didn't bother counting them, but knew from previous practice that anywhere from perhaps twenty-five to as many as one hundred and twenty of the boys, plus one or two dozen men, would not leave the ship, but would, instead, disappear into its sweltering bowels where bunks, uniforms, and arms awaited. Ham was pretty sure he recognized a couple of them from the Cazador Club at his previous military school, *Academia Militar Sergento Juan Malvegui*, near Cristobal.

The old man sometimes speaks and acts as if I am his peer or, at least, potential peer. I have my doubts. I know I can plan small things, and sometimes have a good idea that ought to be obvious to just about anyone, but I cannot quite see myself planning ten or more years out—who knows when he began?—to prepare a clandestine amphibious assault ship, and special light infantry clubs in a half dozen military schools to man that ship, plus refugee camps to hide the boys until needed, plus a hidden reserve of helicopter and hovercraft pilots . . . and those are just a few of the high points.

Other things, even Alena the witch can't guess at. But I remember Legate Fernandez bringing the old man a black box, some kind of electronic control or computer for something, and the excitement that caused. Then, too, I know that he didn't put to death the Earthpigs' high admiral, but has him and one of the other Earthpigs prisoner somewhere.

What I don't know, and what even Alena the witch doesn't know, is what all those things have to do with our target.

Assembly Area Maria, Santa Josefina, not far from Hephaestos, Balboa

Scales change in the jungle, scales not only of distance but of time. Everything is slower, everything more compact. This was as true of the base built near the border between Balboa and Santa Josefina as it was anywhere else. This was mostly because, while little but large trees grew at ground level, those trees were indeed large, as well as thick, and tended to cut off the observer's view relatively quickly. Thus, for example, the base the *Tercio la Virgen* dug for themselves not too far from the border was only about three kilometers across. The defenses were, however, quite dense.

The base wasn't really about defense though; indeed, the defenses, as compared to those further west, were rather rudimentary. Rather, it was about attack or, more specifically, providing support for an attack.

There was nothing in the way of Tauran ground forces nearby. There was a small airport, with a runway just slightly over the minimum for the Tauran Hurricanes based in the country. That airport, the *Aeropuerto Jaba*, however, was almost never used by the Taurans. This did not mean, of course, that they could tolerate its possession in enemy hands.

There was more than the airport to make the place

special, too; not long after the Great Global War, about six hundred Tuscans had migrated to the area to make a living in agriculture. Their influence still held true in several key particulars; the children spoke like La Platans, which is to say Spanish with a deep Tuscan accent; their culture remained Tuscan, and they were one of the few groups in the country who, by and large, supported the Tauran Union's presence.

"So, we're going to teach them a sharp fucking lesson," announced the *tercio* commander, Legate Jesus Villalobos. "We're also going to teach the Taurans a sharp fucking lesson while we're at it."

Villalobos' command group, down to the maniples, stood around a sand table built in the dirt just outside of his dug-in headquarters.

"This," Villalobos said, using a stick to point to the town and the airfield, "is the physical objective, San Jaba. Note the highway, Highway 126, that connects the town and its airport with the capital to the east and the road to Balboa to the north. San Jaba doesn't really matter to us; it's just bait. What *does* matter to us are the Tauran forces here"—he pointed to the battalion facing Balboa across the *Rio Naranja*—"and here, near the capital. We want to kill a couple of hundred of each. That, the destruction of their reserves, is our actual objective.

"How? The short version is that we're going to send out the First Cazador Maniple to screen Highway 126, plus the feeder roads and trails. Cazador commander?"

"Here, sir," answered Tribune Madrigal, commanding one of the two Cazador maniples in the *tercio*.

"That's harder than it sounds. Consult your map; there

are a *lot* of feeder roads and trails. Also, you are not to be seen while occupying your screen line, and you are not to let the civilians escape. I want you to carry enough mines to make use of the roads risky and iffy. Lastly, you need to cut the phone lines and disable any cell towers that service the area. And you are not to be seen, doing it. Clear enough?"

Madrigal raised a single eyebrow. "Clear, sir." *But bitching hard to pull off.* "When can I leave?"

"Twenty-three hundred hours, tonight, which is about twenty minutes after the first moonrise. I think you'll probably need a little illumination, even though it has its risks. Also, all of you, note that we're out of Balboa now, so the Global Locating System should be functioning reasonably well if you need it."

Madrigal nodded, thinking, *Okay, that sounds a little better.*

Villalobos continued, "First Infantry Cohort?"

"Here, sir."

"For you, job one is surround the town and take the populace prisoner. Job two is turn them over to the service support battalion, which will be rolling into San Jaba right behind you. Job three is move east, but behind the *Cazadores'* screen line, and set up a very large ambush."

"Then kill the Taurans when they roll into it?"

"Correct," answered the legate. "I want maximum feasible loss of life here. I want a roach motel, where the Taurans check in, but they don't check out."

"Got it," answered the cohort commander, looking down to peer intently at his acetated paper map.

"Third Cohort, your job is similar, but you're skipping the town entirely and moving directly to set up an ambush just south of the town of Agua Dulce, either side of Highway 126."

"Both infantry cohorts can move out of the base area not earlier than midnight. Also note that each of you will have a river behind you, with a bridge. I want the bridges wired for sound, with a demo guard in place, just in case things turn against us and we have to scurry."

"Now . . . artillery?"

Container Twenty-one, Beloretsk, Volgan Republic

Eighteen long-range bombardment Condors, and the crews to maintain and launch them, had been parachuted into Volga from the ramp of the militarized airship *Casamara*. To everyone's surprise, the container's parachutes had all worked flawlessly. Previously, everyone aboard the airship or watching from the ground or sea had felt the anguish of watching a critically needed container full of war materials plunge into the Shimmering Sea, not far from the small port of Mataca, Santa Josefina.

They'd been met by an odd character with an odd walk, the walk being the result of having lost both legs on a raid in Santander, the legs having been replaced by high-end prosthetics. The character, Anton Pavlov, and no relation to the Volgan aviation officer, also called "Pavlov," was a warrant officer, one who had been medically retired as a sergeant, but then elevated, sent home, and remaining on the clandestine strength of Fernandez's organization.

He'd seen to it that the eighteen Condors and the ground crews were loaded on trucks and scattered into rented barns and warehouses across some forty thousand miles of territory. None of them but Pavlov actually knew where all the Condors had been stashed. Moreover, the crews had been split up into three groups, such that the loss of one would not interfere with the continuing program of launches to sting the Tauran Union into helpless fury.

None of them, not even Pavlov, knew how many launch sites there were. None even knew how many of the Condors had been manufactured, let alone the number of drone versions.

Number Twenty-one of this package, however, they knew everything about. It sat, fueled and armed, just outside a barn on a former collective farm, now gone pretty much to seed.

"What's the load on this one, Vera?" Sergeant (retired) Pavlov asked of Sergeant Dzhugashvili. He spoke Russian, which Vera had learned in the home from her parents, even though she considered Spanish her first language.

"Five-minute bomb," she answered, simply.

"I *love* those," he said.

"We all do. They don't hurt anybody . . . well . . . hardly anybody, but they hurt the enemy, *bad*."

"What's the target for today?"

"More like the target for this week," she answered. "We don't really have that many drones."

"Oh, yes, I know. I got them all moved, remember?"

"Yeah, sorry; anyway, this one is for Lumiere, the Capital of Gaul. City Hall, actually."

"Oooo, that's going to piss them off."

Tauran Defense Agency Headquarters, Lumière, Gaul, Terra Nova

Campbell ignored the sirens that filled the air around the headquarters. *After all, the anti-aircraft guns they dug out of storage haven't kicked in yet, nor even the machine guns. Not that they'll hit anything, of course.* Instead, she scanned the extensive reports given her by the Volgan, Vladimir; the sheer scale of the purchases, and the sheer age, in both senses, of some of them, took her aback.

"Does anybody really start planning and getting ready for a war that far out?" she muttered.

"*Quoi*?" asked Captain Turenge, absently, as she worked on a report to Janier on the subject of interallied cooperation within the Tauran Defense Agency and the lack thereof.

"It's the defense purchases made by the enemy, Captain. They were always several steps ahead of any reasonable need. Some of it wasn't obvious at the time, of course, because they made purchases but didn't bring all their 'shopping bags' home with them. Hmmm . . . wait a second and let me show you what I mean."

Jan fiddled with her desktop computer, one that could only access and be accessed by the files and computers in the headquarters itself. There were other computers within the headquarters that could reach out to the global net, but those were completely disconnected from the internal net she was using.

"Come, let me show you," Jan said, gesturing with her fingers.

Turenge walked over and bent slightly at the waist to rest her hands on Jan's desk, also bringing her face lower to see the screen.

"No, no, pull up a chair."

Jan waited until the captain had, and was seated next to her.

Jan entered a query. The screen almost instantly showed a Volgan helicopter, in civilian markings, lifting a slung pallet, somewhere over what looked to be very dense jungle.

"That," Campbell said, "is a helicopter of SHEBSA, the *Servicio Helicoptores Balboenses, Sociedad Anonima*, which is to say, 'Balboan Helicopter Services, Incorporated.' It was always part of their hidden reserve and we knew about it almost from the beginning, too.

"But here's where it gets weird. SHEBSA only had so many helicopters until the war began. They doubled their numbers almost overnight. Where did the helicopters to double their numbers come from?"

Jan pointed an oval-shaped, red painted nail at a paragraph on a particular page of Vladimir's report. "They bought them back in '63 and '64 and have been storing them, probably in nitrogen and shrink wrap, ever since."

"That *is* foresight," the captain agreed.

"That's not exactly right," Campbell corrected. "Foresight is when you get ready for what might happen at someone else's initiative or by chance or fate. '*Planning*,' on the other hand, is what you call it when you are getting ready for something at your own behest."

Turenge shrugged off the correction. "I think," she said, "that even if the general 'ad 'opes for peace, you and I already knew this Carrera person intended war all along."

"Not just intended to fight a war," Jan said. "He intended and prepared to win it."

Jan's eyes glanced over the several thick files given her in Saint Nicholasberg. "Are you about done with your report on 'interspecies cooperation and amity'?" That was their internal code phrase for physical intimidation of the otherwise uncooperative.

"Very close to done, *oui*."

"Okay, finish it up and then you and I are going to split the files, then do some math, read some intel reports old and new, and try to figure out just what our armies are facing based on what the Volgans gave me and what we think we already know. We need a solid case because, since Janier's swung over to the belief that he really did sucker the enemy, this time, he may be a hard sell."

Through the glass of her office window, Jan felt more than heard the sound of a very large bomb going off somewhere in the city, followed by ambulance and fire sirens. Mentally, she recited the grand joke, *Attention, please. I am a Five-Minute Bomb. Attention, please. I am a Five-Minute Bomb. Evacuate the area quickly. I am a Five-Minute Bomb. Evacuate the area quickly. I am a large Five-Minute bomb. My delay is fixed at a maximum of five minutes. It could be less. Leave the area now! Four minutes, fifty-nine seconds . . .*

**United Earth Peace Fleet *Spirit of Peace*,
in orbit over Terra Nova**

Intel, thought High Admiral Marguerite Wallenstein, looking at the main screen of the bridge. *Must go talk to intel.* At about the same time, the intercom sounded off with, "High Admiral? Khan, husband, in intel. There's something you need to see."

The bulk of the ship spun around a hollow central axis, a cylinder, called for reasons both practical and traditional, "the keel." The keel actually contained the bridge, the sail mechanism, some elevators, auxiliary tactical propulsion, and such. It could contain the hangar deck, too, but normally that rotated with the rest of the ship. Outside of that, filling up the bulk of the two-hundred by three-hundred-meter ovoid starship, the decks rotated in what was the only way yet found to provide artificial gravity in space.

To leave the bridge, Marguerite Wallenstein stepped out into the cylinder of the axis, then used handholds to pull herself to a transition chamber. Entering this, she reoriented herself so that her head was toward the portal through which she'd just entered. Then she grabbed another set of handholds and announced to the ship, "High Admiral, going to the lowest gravity deck."

The chamber immediately detached itself from the inner axis and locked itself to the rotating bulk of the ship, then moved slowly in a large groove within the keel. Given the lack of gravity, had she not been holding on tight to the handholds, Marguerite might have fallen to her shapely posterior. A hatch chimed open, giving her notice to move so that the chamber could reattach itself to the cylinder. She pulled with both hands, the movement being more sail than step. To someone on the deck, it would have, indeed, did appear that the High Admiral had dropped, feet first, through the ceiling.

The ship, sensing the chamber was empty, promptly closed the safety hatch, reattached the chamber to the cylinder, gave the cylinder a little nudge in the other direction to make up for energy gained in the lock-unlock process, and then gave a very tiny burn to some external rockets to make up for the tiny bit of energy lost to the rotation of the gravity decks in the process.

There were eight such chambers within the keel. The ship's computer could usually direct them in such a way as to minimize energy loss and fuel expenditure, while maintaining rotation, hence gravity, to the higher decks.

It was always a bit disconcerting to transition even to the lowest of the gravity decks from the microgravity of the transit chambers of the keel. Moreover, the gravity here on the "bottom" decks was so low it was hardly useful for any real purpose.

There were a number of elevators to move crew from that lowest gravity deck to the higher decks where both serious work and most living were done. Marguerite even had one dedicated to herself and her immediate staff. She usually spurned this, using the curved tubes that also connected the decks because, as she thought, stepping into the tube, *It's just so much damned fun to shoot up the decks under my own power and Coriolis Effect. It's nothing like skiing and yet it is almost* exactly *like skiing. Wheeeee!*

Hatches and numbers shot by, *2* . . . . . . *3* . . . . . . *4* . . . . . . *5* . . . . . *6* . . . . . . *7* . . . until Marguerite began to close on the deck she wanted, Deck 19. She put her hand out and overhead, fingers catching and then releasing handholds to slow herself down, *8* . . *9* . . . *10* . . . . *11* . . . . . *12* . . . . . . *13* . . . . *19.*

Marguerite paused at the hatch, catching her breath and applying a disciplinary palm to unruly hair. Then, happier than she'd been on leaving the bridge, she stepped out under noticeable and stabilizing gravity, walking briskly and with an approximately normal step to the intelligence shop.

CHAPTER TWELVE

"There comes a point during the course of the war when the people, especially those in the comparative safety of the towns, have to be informed in no uncertain terms who is going to be the master."
—Sir Robert G. K. Thompson, *No Exit From Vietnam*

Intelligence Office, UEPF *Spirit of Peace*, in Orbit over Terra Nova

The map showed on a screen darkened to indicate that it was night time below. Even then, there were glowing marks, red and white, blue and green and yellow, to indicate activity down there.

Khan, the husband, was there, posted by the screen, as was one of his assistants, Commander Spiro.

Khan said, "High Admiral, you wanted to know when or if the Balboans—or, more technically, their Santa Josefinan troops—began moving out of the little enclave they built at that bite in the border. They have. It's only patrols but there are a lot of them, they subdivide as they

223

move forward, and they seem pretty aggressive. They're also moving faster than I usually see them move at night in that kind of terrain. It's like they have a long way to go before morning."

Wallenstein leaned back against a desk affixed to the deck, crossed her arms, and stared intently at the screen. "Have we," she asked, "figured out where they're heading?"

Commander Spiro answered. "There's no obvious terrain features they're shooting for, or, at least, no contiguous set of them. I have, on the other hand, made a guess of where they'll be—or could be—by dawn, based on their speed." Spiro touched some button or other and suddenly an irregular arc appeared on the screen, in red. "They're not going past that, anyway."

"They're . . . what's that term when a force on the ground sends out patrols to report but not necessarily to fight?" she asked.

"Screen," Khan replied. "And, yes, that's my surmise. But is the screen to defend the base they constructed or to cover and provide warning for a movement out?"

"What's going on inside their base?"

Khan shook his head, "No clue. We could keep fairly close track of them in Balboa, but they did something in their enclave before we noticed they were moving that makes it nigh impossible to sense anything. They were using their radios fairly liberally in Balboa, and kept up a similar level of chatter from the same locations during their move. Frankly, they fooled us there. What they did to the enclave they moved into . . . well, I think they put something in the trees to defeat radar, probably whatever

they did in Balboa, and there isn't much heavy equipment
to triangulate off. Also, go figure, the skimmers can't see
much of anything through the jungle canopy. And, though
I put some effort into trying to intercept their radio
communications, they haven't uttered a single electronic
peep.

"Moreover . . ." The intelligence officer stopped short
as the screen began to provide a series of Vs moving east
out of the area marked as their encampment. "Okay, well
it's not just a screening line." He did some quick number
crunching in his head, even as more and more Vs
appeared. "Okay, they've got what looks dense enough on
the ground to be a main force battalion, moving to take
that town . . ." Khan hesitated briefly, " . . . San Jaba."

"If you can't intercept the Balboans' communications
in Santa Josefina, what about the Tauran forces there?
Marciano's headquarters?"

"Now theirs we *can* intercept and decrypt. Not a peep,
rather, nothing out of the routine. They're not aware of
the movement out, as far as I can tell, though they've
known at least a little something about the base for a while
now. They probably worried about it no more than we did,
having enough problems not to want to borrow trouble."

Marguerite began tapping her nose with her right
index finger, middle and ring fingertips pressed to her
lips. Reaching a decision, she said, "Get Esma and issue
her a communicator. Have my barge take her down to
Aserri, in Santa Josefina. I want the embassy there to get
her put in touch with General Marciano and act as a
liaison with him, feeding him intelligence reports from
us."

"Why not just have me break into the radio net?" Khan asked.

"Two reasons. One is that I don't want our enemies— nor even our friends—to know we can. The other is that I don't want to trip the Federated States' paranoia switch by seeming directly to help the Taurans there."

Khan nodded. "I'll also notify the embassy in Aserri to make a car and driver, plus security escort available to Esma. But we shouldn't use your barge. Instead we should use whichever one makes the normal mail and supply run."

"Good. Do it that way."

"There's something else, too, High Admiral. Listen."

Khan touched a spot on his screen and a voice began to speak, in Spanish. He let it run briefly, then stopped it, saying, "That seems to be just a meteorological message." He then started an automatic audio translation program and advanced the recording The small speaker brought forth, "Terra Nova, Terra Nova, this is Radio Balboa calling to our friends around the world. We have the following notifications and messages: Bellona is made of green cheese. I say again, Bellona is made of green cheese. Tilly has a very tight orifice. I say again, Tilly has a very tight orifice. Colin salts his friend's penis before eating it . . ."

Khan stopped the recording. "It's troublesome. This has been going on since the Zhong landed on the mainland. We have no idea who the messages are for, nor what they may mean."

"Why not?" Wallenstein asked.

"They all seem to be one offs, meant for one recipient

or a small group. And they never repeat. We think many of them, too, are purely spurious, meaning nothing to anybody, but we don't know that."

United Earth Embassy, Aserri, Santa Josefina

It was past dawn before the shuttle touched down on a broad green lawn. Five of the uniformed security staff met it at the landing pad. The senior of those guards slapped the side of the shuttle, hard, and told the pilot to take off immediately. Meanwhile the other three, trying to surround Esmeralda on all four sides, began to hustle her at a near run, out of the open and into the main building.

The last one to enter the building was the sergeant in charge, also bearing Esma's overnight bag. He slammed the heavy door behind him and then directed the rest of his crew to take Esma deeper into the building for safety. In was at about that time that she realized the windows were all sandbagged.

She stopped, nonplussed. "What has been . . ."

The sergeant's accent said he was local. "Snipers and mortar fire, ma'am, almost daily for the last couple of weeks. We haven't lost anybody but we can't afford to lose one—you—now either. Sorry for the rough and ready treatment."

"It's okay, sergeant. Needs must and all. I had no idea things had gotten this bad here. Certainly, the high admiral doesn't know."

Rather than answer in words, the sergeant flicked his eyes in the direction of the ambassador's officer.

"Oh, I see." Esma sighed, then asked, "If this place is under effective attack at all hours, how do I get out of the compound and to General . . ."

The sergeant shook his head. "It isn't all the time. There's been several lulls every day. The next one due is when the local staff reports in, which will be in about an hour. We can slip you out then. It's going to have to be in a plain, unarmored car though.

"Most of the city—most of the country, in fact, all of it that doesn't have anything to do with us or the Taurans— is actually pretty quiet and safe, ma'am. You'll be fine once you're half a kilometer from us."

Esma caught sight of her friend, Estefani Melendez, the ambassador's private secretary, as she was seen to her overnight quarters. Estefani, "Stefi" to Esma, ran to greet her, throwing both arms around the Earth girl and kissing both cheeks.

"Isn't it awful?" said the Santa Josefinan girl. "It's like it isn't even my country anymore around here. Did you know they've tried to suborn even *me*? Really, they cornered me on my way to work, two of them, and demanded I give them a list of embassy personnel. I refused, of course."

"How is it away from the embassy?" Esma asked.

"About the same as always. It's only here . . ." She let the words trail before asking, brightly, "Will you be here long? Can we maybe escape this prison and go have lunch or go shopping someplace safe?"

"Maybe when I come back through," Esma answered.

Escuela Maria, Madre de Dios,
San Jaba, Santa Josefina

When you engage in an atrocity against mostly innocent parties, thought Legate Villalobos, *it's at least a minor balm to your conscience when your victims are cultural foreigners.*

As if to punctuate the thought, there came a brief and ragged rattle of musketry, followed by the mass screams of what sounded like women and children. As if on cue, because it *was* on cue, a San Jaban man, hands tied behind him, was led out between the blue- and beige-painted square pillars that held up the gate and this end of the covered walkway, flanked by two guards, with a third pulling on a rope leash around his neck. The future victim tried to maintain dignity, and kept an admirably stoic face. Yet dignity was hard to maintain when every pull of the rope caused a stumble.

The irony of doing the court-martials in a school dedicated to the Virgin Mary, the executions in a play yard nearby, all by a regiment named for the Virgin Mary, was not entirely lost on Villalobos. *I do wonder what she thinks of all this.*

He decided to follow along. *If I can order it, I can at least force myself to watch it. I've already spent enough time watching the "people's tribunals," in any case.*

The informal little procession followed the street west, past a tree line to an open field, that field bisected by a creek, and with a few stout individual trees growing here and there. Some playground equipment, a brace of see-saws, a jungle gym, and a brightly painted, polychrome merry-go-round were there as well.

Incongruously, a firing squad, six men and a tribune, stood at ease in a line, perhaps fifteen meters from one of the trees.

A crowd of women and children were waiting and wailing, held back from coming closer by a line of rifle-wielding men. Villalobos saw, too, that a camera followed a small party, just two men, dragging a body bundled up in a sheet along the ground. They passed by the line of soldiers, depositing the bundle among the women and children, and then retreated to lay another sheet at the base of the tree, then waited for the next delivery.

Back amongst the crowd, the women, some of them, bent over the sheet. The wailing instantly grew to a crescendo as the cameraman turned his and its attention back to the tree. The sound dropped as some of the women and boys cradled the body gently, lifting it to bring it home.

Villalobos shook his head; he was not a man without pity.

The next victim, the mayor of the town, was led to the tree near the firing squad. The rope remained around his neck, but was given a turn around the tree, and then used to tie off his torso.

Then came the commands ". . . *apunten . . . Fuego!*"

The crowd moaned between the words, which moaning changed at the final command to a long shriek as Villalobos' soldiers fired. The body was battered against the tree, then slumped into the ropes. Villalobos thought the man might still be breathing, a guess confirmed when the tribune commanding the firing squad marched to the tree, drew his pistol, and fired a single shot into the mayor's head, spraying blood, brains, and fragments of bone out the other side.

And what was your crime, Mister Mayor? thought Villalobos. *You spoke in public in support of the current government and the Tauran Union forces here. It was possibly understandable, but was completely impermissible. Tsk.*

Villalobos noted the cameraman stopped to change the batteries on his camera. *Necessary, I suppose, given the power required to send the record to the globalnet from here.*

Task Force Jesuit Headquarters, Rio Clara, Santa Josefina

The name, officially, was Tauran Union Security Force— Santa Josefina. The alternate name, Task Force Jesuit, for "SJ," had begun more or less as a joke, but then stuck. That General Marciano was, himself, a religious man, probably helped with the sticking.

Watching the video of the murders—*formal murders, yes, and with a degree of protocol attached, but murders nonetheless*—caused him to wince at each command to fire. It was made worse, somehow, that the people being shot on screen were, by blood and culture, his own. He even shared a language with the older ones, though only half a language and most of an accent with the younger.

*And I know why they're doing it, too. At least I think I
do. It's to bait me in, to make me take some portion of my
overstressed pocket division and try to stop the killings. If
I don't try, the TU and the local government*—and here
Marciano made a small pause to mentally spit—*look weak
and helpless. If I do try and lose we look worse. Even if I
try and win*— *and I do not like our odds for beans here*—
I doubt I can save many of the condemned.

A phone rang with the peculiar *rattlerattlerattle* of a
field telephone. The duty officer picked it up and
answered it, before announcing, "President Calderon for
you, sir."

"Have it transferred to my quarters."

Claudio rarely tried very hard to hide his contempt for
both Santa Josefina and its president. He didn't try now,
either. No sooner had Calderon begun to berate him for
his inaction over San Jaba, then the general began beating
his phone on his desk. He stopped briefly to ask, "Have
you got the message, Mr. Calderon?" before beginning
the beating again. He went through this routine three
times before the president shut up and apologized.

"Good. Now what do you want? . . . Yes, I am getting a
relief column ready . . . no, I don't need anything from
you . . . if you had wanted to help, you should have started
building your own army so that I'd have more than a short
battalion to throw into this . . . no, in fact I may not launch
the relief column . . . yes, you should get to work on a time
machine . . . or you can ask the Federated States to
commit troops to your defense, but I wouldn't hold my
breath on that one.

"Now, if you'll excuse me, I am busy today."

After a brief knock, Marciano's operations officer, Stefano del Collea, asked, "Are you too busy to talk to a charming young lady, General?"

It was a sufficiently silly question that Marciano replied, "Send her in." He was rather surprised to see the beautiful young woman he knew as Esmeralda, High Admiral Wallenstein's cabin girl become aide de camp.

Before he could so much as utter a greeting, Esma pulled a communicator from her pocketbook, saying, "My High Admiral has information she wants to give you that you need to have, sir. This was the only way she thought she could safely get it to you." *Though it wasn't all that safe for me.*

"Let me talk to her, then, please. And, Stefano?"

"Sir?"

"No word of this, and bring me a map and some alcohol pens, would you?"

"Sir."

"So an ambush on both the high speed avenues of approach into the town, and an anti-helicopter ambush close to the town?"

Khan answered, "We really think so, yes, General Marciano. Do you have the means to fight through them?"

"No," he answered. "If I had even half my command available maybe, but about a third of it is guarding airbases for the war in Balboa, and for which my forces were not increased. Another third is engaged in containing the guerrillas in the south and, since their message spreads by non-physical means and their arms by clandestine ones, not having a great deal of success. The remaining third is mostly stuck facing Balboa to the northwest, though I had thought to break away a task force of a couple of companies for San Jaba. But that's not enough, is it?"

"Not really my area of expertise, General," Khan replied, "but, on the face of things . . . just a guess . . . probably not."

"Can I speak to Wallenstein?"

"I'm here; I've been listening."

"At least somebody is," Marciano said, not bothering to keep the bitterness out of his voice. "Since you *are* listening, High Admiral, can you get Janier or the World League or *somebody* to send me about twelve thousand more men, half of them in the form of eight or so infantry battalions and three more artillery? Because, with guerrillas growing up behind my so-called lines, with the people getting a graphic demonstration that we are not going to win and that the price for our not winning will be death to those who supported us, with that worthless shit Calderon unwilling to raise an army to help us . . . well . . . without those troops I'm going to have to pull back to the capital region and try to hang on to that and the port. Anything else is soon going to be beyond my powers."

"No promises. I'll see what I can do."

Academia Militar Sergento Juan Malvegui, Puerto Lindo, Balboa

Schools were in many ways ideal for military headquarters. They had auditoria, classrooms for offices and billeting, mess facilities, sometimes medical facilities, internal communications, parade grounds for helicopter landing and pickup zones, storage areas, etc. A military school like this one, though, far exceeded the normal school standard for military utility by adding arms rooms, ammunition storage bunkers, heavy vehicle maintenance bays, bombproofs, actual barracks, tunnels to move between the buildings . . . it was simply perfect for its new role.

It even had a small mansion for the former commandant, though Janier thought that too obvious a target. It was left empty. He made do, instead, with an office in the main academic building, next to his command post.

It was in that office that he used his communicator to speak with the High Admiral of the UEPF on the subject of Santa Josefina. Janier absolutely didn't want to send troops to Santa Josefina that he was likely to need in Balboa.

"I am fairly certain," said Wallenstein, "from speaking with him, that Marciano is going to pull back immediately if he doesn't get a firm commitment to add the forces he demands, and will pull back within a short time if they don't start materializing. My aide was there and spoke to me after. She said he 'exudes sincerity.' What's *that* do to your plans, Bertrand?"

"It will cut into our air support," said the Gaul, "but not so badly as all that. I had hoped that the Zhong would have been able to clear the road from Santa Josefina to supply an attack on the Balboans' western flank but, since they seem to be completely tied down in a guerilla war themselves, amongst that half-million civilians into whom were apparently interspersed several thousand soldiers of both sexes, there's nothing to be gained for us that way."

The "half-million civilians" referred to the collection of refugee camps, outside of his own defensive perimeter, that Carrera had set up expressly to force the Zhong to feed them, thereby straining their logistics. It also meant the couple of thousand *Amazonas* and *Cazadores* he'd mixed in among them to make feeding both the refugees and themselves highly problematic.

"The thing is, you see, Marguerite, that if we win in Santa Josefina but lose here, Santa Josefina will be lost soon enough, too, while if we lose in Santa Josefina but win here, we can recover Santa Josefina in short order. I'm afraid Marciano is going to have to do the best he can to buy us time to win here. After that he can have fifty, even a hundred battalions, if he wants them."

San Jaba, Santo Josefina

The court-martials there being finished, and the nearby executions done, the *Tercio la Virgen* also set up headquarters in a school. It was big enough for the purpose and, since the Taurans couldn't be sure they'd moved out all the children, even at night essentially immune to aerial bombing or artillery strike.

The lunch room now served as the unit's tactical operations center, with some of the classrooms set aside for quarters and specialty shops.

Similarly, the medics had moved into the town hospital,

a blue-painted concrete facility of about twenty-four thousand square feet, complete with an emergency room and trauma center, plus wards equal to thirty-three beds.

In the headquarters, Villalobos listened absently as the reports of the Cazadores on the screen line came in by wire. All was quiet along the "front."

If they were coming, thought Villalobos, *they'd have been here by now. So, I think I can assume that they're not coming. Still, this wasn't a waste, not even having those poor bastards shot. We've got a liberated zone. We've taught collaborators, real and potential, a pretty sharp lesson. We can maybe even claim belligerent status, ask for recognition, and import arms openly. Could be worse.*

I really expected them to fight me for the town and to do something to try to push us back over the border. I was wrong. And that's what I planned for. So where do we go from here?

**Task Force Jesuit Headquarters,
Rio Clara, Santa Josefina**

And demography and geography, under their child, logistics, dictate, fumed Claudio, studying the big, wall-mounted map in headquarters. *I cannot stay where I am. Not only am I outnumbered in both areas, with guerrilla movement rising behind us, but I cannot move my crappy reserve quickly enough to either reinforce either east or south, nor to clear a road to withdraw them if the enemy keeps trying to infiltrate.*

On the other hand, if I try to pull back to near the

capital, my road net, for mobility, is fine, but I'll have granted the enemy a potential hundred thousand young male recruits, and an absolute moral ascendency.

Speaking of one hundred thousand new troops, I wonder if the Zhong might provide me . . . ah . . . never mind; the word from Balboa is that they have a very heavy, and not all that effective hand when it comes to counterinsurgency. That might work for them when they don't have to deal with a free press and the TU government. Nothing but trouble for me, however.

Hmmm . . . I could try the firebase and strongpoint approach, guard each of the avenues of approach to the capital with a single strongpoint, all within range of an artillery battery located on a different strongpoint or firebase. I'd have to pull back there, too. Except . . .

Marciano made a compass of his right hand's index and baby finger, spread them along the distance scale, and then started measuring artillery ranges against useful spots for strongpoints and came to the conclusion, *No. Worse, even if I did, I have good reason to know they're aggressive patrollers. Given that and numbers, they'd drive my patrols back into our strongpoints, then bypass us at leisure. And that's not even counting what thirty or forty heavy mortars—eighty or more if we count their one hundred and twenty millimeter jobs—could do to a battalion strongpoint in the course of a week or so.*

Can I somehow starve them back to Balboa? Mmmm . . . eventually, maybe, but the regiment in the south probably brought five or six thousand tons of food on their ship. Starving them out could take two years unless I got very lucky and found a bunch of their food caches . . . without them destroying the patrols looking. And the other regiment, the one my staff tells me is named for the Virgin Mary; they're being supplied from Balboa, of course. There's no real way to stop that, no useful way, anyway. They sit near the border and remain fully supplied or they go back across the border, still present a threat to us, and remain fully supplied.

Marciano turned over those and half a dozen other options in his mind before deciding, *Okay, so there's no static campaign that would have a chance. No campaign aimed at their logistics that would have a chance. So . . . is there a mobile one? Risky, risky.* Marciano rubbed nervous and sweaty palms together. *But everything else is doomed . . . and in the kingdom of the doomed, the risky must be king.*

Then, too, as long as that lovely young lady is here, I'll have some pretty good intelligence from on high.

So, what now? Now, I think, I abandon every air base but the most easily defended one that I can use myself. If the war in Balboa won't aid me, they can kiss my Tuscan ass. Okay, that frees up a battalion. So, I'll have one facing south, one west, and a mobile force of nearly three battalions, including the artillery, four if I count the commandos and tanks. If they probe one of my forward battalions, or attack it, I'll have them fall back. Then, with my three, one vehicular, one airmobile, and the artillery, plus the engineers and commandos, I can hit back when they're overstretched.

Yes . . . yes . . . I can see possibilities here.

I can hardly wait to tell Janier that I won't pull back from our current positions, but all the guarding of air bases is going to fall on him; let them stand or let them fall, no matter to me. They wear our notion of being an independent protective mission pretty damned thin, anyway.

And, just maybe, I can feint a withdrawal—no; think "Cannae"; withdraw only under pressure; anything else is too suspicious—and use it as bait for my mobile force . . . and a touch of disinformation? Trebia? Trasimene?

"Rall! Del Collea! You two! In my office! Now!"

CHAPTER THIRTEEN

"Timeo Danaos et dona ferentes."
—Virgil, *the Aeneid*

**Tauran Defense Agency Headquarters,
Lumière, Gaul, Terra Nova**

One entry in the spreadsheets and reports given her by
Vladimir puzzled Jan Campbell deeply. *What*, she
wondered, *is an SPM-7b? It's a fairly recent purchase. It
doesn't have a motor. It has no caliber. It seems to use a
kind of fuel cell. It comes in a . . . hmmm . . .*

She took the file with her as she left her office. Captain
Turenge, deep in her own number crunching, looked up
but said nothing as Jan left.

*And why would they need twenty-four of them? And
why are they so expensive?*

The elevators in the old building were iffy, at best. Jan
took the nearest set of stairs, then *clop-clop-clopped* down
their granite risers to the basement, to where the open
source, which was to say, globalnet-connected, computer
room lay.

Houston, loafing outside his own office, saw her and instantly ducked out of view.

Flashing her badge at the attendant, she neglected to sign in. Instead, she went straight to one of the small closets that held a computer each, and logged in with a spurious account she'd set up for herself some months prior.

SPM-7b, she typed in.

Hmmm . . . nothing. Let's try SPM alone , no numbers . . . well it's not likely to be a Kashmiri civil decoration or a band from Wellington. Hmmm . . . okay, narrow it to SP. Nope. Okay, expand to "SPM Volga."

Bingo; a spacesuit or, rather, two dozen of them. And new, apparently, based on the price. Hmmm . . . almost latest model . . . and maneuverable in zero G. Now how often do the Balboans buy new? Must be important. But why in the name of the mythical purple-suited Elvis would Carrera need space suits.? He's done a lot—credit where it's been earned—but a space program he doesn't have. Planning ahead? Well . . . he does plan ahead, but this is an order of magnitude more. This is like planning for powering the planet with magic unicorn farts. You can set up all the fart collection stations you want, but since there are no unicorns . . .

She considered contacting the Volgan agent, Vladimir, from the computer in front of her but decided, *No, that might be a needless risk. I'll use my computer at home, after work. However . . .*

Campbell carefully removed the sheet from the file, folded it into a small package, and tucked it down between her breasts.

***

It was late when Turenge and Campbell decided to call it a day. The more they'd delved the more difficult things had gotten. After all, "What does i' mean," Turenge had asked, "when you find an entry for five-'undred and seventy-two eighty-five-millimeter barrels but can only find about 'alf that many carriages?"

"Ask an artilleryman," was Campbell's parting advice.

Mostly as an indicator of personal esteem, but also to maximize her productive workday, Janier had arranged for a driver for Campbell. That poor sod had little to do besides fetching her in the morning and wait around, ready to take her anywhere she wanted. Fortunately, there was a nice little *brasserie* not far from the headquarters, with waitresses pretty, saucy, and well-built, so the driver didn't feel too abused. An occasional lunch purchased for the door guards, too, and he could count on early warning of when *la petite fille ecossaise* would need transport.

He was, in any case, standing by at the side door when Jan emerged. She'd come to take that for granted by this point, but still rewarded her driver with a brilliant smile. He held the door for her, closed it, then walked around to the driver's side. While he walked, she sniffed. *My God, heavenly. What is that . . .*

"It was a late lunch special, madame," the driver said. "Two for one, so . . ."

"*Merci*," she said, rather warmly, while thinking, *Good because I am not only a wretch of a cook, but too busy tonight to go out.*

By the time city traffic permitted her driver to pull up near the door to her apartment complex, in reality an old mansion that had been subdivided, a light rain had begun to fall.

"Don't worry about the door, Marcel," she said. "No need for both of us to get wet."

"As you wish, Madame."

Flinging the door open, Jan ran for the awning over the main door. Inside, she was greeted by the rather fine stone and plasterwork of a bygone era. She had never really acquired a taste for that kind of finery, though. Oblivious to it, she entered the main lobby elevator and punched in her floor.

A thumb-driven lock clicked open. She entered, automatically nudged the door shut with her hip, then went to sit down at her computer desk.

Opening the system, and then logging in to the email address Vladimir had given her a password for, she composed a message that read, simply, "Why twenty-four spacesuits?" Then she saved the message as a draft and signed out. Fifteen minutes later she signed in again. There, under her own draft, was the message, "We haven't the faintest clue. Let us know if you figure it out."

Isla Real, Balboa

A heavy shell landed outside the even heavier bunker Colonel (Brevet) Wu had taken over to serve as a command post. Wu really wasn't sure why he and his little command were still alive or uncaptured. *They had us. They still have us. Why didn't they finish us off?*

Wu had landed on the island as a major, but a

combination of casualties, failures on the part of the generals and colonels commanding the landing, plus his own determination and an unusual helping of luck had seen him survive to be promoted by Admiral Wanyan. He had, in any case, made the only real gains of the landing that were not quickly wiped out or later abandoned as untenable.

By the evening of that first day Wu had had about five thousand men under his shaky command. By the next day, another three thousand badly shocked stragglers had crept in. They continued coming, too, for the next week, in dribs and drabs. At the moment he, a mere brevet, which was to say not even a real and permanent, colonel, had a decent sized division under his command. And Admiral Wanyan was talking about jumping him yet another grade, to brigadier general.

And the Balboans still ought to be able to toss us into the sea if they pushed matters. But they're not. They're not even interfering with the nightly supply run, twelve to twenty helicopters that bring me the thirty-six tons I need and without which we begin to die.

And then there's this. Wu looked down at an official-looking certificate which had been brought through the lines by a parlementaire and which read:

"THE TIMOCRATIC REPUBLIC OF BALBOA IS
BOTH PROUD AND PLEASED TO AWARD TO
MAJOR WU ZIXU
OF HIS IMPERIAL MAJESTY'S MARINE CORPS
THE CRUZ DE CORAJE EN ACERO"

This was followed by a fairly accurate rendition of the actions on the day of the first landing and signed by Legate Puercel, the man who was, apparently, in charge of all the defenses of the island and the *Mar Furioso* coast, near the capital.

Wu shook his head. *And over on my desk is a unit commendation for everyone involved in the landing who made it off the ships; they called us "Task Force Wu." Does an enemy get to tell you what your unit is called? And the men have taken it up since the Balboans distributed copies, with translations, all along the front.*

They've also offered me a four-hour ceasefire, if I need that much, to either turn my badly wounded over to them, evacuate them to a single ship which must be identified in advance, or at least fly in or land enough medical personnel to care for them.

Wu heard a knock. It was nearly silent, just as one would expect on concrete. It was former sergeant, now Sergeant Major Li, who had become something of a right-hand man since the day of the landing.

"Yes, Sergeant Major?"

"We've worked out the details of the evacuation with the enemy, sir. One square kilometer of beach and the ship—the *Qin Shan* is apparently seaworthy again—will not be engaged from eighteen hundred hours to midnight. And, yes, they expect we'll use that window for our nightly supply run and said, 'That's fine, what's a mere thirty-six or so tons of supply?' How do they know shit like that?"

Wu, again, shook his head, then offered, "Prisoners? Maybe some deserters?"

"They also warned us that, rather than let it go to waste,

they're going to use their artillery to paste the shit out of everything else we hold."

"Sir?"

"Yes, Sergeant Major."

"These people are fucking weird but I don't think we should be fighting them."

"Maybe. Have the word passed to expect a pounding."

In a different part of the island fortress, deep underground, well-covered by concrete and steel, likewise well-guarded, were the former High Admiral of the United Earth Peace Fleet, Martin Robinson, along with the former Marchioness of Amnesty, Lucretia Arbeit. Both had been captured in Pashtia years prior, and wrung for any secrets they might know. They were not normally allowed to speak to one another and never alone.

For quite some time they'd been both somewhat unhealthy and pasty white, from never seeing the sun. Eventually Fernandez had placed sunlamps in their quarters, and provided Vitamin D supplements. Even with that it couldn't be said they looked healthy, for all that each looked to be fairly young.

Lack of exercise had made each of the prisoners go somewhat to fat for a while, though they'd never become exactly obese. For the last several months Fernandez had provided a legion physical training expert to whip them back into shape. "Whip" was actually very much the right term, as the normal response of any flagging on their part was, "Warrant Officer Mahamda's assistant is waiting to see you."

They'd both met Mahamda, the Legion's chief

interrogator for hard cases. They also knew that what that meant, non-euphemistically, was that he was the chief torturer. It was amazing how much further and faster someone could go on an exercise bike if he thought the alternative was a session in Mahamda's chambers, perhaps strapped tightly to a dentist's chair, with the mouth held open by an adjustable framework, a drill whirring away, and no Novocain in the offing. Being sent to the assistant was not an improvement; the current assistant lacked Mahamda's finer sensibilities, as well as his humanitarian instincts and feelings.

The island, itself, was the legion's home, if any spot on the planet could be said to be. It had also been their main training base. As such, it had once boasted a battery of tailors to prepare uniforms for young officers and old centurions. Most of those were now either with the colors or evacuated to one or another refugee camp. Two, however, had stayed on. These were, even now, measuring Robinson and Arbeit for new uniforms, based on their ragged old ones and using insignia salvaged from those. The old uniforms had been seriously trashed in the course of their capture and early imprisonment. Indeed, Fernandez, on Mahamda's advice, had left them in the same clothing for months to help break their spirit. For many years since they'd worn only the simplest prison garb.

"Do you dress to the left or dress to the right, Admiral?" asked one of the tailors, in Robinson's cell. He actually had to think about it, it had been so long since he'd had a fitting. Then, too, the prison garb was sufficiently baggy that the question of where to hang one's testicles had never quite arisen. After a minute's though he'd answered, "Left . . . I think."

The tailor had duly noted in his notebook, *Left but leave some extra room just in case.*

"How long until the uniforms are ready?" asked the tribune, Ernesto Aguilar, in charge of the project and the prisoners. Aguilar was a secondment from the *Escuela de Cazadore* to Fernandez's organization, and before that a secondment from the Fourteenth Cazador tercio to the school. He'd been out of the line and working on this project so long that most back in his home unit had probably forgotten he existed.

"Two days," the tailor replied. "For this one. I can't say about the woman."

"That's quick. Why couldn't I ever get my uniforms done up that fast?"

Shrugging, the tailor said, "It's not like we have OCS and CCS"—Officer and Centurion Candidate Schools— "cranking out signifers and centurions in job lots lately."

Aguilar shrugged preposterously broad shoulders. He'd been a big man, at least in Balboan terms, before Fernandez had grabbed him. The physical training regimen they'd been put through—he and the other thirty-five *most* carefully selected *Cazadores*—had put a great deal of muscle on since then.

Only twenty-three of the thirty-five would be going on the mission, assuming it was given clearance to proceed. There were three pilots over and above needs, plus nine extra grunts.

And I am so not looking forward to the final selection, thought Aguilar. *They're all great guys, even all my friends, and we've all been getting ready for this since about two years after we finished up in Pashtia. I wish we had more or better transport.*

"You done with this one, Señor?" Aguilar asked of the tailor.

"*Si*, done, at least, until two days from now when I bring them back."

"Okay." Aguilar turned his attention to the Earthpig. "Admiral, you have an appointment with your physical trainer. Please don't disappoint him."

Tauran Defense Agency Headquarters, Lumière, Gaul, Terra Nova

Campbell and Turenge decided to lead their report for Janier with a litany of the anomalies, these ranging from more than double the required numbers of barrels for mortars and towed artillery, to unaccounted for long-range multiple rocket launcher systems, to acrylic probably intended for Meg Class submarines but well in excess to needs for the number believed to have been produced, to where the steel from scrapped Volgan warships went, to scores of others. Oddly enough, one of the anomalies was not included.

Why, asked Campbell, for about the five-hundredth time, *why did they need twenty-four spacesuits?*

She couldn't answer the question. No theory she came up with made sense. *But they cannot be oriented at us; we hardly have a space program worth ruining. They could maybe be used underwater but there are cheaper and better solutions. And, as far as using them on the planet, I cannot imagine how someone would lug three or four hundred pounds around and expect to accomplish anything.*

No, there is only one target that makes sense . . . and that doesn't make sense.

The sirens began to blare, as they did every few days to every week or so. There was seldom much warning, as radar couldn't pick up the slow drones the Balboans called "Condors."

And that was a clever thing, the air force types tell me, gaining stealth by substituting random chance and polystyrene foam for extremely careful engineering and manufacture. We can't pick them up, except visually, and the Earthpigs tell Janier they can't, either . . . now isn't that interesting?

Jan went back to the report about to be sent to Janier. *We know some equipment went to Zion, and we know a shitpot's worth were transshipped through Cochin. But how do we know what was not transshipped through Cochin? Or how much was? Or how much might have been diverted, hence how much can be in country? What we have identified, or the Volgans gave to me, doesn't match—rather, it overmatches—their order of battle as we can see it.*

"I need to take a brief trip," she said to Captain Turenge. "Maybe three weeks. I'm pretty sure you can handle the shop until I get back."

"No problem," answered the female Gaul. "Anything I can do to 'elp?"

"No. And I'll take only Greene and Dawes with me; the

rest of the direct-action team I'll leave with you in case somebody"—she looked pointedly down toward a particular section of the basement—"should happen to get uppity."

"*Merci.* Though I still think we'd 'ave been better off if 'e and the other one 'ad died in a fight to the death over *moi.* If only as a lesson to the others."

Air Gaul Airship *Jeanne d'Arc*

Jan knew she was close, at least, to the former base of the Salafi Ikhwan, the base Carrera had raided and destroyed, bringing the ultimate act of the war against the terrorists to a close.

And that, she reminded herself, *is suspicious as hell, too. There's a cross border attack, against an enemy base in an allied country—well, "officially allied"; everyone entitled to an opinion knew they had to play both sides— and suddenly the old high admiral, Robinson, disappears and new high admiral Wallenstein is in his place? And a few days later a nuke goes off in Hajar, right in the compound of the clan to which the head of the Salafi Ikhwan belonged? How did that nuke get there? The official story, that Mustafa had gotten one from who- knows-where and it went off accidentally, stinks to the high heavens. Nukes are hard to make go off; one going off accidentally beggars belief. But if it didn't come from there, why was there no trace of . . .*

Mentally, she replayed the warbling sirens in Lumière. *Well, it's plausible anyway. But if so, where did he get a nuke? And if he had one, I wonder how many more he might have? Enough to destroy the TU? Or only enough to destroy my home? I've never been cleared for the information, but I wonder if anyone I know is. And, if so, how would they know? But, now that I think on it, I'm not entirely sure the reluctance to use nukes against Balboa was purely the result of enlightened sensibilities.*

Of course, the Volgans didn't give me any information on that, but then, they wouldn't, would they?

The flight took a little under two and a half days. Though, in truth, she'd wanted to take a trip on a luxury airship for years, just for the experience, it was also true that such a craft was a better cover for her, in her portrayal of an upper-class dilettante, or someone with an interest in global shipping and ship building *playing* the dilettante, than a faster jet would have been. She'd also booked the trip as SOPH, Starboard Out, Port Home, to avoid the worst of the sunlight. It had added several thousand drachmae to the cost but, *What the hell, the TU is paying.*

It also tended to play to both her covers that Dawes and Greene could serve as bodyguards, while publicly acting like boy-toys. Whatever their social background, they'd both served long enough in Anglian special operations, and both been well-trained enough, that they could present the right image. She felt bad that one of them had to sleep on her cabin floor every night, just in case the Cochinese—a very suspicious bunch—were vetting passengers, but, after all, *needs must . . .*

Dawes and Greene could pull off their parts easily enough. But Jan wasn't sure she could pull off hers with anyone who grew up to know better. Thus, she took her meals in her cabin, for the most part, the two non-coms taking turns picking them up, thus avoiding social contact with the other passengers.

I suppose I'm missing a great part of the experience, and, moreover, an experience without financial guilt since the TU is paying my way at first class plus. Why, it's almost like being a left-wing activist working for the World League or Save the Terrorists. But to hell with it. And besides, the scenery you can see this way is entertainment and education enough for a poor girl from a hardscrabble fishing village not far from Saint Mungo. At least, it is when I'm not studying the nuances of international shipping, shipyards, and shipbuilding.

Prey Nokor, Cochin

The town was a riverport, well inland. Jan could smell it before she could see it. Indeed, given that she was arriving at night, and liberal provision of electricity was something that, like poverty, the formerly socialist Republic of Cochin aspired to, she couldn't have seen it if her cabin had been facing the wide river.

There's something else there, too, beyond the stink of the mud and the marsh. I smell poverty . . . a trace of what I grew up with, wood smoke and piss and shit that nobody bothers to bury or cart away . . . garbage . . . maybe disease and bodies . . . unwashed bodies, too, even if healthy. Onions. Those are very poor people, down below.

She sensed the engines of the airship were having to

strain a bit. *So, we're downwind. That might explain the stench.*

After a bit, the stench was gone but the strained thrumming of the engines remained. And then she felt the huge lighter-than-air craft begin a lazy circle to port, finally revealing the few main thoroughfares of the city that were well-lit with both streetlights and nightlife. At that point, the airship's descent became relatively quicker than it had been, quick enough to give some of that sense of an elevator going down. Even as the descent accelerated, the engines went neutral, and then reversed at low power to fight the tailwind. When the ship finally touched down into its concave landing pad, Jan hardly felt it.

Customs was a fairly painless passage. In the first place, the first-class passengers had a separate—and very quick and courteous—line, paid for as part of the price of their fare. But in the second place, Cochin wasn't worried too much about people smuggling drugs in, since few of the people could afford any such thing. They were far more concerned with people trying to smuggle things—antiquities and young sex slaves—out, actually. And their one external threat, *Ming Zhong Guo*, had few tourists, few enough for them to be watched like hawks. Of course, the Cochinese took a keen interest in the activities of the Zhong embassy staff.

In any case, for Jan, being neither a Zhong tourist nor a member of any official delegation, there was no tail. She was easily well-trained enough to have spotted one, and even had she not been, both Greene and Dawes were.

None of the three spotted anything remotely like a tail, on the taxi ride to their suite at the Hotel Daydream, which was, arguably, Prey Nokor's finest. Its decor was, interestingly, far more influenced by Tuscany than Gaul.

I wonder if that's a deliberate slight of their old oppressor.

Jan had had her secretary, back in Lumière, make a number of appointments with various concerns in Cochin. The secretary had done so posing as part of the staff of a long-existing, but completely spurious Anglian shipping company, with interests also in ship-building. That spurious company, itself, was a temporary borrowing— with permission—from Jan's official chief, Sidney Stuart-Mansfield.

She went through appointments with three builders and two chandlers and a scrapper. Only one of those was useful, when the scrapper mentioned three more companies that were allegedly skilled in modifying ships for original uses. One of these turned smaller freighters and coasters into yachts.

Hmmm . . . I wonder if . . . no, probably not; the legions seem to have used others for that kind of work.

Two others did more substantial modifications. Of these, one, a Mr. Nguyen, who was also a cousin of one Commander Nguyen, seemed to Jan a little greasier, a little greedier, and perhaps not as conscious of his previous client's security as he might have been. He also seemed confidently competent. Moreover, his French was at least as good as hers.

"I no longer have them here to show you," said Mr.

Nguyen, "but my company can and has turned a warship into a freighter and a civilian freighter into a warship. We have the architects. We have the welders and fitters. We have everything. Whatever you want or need done, we can do. Most of my people learned their jobs from the Federated States Navy."

Something in his phraseology . . . aha . . . inspiration strikes.

Jan's face became very serious. "Let me get to the point," she said. "My cover as a dilettante is only that. I am here on *serious* business. What my company is interested in, Mr. Nguyen, is making a proposal to the Federated States to provide for them what their existing arsenal ship program is failing at; a low cost, heavily armed bombardment ship, mounting either cannon or guns or both, to assist in clearing the beaches for opposed landings for their marines. We think there might be considerable profit in this, the more so, of course, if costs can be kept low, which Cochin's cost of living says is possible."

Jan didn't have to feign interest when she asked, "So explain to me how your people go about such a job, from the very beginning . . . Ah, yes, of course I understand your time is valuable and of *course* my company will pay for it *most* willingly."

And so where did that ship go? Jan wondered. Where did that ship go, with its squadron of nitrogen-preserved attack and transport helicopters? With its hovercraft? With its almost nine hundred long-range rockets? With its Volgan infantry fighting vehicles that are more powerful than any tank of the Great Global War? And where did it pick up its infantry? Because somewhere, it is picking up twelve to fourteen hundred infantry.

How do I find it? Nobody knows who owns any given ship. There are civilian ship watchers who do a better job of tracking ships than any intelligence service, but they're usually anywhere from a couple of days to a couple of months behind. And we of the intelligence community? Nobody pays enough attention. Some of us try. Most of us usually fail.

Maybe more importantly, if the target is who I am beginning to suspect it is, do I tell anyone or just keep my pretty little mouth shut?

In any case, I have time to think about it; the next few days are filled with appointments and bribes for heavy duty scrap metal dealers, and then one who deals in slave labor.

CHAPTER FOURTEEN

"I am driven on by the flesh, and he must
needs go that the Devil drives."
—Shakespeare, *All's Well That Ends Well*

Headquarters, Task Force Jesuit,
Rio Clara, Santa Josefina

In the command post, Marciano looked at Esma carefully.
It wasn't because she was something of a vision, though
she was. No, it was something else about the girl that
disturbed him and he could not quite put his finger on it.
She'd been with his headquarters several weeks now and
never been anything but admirably sweet, pleasant, and
attentive to her duties. There was nothing actually *wrong*
with her, and yet . . .

Then he realized, "Young lady, why are you here
without so much as a pistol to defend yourself with?"

"I didn't think . . . ummm . . . nobody issued me one."

"I see." Marciano stood up. "Come with me, please. Do
you know how to shoot?"

Esma shook her head in the negative. "I've never so much as held a firearm in my hand."

"I see," said the general. "Stefano!?" he shouted out.

"Sir?"

"My quarters, one good sergeant, married, religious, faithful, who is also a good arms instructor."

"Sure, sir. Be a few minutes to find this paragon of whom you speak."

"No dawdling. And have him draw five hundred rounds of nine-millimeter from the ammunition people." Turning his attention back to Esmeralda he repeated, "Now come with me, please, miss."

In another time, on another planet, Esma would have assumed that any man in a position of authority who gave her an order to follow him intended rape. Marciano, though, had been thoroughly decent since she'd shown up at his command post. *He treats me . . . he treats me very much the way the High Admiral does, as a kind of daughter. How can the wrong side have so many decent people in it? How could they be the right side when they have so many demons in human form?*

At the general's spartan quarters he pulled a chair out from his desk—not a typical folding field desk but something much more substantial that a group of his soldiers had skillfully built for him—and invited her to sit. Then he went to a simple green-painted footlocker that *was* atop the expected folding field desk and opened it. From it he took a pistol mostly concealed by a leather holster made to clip to a belt. He held it contemplatively for a short while, hefting the weight in his right hand before withdrawing the pistol from the holster. He stared at the thing for a few moments, then cleared it, dropping the magazine and jacking the slide. Then he turned to Esmeralda and showed it to her. She saw bronze-colored metal, with beautiful silverwood grips, the same material as on the walls of the High Admiral's conference room on the *Spirit of Peace*. The grips were grooved to accommodate fingers. There was some engraving, too, but it was in a language she really couldn't read.

"This is special to me," Marciano said. "But it is also probably the only woman's gun you could find in this encampment. Oh, you'll find women carrying pistols, but they're big-gripped jobs, holding double stacked magazines, and really not comfortable for a female hand.

"It's a loan," he advised. Then he smiled broadly, adding, "Unless of course, I am killed, in which case, keep it with my blessings."

"General, I can't . . ."

"Hush, young lady," Claudio said, forcing the pistol into her tiny hand. "I'm a general, even if only a ground-bound one, whereas you are a mere ensign. You must do as you are told, no arguments."

"Yes, sir. Thank you, sir."

The general looked up then, perhaps out of embarrassment, and saw a middle-aged, maybe slightly paunchy, and balding sergeant standing by with a filled haversack containing what appeared to be, from the sharp corners poking the material, a fair amount of ammunition.

"*Maresciallo* Bertholdo, sir." *Maresciallo*, or Marshal, was the Tuscan equivalent of a master sergeant. "The Operations Officer gave me certain instructions . . ."

"Ah, very good, Sergeant. Please take Ensign . . ."

"Miranda, sir," Esma supplied.

"Yes, of course. Please take Ensign Miranda and teach her how to shoot and care for that pistol."

"Yes, sir." The sergeant looked at the narrowish weapon. "General, is that a Helva P21S? I love those guns. Miss Miranda, this is going to be a fun afternoon for both of us."

Esma turned to go, then turned back. "If I may ask . . ."

"It was my grandmother's."

There was a protective berm not far from his headquarters, Marciano assumed, from the somewhat erratic *poppoppop* coming from that direction, that Sergeant Bertholdo had selected that for the training session. He, meanwhile, was in discussion with his exec and operations officer, Rall and del Collea, respectively, on the Santa Josefinan guerillas' maddening refusal to take bait.

"Why should they," insisted Rall, "since they're winning without it?"

"How do you mean 'winning,' Rall?" asked Marciano.

Del Collea was nearest the map, so answered for both the Sachsen colonel and himself.

"The action, sir, is all behind us." Del Collea began tapping the map. "Ten days ago, ambush here, right inside the town of Irazu. Yes, sir, the very same Irazu—"

Rall interrupted, first with a cough and then with, "Told you we should have rounded up and done away with a thousand of them."

Del Collea continued without more than the slightest pause, "where we were ambushed before. This time, instead of a tank, it was a fuel truck, two rations trucks, and a trailer load of ammunition, mostly small arms." His finger moved several inches east on the map, or about five miles in real distance. "That afternoon, a Santa Josefinan police checkpoint was assaulted. We have no idea where the officers are." Again, the finger moved, this time to the capital. "Sniper killed two and wounded one of our men in the red-light district in Aserri . . . avoiding the main roads, two of our vehicles ran into mines in dirt roads . . ." Move, *taptaptap*. "Mortar attack against the port. Didn't do any damage but cost an afternoon's work unloading." Move, *taptaptap*. "North of Pelirojo; firefight between an estimated platoon of guerillas and one of ours. We had one dead, four wounded. We have no idea what we got of theirs, or even if we did."

Del Collea's tapping finger continued to punctuate the litany: "Ambush . . . bombing . . . mine . . . improvised explosive device . . . sniper . . . kidnapping . . . murder of civilian . . . murder of civilian . . . sniper . . . mine . . .

"Note, sir, that every one of those was in what are supposed to be safe rear areas for us.

"I'd like to be able to say that they could all be the same platoon, or a platoon from each of the guerilla regiments, except that they've hit us in more than one place near each 'front' simultaneously and they've hit us in areas too far apart for it to have been the same crews. I think a lot of it is classical guerillas, probably raised and led by people from the two enemy regiments we know about."

Rall stepped up then, using his finger to draw supply routes. "Sir, if this keeps up or, God forbid, gets worse, we're not going to be able to supply the forward battalions for much longer. We're already getting overly reliant on helicopters to keep them in beans and bullets. And those tend to break down under heavy use. Worse—"

It was now Rall's turn to be interrupted as one of the women manning the bank of radios at the far side of the headquarters announced, very loudly, "Enemy attacks! Multiple enemy attacks in the capital! It looks like they're going after embassies."

Near the United Earth Embassy,
Aserri, Santa Josefina

Almost the entire platoon was huddled in a garbage-reeking indentation off an alley that led directly to the perimeter of the embassy. Near the edge of that indentation and nearest the objective, Corporal Esteban Sanchez, Second Cohort, *Tercio la Virgen*, figured that the Earthpig Embassy staff never quite figured out that the sniping and the mortaring were about keeping their heads down so that recon parties could do their jobs unimpeded. *That's how we found this little spot to assemble. Same for the bulk of the Tauran embassies, too, I guess.*

He glanced down at the rifle in his hands. It was a Tauran job, confiscated from the hold of one of the interned ships of Balboa's *classis*, as was only right, proper, and within the laws for internment of combatants, then distributed to the men of the Second Cohort who had lined up at the border to go home some months prior.

Sanchez had been assigned his, along with a decent load of ammunition; web gear, and new uniforms of the liberation army, in the same bar, *La Cascada*, where he normally picked up his pay. They'd been assigned there, but almost everything had been brought to the alley's opposite entrance in a couple of automobiles. Indeed, only the uniforms had come with the men, and those had been hidden under civilian clothes now piled in bundles at the back of their little assault position.

It was all weird, but the uniforms were especially funny. They'd been made locally, and to a somewhat different design from the legionary battle dress uniform Sanchez was used to. But the same company had done up quite a number of them for some of the contingents of Task Force Jesuit, not least the Task Force's contingent of Cimbrian commandos. That civilian company had also long been a subcontractor for the legions and had been using for both sets of battle dress excess and leftover material that had proven impossible to forward to Balboa. Thus, if the *Tercio la Virgen* were violating the law of war, by using Cimbrian uniforms, what of the Cimbrians' own violations, stemming from their using the same material and general cut as Carrera's legions?

What the fuck, it still beats carrying a shotgun and wearing denim trousers, a dark blue shirt, and a fucking stupid-looking blue baseball cap. And fucking clever of the Duque to have put the Taurans in this position.

Sanchez and anybody else who believed that would have been surprised to know that the thought had never occurred to Patricio Carrera. Possibly it should have but, in fact, it was just part of the serendipity of war on a grand scale. Sanchez wasn't up to worrying about war on the grand scale, anyway. He was, on the other hand, pretty damned good at war at the micro scale. Not everyone could say that.

Those stupid motherfuckers in the Earthpig Embassy, for example, don't know shit about the subject. True fact.

Among the various implements and supplies of war that had come to Second Cohort from the interned fleet were also a hefty quantity of demolitions material. Sixty pounds of that, exclusive of carrying case, fuse, blasting cap, and pull igniter, Sanchez had turned into satchel charges to breach the high concrete wall around the embassy. Sanchez wasn't an engineer; he'd never even attended the assault demolitions course the legion ran for non-engineers. So, he pulled out the manual and decided that Factor P, for plenty, should be his guide. Thus, three satchels, rigged to connect on the objective with hanging lengths of demolition cord, themselves hung from pairs of light poles ranging from three to six feet long, connected at their bottoms by short lengths of heavy-duty string. Three of Sanchez's four men each carried one of those, while he and another free man, Vargas, the light machine gunner, would provide left and right security, once the order came.

Sanchez's platoon leader, Centurion Mora, whispered a word into the radio that linked him and one of the maniple's light mortars. Seconds later, Sanchez heard a distant *thump*, soon followed by half a dozen more. But for timing they could have been a car backfiring. No car backfire, however, sounded remotely like the *bangs* that came from inside the embassy walls, about fifteen seconds after the first *thump*. Other, more distant thumps and crashes told of still other attacks kicking off. Sanchez knew of six that were planned, but there may have been more.

The corporal was close enough to Mora to hear the words come through the radio, "The Earthpigs are all running for cover. Nobody's watching the wall. There were some civvies but they're all running like hell. I think you can go for it."

"Sanchez," ordered Mora, "move out."

"Roger, Centurion. C'mon, motherfuckers." Sanchez took off at a brisk jog, the footsteps of booted feet behind telling him his men were following. In a single line they emerged from the mouth of the alley, dodged between parked cars, and sprinted across the street for the embassy wall.

They'd rehearsed this a dozen times. Unfortunately, little details missed in rehearsal can prove problematic in action. They'd forgotten to have a curb edging the sidewalk outside the wall for the rehearsal. Thus Vargas, racing between two parked cars, tripped on the curb and fell face-first to the concrete sidewalk. To his credit, the gunner had the discipline not to cry out, despite the smashed, blood-running nose he'd acquired and the two chipped teeth he had to endure. The rest, hearts pounding, just stepped on him in their course.

Other than that, though, things went smoothly enough. The first man to reach the wall had the shortest poles, about three feet. He used them to prop the charge against the wall at a height a bit over two feet, spreading them at their bases for stability. He pulled a brick from a pocket and propped up the bottom of the sticks, then turned left to guard from that direction. The next man propped his up not quite a foot above the first, then connected the short line of demolitions cord to a blasting cap in the bottom charge. There wasn't time to crimp the cap, which was crap procedure but—so the corporal had decided— better than trying to run with them connected. He then faced to the right and moved out five meters to clear the way. The third man did much the same, placing his charge above the second and connecting it to it. Sanchez and the third man, together, each grabbed one of the two pull igniters. Looking at each other, Sanchez consulted his watch and said, "Together on three . . . one . . . two . . . three." While shouting "Fire in the hole!" was all well and good for training exercises, or demolitions not conducted under fire, under the circumstances, it would have been like initiating an ambush with the order "open fire": silly in other words. Instead, on "three," they simply said, "let's go."

They pulled the igniters and were rewarded with a bit of smoke and some bubbling fuse.

"Help me with stumbledick," the corporal ordered. He and demo man number three each bent and took one side of the still-stunned light machine gunner. One of the other men grabbed his gun. Then all five took off as fast as feet would carry them for the alleyway.

"Hurryhurryhurryhurryhurry!" Sanchez encouraged. In rehearsals they'd had plenty of time. Half carrying Vargas was tougher, especially between the parked cars. "Shitshitshit! Hurry!" Demo man number three then bent and grabbed Vargas' feet.

"We can carry him faster this way!"

"Hurryhurryhurryhurryhurry!"

They made it with one and a half seconds to spare. And there was a great, Earth-shattering—in more senses than one—*Kaboom!*

After giving flying shards a dozen seconds to settle to the ground, Mora risked a look out at the embassy wall. "Nice," he said, upon seeing a roughly man-sized, rough-edged oval in the wall, as well as half a dozen cars, flipped and, in most cases, furiously burning. "First squad, go!"

Sanchez didn't particularly like the next part of the job. Two of his men, including a now somewhat recovered Vargas, took up security on the outside, near the breach. Two more posted themselves inside, scanning the compound. While second squad cleared the grounds, and first squad—reinforced, for prisoner control purposes, by half of third—went for the embassy building, the corporal took a can of spray paint and wrote "COLABORADORES" in red on the inside wall, not far from where they'd made the breach. The paint ran, but not so much that the word couldn't be made out easily.

From inside the embassy building came the sounds of shooting, of small explosions from grenades, and a great many screams. After what seemed half an hour, but may have been less, the other half of third squad appeared, with the squad leader, herding about three dozen civilians out of the building. Some were female. Of those, a couple were young and pretty. Others were male, ranging from late teens to early seventies. Age or sex notwithstanding, all seemed to be in shock and not a few, male and female, both, in tears. All, too, were herded to the wall and made to stand under the freshly painted word.

Centurion Mora, carrying an Anglian submachine gun not notably different from the Pound used by the Legions, began at the left. "What is your name?" he asked one young woman.

The girl—she'd have been pretty were it not for the tears and snot running down her cheeks and chin—was shuddering and choking with fright so badly that it took her quite a long time to get even her own name out. "Es . . . Es . . . Estef . . . tef . . . tefani . . . Estef . . . Es . . . Es . . . Estefani . . . Me-Me-Mel-Me-Melendez . . . Melendez-Ri-Ri-Ri-Ri-Rios."

"Ah, now that name rings a bell. You were on my special list. You were the Earthpig ambassador's private secretary," Mora accused. "And yet, did you help the revolution? No. Why should you not be shot for crimes against the people and collaboration with the enemy?"

Mora didn't even wait for the answer, but turned to the next person, an old stooped and graying man. "What is your name and what was your job?"

"I was a janitor, sir," the old man replied. "My name is Pablo, Pablo Escobedo. I needed the job to support a sick wife. If you kill me, who will take care of her?"

"The revolution is not heartless, Pablo," Mora said. "Go and take care of your wife. But"—Mora looked around the compound; flames had begun shooting out of the embassy's upper story windows—"I think you're going to have to find another job.

"Now go."

At that time the squad that had gone into the embassy building emerged, pushing the ambassador and a few of her assistants. They were pushed toward the breach in the wall from whence they'd be led to cars and captivity. Each of the prisoners was heavily laden with files and, in a couple of cases, cabinets.

Mora turned to the next. "You; what is your name and job . . ."

In the end, Mora let seventeen of them go. Nineteen, including the ambassador's secretary, remained standing under the word on the wall. The numbers were deliberately chosen for the message, "The revolution is not without mercy, but your odds of survival if you work with the enemy are less than half." Seeing the last of them off to the breach, Mora joined the third squad's firing line.

Out of her wits or not, Estefani realized the implication. Her bladder let go as she sank to her knees, eyes tightly closed and mouthing, "puhpuhpuhpuh." She was still doing so when Mora steeled his heart and gave the command, *"Fuego!"*

It took a day and a half for Marciano to turn his columns toward the capital, march there, and fight his way to the embassy district. It would have taken longer but for the timely intelligence provided by Khan and company, and relayed through Esma.

Marciano's first intent was to get to his own country's embassy, that of Tuscany, but the United Earth embassy was on the way to that, indeed, only a quarter of a mile before it, so that was what he'd reached first. He stopped in front of the Embassy's wide-open main gate, two security guards sprawled in undignified, bloody death in the opening. Esma recognized both of them from the party that had escorted her from the shuttle to shelter, not so long ago.

"High Admiral Wallenstein is going to want an eyewitness report," she'd said to Marciano, "and I'm probably the only one available."

Shaken with both the completeness of the disaster and, from the limited reports he'd received, the shocking ruthlessness displayed by the guerillas, Marciano just told del Collea, dully, "Get her a platoon for security."

Del Collea answered, "Yes, sir," then his eyes flicked back and forth for a few moments as he pulled up some memories. He ordered into the radio that such and such platoon of a particular company was to come forward. It meant nothing to Esma until she saw a familiar and friendly face dismount from a wheeled infantry carrier.

The platoon proved to be under the leadership of a saluting, "Maresciallo Bertholdo, reporting as ordered."

Del Collea returned the salute. As he did he stole a glance at Marciano. *No, no; the general is not up to detailed orders to individual platoons at the moment.* Then he said, "Bertholdo, escort Ensign Miranda into the Earth Embassy. Don't let anything happen to her. While you're doing that, make sure the enemy didn't leave behind any snipers or bombs or booby traps."

"Yes, sir."

The diesel and gasoline-driven roar of Marciano's column continued on up the boulevard, behind them. The pavement of the road shook with their passage. The stink of exhaust was heavy in the air.

Bertholdo went through the main gate just ahead of

Esma. Before she'd passed, a couple of soldiers dragged the bodies out of the way to allow passage for their carriers without mutilating the dead. Thus, he saw the large word, "*Colaboradores*" before she did. He wasn't sure what it meant until he saw the distortion, looking something like heat distortion, of a huge swarm of flies buzzing around between the word on the wall and the ground.

I've got a very sinking feeling about what we're going to find over there.

"Miss," he turned and put up an arm to stop Esma, then said to her, "why don't you wait here, inside one of the armored vehicles, until we can make sure it's safe?"

Esma leaned to one side and saw the same pseudo-heat distortion and the same huge, spray-painted word. She, too, had a pretty good idea of what she was going to find. She pushed past Bertholdo, then began to race, then sprint, for the spot. Frantically, the Maresciallo began gesturing and ordering his vehicles and men to position themselves to cover and secure her. Then he, himself, clutching his rifle, began to follow at a jog. He picked up to a sprint, too, no mean feat for a man of his age and weight class, encumbered by full fighting equipment and armor, when he saw the ensign cover her mouth with both hands and sink to her knees.

The nearest body, Bertholdo saw, was female. Her face, whatever there might have been left of it, was covered by a layer of blood-lapping flies. More flies feasted on the sticky red stuff across her ruined chest.

He looked then at the Earth girl, who was rocking back and forth, face still half-covered, and tears running down her cheeks.

"Did you know this one, Miss?" the maresciallo asked.

"I can't remember her last name," Esma managed to get out. "I'm ashamed, but I just can't remember it." Stifling a sob, she continued, "Her first name was Estefani . . . 'Stefi,' I called her. She was the nearest thing to a friend that I had on this world, outside of some of you. She was kind of dumb, I suppose, in some ways, and kind of innocent, too, in others. But she meant well and she didn't ever in her life do anything to deserve anything like this."

"Almost nobody does, Miss. I'm sorry for your friend."

"Why would anyone do this? *Why*?"

Bertholdo sighed, wearily. "I've seen this before, in a few places . . . Pashtia . . . Xamar . . . couple of others. The key is in the word on the wall. That, and the bodies, mean 'do not collaborate with the enemy in the slightest or you will pay a price.' In effect, these score or so bodies were not people; they were just stationery."

"Does it work, that message, when they send it this way?"

"I'd like to tell you it doesn't," Bertholdo said. "I'd like to but I'd be lying. It works more often than not."

Esma began to stand, saying, "She wanted us to go to lunch together, when I passed through here, but I didn't have time. And now she has no time and . . . and . . . and . . ."

Bertholdo caught the tiny girl before her wilting body could hit the ground.

CHAPTER FIFTEEN

"The long march through the institutions"
—Rudi Dutshcke

Oppenheimer Mosque, Sachsen

"May Allah grant you peace and security, and may His Mercy be upon you."

So said Khalid to the man to his right, his assistant, Maytham. Turning his face to the left, he repeated to his other follower, Bandar, "May Allah grant you peace and security, and may His Mercy be upon you."

The *Asr* then being finished, and after a minimally decent pause, he rocked back onto the balls of his feet, then stood straight up, even as his feet rocked further back to rest flat on the thick rugs beneath him.

Taqiyya-wise, thought Khalid, *Muslims have nothing on Druze*.

The imam of the mosque, one of the largest in Sachsen, older, and less fit, indeed, rather pudgy, was helped to his feet by two acolytes who had performed the afternoon prayer in the foremost spots of the two central rows behind the imam. The iman, somewhat unsurprisingly named Mohammad, had the lump on his forehead called a "*zabiba*," or "raisin," which indicated a life of devotion and enthusiastic prayer to his god.

Turning to Khalid, Mohammad made the palm down, finger gathering motion to come or to follow. He then walked toward a side door, in confidence that Khalid and his assistants would.

Through the door a broad set of marble stairs led to a basement. Motion sensor-driven lights came on automatically as they descended and as they walked the somewhat plainer corridor to the imam's office. On the way, they passed a locked storeroom containing, *If I recall correctly, one hundred and fifty rifles, selective fire, thirty-two light machine guns, an even dozen medium machine guns, a dozen sniper rifles, twenty-nine submachine guns, fourteen pistols, eighteen anti-tank rocket launchers, two hundred and twelve thousand rounds of ammunition, four hundred pounds of assorted demolitions, twelve hundred grenades, hand thrown, three hundred rocket-propelled anti-tank grenades, and—if the imam and his committee of jihadists have been listening—thirty or forty radios and a thousand liters of gasoline, with bottles. Couple that with the shotguns and hunting rifles the imam has been advising his followers to obtain, and there's probably a smallish battalion for this city.*

Khalid mused further, *A fascinating place, Sachsen, really. Reputed to be tied for first place in terms of abiding by the law, it is nearly as well armed a group as Balboa but three-fourths of the arms are illegal and, rather than being in criminal or military or police hands, in the hands*

*of otherwise upstanding and law-abiding civilians . . .
which is to say law abiding except insofar as they refuse
to be disarmed.*

*This place is going to be a horror story once the revolt
kicks off.*

*If they had two brain cells to rub together or, rather, if
their rulers did, no mosque would ever have been given
the chance to amass the kind of arsenal this one has. Of
course, they couldn't, because they might have been
accused of racism. Now Druze, we may be a race, but
Moslems are not; they'll take anyone.*

But there's no reasoning with a Kosmo—a cosmopolitan
progressive—*where his fantasies are concerned.*

*I suppose by now the Tauran police forces probably
have some idea of what's been building underneath their
feet, but are probably afraid of the civil war it will kick off
if they started to violate the mosques' sanctity.*

*Silly folk, Tauran elites; they really think they can hide
from what's coming.*

*Too, even if they didn't want to enter mosques to
search, they could have cut off the flow of arms, but that
would have been racism, too, if they'd found anything or
not. I can almost hear the words, "The Moslems only
started stockpiling arms because we've made them
afraid . . . and you're only looking for their cars and boats
because you're a racist."*

Idiots.

"What was that, Khalid?" asked the imam.

"Did I say something? I must have been thinking out
loud."

"Thinking about?" Mohammad prodded.

"What idiots our enemies are, to permit what we are planning."

"Allah has stolen their wits," the imam said.

"It must be so." *And, in truth, old man, I agree with you.*

"*Il hamdu l'Allah.*" To God be the praise.

"My arms deliveries are complete now," Khalid said. "Your other preparations?"

"I cannot speak for the other half dozen mosques in the city," Mohammad said, "but for my fifteen thousand we have the radios, the medical supplies, and the food you suggested."

"How much food, actually?" Khalid asked.

"Thirty days' worth," the imam replied, "or about seven hundred tons. Only about one hundred tons is here, the rest is in various warehouses and safe houses."

And that shows the Tauran rulers are doubly idiotic. Arms? Anyone can have arms. When people start stockpiling food on that scale it means they're serious.

"Most of my fighters are uniformed, as well. They're not fancy uniforms, just stout working clothes, gloves, boots, and hats. We don't have body armor, except for a few. It isn't so much tightly controlled as simply unavailable."

"It is enough," Khalid said. "Allah will smile upon you and yours for your foresight." *Though He's unlikely to be too happy with Fernandez and myself for ours.*

Global Court of Justice, Binnenhof, Haarlem

There was a considerable international crowd gathered

outside the halls of the Global Court of Justice, or GCJ. The chants and banners varied from "Peace now!" to "Save the rainforest!" to "Stop the bombing!" to "Death to the Tauran Union!" Even in the innermost depths of the building, the chanting could be felt. In the main courtroom, which abutted on an exterior wall, the chanting made it hard to hear oneself.

Carrera's Staff Judge Advocate, Puente-Pequeño, had engaged the Sachsen law firm of Litten, Heinrich, and Kipping to press a lawsuit to ban the Tauran Union from using either aerially dropped munitions, or artillery, in such a way as would damage the Balboan rainforest. There was a protocol to a climate treaty to this effect, called, simply enough, "The Protocol to Protect Indigenous Fauna, Flora, and People of the Rainforests," duly lodged with the World League, and subsequently ratified and signed by every member of the Tauran Union and a good chunk of the rest of the planet. It was a matter of some speculation to what extent the Treaty, in turn, had been derived from a set of treaties on Old Earth.

The language was somewhat ambiguous: "No party to this treaty shall permit the cutting of timber on its territory, nor the destruction of habitat, nor the destruction nor displacement of less developed peoples, nor the processing of products on the rainforest. Neither shall they permit their nationals to do so, in their private capacity, either within their own territory nor anywhere on the planet."

War, of course, hadn't been remotely within the consciousness of the Kosmos drafting the treaty; they were of a class for whom war was a horrid abstract, unfit for discussion in polite company, but not an actual problem to consider and deal with. Similar sentiments had made the anti-landmine movement—and there was remarkable commonality between the supporters of both—a bit of precious nonsense.

Hence, the suit.

Carrera had explained to Puente-Pequeño that, while it might be nice if the courts would order the various national armed forces of the Tauran Union to stop bombing, that wasn't the objective of the suit. Instead, the objective was "to drive a wedge between the Tauran elites and their ecofreak minions. I want more riots to add to the other ones we'll be fomenting. I want their society as disrupted and fragmented as possible. Also, the suit, win or lose, must delegitimize their leaders and the institutions of the Tauran Union in the eyes of the people."

Ordinarily, the Global Court of Justice didn't have jurisdiction over or between individuals, but only between states and, occasionally, supra- and sub-national organizations. Moreover, for Balboa—the same country which had sentenced to death for treason various Tauran pacifists aspiring to human shield status—it would never do to appear to be hiding behind an international treaty. Thus, state versus state legal action was right out . . . for Balboa. However, the other states of Colombia del Norte, not being at war with the Tauran Union even though they provided some rather elite troops to help defend Balboa, didn't live under the same moral memetic onus. Therefore, the documentation delivered by Litten, Heinrich, and Kipping, included the signatures of almost every Spanish and Portuguese-speaking state on the planet.

The President of Atzlan had pretty well summed up the general feeling, "Those do-gooding, self-righteous, posturing Tauran assholes have been using this crap to try to limit our use of our own resources, to develop our own economies, to feed our own people, for decades. Let's see how they like it when it's used to harm them!" He then signed with the words, "Gander, meet sauce."

In any event, with the roar of the crowd outside ringing in their ears, fully armed with the righteous anger of the yearning masses, this in the form of a multiply presidentially signed motion for injunctive relief, specifically to order a halt to the bombing of the Balboan rain forest, Lawyer Johannes Litten, brief under his left arm, flanked by his legal cohorts, Beate Heinrich and Karlie Kipping, marched to the carpeted marble grand staircase that led up to the courtroom of the day. At the end of the first dozen steps the party came to a landing, also carpeted, from which more steps led to the right and the left. Litten looked right, then lifted his chin to look down his nose at that set. Saying, "Come, ladies," he, instead, turned ostentatiously to the left, ascending those stairs.

The fifteen judges sat along a long bench, under a trio of stained glass windows, with a marble wall behind them and framing the windows. Behind the judges hung a portrait of the current president *pro tem* of the Tauran Union, Monsieur Gaymard.

With the slightest of smiles crinkling his lips, Litten cocked his head to the right slightly, looked up at the painting and said, *sotto voce*, "Ah, I have long been in favor of hanging him up high."

Then, amidst the twitters of the onlookers and even a few judges, Litten paced forward and, far more forcefully than might be considered polite, slammed a copy of the motion in front of the chief judge. (This— the delivery, not the slamming—was a formality of this particular court; the judges and clerks had had copies for several weeks.)

With that, Litten and company retired to their table, to await the judges' pleasure.

Conference Room, UEPF *Spirit of Peace*

The walls were paneled and the wood made of frightfully expensive, and now endangered to the point of approaching extinction, Terra Novan silverwood. At one end of the long conference table, seated under comfortable high gravity, with the huge Yamatan Kurosawa screen on the right-hand wall, was the high admiral.

"Was it an inside job?" Marguerite asked, forehead propped by the digits on one hand. She carefully kept her face impassive, lest any fraction of her surprise, anger, and hurt leak out. In this, she was not entirely successful.

"We don't know," said Khan, husband. "It seems at least plausible, though."

"How many embassies do we have that are at high risk? Minus the one in Santa Josefina, I mean; I have no intention of reopening that one."

Khan thought about that for a moment, then punched

up a map. Studying that for a long couple of minutes, he highlighted most of the countries showing, then answered, "Sixteen. Oh, there's risk in the Tauran Union or Uhuru or anyplace—we simply don't know the enemy's full reach—but those sixteen are places where the local government might grab our people for bargaining chips or Carrera may have inserted a team. It's even possible that, as the Taurans inflict casualties on their contingents in Balboa, the local people might be inspired to riot."

"How many guards to defend one? Our own people, I mean, not locals who might be infiltrators."

"About five hundred, I suppose, would do the trick; twenty-five or thirty in each at-risk embassy and a reaction force of a small company. But we hardly have anyone aboard our ships capable of ground combat. And taking that many from Atlantis Base would be . . . well, no, I suppose with all the defenses being automated we could take them from there."

"Give the orders."

"Yes, High Admiral. Now what do we do about the ambassador? The guerillas in Santa Josefina say they're going to start returning her a piece at a time unless we cut off all support for the Tauran Union and denounce their invasion of Santa Josefina."

Marguerite's mask slipped just that much more with those words. *Clever, clever bastard, my enemy. Note how carefully they did not demand an end to our support of the Taurans in Balboa. They don't have to; denouncing the Taurans under Marciano will ruin our relations with the ones under Janier.*

I can't help but wonder, too; is this my fault? Did the

support I gave the Salafi Ikhwan in their campaign of
terror teach Carrera to use terror the same ways? I
know that I have a hefty share of the blame for the war
as a whole, and for his rise, but did my actions cause
him to pick up the techniques? Elder gods, forgive me if
I did.

"What if I don't?" Wallenstein, raising her head, asked
of Khan, wife.

"I believe they'll carry through on their threat," she
said. "I think that there are two—well, three—problems
with that. The ambassador, herself, doesn't mean much;
that's why she was posted to the nothing much embassy
in Santa Josefina. But she has connections and family back
on Earth. They'll be trouble for you . . . eventually."

"'Eventually.' I can live with 'eventually.'"

"The other problems," Khan, husband, said, "are more
immediate. Consider, High Admiral, the effect of her no-
doubt miserable and graphic death on morale of both the
fleet and Atlantis Base, and the probability that, to avoid
that, or try to, she'll spill her guts about everything she
knows, make any statement they want her to, to boot."

Marguerite had a sudden, horrible thought. "What
religion," she asked, "if any, was the ambassador?"

Khan, wife, had no need to consult her tablet.
"Orthodox Nanauatli."

The Nanauatli, Aztec-based sun worshippers, were
chief among the religions of Old Earth that favored
human sacrifice. Some actually believed it was necessary
to the maintenance of the universe. More, Wallenstein
was convinced, just used it to terrorize the people into
submission.

"Crap," she said. "Just crap; anything but Orthodox Nanauatli."

"She's a relation of the Castro-Nyeres," Khan, husband, said. "That's probably why she got picked for this particular sinecure; her native tongue was close enough to Santa Josefinan Spanish."

"The Castro-Nyeres?" Wallenstein fairly spit. "Could life possibly get any better?" Her head once again sank, dispirited, to be supported by her left hand's fingers.

Along with their many, *Oh many*, other crimes, the Castro-Nyere clan ruled TransIsthmia, Esmeralda's home, back on Earth, with blood-dripping hands. It was, in fact, their fault that Esma's sister had been sacrificed and turned into a large cauldron of chili, as had almost happened, too, to Esma.

If I ever have the chance, I will hang that clan down to the tiniest brat sucking on its wet nurse's tit.

"They're a vile enough crew," agreed Khan, husband, adding, almost as if he'd read her mind, "If ever there was a case to be made that evil can be genetic, they would exhibit one."

Wallenstein just grunted agreement. "Speaking of their crimes, how is my girl, Esma?"

"Knowing you would be concerned," said Khan, wife, "I inquired. There's nothing medically wrong with her, according to the barbarians' medicos, below. But she is very upset, depressed, and uncommunicative. She has no appetite and is losing weight. They think she needs a break, a week or two, from any duties."

"Cut orders to send her somewhere peaceful, beautiful, and—above all—safe," the high admiral said. "My personal tab. Let her stay anywhere from a few days to a few weeks, whatever she thinks she needs. And give her some of the local cash."

Wallenstein looked over at the captain of the *Peace*, Richard, earl of Care and Esma's regular lover. Richard had, so far, been silent. "Would you care to join her, son?"

"If you think you can spare me for a few days, High Admiral, yes, please." In a civilization replete with sex masquerading as love, and that rather poorly, Richard, quite young himself, was actually in love with the still younger Esmeralda, so much so that he'd long been considering taking a discharge here on Terra Nova and contracting an old-fashioned marriage with the girl. It would be better than subjecting her to the snobbery of his own class, in any event.

"Consider it an order."

Wallenstein looked once again to Khan, the husband.

"Back to the ambassador. Open up a line of communication with the people who hold the bitch. Offer them a substantial amount of money. Explain that they can have that, and give up the ambassador, or they can kill her, however they choose, and get nothing for their pains.

"Those are my final words."

"But what if they torture or threaten her into making statements?" Khan objected.

"If it was known down below what our home planet and most of our ruling class are like, they'd unite as one to exterminate us. So, no, they won't have that cajoling them into holding out. Even so, make it a *lot* of the local money."

Hotel Edward's Palace, Island of Teixeira, Lusitania, Tauran Union, Terra Nova

"I need to talk to you," had been the message Esma left on the email drop for Cass Aragon. It included the name of the hotel and said, "Pool. Just after noon. Every day. If I am talking to someone male, back off until he goes away. Important!"

Cass had used an exclamation mark, too, in her message to Legate Triste. In fact, she'd used two of them. One was to indicate the importance of getting to their prize mole, Esma. The other was a plea for money to cover the trip.

Money had been provided, but she'd frankly lacked imagination.

Getting out of Santa Josefina had been a problem. In the first place, a series of mortar attacks on the airport, Julio Asunción, had shut it down for all but military flights. Hence, she'd had to take a bus. But with all the people fleeing the war in Santa Josefina, and heading for some newly established refugee camps across the border, in Córdoba, bus space had been at a premium. The bribe needed to get someone else kicked off to free up a seat had been large enough to make her pause. *The legions had better win the war or I'm in deep financial trouble.*

Another bribe had been needed at the border itself. Not that there was anything wrong with her passport. Oh, no, she'd just looked healthy, and well-enough fed, and so the customs people on the other side had decided she'd be a soft touch. She was pretty sure she could have traded sex instead of money, but a girl had her dignity, after all.

From there things had lightened. Air passage from the airport at the capital, Managua Nueva, had been fairly easy and not too expensive. From there it was even easier to get to the Federated States and then catch a flight to the tourist haven of Teixeira.

The problem was that it took five days to make the entire trip.

To say that sex wasn't an important thing for Esma would have been an understatement, this despite being of an age when sex bid fair with most boys and girls to overwhelm their thoughts and lives. Unfortunately, in the society she'd grown up in, as a beautiful but powerless girl, of a peasant family, and unconnected, sex had begun rather too early and very much badly. Moreover, until Richard had come along, she'd never once been asked. Instead, her lot on her family's small farm, and later, in the slave pens of Razona Market, had been that of an ambulatory piece of meat. It would have been worse if that hadn't also been the lot of every girl of her class that she knew. There was no special shame, after all, in what everyone endured.

Still, Richard was kind and she tried to put on a decent show for him. She wasn't sure how well the show actually worked. And, after five days of pretense, she was just as glad when his short liberty was over and he had to return to the *Peace*.

And, to be let in peace, to sun herself by the pool, in a bikini less there than not, was probably exactly the

medicine she needed. She was almost sorry when a
weary looking Cass Aragon lay down on the lounge next
to hers.

"We can't talk here," Aragon said. "Get up and leave
but wait for me in one of the chairs by the elevator. I'll
come along in five or ten minutes. When I do, get in the
elevator. I'll follow. Then go to your room."

"You want *what*?" Aragon demanded of the girl halfway
to hysteria.

"I want out," Esma said, shrilly. "I saw things, in Santa
Josefina, that let me know you people aren't a whit better
than old Earth. I saw the murder of an innocent young
girl. I saw her body, anyway. I know about people shot for
voicing an opinion. Or selling food. Or serving a Tauran a
drink in a bar. You're just as rotten as the Castro-Nyeres,
back home, and none of you is as decent or kind as
Admiral Wallenstein. So, I'm out of this. I won't help you
anymore."

Aragon's first thought was, *You're out of an airlock if
we tell your oh-so-decent and kind High Admiral that
you've been spying for us. But my orders are "kid gloves."
I'm pretty sure arranging for your death won't quite fit
into those.*

Instead, she asked, "Please tell me what happened."

Esma did, at length and bitterly, dwelling particularly
on the sheet of blood-lapping flies covering the ruined
body of her friend, Stefi.

"They may have exceeded their orders," Cass pointed
out, reasonably. "They may have been following orders of
their own. They could have let their anger at what they

saw as treason get the better of them. I don't know. I don't think we actually have day-to-day control over what the *tercios* in Santa Josefina do. I do know that we gave them a course in guerilla warfare run by some Cochinese experts, and they are some hard men and women.

"They had to be that hard to defeat the Federated States and the Zhong. We, too, have to be hard to defeat the Tauran Union and Old Earth."

"Is that what you call it, 'being hard,' when you line a bunch of civilians against a wall and massacre them?"

"I didn't massacre anybody, Esma."

"Your *side* did."

"Do you know how this war really started?" Aragon asked.

"No."

Sighing, Cass continued, "I don't know all the details but I know some. It began when some terrorists killed Carrera's wife and kids. Do you know who was supporting the terrorists, Esma? The United Earth Peace Fleet. That's right; *your* side killed thousands of innocent women; children, too. Nobody has clean hands, honey, but that's not the question."

"What is, then?"

"The question is what does the world—or what do the worlds—look like depending on who ultimately wins. We don't murder innocent young girls like your sister for no better purpose than to turn them into . . . how did you put it? Oh, I remember; 'a bowl of chili,' you said.

"That's not going to happen with us. But you know what the world of the other side looks like. With them it's probably unavoidable."

"Maybe so," Esmeralda answered, "but I'm still done helping you."

"Is there any way I can get you to reconsider?" *Other than, that is, threatening to turn you over to the other side or having you killed by our own?*

Esma thought hard for a few minutes, thinking of the most impossible thing she could ask for. Finally, she thought she had it. "Sure. Tell your big boss, Carrera, to come see me and explain it to me."

With a frustrated and helpless shrug, Aragon said, "I'll put in the request. If he agrees, and he probably can't or won't, are you picky about where?"

**Headquarters, Tercio Amazona,
deep in the Balboan jungle.**

The tercio commander listened to the nightly messages from the capital with only half an ear.

"Terra Nova, Terra Nova, this is Radio Balboa calling to our friends around the world. We have the following notifications and messages: Athene's orifice is stretched wide. I repeat, Athene's orifice is stretched wide. Yvette always swallows. I say again, Yvette always swallows. Delong has de very little penis. I say again, Delong has de very little penis. Hecate is cheddar to the core . . ."

"I do not," said a young woman manning the radios. "Never. It's disgusting."

The tercio commander shrugged, saying, "Don't knock it, Yvette, if you've never tried it."

The girl muttered something under her breath.

"What was that, child?"

"I said, sir, that the difference between the legions and the Young Scouts is that the latter, at least, have adult supervision."

CHAPTER SIXTEEN

"The road of life is paved with flat squirrels
who couldn't make a decision."
                              —Unknown

Estado Mayor, subcamp A, *Ciudad* Balboa

Although the Taurans had not, so far, targeted the
Balboan presidential palace, also known as the Palace of
the Trixies, it was too great a risk for Raul Parilla,
president of the Republic, to actually live there. Instead,
he and his wife and a couple of servants made do in a
small but thick-walled apartment, underground and under
a building. The walls, though thick, were possibly not
thick enough to contain Parilla's shouts.

Waving his arms furiously, the president exclaimed,
"You're out of your fucking mind, Patricio. Insane! I
forbid it. I won't even hear of it. Not one fucking word!"

Carrera, standing at ease in front of Parilla's desk merely
said, "Explain it to the president, would you, Fernandez?"

Unlike Carrera, Fernandez couldn't stand. A would-be
assassin's bullet had shattered his spine years ago. He,

instead, sat in what was probably the best wheelchair in the Republic.

"What are you going to do, Mr. President?" Fernandez asked, "Have me shot and relieve me of the burden of living a cripple? No, eh?

"Unfortunately, Mr. President, this is not just any girl. In the first place, as a spy she is a pearl beyond price. In the second, our main enemy, the Earthpigs' high admiral, seems to love her like a daughter. But in the third case . . ."

"How do you know that? How do you know how Wallenstein feels?" Parilla demanded.

"The Yamatans tell me so, though they still refuse to say how they know."

"And you believe them?"

"I do, not least because they don't understand us well enough to lie convincingly. And, as I was saying, in the third case, she is a hefty insurance policy against failure when we make our ultimate move."

Parilla, now aged beyond his years with stress and worry, used one arm of his chair and the opposite hand on his desk to help himself to stand. On uncertain, shaky feet he walked a quarter of the way around the desk to stand on the opposite side of Fernandez from Carrera. There, with his hand on the right-front corner, he stood and shook an already shaky finger at Carrera.

"You; *you* brought this war on us. I never wanted it. And you're not going to aban . . . abando . . . ndo . . . oh . . . oh, shit." Parilla's hand clutched at his chest. He rocked for a few moments and then began to sink to the tiled concrete floor of the place.

Carrera almost knocked Fernandez over in his rush to

support his political chief. He would have knocked him over, too, if the wheelchair hadn't weighed upwards of two hundred pounds.

"Medic!"

"They say he'll make it," Carrera told Fernandez, the two of them sitting over some diluted shots of legionary ration rum in Carrera's underground quarters. "But he's going to be out of commission for anywhere from about ten days to three weeks."

"Two questions, then," said Fernandez, "or maybe three. Yes, three. Do we send you to meet the girl? Do we inform the first vice president to assume Parilla's duties until he's back on his feet? Do we forge a paper in his name to send to the senate to appoint you dictator for six months, per the national constitution?"

"Number three is a case of, 'If nominated I will not run. If elected I will not serve.' If you try to make me I will run . . . to someplace without an extradition treaty with either the TU or Balboa, that is also not a member of the Cosmopolitan Criminal Court. Trust me, here; I know my limitations; I know how to destroy and how to build things that destroy. To build things that better things? Me? No, and in that I've mostly been lucky. Rather, I was lucky to be able to recognize people who can build, and to have them come into my life."

Fernandez nodded. Carrera's self-assessment matched his own of his chief very closely. He asked, "Then what about the first vice president?"

Carrera considered that for a bit, but, reluctantly, shook his head no. "I don't think so. He's not half the man and not a quarter the politician Raul is . . . or was. And, no, we can't jump down to the second vice or the senate, though I think Senator Robles might make a fine dictator, personally."

Robles—a poor boy, once, then turned soldier-turned farmer-turned politician—had been one of a minority of people who had balked Carrera on something important to him. Carrera didn't always trust his judgment, but he always and completely trusted his strength of character and commitment to the country.

"Anyway, if Raul is going to make it, let's not borrow trouble. Things will continue on for a bit without his hand at the tiller. On the other hand . . ."

"On the other hand," Fernandez continued, "you can now visit our mole. Even though we both know it's box of rocks stupid."

"Yeah; set it up, would you?"

"Sure. Now what do we do about rumors?"

"Rumors? Do? Why, we stoke them," Carrera replied, slyly. "But not until I am back."

There really weren't any great options for getting Carrera out of Balboa. The safest was to use one of the medical flights that took some of the more seriously wounded to Santander, La Plata, or south to Atzlan or the Federated states. But that would have been a violation of the laws of war, in Carrera's opinion, a subject on which he was something of a legalistically minded stickler. There were still Meg Class coastal defense submarines not interned with Fosa. But that would have been slow and, since they couldn't really use the Global Locating System all that well when submerged, somewhat uncertain. Fernandez had considered a helicopter, flying nap of the earth, but, what with the sheer numbers of Tauran aircraft hanging about, that was right out.

"And," Fernandez said, "we can't really risk you to an international flight even if we could get you to someplace not directly involved with the war. Your eyes we can cover with dark contacts, and we will, anyway. Your hair we can dye, and we will, anyway. We can and will teach you to walk like an old man with a cane. What we cannot do, or cannot be certain of doing, is beat facial recognition. Hence, the international system is right out. I cannot charter you a plane, either, because they are probably more carefully watched even than public flights. Mind you, it's by no means certain you would be caught, but since I cannot measure the risk I have to assume it is too high."

"And so . . . ?" Carrera had a dread deep in his chest over the answer.

"And so, I've told our handler for the girl, Miss Cass Aragon, to get the girl to go back to Aserri, in Santa Josefina, and to check into a particular hotel near a particular bar. It's a not a whores' hotel but the bar is a whores' bar. Thus, it is frequented by some of our troops there. They can provide security."

That sense of dread grew. "And I get there exactly . . ."

There was a knock on the door. In popped a familiar head.

"Legate Fernandez, you sent for me?" asked flight warrant Rafael Montoya.

Oh, thought Carrera, *I am so fucked*.

★★★

"It wasn't my fault, sir," Montoya insisted, "that time we got splashed near the Isla Real."

"No, son," Carrera agreed, "no, it wasn't. It was just bad luck, only salvaged by your excellent flying. But it *was* bad luck. And, based on some things you said, you have a lot of it."

"That was women, Duque; I have bad luck with women. Well . . . good luck, by some measures, but it never seems to last."

"Yeah, we call that 'bad luck.'"

Fernandez interjected, "I hate to say anything that will go to this young man's head, Duque, but he is probably the top Condor pilot—"

"I can fly anything," Montoya insisted.

"—as I was saying, the top Condor pilot and very good in any of our aircraft except the fighters."

"I was scheduled for those, sir, before you pulled the plug on me."

"Too valuable to risk," Fernandez insisted. "Too *dangerous* to risk, too, on anything less than this."

"So, *what* is your plan?" Carrera asked.

"You and Montoya get into a two-man Condor. They're stealthy enough. Indeed, sir, we know that neither the TU nor the UEPF can see them with anything but the— speaking of luck—occasional lucky set of eyeballs. Montoya will fly dead reckoning to a certain point, then switch to the Global Locating System which, be it noted, nobody in Santa Josefina is interfering with. He will bring you down in a field where you will be met by a platoon from Second Cohort, *Tercio Le Virgen.* They will dispose of the Condor. They are also charged with renting young

Montoya, here, an airplane. It will come with a pilot, but you can get rid of him at pistol point and Montoya can fly . . . say, can you fly multi-engine turboprops like a Pfeiffer Senator?"

"Yes, sir; I can."

"Good, because that's what they've rented."

Fernandez grew a bit contemplative for a moment. "It's funny, you know," he said, "that amidst the war we launched in Santa Josefina, the economy there is still mostly carrying on. Of course, their level of war is less than ours, but still.

"Anyway, the platoon . . ."

San Miguel, Santa Josefina

In the midnight gloom of an open field, now somewhat freshly plowed by a legionary Condor, Centurion Mora was all business as he personally helped Carrera out of the gutted aircraft. "Follow me, please, Duque. Second and Third Squads, obliterate that thing and dispose of the residue *completely*. First squad; get the pilot out and then escort."

"Do you have a medic?" Carrera asked.

"Yes, a regular medic," the centurion answered.

"Well, my pilot is not the sniveling sort, but I believe he took some damage when we flew over what was probably an element of *Tercio la Virgen*."

"Wasn't my *fault*, Duque," Montoya insisted through gritted teeth.

"Yes, Montoya, I know . . . and, got to hand it to you, it

was some great flying that got us this far after we took a few hits."

"Hits?" Mora asked, after summoning the medic.

"Just a couple. Okay, maybe fifteen or twenty."

Montoya must have hit whatever was injured when Mora and the medic attempted to extract him for the rapidly disassembling glider. "One of them went through my foot, a part of my leg, and is, I think, buried in my ass."

"How . . ."

Carrera explained, "Clouds were covering Hecate and Bellona for most of the trip, but there was a break in them at just about exactly the wrong time. Just bad luck, like he said. Somebody on the ground with a machine gun—most likely our own—must have seen us silhouetted in the moonlight and opened up. It was so close when it started that we ended up flying right through it. I had an armored plate under me, but Montoya here said it was too much weight to put one under him."

From the Condor came, "Oooow, Jesus, be careful."

"Oh, stop being such a baby, Montoya," Carrera said.

"We're going to have to carry him facedown, I think, Centurion," said the medic. "I'll get a stretcher made up."

"I'm on it with my boys," piped up Esteban Sanchez.

"Okay," said Mora. "Now, Duque, if you're satisfied that your man will be cared for, will you *please* come with me so we can get you the hell to shelter?"

"Sure," agreed Carrera, then, holding up an index finger, he said, "Oh, one last thing." Turning back to the Condor, he extracted a walking stick.

★★★

The return trip had been much easier for Cass, even with Esma in tow, than the trip out. For one thing, she'd had more time to plan, so had been able to get a better flight to Managua Nueva. That included a first-class seat for Esma, as the girl's boss would have wanted her to have. Then, too, she'd been able to rent a car and driver— oh, the danger pay had cost something—to ferry them direct to Santa Josefina and the hotel. She could have taken a bus, too, for anonymity's sake, there being very few people trying to get *into* a war zone.

The speed and certainty of a single car was better, Cass had thought, not long after crossing the border. She cast a sideways glance at Esma, sleeping with her head propped against a window. *I suppose I should be mad at you, for putting me through all this trouble, and for endangering my side in a life or death war, but I just can't be. You're too nice a girl and you've been hurt too much in your life. And, frankly, if it had been my friend stood against a wall and shot I'd be pretty upset, too. Okay, I'd be more than just upset; I'd be murderous. I just hope Carrera, who I never really expected to agree to show up, can explain it to you better than I could.*

The weary looking old man, a bit stooped, trudged around the corner, leaning on his cane to keep himself upright. An intermittent breeze plucked at his steel-gray hair, which seemed a bit wispy. The gray of the hair stood in stark contrast to his dark skin and brown eyes.

Surprisingly enough, within days of the embassy attacks, the city had returned to about ninety-nine percent of normal. Indeed, the sidewalks were crowded enough that the old man had to dodge, more than once, to keep to his feet.

Thought the old man, *Goddamned good thing Fernandez insisted on the lessons in walking, and in disguise, and the haircut. And the fake tan. And the contacts. And the dye. And the shoes and suit. I don't think even Lourdes would recognize me now. Well, with my clothes on she wouldn't.*

The hotel was only a couple of blocks away. Even at his reduced speed—*I fucking hate walking slowly*—he made it in less than a dozen minutes. There was an unarmed doorman at the hotel's door but, since Carrera was in a good quality linen suit and maintained an air of confidence despite the uncertain walk, the doorman didn't spare the old man a moment's thought, but just opened the door and gave the greeting of the day.

On the other hand, if the doorman *had* recognized Duque Patricio Carrera he'd probably have snapped to attention and saluted. That was to be expected of a soldier of the *Tercio la Virgen*. Moreover, it would have been disastrous, at least potentially.

Carrera had been briefed that the hotel staff was infiltrated by the guerillas, but not as to specific personalities.

I wonder if we'd have been better off with a whore's hotel. Lots of men go to random rooms in those. Funny the girl's handler objected. Well . . . after reading her file, I guess I can understand.

This is also, as Parilla said, really fucking stupid. We think we have secure means of communication with our limited overseas intelligence apparatus, but we don't know . . . well, I suppose we will know if I get away with this. Yeah, yeah, Fernandez said they occasionally dropped bits of bait into the system to see if the Taurans react, and they don't. But they're good at their jobs, too, in general.

Carrera started looking around the hotel lobby, suspicious and suspiciously, before he caught himself. He though he recognized a couple of men from Mora's platoon, but couldn't be one hundred percent sure.

Best thing to do is get out of sight, he thought, heading as briskly as a worn out old man might be expected to for the elevators.

There was no secret knock for the door. Carrera just rapped it a few times until it opened, held by a charming, young . . .

"Aragon?"

"Yes, Du . . . sir."

"Is our . . . ?"

"Waiting in the next room. There's a door between the two. I'll go to her room and get her to come to this one. In the interim, make yourself comfortable. I left a bottle of Ardourgnac and some ice on the table. It's odd, but the liquor selection here is better since the Taurans came."

"I'll do that," he said, entering, then standing fully upright, before taking a seat at the table.

The wait wasn't a long one. Carrera heard a doorknob or latch click and then she was standing there before him, tiny, brown, and perfect.

"They told me to be prepared for a shock," he said, heart suddenly pounding, and breath feeling a little short, "but the warning didn't do justice."

"Sir?" Esma asked, taking a seat opposite his. She noticed immediately that, old-looking or not, she liked his smell quite a bit.

Carrera reached for his wallet. It had no legitimate—though much fake—identification, but it did have some genuine pictures. He pulled a particular one out and slid it across the table to her.

Esma took one look and gasped. "How did you get my picture? And how did you get me in a gown the like of which I've never worn? And why do I look several years older than I am?"

"It's not *your* picture, girl; it's my late wife. I'm not sure how you two ended up looking so much alike. Maybe because you're from the same area, so about the same gene pool, on Old Earth that her multi-great grandfather and grandmother came from. Maybe something else, but I'll have to ask a priest about that one."

"Cass told me she was killed and that's what began the war."

"I'm not sure you understood her." Carrera shrugged. "Or maybe she didn't understand. My wife—Linda was her name—was killed along with our children the day the war against the Salafi Ikhwan began. That war led to this war, yes, but they're not the same war. Well . . . they're not *exactly* the same war. The UEPF was up to its rotten neck in the plot to destroy the building my wife and kids were in. So, my war with them is the same war. But the Tauran Union and I . . . and Balboa . . . were on the same side for the most part in the earlier war."

"I am . . . I've overheard . . . oh, never mind."

"Go on, Esma, you can speak freely."

She looked doubtful, but then relented and spoke. "I've heard things, little scraps and sleep talking, from the high admiral. She regrets her part in that. Yes, she had a part and she is *so* sorry."

"I imagine," Carrera said, "that she's not quite as sorry as I am."

"No . . . no, I suppose she couldn't be. She was . . . your wife was . . . oh, never mind that too."

Carrera almost laughed. He *did* smile. "You were going to say that my wife was very beautiful, but you couldn't because that would be the same as saying you, yourself, are very beautiful, yes?"

"How do you do that?" she asked.

"Been around people and studying them a long time, Esmeralda."

"Please, just 'Esma.'"

"Esma, then. The other part is that your beauty has caused you little but trouble and pain, yes?"

"Yes," she answered, simply, letting her delicate chin fall to her chest. "I'd say you have no idea, but I suppose Cass put it in her reports on me."

"Yes, though it wasn't exactly about you; more about the way Old Earth is. Still, it wasn't hard to figure that Aragon's witness was you, and that the things described happened to you . . . well, you and your sister. They kill people, hang them or burn them or cut their hearts out, either to appease old, false, barbarian gods, or to terrify commoners like you, or both, yes?"

Chin still resting on her chest, Esma answered, again, simply, "Yes."

"And some of them eat them?"

"Yes."

Carrera saw a single tear form and then run down the girl's face. He reached out a hand and patted hers. The touch was electric enough—*it's like having my Linda here again, in the flesh*—that he withdrew his hand quickly.

"Tell me, Esma, what would you be willing to do if you could have your sister back?"

She wiped the same hand across her cheek—she thought, *he does smell interesting*—sniffled a couple of times, and answered, "That's impossible."

"Yes, I know," Carrera said, "but *if*?"

"I don't know."

"Are your parents alive?"

She shook her head slightly. "I don't know that either, not for sure. The high admiral said they were and that she'd given orders to move them somewhere where they'd be safe from the rulers of TransIsthmia, the Castro-Nyeres. But we've been gone a while now, so . . ."

"So if something were threatening them what would you do to protect them?"

"Anything."

"You're a good daughter. So tell me, would it be right for someone else to do 'anything' if he were trying to protect a lot of people he cared about from what happened to your sister or what may happen or have happened to your parents?"

"I don't know." She lifted her chin slightly and, brown eyes flashing, looked directly at Carrera. "But if you're talking about the guerillas here murdering my friend, I don't think that was right. Who were they protecting from what that required her to die? Nobody! Nothing!"

"Ah, but they were, though," Carrera insisted. "No, no," he continued, seeing the anger writ plain on her face, "hear me out. Your friend was innocent, yes, I can agree to this, at least insofar as she intended no one harm. But let me ask you a question or, rather, a few of them.

"If you knew, maybe not to a certainty but pretty damned well, that something bad was going to happen, would you have a duty to prevent it?"

"Maybe," she conceded, "if I knew how and I could."

"Well," Carrera continued, "we know . . . *I* know, to a considerable degree of certainty that if the Tauran Union and the Peace Fleet win this war something very bad is going to happen. That bad thing is that we will become a lot like your old home. We might differ in the details, here, but we can be pretty sure that once power is handed over to a bunch of unelected and unaccountable bureaucrats, competent only in corruption and corrupt as a piece of meat left in the sun for flies, things get very bad indeed. You've seen it. At least you've seen the result of it.

"The people that will happen to, Esma, those future people, won't be much different from your sister and your parents, or from anyone else you met in the slave market. And they'll be innocent, too.

"So, if those are the choices—totally innocent people suffer or people who have good intentions—I'll concede your friend had good intentions—that are going to turn out bad, who is better to have to suffer? Whose suffering is most likely to do some good?"

"But you don't know those bad things will happen."

"Well, no . . . but tell me this, if they do come to pass

and I were able to stop it, do you think people will think it was my fault for not stopping it when I could have?"

"I don't know. I know you don't know the future."

"Neither of us can really know the future, Esma. All we have to go by is the past. The past tells us that when people like the people who run your planet take over, they ruin everything and everyone but themselves."

"That may all be so," Esma said, "but I'm still not going to work for you or your side anymore."

Carrera smiled, sadly. "And now which of us is making a prediction about a future we cannot see? Hmmm . . . let's keep this simple. Let me show you something else."

From a pocket in his jacket Carrera pulled out a small folded sheaf of photocopies. He opened them and passed them over to Esma. She looked at the first one and gasped. Her little fist flew to her mouth. She bit down on it to keep from crying out.

The picture was of rescue workers extracting the remnants of a young family from a collapsed building. Centered in the picture was a small baby, perhaps three months old, covered in blood and with its head deformed from some kind of trauma.

"That was taken in *Ciudad* Balboa, about two weeks ago. The building collapsed from a bomb dropped by a Tauran Union airplane. That plane flew from here in Santa Josefina."

The girl started to answer, then though better of it.

"Go to the next one," he commanded.

Reluctantly, she did. That next image was of the inside of a bomb shelter that had been penetrated by a bomb before it went off. There were several hundred bodies shown, some incomplete.

"The next few are of the same place, but closer up and in more detail."

She looked, horrified. There were women, children, old men. Almost all of them seemed slightly cooked in the picture. Their color was a little off, in any case, though it was most noticeable in the lighter-skinned ones.

"That was another plane that flew from here."

"How do you know?" she demanded.

"We have radar, spotters, and spies," he answered. "We have command centers to track the incoming attacks."

"Then why didn't you stop those attacks?"

Clever girl, he thought. "Limited ability," he answered, truthfully, "and for not very long, which is why we have to use other means to stop them from using Santa Josefina as a base against us. And killing your friend, who was, in her own small way, working to keep Santa Josefina as a base for them, was a step toward stopping that use and"— Carrera gestured at the pictures—"a way to stop that from happening for much longer."

How much do I dare tell her about the really big things? Carrera wondered. *I think maybe no more than we already have, which is, I hope, nothing.*

"I don't know," Esma said. What it was she didn't know wasn't entirely clear. She looked up at Carrera. "You took a big risk coming to talk to me."

"Not small," he agreed, *though worth it if only to feel like my Linda is here with me again, even if she isn't.*

"Was it just to talk me into doing your dirty work for you?"

"No," he admitted. "No, it wasn't. I wanted to see . . ."

"Your wife again?"

"Yes."

"I'm not her."

For a moment, Carrera's face grew stone-hard. "I know, but you're painfully like her."

"This is hard for me, too," she said.

"The question of right and wrong?" he asked.

She looked down, embarrassed. "No, the question of if I am too young for you."

"I am flattered . . . but you are."

She flashed a smile, brilliant white against dark olive skin. "Only an honest man," she said, "would have admitted that. A dishonest one would just have picked me up and carried me to the bed."

"What if I had?"

The smile faded slightly. "Only an honest girl would tell you I wouldn't have resisted."

Next incarnation, maybe, Carrera thought, mentally sighing at what could not be in this life. "You need to be honest with yourself then, Esma, too, and honest about the world—the worlds—as they are, and honest about the future."

His words dripped with sincere desperation. "You *know* what a horror story Old Earth is, Esma. You *know* that if we don't win here then we'll become the same. I am sorry, truly and deeply sorry, for your friend, but I'd order it or do it myself a thousand times over to prevent what has happened to you, to your sister, and to your old country from being repeated here, and inflicted on ten billion girls just as innocent as your Stefi."

Esma sighed, deeply. "I'll think about what you've said. I can't agree to more than that. It would help," she added, "if you would give orders to stop the murders."

"You're that important," Carrera admitted, "not just to me because you're my late wife in the flesh, but that important to our cause, that I can give the orders to stop the extra-judicial killings," Carrera said, "and, for your sake, I will. But I cannot guarantee they'll be obeyed. It's a guerilla war, after all, and that war still goes on. And, in this kind of war, it's a fine line between a murder and a legitimate combat action."

Then, too, though you don't know it, we've probably already gotten everything we need out of our little foray in specific terror.

"Then I'll try," Esma said, "yes, I'll try to keep helping, just as long as the killings are not massacres, not wanton."

"Best we can do, I suppose," said Carrera. "And, dear, for your own sake prepare yourself mentally for the day you're going to have to do something you would really rather not, because your duty or your personal safety demand it. And don't forget the advantages of the simple and direct."

CHAPTER SEVENTEEN

"Diplomats are useful only in fair weather. As soon as it rains, they drown in every drop."
—Charles de Gaulle

Headquarters, Task Force Jesuit, Rio Clara, Santa Josefina

There was an unusually large amount of radio traffic echoing through the command post. Most of it sounded acrimonious.

"You're shitting me," Marciano said to del Collea. "Tell me you're shitting me. You've *got* to be shitting me."

Rall shook his head. "No, sir. It's no joke. Every nation contributing to Task Force Jesuit has ordered its national contingent to detach anything from one platoon to two companies to secure their embassy. In addition, the Tauran Union has demanded one more company for the security of its mission. Combat troops, too, mind you; there'll be no transferring our support troops to embassy duty and using embassy grounds for our field trains."

"What's it work out to?" Marciano asked.

Del Collea replied, "Just over a thousand infantry or engineers or commandos to be detached, or about a third of all ground combatants we have. But it's worse than that, sir; every combat unit will be losing a key ability, battalions reduced to two companies, many companies reduced to two platoons. Nobody will have the depth of organization to maneuver, to maintain a reserve, to serve as a covering force. We'll be going from a square organization of triangular subordinates to a square organization of flat subordinates."

Marciano chewed for a moment at his lower lip. "And they just bypassed me? Went straight to their units here?"

Del Collea's face took on a mixture of shame and disgust. "Yes, sir. They went straight to their own people."

"I see." Marciano walked to a chair and sat down heavily.

"Sir, for what's it worth, something over half the subordinate commanders affected have said they'll ignore their orders on your say-so."

"And expose themselves to court-martial? Or relief by some political hacks without the first clue as to our war here? No. The war here was probably never winnable, anyway, but no sense in making the bloodletting any worse than it has to be.

"Draft the orders, gentleman; we're abandoning the rest of the country and pulling back to the capital. Rather, we're pulling back to the embassy district and the road to the port. There's no sense in leaving ourselves out here to be chopped up in detail. At least back there a platoon of

Cimbrians in their embassy can fire in support of the company they came from."

"I'll see to it, sir," Rall said.

"Also tell the quartermaster to start planning for supply by aerial drop."

"Sir?"

"We're not going to be able to hold the road open for very long."

"Yes, sir."

"Oh, and Rall?"

"Sir?"

"Fuck the Kosmos. When we pull out, before we turn the troops over to being embassy guards, and before the guerillas catch up with us, I want to put about three battalions and all the artillery into rounding up those fuckers who crossed the border openly a while back and who made up the groups that attacked the embassies in the first place. And then we put our *own* guards on the interned Balboan fleet. Maybe a platoon of tanks among the guards, too."

"Yes, *sir*! Oh, and sir?"

"Yes?"

"Miss Miranda, the High Admiral's aide is back. She's back in the hut she was assigned before. Bertholdo has her pistol and is bringing it to her."

Esma hadn't been able to get a ride from the United Earth embassy back to Marciano's headquarters; there was neither an embassy to go to nor a staff to drive her. She, herself, hadn't the first clue of how to drive a car, except that she sensed it was important to stay between the lines on the road as best one could. She'd been about to ask Cass Aragon for a lift when she'd realized on her own that, of all the things she ought not do, being seen in public with someone who just might be known as an enemy agent was probably among the worst.

As he often did, Richard had come to her aid, calling her on her communicator and offering to send a shuttle to bring her home to the *Peace*. She'd declined the offer to return home but had asked if she could be brought forward to Marciano's headquarters. Richard hadn't done the best possible job of concealing his disappointment, but had arranged through an embassy that hadn't been smashed to get her a ride.

And I, thought Esma, *didn't do the best possible job of pretending it was a hardship to me not to go back. It isn't. I've met the one I want, even if he's far too old for me. I am not sure I could stand being touched by Richard . . . and Richard doesn't deserve being rejected like that, either. Then, too, I've been betraying the high admiral and, if I decide to continue to work for Carrera, I would be continuing the betrayal. I don't want her to have the chance to sense that.*

This was all much easier when it was just revenge and I didn't have to think about the circumstances so much. It was easier, too, before I met . . .

Esma's thoughts were interrupted by a knock on the door to her hut. It was Bertholdo. He held up her loaner pistol. "I brought you something, miss," he said, "something that I think you wouldn't want to lose."

Esma jumped up, excitedly. "I thought they'd stolen it at the hospital!"

"No, but the smart money would have bet that someone

would have lifted it, given the chance. I took it from you when the field ambulance came for you." He passed the thing back to her. "Oh, and I got you a special treat."

She cocked her head, quizzically. "A treat?"

"Yes, miss, a treat of sorts. I or the general should have thought of it before. See, a pistol isn't really all that great a weapon, and, at the range you're likely to use it, needs to be able to put someone on their posterior pretty much immediately."

"Okay." She'd never really thought about that aspect before, but she supposed it made sense.

"There are a couple of ways to do that. One is to use a large caliber, ten millimeter or better. Your pistol—the general's pistol—is only nine-millimeter and that's not really good enough. You wouldn't think one lousy millimeter would make that much difference, but it does or, at least, it can. I nosed around for a bigger caliber pistol for you, with a small, single-stacked grip, but nobody has one in the arms rooms so we're stuck with that one."

She clutched her pistol defensively. It was so pretty compared to others she'd seen that she couldn't see using the word "stuck" where it was concerned.

"There's another way, too," Bertholdo continued. "And that's to use a trick bullet, a hollow point, say. Those, however, are against the law of war except for some odd exceptions that don't fit you. Wouldn't fit me, either. Enemy catches us with one of those in our possession and they'll shoot us on the spot unless they decide to wait long enough for someone to find a rope."

Pistol held loosely in her right hand, Esma's left moved up almost of its own accord to massage her neck.

Bertholdo caught that. "Yes, exactly. So, I hunted around and found a few boxes of these." He bent and pulled out one box from the cargo pocket of his right leg. This he held up before her eyes.

"Frangibles," he said with a trace of knowing triumph in his voice. "About as good as hollow points, maybe even better, and they look normal enough that you won't be shot out of hand for having them." He passed over that box, reached for another that he tossed on her thin bunk, and then dug some more for her magazines.

"I took the liberty of getting rid of the old ammunition and loading the frangibles in your pistol and the spare magazines," he said.

"And . . . 'frangible,' did you say? What does it do?"

"Turns into small particles when it hits something. All the energy gets dumped into the body but it won't go past the body. The downside is it won't penetrate walls for beans, but that's a good thing for a pistol, most of the time."

Smiling, still holding the pistol in her right hand, Esma flung her arms around Bertholdo, giving him a quick, light hug. "Thank you. From the heart, thank you."

Clearly embarrassed, Bertholdo said, "Oh, miss, it's all right. You're a nice girl and you are *very* welcome. And . . ." Bertholdo heard the sound of sirens. "Oh, crap, never mind, miss. We've got incoming. Let me lead you to a shelter."

La Caféothèque, Lumière, Gaul

Tranzitree wax candles burned on every table, adding a fragrance that totally belied the fruit's deadliness. Next to the candle were several rolls of chorleybread, and a generous dollop of butter. Though the chorley tasted buttery, on its own, that wasn't nearly enough for the Gauls.

The spacesuits were still troubling Jan, but there wasn't much she could do about that at the moment. She had a suspicion she needed to talk to someone who had been on one of the Earthpig starships but she knew of none, or none that would talk to her, anyway.

Sirens sounded. From her table, Campbell looked up toward the large plate glass window of the coffee shop. Customers rushed out of the coffee shop and into the street. People were abandoning cars in the streets and running for the shelter of the metro stations and various marked bomb shelters. The proprietor, older, balding and with a bit of a paunch, simply sighed with exasperation and went back to cleaning cups and saucers.

Paunch or not, he has a military bearing, doesn't he? I'd bet a thousand pounds he's been through some of this before.

It was daylight outside. A daylight attack was something that surprised Jan not at all. The gliders almost always came in under the sun, probably the better to interrupt the workday.

Campbell shrugged off the sirens. *Big city, small me, and I have work to do.*

The coffee shop had free connection to the globalnet; that was the big thing. Not that it was free, but that "free" probably meant untracked. Coupled with her pawn-shop purchased tablet, it enabled her to check things she really didn't want the Tauran Defense Agency to know she was looking into.

I wonder, thought Campbell, twisting her neck to look as far up as she could, in hopes of a glimpse of the incoming robot bomb, *I truly wonder just how much one of those costs, as a percentage of Balboa's prewar gross domestic product, compared to what it costs the Gauls, or Anglia, or Sachsen, or any country in the Union to have maybe half a million workers sit in a bomb shelter for a quarter to a half a day, and lose all that work. My guess would be it costs the Balboans a slightly bigger percentage, but that they don't care, that they're waging moral rather than economic warfare . . . and there, they're winning.*

She heard the *crumpcrumpcrump* of an old-fashioned anti-aircraft gun, pulled out of mothballs. A few more of the relics soon joined in. She was pretty sure they were firing only to bolster the morale of the people of the city; the gliders almost always came in so low that machine guns had a much better chance. They even occasionally got one to crash or detonate prematurely.

Campbell shrugged with a mix of indifference to the small risk of the bombs and impatience at the long delay as her untraceable tablet pulled up another site that concerned itself with ship spotting. It seemed almost an exercise in futility. *There are tens of thousands of merchant ships on this planet, almost none of them traceable, and I don't even have a good description—nor even a likely name—of the one I am looking for. All I know is it's a freighter, within a couple of thousand tons of twenty thousand. It's not a lot to go on, really. The only Cochinese who would talk to me was a security guard who didn't have detailed knowledge of the sea or of ships. He didn't even know the difference between a Ro-Ro and a break bulk. He could only tell me how much of the dock it took up, and about how wide it was. And some of what it took on, too, of course. The twenty thousand, give or take, tons, is just my best guess. Has to be my best guess, because if I go to the Navy and ask they just might figure out why I want to know. Or get suspicious enough to try, anyway.*

Oh, and the guard could also tell me that many, many large rockets disappeared into it. I am sure there were other people who knew a lot more, but if one of them spoke English or French I never found him. And using a local translator is what we call a bad idea in general.

In her search for the ship, Campbell had started with the obvious stuff. She didn't really expect it to work; nobody had even noted the ship leaving harbor, but, *I'd have felt bloody fucking stupid if I hadn't looked and later found it had been there all along.*

That having failed, she was using a combination of "Bronze Bild," a Sachsen image matching program, several ship-watching sites, and an intelligence program for sorting data. Those had narrowed the field down to, *Oh, call it about five thousand ships that could be it. Five thousand . . . shit.*

She had worked with those for several hours, feeling no closer to her goal at the end than she had in the beginning, *Or even in Cochin, for that matter. This is hopeless for one girl on her own. A couple score could work through the problem in a few days, I imagine, but I cannot risk that many people suspecting. I can't even risk Turenge knowing. Those spacesuits . . .*

So what else might work? How about if I look into known Balboan contacts, formerly used ports, and sources

*of supply? Well, start on that one tomorrow night, since I
can only duck out of the office occasionally during a duty
day, while Janier is still—pretty reasonably, in my humble
opinion—stressing himself into an early grave over trying
to clear the port of Cristobal while not really knowing
what's behind him.*

The ancient anti-aircraft guns cut out, which cease-fire
was followed by a substantial boom, surprisingly close.
The large plate glass window rattled but held.

Leaving the few small coins that constituted her
change next to the cup, Jan got up and left. She supposed,
in retrospect, that while ignoring the incoming bomb, in
general, was sound, given the odds, staying in a place with
a plate glass window, which would have made even a fairly
distant miss potentially quite deadly, was *dumb as shit.
Note to self, new coffee shop tomorrow.*

The new Defense Agency Headquarters wasn't far.
Rather than calling for a taxi or for her usual driver, she
decided to walk it. *And besides, if someone gets inquisitive
about my whereabouts, I'd rather not give them a coffee
shop's account and records to check.*

As she walked, she passed several shipping containers,
sandbagged against blast and fragments, plopped down
wherever there might be space. They served as convenient,
cheap, and, once reinforced, reasonably effective bomb
shelters. The sandbag layers appeared to be about half a
meter deep, on all sides, but heavier on top. More sandbags
formed dog-legged entrances, sheltered against fragments
but a little precarious for the blast from a near miss.

As the all-clear sirens sounded, people began to
emerge, frightened and shaking from the experience. A

few looked at her as if she were a madwoman, or too stupid to take shelter. Her own face didn't show her feelings. *Pussies, the odds of getting killed or even hurt were small. Stay at your jobs. More people are being hurt by stampedes than by the bombings.*

A bit closer to the agency headquarters, she came to a still smoking crater and a number of burning cars. People were coming out from a brace of shelters, on opposite sides of the street, not too far away from the crater. Some wept. A few staggered. There were even a couple of people bleeding from superficial wounds. All looked to be in shock. Jan's face remained impassive and indifferent.

That is, Jan's face remained impassive while taking in the mice who walked like men, scurrying away. She looked back at the shelters though, and suddenly smiled. Turning, she walked to the dog-legged entrance to one, the sandbags of the leg, itself, having been knocked over. She looked inside. *No bodies. Not even one.*

She recalled seeing a largish number of shipping containers during her brief captivity in Balboa. Then she called up the memory of some intelligence reports she'd seen.

Twenty-five to thirty good-sized freighters came to Balboa between the invasions, not counting the ones we know were late contracts to bring in non-military, or at least not obviously military, supplies. Twelve were container ships, ten as big as would fit the country's transitway and the other two ultramaxes carrying over seven thousand twelve-meter containers each. At least forty thousand prefabricated bunkers, anyone? Yes, about that many; they came in full and we know they left empty.

I think the general needs to know that, whatever the flyboys are telling him, losses-wise the aerial campaign probably counts as "mere" in the Balboan ledgers.

Campbell continued on her way. When she reached the Defense Agency headquarters and her own office, a message was waiting for her from Janier. It seemed he was most unhappy with the performance of Claudio Marciano and wanted her to go see what was going on in war-torn Santa Josefina, with an eye toward getting Marciano recalled.

"This kind of thing is hardly my purview," she'd wired back. "I'm intelligence, but not a head hunter."

His prompt response had been, "We're bleeding like stuck pigs trying to take the port of Cristobal, nobody more so than your own boys. I know Marciano needs more men but they aren't available. I need someone there who will hang on until the war here is over. I know you're intelligence, but more importantly you're *intelligent*. So go either make sense to Marciano or get me grounds to remove him."

Hmmm . . . when he puts it that way. And it can't be too difficult for Stuart-Mansfield to get me press credentials. I just hope there's nobody in our contingent in Santa Josefina who knows me . . . in any sense.

Headquarters, Task Force Jesuit, Nacientes, Santa Josefina

The old base at Rio Clara had been abandoned and

burned over the course of several days. The new one wasn't much yet beyond tents and some motor pool areas, barbed wire, a defensive berm, and a bunch of radio antennae. To Jan Campbell it seemed almost homelike.

Campbell's trip had been considerably less stressful than Aragon's in either direction. Armed with credentials—*and, my, wasn't that quick?*—and authorized to fly military as an ostensible civilian, she gone in directly to Julio Asunción Airport on a Castilian medical flight. A half hour of talking to Rall and del Collea later by the main map—Marciano was too busy to bother—and she'd messaged Turenge to forward to Janier, "He has no choice. If he doesn't either get more force or shorten his lines, Task Force Jesuit won't last ten days longer. If that happens the equivalent of a very large and unusually powerful division, plus more than a corps of what amounts to home guard, will descend on the Zhong from the east. After that, they won't even be able to give a pretense of fixing any of Carrera's legions, all of which will then be free to face you."

Janier's response, in turn, was pithy. "*Merde.*"

Jan almost echoed that sentiment, "Shit," when she first caught sight of the black uniformed girl hanging around the headquarters and occasionally consulting with Marciano or one or both of his two chief assistants. *I'm as straight as they come,* thought Campbell, *but if I did prefer girls, that would be the kind of girl I'd prefer to prefer.* That was her first thought. Her second came as a surprise. *Crap, I missed the uniform. She's one of them, the Earthers. She knows their ships. It's things like this that* so *complicate the case for the nonexistence of God.*

Bide my time a bit, yes, but I need to talk to her.

Jan's chance came the better part of a day later, at early breakfast in the officers' mess, of which she'd been made a courtesy member. She very rarely heard her native accent in her thoughts but in this case, *Bludy bastards just like 'avin' me tits around.*

Seeing Esma alone, she sat down opposite her at a square folding table. Fortunately, she'd picked up enough Spanish in Balboa to get by, as well as enough to avoid her own thick accent in her own tongue.

"Do you mind, miss?" Campbell asked.

Esma, shy as was often the case, just quietly shook her head in the negative.

"Thank you," Jan said. "I couldn't help but notice you and your uniform. You're with the Peace Fleet, yes?"

Swallowing to clear her unreliable throat, Esma answered, "Yes; I work for the high admiral. Ensign Miranda," she added, holding out her hand.

"Jan Campbell," Jan answered, shaking the girl's hand in an informal and friendly way. "*Daily Post.*"

There had been some question over using her real name but, as Stuart-Mansfield had pointed out, if she was recognized under her own name, "Oh, I left the army and am working for the *Daily Post*," was a lot less suspicious than, "Oh, I left the Army, went to court to change my name, and now work for the *Daily Post*." She'd considered and rejected herself the other possible line, "Well, I got married." She wasn't the type to give up her own name for anybody.

"You work for the high admiral in an office of some kind or more . . . directly?" Jan quizzed.

"Pretty direct," Esma said. "I'm detached as an observer—officially I'm an observer—to General Marciano. Normally though I'm somewhere between a cabin girl and an aide de camp."

"Ah . . . well . . . in that case, you're going to know a lot of things you have no business telling me or anyone else. Okay, Jan, no pumping the girl for operational information."

That got a laugh from the girl. "Thank you," she said.

"But can I pump you about some things that aren't secret? You can tell me to butt out any time but . . . well . . . I've been in love with the idea of space travel, travelling to new worlds, since I was a little girl. Can you *please* tell me what it's like to live, work, and travel on a starship?"

My, thought Jan, as she digested the information she'd gained, *wasn't that a lovely little intelligence gathering cum interrogation session? So, yes, the space suits are for an assault on the ship, either from outside entirely or from a possibly unpressurized hangar deck. No air on that latter if the captain doesn't want there to be. So now the question is, how the hell do they get from the planet's surface to the ship, whichever ship they're targeting, in orbit?*

It's possible, I suppose, that they have only an intent, but not a real plan. I could see them buying the suits against the chance of someday being able to launch a ship

*of their own, or capture one from the Peace Fleet. On the
other hand, those suits cost a lot of money. Something I
think people miss about Carrera; he looks like he spends
like the prodigal son, but he's cheap as dirt as an
instinctive matter. He'd not have spent the money if he
didn't have a plan and either the means or a way to get
the means.*

"And *that* means . . ." She gave a long, eloquent whistle.

*That ship; it's going to get him the means to get into
space.*

*And how do I actually feel about that? Do I care a fig
for Old Earth? Not a bit of it. Are they our allies, to whom
I owe some kind of duty? Not remotely, they've been using
us and our soldiers like cheap whores. Win or lose on the
ground in Balboa, is my country hurt by the Earthpigs
being hurt or even destroyed? No; no, it will all be done
one way or another, and independently of what happens
here.*

*So fuck 'em, the arrogant pricks; we're all better off
with them out of the picture.*

Julio Asunción Airport, Aserri, Santa Josefina

"Better than nothing, I suppose," said Rall, as five new
battalions, two gendarmie from Gaul, two carabinieri from
Tuscany, and a battalion of police from Sachsen formed
up in ranks on the tarmac outside the cargo airship that
had brought them. From behind the airship light armored
vehicles, wheeled for the most part, disgorged themselves.
A number of helicopters, partially disassembled and

mounted on rollable frames, came out the rear ramp as well.

"The Tuscans and Gauls are better than regular infantry," del Collea corrected. "I know you Sachsens don't have them, nor anything like them, but these guys, a mix of policeman and light infantry in their organization, training, and equipment, are the best, just the best, for guerilla suppression and rear area security."

"One battalion to embassy security," commanded Marciano. "We'll rotate them in and out for a rest. For the other four, send them to the assembly area for the troops we're going to launch at the fuckers who attacked the embassies. Let's see how that one battalion likes dealing with seven. With artillery.

"Rall?"

"General?"

"Curb your prejudices and think of these men as professional light infantry with some additional skills."

"Yes, sir. I'll try, sir."

"General, we've got a breathing space now," del Collea said. "Instead of attacking into about half a vacuum I'd suggest putting the gendarmes and carabinieri into intelligence gathering, en masse, so when we strike we hit something. We probably only need to keep one infantry battalion for that; the rest can reoccupy our old positions to the northwest."

Marciano thought about that for a while, eyes squinting against the sun but focused on the lean, sunburned, and tough faces of the new arrivals.

"They are pretty good at that kind of thing, aren't they? All right, we can do that now. And set me up a meeting with the commanders of all five new battalions; I learned a lot about guerilla suppression in Pashtia from Carrera and I would like—oh, I *so* would like—to pass some of those lessons on."

"Yes, sir."

"And Stefano?"

"Sir?"

"Send a case of wine from the officers' mess—no; instead make it my personal stock—direct to Janier. The frog son of a bitch went way out on a limb for us this time and deserves a reward."

CHAPTER EIGHTEEN

"There are no absolute rules of conduct, either in peace or war. Everything depends on circumstances."
—Leon Trotsky

Internment Area, Puerto Bruselas, Santa Josefina

In the shadow of the aircraft carrier *Dos Lindas*, stood two men in the denim uniform of local security guards. The senior of the two, sometimes called "Centurion Mora," was unarmed. The junior, Sanchez, was armed only with a shotgun. Both watched the newly arrived Taurans fanning out to take up positions all around the shoreline.

Said Centurion Mora, "Colonel Nguyen told my class that it was the police, not enemy infantry, artillery, or tanks, that were the most dangerous opponents of the revolution."

Sanchez nodded, slightly. "Not immediately; for a little while they'll be in the dark."

"But only a little while," Mora added. "We see them so often directing traffic that we forget too readily that police

331

are, in good part, intelligence gathering organizations. And I wonder how much intelligence they already have. Do you think they know we're actually part of the resistance, operating under the cover of idiot law?"

"Yes," said Sanchez, pointing with his chin. "And I think they're coming to arrest us now. Fight?"

Mora looked at a small column of uniformed Taurans, maybe in platoon strength, marching toward them, rifles held in front of their chests at port arms.

Weighing the impossible odds, Mora commanded, "No, don't fight. Bluff, lie, whatever it takes. But I think we're going to be out of work for a while."

He pulled out his cell phone, pressed a few buttons to dial up his platoon sergeant, and then, after a brief pause, said the word, "*Conejo*," or rabbit. That was the code to get low and in the shadows and hide for a while.

"Oh, well," said Mora, "we had a pretty good run for a while."

"Yeah," agreed Sanchez. "You know, those guys give off the feel of a real force, one that acts like an infantry company because they live like an infantry company. I wonder how many units like that the Taurans have."

"No clue, but it's a good question. Unfortunately . . ."

Mora shut up as the approaching Tauran column halted about ten meters away. Their leader then gave a command. The leading man on the right of the column stepped out, gave a command of his own, and then nine men fixed their bayonets. On a second command they rushed the two "guards."

The Taurans formed a ring about Mora and Sanchez, most leveling their bayonetted rifles menacingly. Two, however, took ostentatiously careful aim. Their leader stepped past the ring, snatched Sanchez's shotgun, and announced, in very badly accented Spanish, "I am *Vice Brigadiere* Martone and you two shits are under arrest."

Nacientes Internment Camp, Santa Josefina

With Task Force Jesuit rolling forward to reoccupy their previous positions to the south and northwest, Marciano decided that part of the never completed and not yet abandoned headquarters camp would, with the addition of some towers and barbed wire, make a fine holding pen for the guerillas and their sympathizers being rounded up daily. The president of the country, Calderon, of course, objected, as did any number of human rights lawyers and other very sensitive and caring people.

Sister Mary Magdalene of *Pax Vobiscum* was one such. Sadly for the cause of human rights, the Gallic gendarmes were not cut from the same cloth as the usual Gauls she, Father Segundo, and their organization normally dealt with. Indeed, the entire organization, already under deferred sentence of death in Balboa, was picked up within the space of a dozen hours, each member being handed a plastic cup and bowl, as well as a spoon, before being unceremoniously pushed behind the wire.

Along with *Pax Vobiscum* went into the holding pen some seventeen human rights lawyers, thirty-one peace activists from the Federated States, fourteen Santa Josefinan police, including the president's military advisor, Lieutenant Blanco, and, to date, two hundred and seventy-one previously clandestine members of Second Cohort, *Tercio Le Virgen*.

All were subject to considerable interrogation by men and women who were, unlike most military interrogators, long service professionals of vast training, considerable experience, and no little skill.

"Well, of course you can be hanged or shot," said Adjutant de Gaullejac to Corporal Sanchez. She was tall and slender, sexy in her own way, albeit no longer young.

"We know your unit was involved in the terrorist attacks on the embassies. We even know which embassy you, personally, were involved in attacking. Tsk." That was a lie, of course, but it would suggest to the captive that someone in his group had already broken, and he couldn't refute it by asking "which one" because that would be an admission of guilt for someone. "We both know your people murdered several hundred innocent civilians. As part of those organizations, as a co-conspirator, you're as guilty as any man who pulled a trigger. You'll get a trial, of course, but don't expect it to be much. And—exigencies of war and all—you won't get an appeal and your execution won't be advertised in time for anyone to make a deal for you."

Sanchez sat quietly defiant. He didn't feel like a hero, but he was pretty sure he could keep faith at least until the hot pincers came out. He felt his resolve weaken a bit as he heard the faint commands and rattle of musketry that suggested an execution.

"Can't you give me *something*, Corporal, anything I can use in your defense? It's so goddammned silly for a young man like yourself, with a full life of peace ahead of him, to be butchered and shoveled into an unmarked, lye-filled grave. And for what? We've come in in strength now, and to win. Your death will be meaningless, especially since no one who matters to you will ever even know."

That got to him more than the next rattle of musketry. *I've been a good soldier since I joined up. But to be shot like an animal, extinguished like a cockroach . . . there are limits on what I am prepared to endure. But what can I give that I can in good conscience give? I don't know much. I don't know, for example, where the embassy folk we took prisoner are being held. I don't know exactly why the Duque came here, though it must be . . . ah . . . maybe that.*

"Carrera was here, you know, Ma'am," Sanchez said. "Supposedly he had to have a meeting with someone. I don't know who. And even if I was involved in the attack on the Earthpigs' embassy . . ."

Esma overheard Rall say to del Collea, "Now, isn't that interesting? One woman got all that from one of them and that quickly."

"I told you they were good," said del Collea. "Better than we are for a lot of things. Still, fascinating; I wonder who Carrera was here to meet."

Since she knew who, Esmeralda Miranda felt a sudden rise in blood pressure. *Oh, no; they're going to find out it was me and then . . .*

"And the dumb ass who told us that also told us that he, personally, was involved in the Earth embassy massacre."

"Well, he was only a corporal," Rall said, "You can't expect too much."

Oh, shit; what if the corporal knows why . . . who . . . me? Well . . . I do have an excuse, if it comes to that. Esma's hand instinctively stroked the pistol loaned her by Marciano.

Leaving the soon-to-be-abandoned command post—the radiomen were already dismantling it in part—Esma made her way to the prisoner's compound. The interrogation cells stood well away from the wire. These were field expedients, a couple of soundproofed six-meter shipping containers helicoptered in for the purpose.

But it has to look right. I can't just walk in and shoot somebody looking like somebody trying to tie up a loose end. I have to look furious, bestial, beyond reason, inhuman.

She waited, watching for a while, until one of the containers opened up. From it emerged two men, one in civil dress and the other in the field uniform of a Gallic Gendarme. With their departure, that container was empty. *So it's the other one.*

It's me or him, Esma told herself. For a moment she thought about shooting the interrogator and the captive, both, but then realized, *No, he can't have grabbed the interrogator's gun and shot him or her, and then me shot him, because I have those different rounds, "frangible," Bertholdo called them, that the interrogator is unlikely to have. Oh, well, "simple is best," as someone told me.*

She put on the very bestial and enraged face she knew she'd need for her after-the-event excuse. She was a little surprised to find her emotional state changing to match her face. She then stormed to the metal door. There, she eased the door open and stepped inside. She carefully half-closed the metal door behind her.

The prisoner, unbound and sitting in a chair, looked like he could have been a cousin from back home. "Well, no, I don't know, as I said. I did hear a rumor . . ." He shut up and looked up when he saw Esma framed for a moment in the light of the cracked open door.

The interrogator, a tall woman Esma hadn't noticed in the camp before, noticed Sanchez looking at the door, then turned and began to ask, "Who are . . ."

Esma drew her loaned pistol and screamed at the top of her lungs, "For murdering my friend!" Then she took aim and fired three shots at Sanchez, two of which hit. She fired so quickly that the chair was only a quarter tipped over before she ceased fire.

"He murdered my friend," she explained, to the interrogator, chin lifting and her voice infused with a surreal calm. The interrogator had her hands raised over her head.

"Justice is done."

So that's how someone commits murder for a cause or to protect themselves. It isn't as hard as I thought.

Café de Flore, Lumière, Gaul

Mission in Santa Josefina more or less accomplished, Jan had ducked back to Gaul on the first thing smoking. Stuart-Mansfield had been a help there, too. Once home, she'd begun a hunt for a safer venue for her research. It seemed that the plate glass windows fronting coffee shops were inevitable. At least, Jan hadn't been able to find a place without one. *Is there some kind of unwritten rule? Is it the Gallic penchant for girl watching? Clearly, some other kind of venue is needed, eventually.*

Window or not, she'd had an idea before being sent to Santa Josefina that needed exploration. The ship she wanted had disappeared from Cochin as completely as something could disappear. *Even if we had the satellite imagery for the last couple of years, we—at least I—don't have the manpower to check it. I doubt even the Peace Fleet does.*

So let's jump ahead, way ahead. Any troops that are going to get on that assault transport probably—no, certainly—came from Balboa. Carrera will use his allies, as long as they're being watched, and under supervision of people he does trust, but everything we can see of how they've been parceled out says he doesn't trust them out of view. So, there are a few ways to see who's left Balboa.

She went to satellite views of the airships Balboa had used mostly for the purpose of moving—*there they are again*—shipping containers and other supplies from the two ports to the area between them. From Balboa, some had picked up humanitarian supplies and women and very young children and moved them to various spots around Colombia Latina. Some of the children weren't all that young. She tracked something over one hundred such humanitarian flights before giving that up as a bad use of her increasingly limited time.

Okay, maybe he moved some of his cadets out that way. But the numbers are too small and the total numbers moved by air not much cover. And there really weren't that many cadets to move. On the other hand, my Volgan reporter reports that not only are one of the two heavy Balboan legions made up almost entirely of cadets and Young Scouts, but they have expanded all the cadet regiments with massive numbers of Young Scouts and placed those regiments throughout their entire force.

Jan began to say, "There ought to . . . ," when she realized that there *was* a law and Carrera simply ignored it, as he tended to ignore every aspect of law of war that was Kosmo-man-made rather than common law.

Okay, so I can't judge based on numbers or bodily size. Let's try another tack.

It was difficult for her to say, initially, which of the ships that pulled into Balboan ports during the truce between invasions was a long term hide for major equipment and which was a late negotiated contract for non-military supplies. As she reviewed older satellite imagery, though, something became quite obvious.

Tanks and infantry fighting vehicles don't just materialize on a Ro-Ro overnight. They were bought, loaded, and stored against the day, long, long ago.

But that was only a few. There were more Ro-Ros that were in regular service but broke their contracts, off-loaded their civilian cargos, and picked up whole motor pools of less obviously military equipment before delivering it to Balboa.

No matter, no matter; they all came to Balboa and dropped off equipment and supplies and, in a few cases, formed battalions and brigades of other Latins come to help their brothers.

Where did they go from there?

Hmmm . . . a number of them went for additional cargos. Some went back into commercial service. But . . . aha . . . there's one off the coast of Valparaiso . . . a number of them carried civilians to refugee camps out of harm's way to both coasts of Colombia del Norte and Colombia Central. Interesting—and we should have picked it up— that none of them went to Santa Josefina. I suppose Carrera already had that war well thought-out.

So, let's track one.

Jan followed the progress of one such ship, the MV *Leaping Maiden*, from Balboa to Valdivia, where she disgorged what had to be twenty-five thousand people.

She fiddled some more with her, as far as she could tell, untraceable tablet. "Hmmm . . . let's fast forward a bit . . . yes, right about two thousand tents so something like twenty-five thousand people. Maybe a bit less. Okay . . . now what?"

She was disappointed to discover that "what," in this case, was the *Leaping Maiden* disappearing into the stream of commerce, with nothing further to do with the Balboan war or humanitarian efforts. At least, there was nothing obviously to do with either.

Bastards.

Nonetheless, a number of freighters—seven, she thought, though the shell game being played meant it could have been twice that—did continue plying those coasts, bringing supplies to the refugee camps.

And then, at the port of Saavedra, Valdivia, she spotted something odd. This was a ship, maybe a little larger than some so engaged, disgorging humanitarian supplies but also apparently picking up some. *Okay, well maybe they made a mistake and sent too many widgets to Saavedra and not enough to wherever. Buuut . . . the loading in both directions is being done by* . . . she dialed back her tablet in time and tracked a convoy of some common trucks carrying what were probably boys to the port from a refugee camp. There was enough detail to count twenty-five heads per truck, and sixteen trucks in the convoy.

"But fast forward, shall we, lass?"

The same sixteen trucks left late that same day, but she counted only fifteen heads per, back in the cargo area.

"Bingo!" *I have the ship. Now let's see where else they've been and where they are now.*

MV *ALTA*, Mar Furioso

Along with a number of other uncanny abilities, the woman Alena, so-called, "the witch," could generally find Hamilcar Carrera whenever she wanted to, provided he was within half a mile or so. She didn't know how she did it either, but ever since she had decided that the boy, then about three years old, was her people's long-awaited savior and god, Iskandr, the two had been linked by an almost psychic bond.

She found him this time on the missile deck, the place where the Cochinese shipyard had installed seventy-three fourteen-tube, long-range rocket launchers in the five-hundred-and-fifty-pound warhead range. They'd only put in the tubes and the elevating and traversing mechanisms; the trucks that normally carried them had been outfitted with dummies made of painted tree trunks and parked somewhere to rot in Cochin's sweltering climate.

Reaching Ham, sitting on one of the tube assemblies and contemplating another, she started to do full proskynesis.

Ham held up his hand to stop her. "Please don't, Alena; you know I neither like it nor need it."

The woman stopped about halfway to her knees and went back to a full upright position. Alena was a princess, more or less, of a barbarian people who traced their culture and their genes back to Old Earth's Afghanistan and, pushing far enough back, the army of Alexander the Great. She was completely pagan, as well, but her people retained, as a general rule, the nobler aspects of paganism, and none of the cobbled together scraps of paganism that had Old Earth's Orthodox Druids and neo-Azteca Nanauatli murdering the innocent to appease gods they themselves rarely believed in.

"You should not wander off, Iskandr, without telling Legate Johnson where you are going. This ship is a dangerous place and he worries."

"Did he send you to find me?" Ham asked.

"No, he just wondered where you were, aloud, and I took it upon myself to find you. Don't ask why; you already know: because this ship is dangerous and *I* worry."

"Ah, but if I am, as you insist, a god, my mother in all but womb, how can anything here hurt me?"

"The original Iskandr was a god, too," the woman said, "and yet he was done to death, and his people—my people and yours—were deprived of him for almost three thousand years, possibly by a lousy mosquito. You owe it to us, this time, to be more careful.

"What, by the way, did you come *here* for? This place is as alive as a tomb."

"I realized that we made a mistake, and possibly a disastrous one."

"Your father, even if he is not a god, like you, doesn't make many mistakes that I have seen."

"I'm not sure it was him, or, if it was, that it was something a non-naval man who is also not an artilleryman could be expected to have seen. And maybe it was just unavoidable."

"And that mistake was?" she asked.

"All of these rockets fire only in one direction, to the left, or 'port,' as the swabbies would say. That means a long slow turn to put us in position to fire, or going to the other side of the target than we'd planned on. I suspect there's a possibility that we'll have to keep turning as we fire to take out enough for a window into the target."

"Have you brought your concerns to Legate Johnson?"

"No, no yet. I wanted to see if I could come up with a solution."

"And have you?"

He shook his head regretfully. "No."

Alena's voice took on a note of concern. "Will we fail because of it? Will you be endangered?"

"Probably not, for either," Ham said, "though probably doesn't mean certainly."

Ham hesitated, a gesture Alena was sure to catch.

"Yes, Iskandr?"

"I heard the news about the embassy attacks in Santa Josefina, and about the massacres during them. Do you suppose it's all true? Did my father order it?"

Alena didn't hesitate. "Of course, he knew and, if he didn't order it, it was certainly the kind of thing he might order. He is a ruthless man, your father, and bent on winning and bending the worlds to his will."

"Hajar," said Ham, distantly and softly. Hajar was a city—had been a city—in Yithrab. Hamilcar's father had destroyed it, he was sure.

"Yes," said Alena, "Hajar. You do know . . . ?"

"Yes, I know. And I know I may end up doing the same thing at our target's capital."

"You may," she said. "And like your father's ruthlessness in launching a war in Santa Josefina, launching it and carrying it on, you must be ruthless."

"If I am a god by your people's reasoning, Alena, is my father, as well?"

"No . . . no; I'm afraid your father isn't human enough at the core to be a god."

**Headquarters Task Force Jesuit,
Rio Clara, Santa Josefina**

Marciano was livid. If looks could burn, the scrunched-up piece of paper in his left hand would have gone *poof* in an instant.

"God*damn* it!" he shouted, loud enough for the gate sentries to blanche. "And Goddamn that frog bastard, Janier, too! We finally, *finally* start to make a little progress here and he orders four of the five battalions we were sent as reinforcements to Balboa! Now fucking what?"

"We comply," said Rall, with an indifferent shrug. "But since the battalion he's not taking is the Sachsen battalion of police, we put them on embassy duty and continue with what we were doing before the attacks.

"Besides, he's right, you know. If we can hang on here long enough for him to win there we'll eventually have a quarter of a million men at our disposal."

"Traitor," said Marciano, but without any heat. "Fine. Send the word to the troops moving on the guerilla base to hold positions, then get them back to where they were before everything started to look like it was coming apart."

"And it isn't a total loss, anyway, General. We've now got about a thousand guerillas, sympathizers, and general troublemakers locked up behind wire. We won't have the problems with rear area security we did before, either."

"Color me skeptical," said the general.

Rall forced a true shit-eating grin. "*Ja* . . . there's a hearing tomorrow concerning our right to keep our prisoners, too, so . . . maybe we'll see our efforts undone there, as well."

"Goddamn it."

"And speaking of that," piped in del Collea, "what are we to do with the charming and lovely, but, as it turns out, high strung and murderous Ensign Miranda?"

"We're going to do exactly nothing," said Marciano. "I'm not even going to reclaim my pistol. The interrogator was quite certain that he was involved in the attack on her embassy, hence responsible for the murder of her friend. I think no court-martial we could empanel would convict her for doing what every man in the task force would love to have done for himself.

"And besides . . . I need her for the intelligence we get from the peace fleet."

Global Court of Justice, Binnenhof, Haarlem

Johannes Litten and Beate Heinrich kept their seats while their colleague, Karlie Kipping, summed up the argument for the current issue. This concerned the illegal imprisonment, without trial, of Santa Josefinans, and Tauran and Federated States civilians, who were currently languishing in durance vile, "contrary to the laws of war as they currently exist," insisted Kipping, "and contrary to interplanetary human rights law." The current motion had been appended to the earlier one, designed to stop the destruction of the rain forest.

She flipped a page on the folder in front of her. "The law is settled, Your Honors, with the entirety of United Earth, and the overwhelming majority of nations on Terra Nova having agreed to the ancient codicil to the law of land warfare, Protocol Additional One to Geneva Convention Four, concerning wars of an international character, must be considered customary law of war. As such, it is binding upon all states and parties to such conflicts."

Kipping looked up from the paper to gauge the faces of the bank of judges. *Ah, good; with me so far.*

"Of course, there was no question that it is binding upon the Tauran Union forces in Santa Josefina, as every armed force there aligned against the freedom fighters is from the Tauran Union. Let there, therefore, be no claim that either the Protocol is non-binding nor that this court lacks jurisdiction.

"To the particulars. Per paragraph fifty-one, section three, civilians remain civilians, for all and any times they are not actively engaged in hostilities. As civilians, they are entitled to all the protections of civilians caught in a war zone. Per paragraph seventy-five, section three, those persons being held are entitled to be informed of the charges against them, to a speedy trial, or to be released post-haste . . ."

Assembly Area Maria, Santa Josefina, not far from Hephaestos, Balboa

It had been a bad few weeks for the *Tercio la Virgen*. With so many better armed Tauran units freed up from nonsense missions and with their rear areas secure for a change, it had been all Villalobos could do to escape with his regiment and some of their new recruits. Casualties on the long route back to their base had been non-trivial.

Fucking Taurans can do okay when they're given half a chance, can't they? thought Villalobos, huddling in about as deep a shelter as his men had been able to dig before moving on San Jaba. The ground shook and rocked with the impact of aerially delivered Tauran bombs, even as dirt and sand filtered down between the logs used for the overhead cover.

The falling clods and clouds reminded Villalobos, not that he needed reminding, that, *God, getting killed is one thing, but* please *don't let me get buried alive down here. I'm not afraid of much but I am* so *afraid of that.*

Sometimes, particular near misses had set not just some of the other denizens of the shelter, but Villalobos, himself, to vomiting. The place reeked or, rather, *It would reek except we've been hiding here long enough to get used to it. We've been—hey, what was that?*

What "that" was took Villalobos long minutes to recognize. When he did he turned to a private, ghastly pale even in the dim artificial light, and asked, "When's the last time we didn't hear at least a plane overhead?"

For the first time, also, in several days, an antania stuck its head out of its nest to cry out, *mnnbt, mnnbt, mnnbt.*

"Been a couple of days, sir," gulped the private.

"Yeah . . . at least a couple of days. Hold the fort here; I'm heading to the command post."

Stepping over men still lying prone or sitting against the bunker walls, Villalobos made his way to the entrance, a zigzagging cutout through the earth itself. Hesitantly, ready to race back inside should he hear another attacking aircraft or falling bomb, he stuck his head out into daylight. Indeed, it was an unusual degree of daylight for this spot because so many trees had been bombed to splinters and so much damage done to the thick canopy that had been overhead.

He looked up and saw a good deal of sunlight peeking through the gaps in the trees. The whole area reeked with the smell of explosives, the fumes of which, *Come to think of it, are not all that safe to breathe.* Villalobos put on his gas mask and continued outside.

His operations officer had been killed in the long

retreat so he'd promoted Tribune Madrigal into the position. It was an easy pick since most of Madrigal's maniple of *Cazadores* had also been lost covering the retreat.

That same tribune met him at the top of the entranceway. Somehow, he was enduring the fumes from the bombing without his mask.

"Sir," he said, "you're not going to believe this, but the Tauran Union's Global Court of Justice has issued two injunctions. They're forbidden from bombing the rain forest"—Madrigal looked up and scanned for a bit—"or whatever's left of it. And they have to release our people they've been holding."

"Holy shit." Villalobos paused briefly, then said, "You know, Madrigal, it's things like this that really complicate the case for atheism."

CHAPTER NINETEEN

"The secret of all victory lies in the organization of the non-obvious."
—Marcus Aurelius

Field Tactical Operation Center, Task Force Jesuit

"You know something, Stefano?" Marciano said to del Collea.

"What's that, sir?" asked del Collea, as he pored over his map, looking for a place to make a stand, at least for a while.

"Weeks like this complicate the issue of religious faith *enormously*."

"Yes, sir," del Collea agreed, without really having heard a word. "Sir, I think we can gain at least a day or two, or probably even three, on our retreat by taking up a line running from Cerro Presinger, northeast for about fifteen kilometers, then curving around, following the river, above Zeledón. We can refuse outright flank for a good distance." With a couple of invisible ovals, del Collea also showed the prospective battle positions—defensive positions, in fact and practice—the battalions would take up.

"Let me see," Marciano said, unconsciously straining his neck to look over del Collea's shoulder. The junior officer twisted his body to bring the map around, then used a sharp piece of plastic, the cap for a pen, to show the trace he had in mind.

Marciano whistled, softly. "That's a long line to try to hold with what amounts to a reinforced brigade, Stefano."

"We've discussed it before, sir, months ago. It's the last position we can hold that covers both the main highway to the capital and the branch that runs to the coast and then to the port. I'd say we should stay here as long as we can—forever, if we could—but, of course, the guerillas will feel us out within a few days and within a couple of days after that they'll be probing into the gap between Cerro Presinger and the town.

"Risky? Sir, we're so fucked if we don't take chances that they'd have to come up with a whole new way of saying it; 'fucked' just wouldn't be strong enough anymore."

Marciano was plainly thinking about the risks. "They can still use the coastal road, Highway 43, from Balboa, you know, Stefano."

"Yes, sir, but they have three problems with that. The first one is that not one fucking meter of that road is through the ever-so-important rain forest, so we can bomb the shit out of them if they try. The second is that if they do try to use it in any substantial way they're risking being outflanked or defeated in detail. The third is that we can get the Zhong to send a couple of destroyers to make using the coastal road an iffy proposition, too. And, sir, those Zhong destroyers include some old three-turret jobs with half a dozen five-inch guns. They can't stop the guerillas from using the road, but they can make it painful if they do."

"I'm surprised the Zhong have any ships to spare after the beating their navy took from the Balboans."

"These are ex-Federated States ships, sir, given to Ming Zhong Guo during the Great Global War. They were as fast then as anything steaming, and as fast, or faster, as most destroyers now. But they're old and tired. Engines worn, aching for a refit. In any event, they needed a minor refit before they could put to sea," said del Collea. "They weren't there for the ass whipping. And they'll be along in a couple of days."

"Ummm . . . I may not want to know the answer to this, but how did you arrange for a couple of Zhong destroyers?"

"Esmeralda, sir. She felt so bad about her little bout of irrationality with that prisoner that she begged for some way to make it up to us. As it turns out, the Zhong Empress is the High Admiral's lover, so our Esma asked the High Admiral who asked the Empress. Sir, that little brown beauty is worth her weight in gold, you know?"

Marciano rather agreed, but couldn't quite say so since the girl was, after all, a murderess.

"And better," continued del Collea, "since the Zhong ships need never touch land, this remains a Tauran Union mission."

"Okay, we'll do this," agreed Marciano, "but with two

modifications. One is—I don't care much where they come from but get me half a dozen Mandarin speakers. If necessary recruit them locally. They get attached to a platoon of Commandos and outpost the road to call in fire from the destroyers. Secondly, take one company from the battalion around Cerro Presinger and put it to block Highway 43, here"—Marciano took del Collea's bit of plastic to point—"at the bridge over the Rio Bravo, near the intersection with Highway 342. In effect, there'll be four companies on the line around Zeledón, with one company in reserve. Lastly, send the rest of the commandos to patrol the gap between our forces at Zeledón and Cerro Presinger."

"Yes, sir. I'll make it happen."

"One other thing, Stefano; get a deep recon team to look at their base near Jaba. I know we can't attack it but, precisely because of that, I expect interesting things to happen there."

Sethlans, Santa Josefina

Tauran aircraft circled overhead, less like scavenging vultures than like hungry raptors, looking for an easy snack.

Villalobos had, to his regret, learned the hard way that injunctions from some Kosmo human rights or environmentalist court were always going to be as narrowly interpreted as possible by the typically anti-Kosmo military. In this case, if they couldn't bomb near the ever-so-blessed rain forest they would double up their efforts on anything they could see that wasn't in the rain forest. Unfortunately, there was barely a trace of jungle within ten kilometers to either side of Highway 1.

Villalobos shivered still when he remembered one of his maniples—he was slightly ashamed of his own sense of relief that it was mostly composed of fairly new recruits—approaching the town of Ojochal, north of the Rio Particular. The boys had been overconfident, gesturing, pointing, and laughing at the Tauran aircraft overhead.

Hmmm . . . possibly the very same aircraft up there now.

Back there, by Ojochal, and without much in the way of warning, the aircraft had dived. *La Virgen's* man-portable air defense missiles had tried to help as they could, but the amount of sophistication that could be backpacked was limited, while the defensive measures that were usually crammed into a fifty million drachma fighter were vast. Villalobos had seen his missiles distracted by flares and fooled by chaff. What less visible measures the Taurans had used he didn't know, but he was pretty sure there had been some. So far as he knew, none had even done enough damage to temporarily ground a plane or draw the interest of a mechanic.

On the other hand, what they'd done to his men! First, several of the Tauran fighter-bombers had dived toward the ground and then pulled up, releasing bombs on the upward leg to lob them at some considerable distance and with a fearsome degree of accuracy. They'd landed, perhaps a dozen five hundred and fifty pounders, all around and through the maniple's dispersed formation. Casualties had been horrific.

Worse, in some ways, was something Villalobos never expected to see; under the weight of that attack his men had broken and run for the river to the south. That was when he discovered that *Jellied fucking incendiaries float pretty damned well on water.*

Charred bodies from that had not only lined the riverbank, they floated, poor shrunken fetal obscenities, downstream to horrify still more of his men.

Again, Villalobos shivered at the remembered image of the waves of liquid fire rolling over his helpless men, turning them into shrieking torches in a bare instant.

The solution was obvious but not easy. Villalobos had sent most of his men into the jungle to either side of the road, and substantial numbers in small packets into the farm towns along and flanking the road, basically to collect taxes in kind—which was to say in food and dray animals—and move it by civilian conveyance to the troops in the jungle.

And that makes progress slow, fumed the legate. *But what choice do I have? It's move slow or move at speed to a fiery grave.*

Command Post, Second Cohort,
Tercio La Negrita, East of Peliroja, Santa Josefina

When we hit, thought Ignacio Macera, *we're going to have to move fast, strike hard, and take our lumps to get prisoners. That's our best defense, at this point, from a pasting from the air once we get out of the jungle.*

Though *Tercio la Negrita* had been driven out of the

town before, they'd never really been driven out of the area. Little by little, they'd dug in around it, consolidating for an eventual siege. Worse, from the Tauran point of view, they also had positions built well to the east to interfere with any attempted relief of the town or to prevent the escape of its defenders.

Worse, perhaps, than that, was that Salas, like Villalobos on the other side of the mountainous central spine of the country, had been recruiting busily for quite some time. He'd had maybe forty-five hundred men to begin with, of which slightly under twelve hundred had been lost to death, wounds, or disease, but which had been more than made up for by the roughly seven thousand Santa Josefinans who had found their way to the *tercio* colors. *Tercio la Negrita* was a light infantry division in all but name.

Of course, the defenders had by and large made good their losses, too, and had likewise been busy fortifying the edges of the town.

And in some ways, thought Tribune Macera, lying in the muck while looking at the defenses through binoculars, *they have built even better than we did. But, then, they'd have to. You* need *a pretty stout bit of overhead cover to stand up to a direct hit by a one-hundred-and-sixty-millimeter mortar. Or a dozen of them.*

Macera had begun the campaign commanding the maniple that had seized the port town of Matama and secured the smallish freighter that had brought the unit's arms. Now, vice his former cohort commander, killed in action, he found himself not only commanding the cohort, but a much-expanded cohort, where the maniples were short cohorts, themselves. He was still a tribune, but promotion to junior legate was just a matter of time.

Not a lot of the Taurans to see, mused Macera. *No surprise there, it's not very likely they didn't know we were coming. I'd be behind cover, too.*

He scanned the binoculars across about one hundred and twenty degrees, catching the occasional glimpse of a crawling soldier or the flash of a bayonet.

Macera had a new RTO, a bright high schooler from the area, fifteen, black as sin, with blindingly pearl-white teeth, and willing to do anything to get the foreigners out of his country. "Sir," said the civilian-clad boy, bearing both a field telephone, and the somewhat improbable name of Billy, "Legate Salas."

"Thanks, Billy." Macera took the microphone and reported, "My second and third maniples say they're ready. My mortars and the ones you shunted me from third cohort are ready. We're ready, Boss."

Legate Salas' voice came from the handset. "I can't promise you we can silence their artillery. But it's only one battery, we're pretty sure. Those captured long-range mortars from Gaul are *probably* in position to range the Tauran artillery once it opens up. And I've got *Cazadores* spread across the jungle where the Tauran gunners, again *probably*, are, ready to lunge at them, too, as soon as they hear it. It'll be anything from twenty minutes to an hour before they can put them under direct fire, though."

"So order your attack, Tribune, and God go with you."

"Roger." Macera handed that handset back to Billy and asked for the radio. When he had it, he gave the orders to begin. He also repeated Salas' "God go with you."

As far away as he was, and even above the booms of outgoing shells, Macera could hear the cry—the French version of "Incoming!"—echoing from the town. He couldn't see the outgoing barrage, though he heard it, what with what arose from more than two dozen throats as the jungle surrounding the town erupted with the fire of no less than eleven one hundred and sixty-millimeter mortars, fourteen one-twenties, and twenty-six eighty-one-millimeter jobs. They all fired from positions dug in and otherwise prepared over the preceding weeks. Security to build those positions had come from dozens of small skirmishes between hostile Gallic and Santa Josefinan patrols that had gradually made patrolling too dangerous for the Gauls inside the town. The Gauls had rarely lost such a skirmish, mind, but the cost of keeping it up was deemed politically unsupportable back home.

Worse, under the guise of harassing them or baiting them out to fight, a number of mortar fire missions had been preregistered by one gun of a platoon or section, which meant that when all guns were in position and laid for a parallel sheaf, all the shells would presumptively hit somewhere between pretty close and right on.

Thus, Macera watched as, one after another, seven Gaul bunkers exploded in flame and fury. Looking past those, he saw the Gauls' mess hall go up in smoke. *That's got to hurt*.

For the buildings in the way, Macera couldn't see one particularly important target from his vantage point, but he could see clouds of smoke rising from the behind the building that blocked view of the town's central park, the place where the Gaul infantry battalion had put its platoon of heavy mortars. The smoke was not just the thin black of the high explosive in most of the shells, but the thick white clouds from white phosphorus. The two landed together in what soldiers on another world, at another time, called "shake and bake."

There were almost always vehicles near a mortar platoon, of course, and Macera did see what looked like a light truck flying end over end above the skyline of the town. It trailed a spiral of flame as it flew.

He was a little surprised to see so few soldiers running for the bunkers and trenches from the buildings they'd taken over as barracks. *I doubt it's because they're quite* that *afraid of the mortars. No, they're already in the positions. This is going to suck.*

Taking the radio handset back from Billy, Macera contacted his fire-support officer and told him to cut short the preparatory barrage and, instead, put a smoke screen just on the outside of the southeastern section of the Gaul trenches.

"Already on it, Boss," the FSO said. "As the observers report 'target destroyed,' unless they've got another key mission, I'm ordering the guns responsible out of action and to their secondary positions. I've got a *lot* of white phosphorus stockpiled at the secondaries."

"Roger; good thinking; out."

At that, Macera heard shells flying overhead that didn't sound remotely like mortar shells. Those freight train rattles were incoming one-o-fives, courtesy of the one Tauran battery assigned to the southern sector.

Slow, he thought. *They should have been on us sooner. Language issues, maybe. I suppose you'll get that with almost any multinational force.* He remembered back for a bit. *Ah, yes, the reports were that the artillery was Haarlemer, where young Haarlemers learn English or German, not French, as a second language.*

Salas called. In the background there was a repetitive blasting as from a machine gun firing on a slow sustained rate. "Ignacio, those Tauran guns *are* in range, as it turns out. We don't have eyes on them yet—twenty minutes for that, I think, or maybe half an hour—but we can triangulate on the sound to pin them to about a five or six-hundred-meter square. Basically, for the moment, we're just tossing out harassing fire. Might help."

"Thanks, sir."

Billy, who had taken to his duties with some obvious talent, updated Macera's map with an alcohol pen and thrust it in front of him. The tactical symbols and markings weren't standard—nobody had had time for the finer points in schooling the new troops—but were understandable, still. Macera shifted his binoculars to the river southwest of the town. The screen hadn't started building yet though he could already see a few rising plumes of white between the river and the Gallic line edging that side of the town. One of his maniples, that had crossed the river some distance to the southwest, moved in single file, hugging the far bank. Someone in that maniple must have been spotted because machine-gun tracers lanced out from the Gallic lines to skip over their heads. The maniple was nearly cohort-sized, and operating fairly simply for lack of trained cadre.

Macera made a call to that cohort in-all-but-name. The commander was a twenty-five-year-old junior tribune—a first lieutenant in most armies—named Henry Morgan, "for family historical reasons," he would explain. How a Welsh pirate would have had a connection to a black family on another planet he never explained.

"Henrique, you heard me order a screen in, yes?"

"Yes, sir."

"When you've got everyone lined up along the river bank—and you need to time it pretty closely to get out of there before the Taurans can bring in much artillery on you—wait for the screen to be established. You don't want to be there amidst a hellstorm of willie peter."

"No, sir . . . oh, shit . . . sir, kill the screen. Kill it now. That's incoming. I have about two minutes to go in with what I have!" Macera heard what was probably an ear-splitting blast through the radio.

"Right. Go for it . . . Billy, get me the fire-support officer . . . yeah, this is Macera. Kill the screen. High explosive or anything you can find to throw at the Gauls' trench line and bunkers."

By the time Macera turned his binoculars back to the scene, two things had happened. One was that a partial smoke screen had gone in. In places it was fairly thick and effective. In other places it wasn't much.

The other thing was that Morgan's men and boys had started coming up out of the river. Macera saw a dozen or so, in as many seconds, leap up only to be shot back—arms flying—into the flowing stream. Others had better luck, making it into a position from which they could direct fire and leap forward in small bounds. They were doing that, too. Taking stock of the distance and the loss rate, Macera thought, *Close; it's going to be close.*

"Where's my fire on the Gauls' defenses?"

Came the answer, "Splash, over."

Macera went back to his binoculars to see that, indeed, a mix of high explosive and smoke was falling along the defenders. Morgan's boys must have sensed a reduction in the fire they were taking, because they began pouring out of the river in a kind of uphill flood, even as the ones on dry ground seemed to be moving faster and making their bounds longer.

That is, they were moving more and faster until what Macera took to be Tauran artillery began landing in their midst, some of it, and exploding overhead, the rest.

Not a final protective fire, judged Macera, from the spacing between bursts. *It's trying to cover three times the ground of a normal battery, and firing slowly, to boot. You can't cover that much ground with a single battery, you just can't. And that makes me think . . .*

He called his FSO again. "Look, in five minutes I want you to deluge the Gallic position closest to the river for a good ten minutes. Use the one-sixties, if they're available and alive. And as many of the one-twenties as you can get to range."

"Roger," came the answer, "we can keep up the H and I"—harassment and interdiction—"with the eighty-twos."

"Good, do it . . . break, break . . . Morgan?"

"Sir."

"Did you hear that?"

"Yes, sir. You want me to break in on the right and roll them up?"

"You have grasped the very platonic essence of my intent, son. Now, can you?"

"Maybe. The maniple, so-called, on my right never made it out of the river, too much direct fire. That means they're fresh where the others are scared shitless and, by now, tired. Let me go there and take charge, myself."

"Do it. You have ten minutes. Is that enough?"

"Plenty, sir, or my miscegenating, city-burning, loot-gathering, multi-great-great-grandfather never raped a captive slave girl."

Oh, so that's what it was.

There was enough smoke covering the field that Macera couldn't make out much detail on the ground. The extra wallop of the one-sixties, though, was distinctive. Mortars were relatively high in explosive filler, as a percentage of body weight, anyway, but the percentage also went up as the size of the shell went up. In a sixty-millimeter mortar, for example, weighing three or four pounds, there might be half to three quarters of a pound of explosive. In an eighty-one, weighing nine pounds, it might be close to a fourth high explosive, or about two pounds and change.

The one-hundred-and-sixty-meter shell went off with a weight of about twenty-four pounds, or two-thirds again more than a medium howitzer. When it buried itself in the earth next to a bunker or trench, not only did the target disintegrate, but an enormous column of dirt and rock was propelled skyward, too.

That column, and the accompanying gut-churning shock of the blast, was as uplifting for the attackers as it was for the defenders.

Billy tapped Macera on the shoulder. "Sir, it's Tribune Morgan."

"Yes, Henrique."

"Sir, if you didn't notice, the artillery has stopped playing across the entire field. I think they know what we're doing and are going to drop a genuine final protective fire here on me. I'd rather not be here for it. We've blown a couple of breaches in the wire. I request that you lift fires, please; I am going to do a wild, screaming, fixed bayonets and firing from the hip charge. Probably no choice."

Macera ordered that to the fire support officer, then told Morgan, "Last rounds pure white phosphorus. Last rounds splash in . . . five . . . four . . . three . . . two . . . one . . . splash.

"Go, son! Go! Go! Go!"

Henrique? I am not an "Henrique," but a Henry. Probably says it to piss me off. Which, come to think of it, it does . . . and at a time when it's probably all to the good to be pissed off.

There was a lot of lead flying about, but little or none of it, on either side, seemed to be aimed. From where he'd taken shelter, behind some farmer's stone wall, Morgan stood straight up. Over the roar of the incoming shells, he shouted out to the troops around him. "Nobody staying here but the dead and those who are going to die. We've got just a few minutes. When the fire lifts, and on my command, we need to charge. So fix bayonets, motherfuckers! Fix bayonets!"

Where the shout only carried so far, the images and the clicks of bayonets being fixed passed all along the line, in both directions from the tribune. He ducked down again, enough to cover his body, while watching that section of the Gallic line take its pounding.

"Macera, sir," said Morgan's radio bearer.

"Morgan."

"That's your willie peter. Go!"

Morgan saw maybe two dozen white phosphorus shells, big ones for this caliber, blossom over the Gaul's line. He stood up atop the stone wall, almost losing his balance to a couple of loose rocks, then screamed, "Chaaarrrggge!"

Pistol drawn, Morgan began to run forward. The sounds coming from both sides and behind said that the men were following. *I wasn't sure until I started if they would. You never really know.*

For all the smoke nobody could much see anything, but Morgan did note a stream of tracers passing about fifteen feet to his front. Some screams from the right rear said somebody had run into them.

He flopped to the ground, crawling under the *bracbrac- bracbracbrack* of the passing bullets. *They're firing blind. No clue where we are.*

Morgan almost ran into the Gauls' tactical wire. *Which would tend to explain why the machine gun was firing along it.* He stood up when just past the flight of the tracers and, lo, there it was, triple standard concertina.

I saw us blow gaps. There has to be one to my . . . ummm . . . right, I think.

He headed that way, still wary of the machine gun that lashed the air to his left a few times a minute. Eventually he came to a gap through which a steady stream of his own men poured.

"Into the trenches! Into the trenches! Clear 'em out!"

The Tauran artillery, delayed for some reason or another, began falling heavily between the town and the river. Some men were caught in it, to live or to die as the dangling dong of destiny chose.

Morgan turned for his radio telephone operator and then realized he hadn't seen the kid in a couple of minutes. Somebody new, meaning a fairly new recruit, in this case, came trotting up with a radio slung over one shoulder and his rifle carried in the other hand.

"He bought it, sir," the new man said to Morgan. "But I checked and the radio works. Tribune Macera personally told me to carry it to you."

"Okay, come on, follow me to the trench line."

Past the wire there were no more lines of machine-gun fire. There were, though, a determined band of Gauls, badly outnumbered, trying to fight off as many as four or five Santa Josefinans each. The odds against the Gauls kept growing as more of Morgan's men passed a gap and joined the fray. They were coming quicker, now, too, because the machine guns had been silenced.

Morgan didn't know the word for surrender in French. He suspected these guys didn't either. Simply swarmed by numbers they'd all gone down to bullet, bayonet, or rifle butt with none of them raising his hands in defeat.

"Take prisoners, goddammit," Morgan shouted to anyone who was paying attention. He wasn't sure anyone was. From their glassy eyes and slack expressions, he judged that the men in the newly captured trench line were pretty much spent.

And they'll be that way for a while, no hurrying any recovery.

Morgan grabbed about as senior a non-com as was likely to be found, a corporal. "Until you find a higher-ranking man, Corporal, you're in charge. Get these men off their asses and into some semblance of a defense. Now!"

Then the tribune, followed by his new RTO, turned to the rear, scanning for a new unit. The artillery, maybe uncertain about continuing a mission so close to friendlies without an observer, ceased fire. *Or maybe the* cazadores *found them.*

Through the thin smoke, Morgan saw what looked to be a maniple-sized "platoon" emerging from the river bank. He recognized one of his own. Cupping his hands, the tribune shouted, "To me. To me," then began a slow trot to join them.

The "platoon leader," Junior Centurion Orrellana, reported in with his name and, "one hundred and twelve men, present or accounted for, sir."

"Good," said Morgan. He listened for few second. *Yes, there's still some fighting to the southwest.* Briefly he outlined the situation as best he understood it, then told Orrellana, "Strike for the railway station in the middle of town."

CHAPTER TWENTY

"Fire must be concentrated on one point, and as
soon as the breach is made, the equilibrium is
broken and the rest is nothing."

—Napoleon

Estado Mayor, Sub-camp C, Ciudad Balboa

Carrera read the short but eloquent message Soult
brought him. It read: "Town of Peliroja taken. Many
Gallic prisoners in hand. Gallic mortars and artillery
captured to the tune of eighteen tubes. Also, two tanks we
might make serviceable again once we hose out what's left
of the crews. Casualties heavy but not crippling. All praise
to Tribune Macera and his men. *Viva la Revolución!*"

"There's a list of requests for promotion, too," said
Soult, "along with awards given by Salas or kicked up to
us. Didn't want to bother you with those, boss."

"You see anything weird in them, or questionable?"

"Nah, it all looked reasonable. The Ops folks have the
map for Santa Josefina updated, if you want to see it."

"Yeah, let's. I've got a decision to make and it isn't a small one."

Carrera and Soult walked the tunnel to the operations office. The heavy concrete shrouded and steel reinforced office complex went to a hush when he was seen. Someone called, "At ease," but Carrera waved a hand and ordered, "Carry on."

He went to a side office, the desk, as it were, for operations in Santa Josefina. His chief of staff, Dan Kuralski, met him there with the operations officer in town.

"I take it you've heard about Peliroja," Dan said.

"Yes, and the question is 'Now what?'"

"It's a sideshow," Kuralski said. "More of the same strikes me as fine."

"Actually," corrected Carrera, "it's not just a sideshow." He studied the map intently for several long minutes, noting the apparent open path to the capital from Peliroja, and the long sweep of the Tauran line from Cerro Presinger to the north.

"He'll fill that as best he can, poor Claudio," Carrera said. "And there goes his reserve."

"Why 'poor'?" Kuralski asked.

His smile was sad as Carrera explained, "Marciano and ourselves, depending on how someone looks at it, could, either of us, look to be overmatched in sheer power. That's not how the history books will read it. He really is overmatched, and won't get credit for fighting a damned fine campaign, under constraints that would have me shooting politicians and lawyers right and left. On the other hand, we, in Santa Josefina—at least in the term we're fighting—really are not overmatched, and will get all the credit there is to give. It's just not fair."

"Put that way, maybe not."

Eyes still on the map, as if reviewing a future history he was certain would happen, Carrera said, "Send orders to De Lagazpi of Fifth Mountain Tercio, via Sixth Corps. He's brevetted upward one rank. He's to take one cohort of 'volunteers,' along with Tercio headquarters and whatever they think they need to support them, and leave a command cell behind to oversee the two remaining cohorts of their own plus the Lempiran and Valparaisan mountain battalions, to guard the highway from Almirante to Cervantes and to go after the ports north and south.

"I want that cohort of the tercio to 'desert' en masse, cut their insignia off their uniforms, except for rank, then volunteer to help their Santa Josefinan brothers. They will cross the border, as soon as practical. Maximum emphasis on not being spotted by our friends in space. Their mission is to take Cerro Presinger."

"Be two or three weeks before they get there," Kuralski observed.

"That will be fine."

"The Zhong and Taurans may move together to clear the highway."

Carrera sighed. "Decision Cycle Theory is almost entirely bullshit. One of the reasons why is that it presumes more or less instantaneous translation of decision into action. But sometimes—and this is one of them—when you *do* account for the time of translation, it has a sliver of truth. The Taurans and Zhong will never be able to change plans and reorient their effort to clear the road in enough time to matter. Friction, the sheer resistance and inertia of their own organizations, will stop it."

"Why the promotion for De Lagazpi?" someone asked.

"He's to take charge of the whole effort as if a legion commander. Put that in his orders, too."

Kuralski didn't say anything but thought, *You're right often enough to rate a pass when it looks like you're sticking your dick in the garbage disposal.*

"One last thing; give Fosa the code to be ready to sail within three weeks."

BdL *Dos Lindas*, Puerto Bruselas, Santa Josefina

Covered with polycarbonate, there was a sword welded to the hull of the aircraft carrier, and the shadowy outline of a very small man. Fosa visited the site, regularly, as did many of the sailors of not just the flagship, but the entire *Classis*. A little brass plaque, also affixed to the hull, told the story.

The old gun tub was gone from the same super explosion that had burned an old man into the hull and welded his sword in place. The new one was the same basic design as the old had been, and solid as . . . well . . . as steel.

Fosa sat in the gunner's seat of the 40mm mounted in the tub. Standing up to pass through the hatchway, he patted the metal on her hull, saying, aloud, "Good girl." He repeated it, more softly but with more enthusiasm. "*Good girl!*"

The ship was ancient, having seen service from the tail end of the Great Global War through a number of brushfire wars after that. She'd taken more than her fair share of lumps since coming into legionary service, as well, including a number of missile hits and near ramming by a suicide freighter packed to the gunwales with explosives.

But, you know, old girl, you're in better shape now than you have been in years. At least in all the major areas, as a ship, you are.

Leaving the gun tub, Fosa made his way to the hangar deck. A small crew of five men pushed their way past him carrying what looked to be several heavy chunks of steel. It was Fosa's own rule that for certain events even the skipper made way for the crewmen.

Down in the hangar deck not a single aircraft was serviceable, per the conditions and orders under which the ship had been interned. Indeed, along with the removal of all armaments, and the draining of all fuel, every single plane and helicopter had had a key component removed, generally a propeller or a rotor blade. These, in specially built frames, were kept under lock, connected by chains, which chains ran to welded padeyes. Every aircraft also sat at something of an angle from missing a tire, so that the straight-faced claim could be made that they were still unserviceable when . . .

"I told you fucking pussies," shouted Sergeant Major Ramirez, the senior centurion of the ship, "that we would continue to do this shit until every motherfucking airplane's propeller can be reinstalled within three hours. We'll be at this shit until tomorrow night, dick-lickers, if that's what it takes."

The hangar crews stood at attention in formation for Ramirez's harangue. They wore a mix of brown, green, blue, green, white, and red. Sweat poured off the men, despite the large fans circulating air. Their color-coded jerseys were all also sweat stained, though probably every man had put on a fresh one that morning.

"My little brother," Ramirez continued, "my no good, black sheep of the family, worthless little brother, the battery commander, is never going to tell me that his guns did more for the war than my ship. Do you faggots hear me?"

"Yes, Sergeant Major!"

"Do you faggots *hear* me?"

"YES, SERGEANT MAJOR!"

Ramirez looked up and to his left to where the ship's chaplain stood. "Padre?"

The priest made a sign of the cross and said, in a volume to match Ramirez's, "May God and the Blessed Tadeo Kurita watch over you and your work, boys."

Fosa folded his arms as Ramirez consulted his watch. After a time, he said, still quite loudly, "All right, you faggots . . . five . . . four . . . three . . . two . . . GO!"

Instantly, the dense formation dissolved into seeming chaos. The chaos sorted itself out quickly enough; this wasn't, after all, their first run. Men trotted to every corner and side of the hangar deck, there sorting themselves into teams. There was sometimes a struggle to unlock the chains and pull them out. Indeed, before the chain had been hauled through more than a few propellers, the crews were sliding the bottom ones out and, in teams of three, lifting them, for portage to the right plane.

Briefly, the chaos seemed lessened by a reduction in visible crew. That lasted maybe seven minutes before men began returning, wheeling everything from machine guns to light torpedoes, bombs to heavy anti-shipping missiles, and chaff and flare dispensers EDM pods.

Fosa walked the edge of the hangar deck to keep out of the way of the laboring crews. At the portside sternward corner, he watched a Turbo-Finch's plane captain position a short stand right under and a little forward of the prop shaft. One of the plane captain's men added an oil seal and moved some lines to particular positions, the value of which he seemed quite set on.

A three-man team bearing the nine-foot propeller maneuvered to put the center about where the prop shaft was, then rotated the propeller slightly to just off the vertical plane. The center man stepped carefully up the little stand, repeating to himself, softly, "clock it . . . clock it."

"Hold on; let me do the linkage first!"

"Roger, I'm just reminding myself."

Fosa was pretty sure they knew what they were doing, even if there was some bickering back and forth.

From behind him Fosa heard the command, "Up Uranus, motherfuckers," He turned his attention to a red T-shirt-clad ordnance crew, using a large rolling jack to lift a Volgan Uranus anti-shipping missile onto one of the Finch's inboard hardpoints. The Finch would carry two, which, together, cost about as much as the plane.

Hmmmm . . . this is a kind of dance, but not exactly an

elegant one. I wonder if adding music might help. Note to self, consult with Ramirez this evening.

Fosa listened and watched for maybe another twenty minutes. He consulted his watch again. *No, no way they're going to make the standard I want them to have, not this run. Maybe I'm being unreasonable. Maybe, too, a little music and a slightly better organization will help. In the interim, God have mercy on them because Ramirez will not.*

From the hangar deck, Fosa sauntered to the flight simulators, of which there were ten for fixed-wing aircraft and six for helicopters. The helicopter simulators were somewhat undertasked, as Fosa had transferred out two-thirds of them in favor of another dozen Turbo-Finches. The Finch and Cricket simulators were, accordingly, somewhat overtasked. Indeed, they were in use when Fosa arrived at that section of the ship, and, so far as he knew, they'd been in use since internment, with only minor breaks for maintenance. An experienced warrant officer pilot ran the flight simulation center. Fosa asked, "Progress is too much to ask for, but how about maintenance of skills?"

"Captain . . . there are some things a simulator just can't do. Engaging a target? Ducking or enduring the incoming defensive fire on a strike mission? We can simulate those, not a problem. We cannot simulate the 'couldn't drive a knitting needle up the pilot's ass with a sledge hammer' fear factor. Same for an actual landing on the roof."

"Yeah . . . okay, but we started with a pretty well-trained group of pilots."

"Yes, sir; and I hope, just like you do, that they haven't lost their edge."

"Anything we can do for that pucker factor?"

"Rotate them out to join the guerillas? No, I'm not serious. But I can't think of anything we have available. I've thought on it."

"Okay. I want a list, then, of the twenty-four Finch and eighteen Cricket pilots you're most sure haven't lost anything . . . with three more and two more of each, respectively, for backups."

"Wilco, Skipper."

And now let's see how the rearm the guns drills are going . . .

High Admiral's Quarters, *Spirit of Peace*,
in orbit over Terra Nova

"High Admiral," said Khan, the husband, through the intercom on Wallenstein's cabin door, "I hate to disturb you but there's something you need to see."

The door whooshed open to reveal a tall and svelte blonde in a considerable state of dishevelment, her body covered in an embroidered silk *cheongsam*, one which almost failed to hide Marguerite's privates.

I wonder if she knows how magnificent she looks like this, thought Khan. *No matter what she looks like, she is a* massive *improvement over her predecessor.*

"Yes, Khan, what is it?"

"I can show you better . . ."

"Oh, right, come into my office then."

Khan did, carefully not noting the small and dainty lump under the covers of the admiral's bed. *And why not? She deserves a little love, though I retain my doubts about whether Her Imperial Majesty is capable of feeling it.*

Khan went directly to the computer and signed himself in, then pulled up a folder.

"We've been picking up an odd amount of radio traffic in the jungle east of the town of Hephaestos, Balboa." He drew a circle with his forefinger broadly taking in the thrice-fallen town—more the ruins of a town now—of Jaba, and ranging east to Sethlans, Santa Josefina. "It hasn't been much, mind you, but there was essentially no radio traffic before. I ordered a skimmer to overfly the area, which, by the way, proved a total waste of effort. But on the way back, the skimmer saw, or rather, didn't see, something it ought to have near Hephaestos, in Balboa."

Khan brought up some images the skimmer had taken, then some color plates quite probably filched from some defense publications on the planet. "Those are the only uniforms we could see, High Admiral. I sent another skimmer down later and those were still the only uniforms we could see." He fiddled again with the picture. "These are Balboan uniforms. The others were Valparaisan and Lempiran. Part of the Balboan Fifth Mountain Tercio— how much I cannot say—isn't in Hephaestos anymore; they've moved into Santa Josefina."

"Shit. Just shit. You know, Khan, it's times like these that I wish to the elder gods that this fleet had something other than nukes—not that we know if any of *those* will work, mind you—to use on the planet. Something, anyway, we could use to, shall we say, influence events."

"Oh, I wouldn't think that a good idea, High Admiral. If the Federated States thought we could target their nuclear space forces with precision, they'd nuke us now on general principle."

"Good point," she agreed, "but I wish there were *something* I could do about what's about to happen to a Tauran dependency, which is to say one of *our* dependencies, in practice. What's Task Force Jesuit got to face that with?"

"Having lost a battalion recently—oh, yes, it was effectively annihilated—General Marciano is stretched to the breaking point. He's got a composite battalion blocking the easy road to the capital and a bit under three facing west. This will break him."

"Can't Janier reinforce him?"

"Yes, High Admiral. *If* he would; he could. But he won't. It seems the good general has gotten some intelligence that has tripped every paranoia instinct Carrera gave him."

"So Santa Josefina is lost?" Wallenstein asked. "Lost beyond hope?"

"I believe so."

Wallenstein felt her maternal instincts kick in and her blood pressure begin to rise. "Then get my Esma the hell out of there."

Headquarters, Task Force Jesuit, Zeledón, Santa Josefina

The shuttle, the High Admiral's own barge, was waiting just east of the town. Overhead, the constellations shone brightly, as none of the planet's three moons had yet arisen.

Marciano drove Esmeralda to the shuttle himself, with just a guard in the back for security's sake.

Outside the shuttle's open hatch, with red light streaming out, Marciano passed Esma her bag, which he'd carried from the plane. "Tell your high admiral," he said, as she took the bag, "that I appreciate the intelligence, and concur in her writing us off."

Esma, who genuinely liked the old man, shook her head vigorously. "I'm sure . . ."

"Please, child. Based on what she sent me before recalling you, she rightly recognizes that I cannot stop the better than four-to-one odds that are coming for me. Tell her I appreciate the communications device, too."

"I wonder," said Esma, "why she ever sent me when she could have just sent the communicator."

"Two-way communications," Claudio answered. "Oh, yes, we could have talked both ways with just the communicator, but with you in the loop she could believe what she was told and, as importantly, *know* she could trust it."

"Ah."

"Ah. Never fear, child; you are young; you will learn."

"Oh . . . oh, I almost forgot." Esmeralda started to undo the holster to return Marciano's pistol.

He stopped her hands physically. "No, Esma. Where I expect to be going I won't need it. You keep it, a gift from me. Maybe better to put it in the bag, though, all things considered." He took the pistol, leaving the holster where it was, and slipped it into her carry-on.

"But . . ."

"My grandmother would have approved. She, you know, was quite a beautiful woman, too. If you ever get the chance, go to Tuscany and find my wife. The Tuscan Army will help. She can show you our family history . . . of which you, now that you own that pistol, are a part.

"Now no 'buts.' Get your shapely little derriere on that shuttle and get yourself to safety."

Esma felt tears forming. She knew what he'd meant when he'd said, "where I am going." Flinging her arms around his neck and laying her head against his chest, she said, "I won't forget you. Not ever."

Marciano's hands stopped just shy of returning the hug, hovering in indecision around the girl's flanks. "Thank you," he said. "Now go before I make a fool of myself."

Spirit of Peace, **in orbit over Terra Nova**

Esma had cried the whole way up. There were people she was leaving behind who had come to matter to her, Marciano, Bertholdo, Stefano were only a few among them. They'd all been good men and good human beings, no matter how trying their circumstances.

And they're all going to die. And my side—if it still is my side—is going to kill them.

But then, Cass was kind, too, and helped me through much. And Carrera risked his life to find me and explain some things to me. And I just don't know what to do anymore except cry. And when I think of that soldier I killed to protect myself . . .

Esma felt the slightly disorienting effect of the shuttle matching the spin of the ship. There was no obvious correlation between the two, but she broke down in a new bout of sobbing, even so, as the shuttle lined itself up on the hangar doors.

The rest of the landing was as uneventful as the pickup and flight. The shuttle pilot applied a certain amount of braking in the form of retros, even as the deck magnets were activated to bring the small boat down. Then it was wait about a dozen minutes as the doors were closed and the deck pumped with air.

Richard, earl of Care, met Esma at the shuttle's hatch as she came out. He couldn't, in the very low gravity of the hangar deck, do what he wanted, which was pick her up in his arms and spin her around a dozen times. Rather, he could have, if he'd removed the magnetic slippers he'd put on outside the hangar, but if he had done both it would probably have set the both of them to flying through the air, bouncing off bulkheads, spinning, and eventually puking until recovered by the crew. The crew really hated cleaning up vomit in zero or near zero G environments, and he hated being more of an ass as captain than the job actually required.

Instead of that, Richard just gathered her in and held her tightly, his chin resting on the top of her head for a long sweet moment.

"I've missed you," he whispered, moving to place his lips near her ear "but before I take you to my quarters to show you how much, the High Admiral wants to see you."

Richard's greetings were welcome, with only that little

awkwardness to be found when a man loves a woman, one who doesn't really love him back, but who still feels a sense of obligation to him.

They stopped off at Esma's spartan quarters, near the High Admiral's, to deposit her baggage. There, Richard said, "I hope to see you in my quarters when she's finished."

Where Richard's welcome back had been warm and loving, Wallenstein's was a mother's, replete with hugs and kisses and strokes of cheek. Three times she held the much smaller Esmeralda's shoulders tightly in her hands while she stood back to just look at her. Esma found this all the more remarkable insofar as Marguerite Wallenstein really *did* prefer girls, but had never come on to her in the slightest degree. She found that love very easy to reciprocate.

Finally, Marguerite, still holding Esma's shoulders, stepped back a final time and studied her face intently.

"What are you looking for?" Esma asked.

"Some sign of change, maybe of guilt, since you shot that prisoner."

Esma sighed, then lied, "I wish I could say I had it, but, at the time, all I saw was the ruined embassy and my murdered friend from down below."

Marguerite nodded. "I understand; it's easier when you're sure they're guilty. I pray to the elder gods that you'll never find out what it's like to be responsible for killing someone innocent.

"Speaking of the embassy, we're recovering the ambassador tomorrow. And speaking of guilt, I'm sending the evil bitch to Atlantis Base to stew on her *latifundia* until I pack her home to Earth."

CHAPTER TWENTY-ONE

FISH and CHIPS—Fighting in someone's house and causing havoc in people's streets.
—British Army unofficial acronym

Magdalena, Balboa

Ruins, charred and smoking, were everywhere. There was hardly a house that hadn't been fought for, hardly an open field without its trenches, tunnels, and bunkers, hardly, for that matter, a sewer that hadn't seen vicious hand-to-hand fighting within five meters of itself or even inside its dank depths.

Surrounded by his aide, Malcoeur, and a few radio bearers and bodyguards, Janier could almost taste victory. He stood in a captured trench, gazing intently through binoculars at the street fighting raging in the ghetto to his south.

It's such a dump, he thought, *why do they fight so fiercely to hang onto it? Dump or not, with this port in hand, we can take the rest of the country, no problem. Perhaps that's why they fight.*

It was no mean task to actually get a sense of progress through the binoculars. Malcoeur had found the best spot available, but even there, at most, Janier could catch a glimpse of an occasional squad assaulting across a street; making it whole, if they were lucky, though few were that lucky. As often as a place was taken, it had to be evacuated as the almost inevitable fires got inevitably out of control in this dry season.

Part of the area under attack was the container port. He wasn't surprised that progress there was slim; the lovely *ecossaise*, Major Campbell, had apprised him of her suspicions that a truly vast number of shipping containers formed the basis of prefabricated fortifications. Indeed, in a few cases, so it was reported, the locals hadn't been content with mere sandbags but had been shipping in entire bunkers in the form of containers, complete with cast concrete innards, with a degree of standoff that defeated both shaped charged and plastic explosives, plus communications links and air filtration systems.

Which, I confess, does make me wonder about what we are going to find in that now untouchable rain forest when we break through to it . . . after we take this port . . . assuming, of course. Speaking—or thinking—of which, Campbell has not been able to find out who was paying for the suit that suspended our ability to bomb. It hardly matters, though, if she gets a confession; we all know who was behind it. What a marvelously unprincipled man is our foe, able to look like the most upstanding soldier in ten thousand years, while secretly so sneaky and underhanded that . . . well . . . I doff my hat to him.

But, on the other hand, if Campbell is right about the

containers, and apparently, she is—Janier watched a brace of them slice one of his squads to ribbons in a street below—*then why should he care about them being bombed? The bombing's just not that effective, given how the global locating system has been thoroughly trashed here. So why should he want to release our planes from bombing one thing, that wasn't all that effective, so we can provide better close air support where we need it?*

Unless, of course, the bombing was all that effective, but when has that ever happened?

Janier considered something he hadn't before. *Or what if the purpose was to sever any ties between the soldiery of the Tauran Union and the bureaucrats who run it and the lawyers and judges who tend to run them? That effect, I am sure it has had, but I don't see how it will make any difference.*

Then, too, if he's the wreck of a man that's been reported to me, he's not thinking about long-term effects or moral suasion or anything. He's not thinking at all. It's possible, I suppose, that this is all unfolding according to an old plan, now sadly out of date. Or even . . .

The general's thoughts were interrupted by a vibrating in the left cargo pocket of his field trousers. Excusing himself, he followed the zigzag of the trench until he could be sure of at least some privacy. Taking the device from his pocket he said, "Yes, Marguerite?"

"It's Khan, General. High Admiral Wallenstein is touring and inspecting the fleet. She said I was to apprise you of anything interesting that popped up."

"I'm all ears." Janier smiled at his joke; though a

handsome enough man, his ears were probably his most notable feature. They were quite large.

"Very good, General," Khan said. "Item one is that some of the Balboan Fifth Mountain Tercio is within striking distance of General Marciano's left flank in Santa Josefina. He has nothing to shore it up with and will be outnumbered to a truly ridiculous degree, in general. I think you can expect the capital to fall within a few days, a week at the most."

"Small change," said Janier, who had, over the months, grown tired of Marciano's ceaseless demands for more troops. "What else?"

"There was one other thing," Khan said, "but I am not sure what to make of it. It seems that your opponent, in person, visited Santa Josefina recently. We have no idea why he did so, though if pressed I would offer that it was possibly a combination of morale raising visit and coordination of orders session. I would . . ."

Janier's heart fell. "He *what*?"

"He seems to have visited Santa Josefina and quite recently."

"Oh . . . oh, shit." Janier's voice sounded more strained than the word would suggest. "Khan, give me your professional opinion. I've been operating to a considerable extent on the belief that our great foe, great in all senses, had collapsed, morally, intellectually, and emotionally, and that every weakness we were seeing was because he had lost his grip. But a man doesn't make a very risky visit to some troops operating as guerillas in a very hostile place when he has lost his grip, does he?"

"I suppose not, General."

"No, I suppose not. I'll get back with you later."

Janier turned back in the direction from which he'd come and shouted, at the very top of his lungs, "Malcoeur! Malceour! I want the G2 and G3—no, the entire staff— to meet me at the forward command post within ninety minutes! And get D'Espérey up there, too!"

The forward command post had been established in what had once been the Magdalena community center, a place offering at least roof and walls, though the roof was charred and the walls rather the worse for wear.

The staff took one look at Janier's face, full of worry approaching terror, and felt their blood pressures begin to rise.

The general wasted no time. Turning to his intelligence officer, he asked directly, "How much of our estimate of enemy intentions and capabilities was based on information that their commander was in a state of collapse?"

The second in command answered, "But he is, sir. From deserters, from intercepted radio traffic, he is a man who has climbed into a bottle and whose personal conduct has demoralized his own army. There is no . . . ."

"Can it," Janier said. "I think we've been fed a line."

"Sir?"

"He's gone to Santa Josefina and returned, and recently. I don't know what he was doing there, but whatever it was, it was not acting like a demoralized drunk. He was there for business. Moreover, that business appears to be about to result in the complete collapse of our forces in Santa Josefina. What's that tell you?"

"That he . . . oh. Oh, fuck. And we're . . ."

Janier completed the sentence. "We're neither postured nor dug in for what's coming. Have you read the reports, the analysis done by Major Campbell?"

"Yes, of course, sir. She's a bit pessimistic but . . ."

"Shut up. Now what kind of artillery train does she say Carrera has."

Whatever his failings might have been, the second in command's memory was fine. His bureaucratic instincts were better still; he had the estimate with him. Opening his tablet, he began to read off, "Well . . . between six and seven hundred eighty-one and eighty-two-millimeter mortars . . . between five and six hundred one-hundred-and-twenty-millimeter mortars . . . one-sixties . . . Volgan-type, maybe two hundred or so, less the number we've destroyed here . . ."

"Speaking of destroyed and captured, how many eighty-five millimeter and one-hundred-and-twenty-two-millimeter guns did we overrun here?"

"That's a little more obscure, but I think maybe a couple of hundred."

"Do not subtract them from your estimates or Campbell's. They were *bait*. Continue."

"Yes, sir. You know the Balboans have been manufacturing most of their own mortars for some time. Those figures may not be reliable. As for artillery, she believed they have between fourteen and sixteen hundred guns from eighty-five to one-eighty millimeter and two-hundred-and-three millimeter. Only a few battalions' worth of the latter two types, though.

"Multiple rocket launchers were tougher. They might

have as many as one hundred and twenty of the huge ones the Volgan make. Of the more usual ones, the one-twenty-two millimeter, forty-barreled jobs, between four hundred and fifty and five hundred and fifty."

"So that's what, three thousand, four hundred guns, cannon, and rocket launchers?" Janier asked.

"About that, sir."

"Now tell me, what is the frontage we're facing between the lakes here, along the Parilla Line?"

"It's quite compact, sir, about eighteen kilometers."

"I make it at about that, too," Janier agreed. "Now, did you know that our enemy is a great student of the Volgan way of making war, at least for certain areas where the Volgans were actually quite good, and the class of the world for an industrially based, citizen-soldier army?"

"I hadn't, sir. It's interesting, of course, but—"

Janier cut his response off. "You've studied the old Volgan ways, haven't you?"

"Yes, sir, of course."

"Ah, excellent. Now tell me, what is the standard Volgan density of guns, mortars, and rocket launchers on an area of front they intend to break through?"

"About two . . ." The intelligence officer suddenly did the math in his head. As he did, his face turned a ghastly pale. "Oh, dear God. That's what they've got. They've got the ability to blast about four hundred square kilometers with what amounts to nuclear levels of destruction over the space of a few hours. Oh . . . oh, Jesus. What are we going to do?"

D'Espérey interrupted before Janier could answer, exclaiming, "It's worse than that, sir! There are areas bounded by the lakes, the defense line, and the Shimmering Sea that they'll know we can't occupy because they're water."

"Yessss," Janier nodded. "In other words, that son of a bitch built an entire army around the bait of that port, and assembled an artillery train to blast an invading army to bits in the area it would occupy to take that port.

"Gentlemen, when they speak of the 'tyranny of logistics,' the pundits usually just mean the limits logistics impose upon you. There's another meaning though; the tyranny is also the predictability logistics imposes upon you. That's how the enemy knew the Zhong would have to take the island. That's how they knew to place a half-million-person refugee camp astride the road and infiltrate it with guerillas. And that's how they knew we had to come here. There's nothing magic to it; it's just competent reading of the logistic possibilities and limitations."

"Now here's what we're going to do and what we're not going to do. In the first place, we're not going to panic. In fact, we're going to congratulate ourselves that, for once, somebody—and in this case, I think the praise goes to Major Campbell—anyway, somebody predicted that bastard's trick before he could pull it off.

"We're also not going to surrender. We're not going to evacuate, either. We couldn't hope to get more than a middling fraction of our troops out before Carrera initiates his attack. Even if we were successful in that, the loss of combat power and support would ensure the destruction of the last three-quarters of our force here."

Smiling inwardly, Janier's aide de camp, Malcoeur,

thought, *And this is why I've followed you all these years, General, even when you were treating me like shit. An asshole you can certainly be, but when you're at your best, you're magnificent.*

Janier continued, without a clue to his aide's thoughts, "That's important, by the way. We cannot tip him off that we know."

"So much for what we're not going to do. Here's what we are going to do. One, we're going to thin the line of the front—we already have, facing the Parilla Line. Two, we're going to keep up the attack to clear Cristobal, but at about a quarter of the intensity we have been. Three, we're going to dig in like moles beginning about two kilometers behind our current front lines . . . special attention, by the way, to ensuring our own artillery survives the pounding. There's going to be a window when his infantry will emerge from their shelters—did I fail to mention that *that* is what that Parilla Line actually is? Where it fits into this? I could kick myself for not seeing it sooner. It's a set of protected assembly areas for an attack . . . anyway, their infantry will emerge from those fortifications and we can hurt them, maybe enough to hang on."

The Three put his hand up.

"Yes?"

"Their patrolling will discover that we've thinned the lines. I mean, any offensive is going to be preceded by recon. Once they discover that . . ."

For the first time since calling the meeting, Janier smiled. "No, they won't. They think they're playing one game, a huge ambush. They won't want to tip us off that it's coming. Hence, little or no recon. Hence, they won't know that the game has changed . . ."

Campo de los Sapos, Cristobal, Balboa

Smoke from burning buildings was everywhere, thick in the air. Ashes and embers rolled above the street or fluttered in the air past Verboom's eyes. There was firing everywhere, too; it never seemed to end in this place.

Verboom, along with a tightly grouped cluster of his men, waited to cross a street to their front. Bodies littering that street said that doing so could well be one of those bad ideas. None of the bodies were his men, but he'd left a dozen in the buildings and streets behind what remained of his platoon, some twenty-three men, including himself, with a pair of machine guns and one remaining recoilless.

Well . . . not twenty-three men; twenty-two, plus van der Wege.

Losses? There were two things true of city fighting; it used up ammunition like water and spent men like loose change.

There were also a number of counterintuitive issues that came up in city fighting. One was that, when fighting in cities, throwing smoke to cover crossing the street was only a warning for the enemy to start firing everything available into the smoke. Given the relative frequency of hard surfaces—walls and streets—the ricochets also tended to make that fire much more dangerous. Another, similar problem, was that when crossing the street, sending over one man at a time just meant that a single enemy rifleman, warned by the first crosser, could wait and pop every subsequent man until the crossers figured out what a bad idea this was. The figuring out usually left one man, stuck in enemy territory, alone, scared shitless, and ripe for surrender.

Instead, the way a group, usually a squad, sometimes a platoon, crossed a street was en masse, with no other concern than to get across quickly; no preparatory suppressive fire, no extraneous commands, no smoke, just, "GO!"

Verboom, Haarlemer Commander, and still a platoon leader since the loss of both his officer and his previous platoon sergeant, was just about to give that command and to lead the way across. It always took some self-psyching up because, playing the odds, which is what the technique was, also included the possibility of the dice falling against you. Since he'd managed to get his men across eleven times now, he figured the odds were getting very long against him and them.

Okay . . . yeah . . . okay . . . right . . . get ready . . . .oh, man . . . why do I get the shakes every time we do this . . . right . . . never mind . . . get ready . . . get ready . . . DON'T shit yourself . . .

"Sergeant Verboom?"

The voice—he recognized it as his radioman—was instant relief to Verboom; if he was wanted on the radio he had a valid excuse not to make the mass rush across the street. *Which means we may get to live an extra five minutes.*

Turning around, Verboom took the radio's handset. It

was his company commander, who was probably only a couple of buildings away.

"Stand down, stand by, and wait for orders, Verboom. I don't have any more than that."

"Wilco." *And bless you and anybody else who was responsible for stopping us before it was too late.*

With arm gestures and more forceful pushes and prods, the sergeant got his men away from the shattered window openings and the door they had been prepared to charge through just a moment before.

They'd only been in the building for a short time, thus had never properly cleared it. Verboom directed, "Since we might be staying here for a while, First Squad, clear the basement for tunnels; you know the drill. Second, get upstairs and look for mouse holes. Third and weapons, here facing southeast, but Third, send a team to the rear in case the bastards come up out of the sewer system again. And watch out for booby traps; remember how de Haan had his balls blown off . . ."

Centurion William Ruiz-Jones, Ninety-Fourth Engineer *Tercio*, held a tiny chemical light over a sketch of this portion of the city's sewer system. It wasn't so much that batteries had gotten a little scarce, though they had, as that a flashlight, even with a filter, was just too bright down in this shit-reeking hell.

Olfactory fatigue hadn't quite set in yet, since Ruiz led his platoon of sappers down into the muck. *And, just imagine, with almost the entire civilian population evacuated, the sewers are* cleaner *than they've ever been. I can only wonder how bad it was before the war started.*

But, at that, shit and piss or not, it's probably still no worse than the stink of unburied rotting bodies up above.

It was, except for the tiny chemical light, pitch black down in this place. The men kept together by holding the combat harness of the man to their front. In Ruiz's case, he kept direction through pace count and his sketch.

Pity I don't have a working set of night-vision goggles, but we just exhausted the batteries for those. Supposedly someone in one of the maintenance tercios is working on either using different batteries in homemade cases or gutting and refilling the worn-out ones we have. Funny how it's always the little things that get you.

He'd stopped keeping up the pace count while mentally bitching at fate. He started again—*one-o-five . . . one-o-six . . . and left here . . . yeah . . . there's the branch line . . . one . . . two . . . three . . .*

At "fifteen," Ruiz stopped again. It wasn't for purposes of complaining, nor even of navigation. He was simply listening for any sound of enemy in the tunnel, as well as of fighting overhead. He took the chemlight between his teeth and stuck the sketch in his pocket. Then flicked on the night-vision scope on his rifle and raised it to his shoulder. *Go figure, incompatible batteries with the goggles. Somebody wasn't thinking the day they bought one or the other.*

The scope was a thermal. Unlike light-amplifying scopes it needed no light at all. Instead, it picked up heat or, better said, differences in heat. The thermal scope, however, did give off visible light; otherwise the user wouldn't be able to see anything. Indeed, it could illuminate the face of the viewer. There was a flexible rubber eye guard which both shielded the eye from recoil and cut off light until it was pressed forward, snug against the eye. As Ruiz pressed his eye into it, creating a seal, it folded forward, moving out of the way the piece of rubber that prevented the escape of light. He scanned back and forth and was relieved that, *Thank God there's nobody down here. If any of us shoot we're all fucking deaf.*

Cover and concealment was not all that a city provided to its defenders. More importantly, it gave them the opportunity to change what could be perceived by an attacker and what could be done to that attacker, as well as where and when it could be done. New entrances could be made anywhere and carefully hidden. Covered and concealed routes for counterattacks could be prepared almost anywhere. They almost became as submarines are at sea, visible usually only by chance, except when they, themselves, elected to appear for an attack.

Satisfied that the way ahead was clear, Ruiz turned off the scope and continued his march forward. On "thirty-two" he stopped and went through the routine with the scope again, but this time he was looking for an exit from the sewer, one that he and his men had carved out and covered while preparations to defend the place were still ongoing. The oval they'd cut was unlikely to be found, except from the sewer, as they'd plastered and lightly wired it into place and then covered all the walls of the basement with a thick layer of grime.

Turning, Ruiz whispered to the next man behind him, *"quietly . . . bayonets."* The whispered words passed down the line . . . *"quiquiieietttlllyyy . . . bayayobayonetsetsets."*

There were clicks, as the bayonets were fastened, but

very subdued as the men held their hands over the
bayonets' butts and lugs.

They had plenty of grenades, but Ruiz had ruled them
out for the first breakout into the basement. He'd decided
so because, *In the first place, nobody might be there, so
why let the enemy know we've arrived before we have to?
In the second place, the blast will be bad on them, in the
open spaces of the basement, but on us, here in this
miserable fucking tunnel, the blast will be catastrophic.*

When he couldn't hear anymore clicking, Ruiz walked
forward to the oval, feeling the edge of the tunnel ahead
of him until his fingers found a wall. The light from the
chemlight wasn't much use for this. He felt around some
more and shifted his position until he was certain he was
within a couple of feet of the wall and centered. He then
spit the chemlight down into the muck at the bottom.

He raised a foot and flicked his rifle, a standard Legion
F-26, to burst. Behind him he heard a barrage of clicks
from the rifles of his men. Then, with a silent prayer to
God, he kicked forward, knocking the oval out into the
basement and letting a subjectively bright light into the
tunnel.

He wasn't blinded. There were at least four men he
could see in the basement. They weren't friendlies, either.
Ruiz fired hyperfast bursts once, twice, from the hip. One
of the Taurans went down like a sack of potatoes while
the other was set to spinning to the basement floor,
spraying guts and blood as he did.

Ruiz charged out with a wordless scream of pure fury.
His men picked up the scream. One of the Taurans fired
and connected, but at this range, with the bullet still

yawing like mad, it hit at a bad angle and failed to penetrate the glassy metal plates of Ruiz's legionary lorica. It still hit at an odd enough angle as to bowl him over. On later inspection he'd find that the bullet had almost penetrated and had, indeed, left a deep gouge in the metal.

The rest of the men poured over their temporarily downed centurion. The Taurans had no possible retreat, so between the—as it turned out—four of them remaining and the couple of dozen Balboans swarming them, the basement descended quickly into an orgy of slashing blades, flashing muzzles, and brain-spattered rifle butts in a matter of seconds.

The last Tauran went down, rather, up. Ruiz saw two of his men spike the poor bastard and lift him up into the air, before tossing him. The man's mouth worked like a dying fish cast up on a beach. Then the basement grew momentarily quiet.

Not so the upstairs, however; though it sounded like men taken by surprise up there, it also sounded to Ruiz's practiced ear like men overcoming their surprise and getting ready to fight, fast. This was confirmed when a pair of grenades sailed down the stairs and went off, almost together.

The twin blasts knocked Ruiz to the floor. The centurion was sure he'd lost an eardrum, and probably damaged another. Lying on his back, he raised his rifle to where he thought the entrance for the stairs might be and began firing burst after burst, right through the somewhat shoddy floor above. His men took up the same thing, though spreading their fire more or less around the entire ceiling. They couldn't hear screams—truth be told they couldn't hear a damned thing—but had the sense of falling bodies, even so.

Verboom never felt anything so agonizing in his life as the bullet that came through his heel, shattering small bones there, and then proceeded up his calf, skimming the bones and splitting the muscle for over a foot. The pain was so immeasurably vast that, after collapsing to the floor, he didn't even feel the next two that went through, in one case, his hip, and in the other, his abdomen. Had one of them been kind enough to have severed his spine, he'd probably have been thankful for it, at least in the short term. As it was he simply passed out, which was as good.

Thus, he didn't see when the Balboans surged up from below, shooting, stabbing, and hacking at his men. He also didn't see it when one of them, about to tear his throat out with a bayonet, had his rifle knocked aside by the leader of the Balboans. Neither did he hear Centurion Ruiz order, "We're stretched thin enough, medically, as we can deal with. Put out a parley flag and shout out to the Taurans to ask if they want their wounded back."

CHAPTER TWENTY-TWO

"Therefore, neither be led astray by current opinions nor meddle in politics, but with single heart fulfill your essential duty of loyalty, and bear in mind that duty is weightier than a mountain, while death is lighter than a feather."

—*The Imperial Rescript to Soldiers and Sailors* (1882)

East of Hephaestos, Balboa

Of course, nobody in the tercio had really been asked to volunteer. Instead, their commander, Legate Antonio de Legazpi, had simply gone to one of his cohorts, plus a few, by maniples, starting with the Cazador and transport maniples, and asked, "Who here is such a cowardly, chickenshit disgrace to his beloved country, our dear province of Valle de las Lunas, and our famous tercio, that when our Duque asks us to go to the aid of our Santa Josefinan legionary brothers, and end a threat to our own borders, would refuse to volunteer? Anybody? Anybody at all? Don't be ashamed, just step forward and I'll sign the papers to discharge you this very instant. Nobody? Good."

That took a couple of days, but the days were not wasted. Rather, the tercio's stable of mules were packed with food and ammunition, in a ratio of about three to two. There were between eight and nine hundred of them, not including their bell mares but including the ones partially funded by the Legion in peace and then called up to serve. Then the bulk of the mules, their bell mares, their muleskinners, and the Cazador maniple, had marched about twenty to thirty-five miles into Santa Josefina to establish caches, before the mules returned to either pick up heavy equipment left behind, to pack more consumables, or take the burden of some of it off the men's backs. The Cazadores, with a very few mules, continued on to scout out the Tauran defenses of the mountain, Cerro Presinger, and its flanks.

This would have been out of the question, daring enough to be labelled stupidity, not long before. But then came the Tauran ban on air strikes in the jungle, the essentially complete fixing of the Tauran forces by the two tercios, La Negrita and La Virgen, along with the rise in guerillas over much of the country. Before, Marciano could have sent his commandos out to interdict and destroy the caches. Now?

"Now, gentlemen," said de Lagazpi, "now he's got to use the commandos just to screen his own flanks. We can get away with a lot more than we could have before. And we have calculated carefully our needs . . ."

Of course, in war calculations tend to fail. . . .

"Shut the fuck up with your bitching, Morgenthaler," said Corporal Martinez, without any real heat. Martinez was, in fact, a very distant cousin of that Martinez who was a likely candidate for senior noncom—"Sergeant Major General," in the parlance—of the legions. Morgenthaler, despite a name that, on Old Earth, would have implied whiteness, was every bit as dark as centuries of surely gleeful interbreeding would suggest.

Said Morgenthaler, struggling to pull himself up a slippery jungle trail, trodden into mud by the several hundred men who'd preceded him, "It's been five days since we crossed the border, and two fucking days since I've *eaten* anything, Corp; I got a right to bitch."

"Yeah, but I have a right not to hear it, and so do the rest of the men. So shut the fuck up or I'll just shoot you to get a little peace and quiet."

In the legions, that threat was rather more real than it would have been in some other armies. Morgenthaler shut up. Moreover, it actually *was* peaceful and quiet in the jungle, but for the sound of the troops. The law of the jungle was more than a phrase; hence the animals of the place tended to clear out when a potential threat got close. In this case, that threat was over a thousand men, spread across a front of about three miles, and most of them hungry and, like Morgenthaler, bitching about it.

"Why isn't there any goddamned food though, Corp? I knew we sent out enough, I helped pack some of the mules."

Martinez slapped absent-mindedly at a mosquito. "We *all* helped pack the mules, Private, at least to the point of carrying dry rations to the staging areas. The problem, so I would guess, is that small sections of *Cazadores*, with mules carrying their food and no equipment on their backs heavier than a radio, simply moved further, faster than we can and placed the caches based on how fast they moved. Simple as that; everybody makes mistakes. We'll eat, I should think, sometime tonight."

"Think we'll get a rest then?"

Martinez shook his head. "Doubt it. We're behind as it is and any rest equals a hungry day somewhere down the road."

"Yeah, suppose so. Oh, well."

Shithead, thought the corporal.

West slope, Cerro Presinger, Santa Josefina

The mountain wasn't actually all that impressive. In the first place, it was set in very high ground, already, such that its more than twelve-thousand-foot elevation was really only about a thousand feet above the floor of the valley below. Moreover, there were another five peaks, all within mortar range and two within heavy machine-gun range. Moreover, that high up, with air that thin and rainfall somewhat iffy, there was a lot of rock, not much vegetation, and what there was rather sparse and dry.

In the opinion of Tribune Delgado of the Fifth Tercio's Cazador maniple, the peak or Cerro Presinger, itself, was the wrong immediate objective anyway. Speaking to his legate, about thirty miles to his east, via a carefully sited half rhombic directional antenna, he said, "The peak's a bitch, sir, just a bitch. Not only is it straight-sided, around about sixty percent of it, but the parts that are more or less easily accessible are well covered by direct fire, while the

straight sides which—yes, we or the line dogs can climb—
are also covered by fire from nearby positions. . . . the
damned mountain is framed by lakes on either side, sir . . .
it's a strong battle position for a maniple or, as they'd say,
'a company' . . . and, sir, I spent the last three days sneaking
around this area. No, the key is a peak about twenty-three
hundred meters to the east-northeast . . . yes, sir, that one,
Glacier Mountain . . . no, there's no glacier there, but there
is a little frost or maybe even snow . . . if we take that, put
in a platoon of mountain guns using direct lay, then the
two peaks to the north-northwest become untenable for
the Taurans . . . yes, sir, . . . and once we get first one then
the other of those, we're in light machine gun range and
the Taurans can't stay on Cerro Presinger for more than a
couple of days at the most . . . no, sir, I don't have the
punch to take that first peak . . . yes, sir, I can cut off some
the trails and ridges and keep them from shifting troops
easily . . . roger, sir . . . no, sir, I only have a few directional
mines per squad . . . yes, sir, wilco."

De Legazpi had pushed his command group and the
one cohort mercilessly to get as far as they had in four
days. He also spent a good deal of time on the radio
talking to Villalobos and Salas, explaining his jump up in
rank and their orders. He'd left his sergeant major with
the artillery detachment—one smaller than normal
battery of mountain guns and a standard battery of
mortars—to push them just as hard, though, of course,
not quite fast.

There was a certain irony in those mountain guns;
they'd been made by Claudio Marciano's own country and

sold to Carrera in the middling days of the war in Pashtia. The irony was that the guns and their shells would soon be pasting the Tuscan troops of one of Tuscany's own generals.

The sun was down and wouldn't be up for some hours.

Behind a thin screen of Cazadores, the maniple of which Corporal Martinez and Morgenthaler were a part took the lead for their cohort's main effort. Another maniple, to the northwest, was moving on Cerro Irbet, but would not kick off their attack until after Glacier Hill was secured.

The maniple was in a diamond formation. One platoon—not theirs—took the actual center of the ridge leading to the peak. The other two were somewhat behind and spread to the left and right. The weapons platoon, with a half dozen mules for ammunition, took up the rear with the maniple commander approximately in the center. The weapons platoon was fairly standard, with three mortars and half a dozen anti-tank weapons, though these usually fired simple high explosive. The difference was that the mortars were some of the comparatively few sixty-millimeter versions owned by the legions. They weren't really much use against fortifications, so wouldn't be used to prep the objective. They *were*, on the other hand, useful for breaking up an assembling counterattack. They'd be held for that eventuality.

Behind that maniple, at some distance, trailed one platoon of engineers and one platoon of those Tuscan mountain guns with some very tired gunners. The latter's guns were carried by some twenty-eight robust and healthy mules bearing special pack saddles. Another dozen mules carried ammunition to the tune of seventy-two rounds per gun. This sounded like not much. However, it was another peculiarity of mountain warfare that direct fire with artillery was often possible without exposing the crews to much in the way of return fire. That direct fire, being much more accurate, vastly reduced the number of shells required for a given job. Put another way, because they were safer, themselves, artillery shifted somewhat away from suppression and toward destruction.

However, the guns would not be mounted on—nor anywhere near—this peak, not until the men of both the artillery and the infantry could dig them some fairly solid firing positions with overhead cover. There may have been a ban on using aerial bombing of the rain forest, but the mountain peaks here were mostly above the rain forest and likely to get some kind of aerial attack. Supposedly, guerillas operating near the Tauran's main air base would make that somewhat problematic. Still, as Legate de Legazpi had said, "Don't expect too much."

The other part of the fire support package were the dozen one-twenty mortars. Those, however, had not accompanied the assault force, but had stayed about three thousand meters to the west-northwest. There they'd carved out a firing position by chopping out enough of the blessed rain forest to allow the shells to sail out to the targets unimpeded. This also had the effect of granting a degree of cover from any return fire, the ballistics of which didn't quite match those of the one-twenties' for a given range and elevation.

***

The defenders were an understrength platoon of Tuscan Ligurini, mountain troops themselves and among the best on the planet. The first warning they had wasn't the rattle of incoming shells nor the astonishingly rapid rate of fire of a Balboan machine gun. Rather, it was a campus of antaniae, Terra Nova's dangerously septic-mouthed winged reptilians, crying *mnnbt . . . mnnbt . . . mnnbt* while flapping away to the east-southeast. The vile creatures flew away in terror of a creature that seemed to be much bigger and fiercer than they were. A few trixies followed the antaniae, killed a couple, and then settled down to feast on the remains.

Thought Private Boneli, manning the platoon's radio and field telephone, *I wonder what spooked . . . oh, oh.* He nudged his platoon leader, *Maresciallo*—or Master Sergeant—Pierantoni. "I think we've got trouble coming," Boneli whispered. "Local wildlife running away from *something*."

"Wha . . . what?" Pierantoni was alert in an instant. "Oh, shit. Look, call the squads and the company and let them know, Boneli. I'm going to troop the line to make sure everyone's up and alert."

He felt his helmet for the night-vision monocular he'd fixed there. The thing added so much weight to the helmet as to make it virtually intolerable to wear for any period of time. With a disgusted sound, Pierantoni rotated it down over his eye, letting the eye guard seal off light before turning it on.

The sergeant stood up as straight as possible inside of the platoon command post bunker—a roughly chest deep excavation, done partially with explosives, ringed by sandbags above and below, with decently thick logs overhead and layers of dirt and rocks over that—and eased himself out the narrow, packed-earth entrance. He stopped just past the edge, his eyes and ears just above ground level, listening. He heard an antania's death shrieks, along with a Trixie's triumphant feasting call. *No, that's not unusual.*

Shortly after that, while ascending the sandbag steps that led up and out, a troop of monkeys scampered by on the ground. Pierantoni stopped again, listening. *No, that's not that unusual around here either.*

Pierantoni turned completely around then, scanning the slope of the mountain. At first, he saw nothing but thin vegetation and some more monkeys. Then he spotted them, what looked to be a squad of men, at least the orange blurs of what was probably a squad, moving hunched over under heavy packs, maybe five hundred meters away.

Now, that's *unusual.*

Pierantoni crouched and walked briskly to the central position of the squad, second squad, in front of him. Making sure the squad leader was awake, he said, "Enemy coming. Go make sure third squad is up; I'll handle first."

Halfway to first squad, Pierantoni met the squad leader who said, "I was just coming to tell you . . ."

The senior cut him off. "Company? I know. Get back to your squad and stand . . ."

Pierantoni's orders were interrupted by a rising flurry of fire, with tracers drawing lines in the sky and across retinae, off to the northwest.

★★★

The maniple commander had control of all three one-twenty platoons for now. There really weren't that many shells for what were voracious consumers of ammunition. He had enough ammunition allocated to suppress the objective and the lesser prominences to his right, but nothing like enough to destroy the enemy on all of them. It wasn't that ammunition wasn't available; there were more than twenty thousand shells still sitting back near Hephaestos. It was that not all that much could be ported; mountain warfare had always required a certain miser's touch where ammunition was concerned. This, too, tended to drive the use of direct lay, where possible.

The other maniple, now apparently engaged, could have asked for support from the mortars. When asked by the mortars themselves, though, the forward observers had said, "Forget it; we're in amongst them already."

"Okay," ordered Martinez's and Morgenthaler's commander, Tribune Chacón, "surprise, if we ever had it, is blown. Hunker down for a bit."

That command came just about in time because Pierantoni's platoon, having targets and seeing that battle had commenced, opened up of their own accord. Tracers skipped through spaces that had been occupied by men seconds before. Even then, a couple of Balboan mountaineers were hit.

Chacón then called the mortars for some high explosive. That came in, within a minute and ten seconds, but had surprisingly little effect. "Right. Switch to delay."

A one-twenty shell hit directly on the roof of

Pierantoni's bunker. The fuse, set on "super quick," which was to say point detonating, passed through sod set up as camouflage and hit the rock burster layer beneath. At that it went off, shattering the rock it hit and blowing most of the others in the burster layer in every direction but down. The dirt below the rocks compressed, and the logs beneath that shuddered and groaned.

For all that, Pierantoni was fairly unimpressed. Yes, they were gut-rattling. Yes, that was unpleasant. Yes, *my ear . . .* "What did you say?"

On the whole, though, they did little actual physical damage. Somebody took a small piece of a fragment that drew a red line across his nose before bouncing off his cheekbone. Another screamed, "My eye! My eye!" before falling to the base of his fighting position, clawing at his face. But those didn't really interrupt the integrity of Pierantoni's defense.

"Besides," as he told his third squad leader before a shell cut the wire, "down in our holes we're safe. If we try to pull out, those things will cut us to ribbons. So, we stay as long as we can."

That estimate changed when he saw a fighting position to his left front collapse even as a huge column of dirt and rocks were tossed into the air. He tried to do an estimate of what was coming in his head. The short version of that was, *They won't get a majority of my positions or my men. What they will get is uncovered holes in the defense they can infiltrate through. Time to leave, incoming or not. Besides, delay is a lot less dangerous to men in the open than superquick is.*

There was a pyrotechnic signal for a withdrawal, in this

case a green star cluster. But any pyrotechnic signal, any signal at all, under the circumstances, was likely to mean only one thing which would be instantly clear to the enemy: begin the assault now.

Instead of reaching for the star cluster, Pierantoni called all his squads. Only first and second answered. "Thin the line, pull out, assemble at the rally point to the southeast."

He gave much the same order to Boneli, then left the bunker and cut left to third squad. With the enemy firing on delay it was almost safe to do so.

Almost, however, wasn't quite the same as completely. Pierantoni stuck his head into the rearward entrance to third squad leader's fighting position and shouted, "Get the fuck out now! Get to the rally point!" Nothing happened. He had to physically reach out, grab, and shake the squad leader to get his attention. Once he had that he repeated the order. Then he got to his knees again to stand and move further left.

At that time a shell landed almost exactly between Pierantoni and the fighting position. Like the other more recent ones, it penetrated into the earth before detonating. He had the visual impression of a wall of dirt and rock closing in on the two men inside the bunker, while tossing their overhead cover forward and up. For himself, the ground suddenly lurched upward with force enough to break both shins and hurl him into the air. He flew, conscious and screaming with pain, the lower halves of his shattered shins spinning, until he arced down to the ground. There he rolled downhill. The rolling twisted his already broken bones, turning them into internal blenders for the flesh and nerves of his lower legs. Mercifully, sometime in the process, he passed out.

All night the skilled engineers worked, aided by the artillerymen themselves, and an infantry maniple that provided both security and scut labor.

In an ideal circumstance, they'd have driven tunnels to the forward face of the ridge from its rear. There wasn't nearly time for that. Instead, they used shaped charges to blow narrow holes up to nine feet into the ridge's forward slope. This was tricky, as the stands for the shaped charges were designed to provide standoff but also to work only in the vertical plane. Getting them to fire almost horizontally into the ridge required a little thought and some scavenged logs. When the holes had been punched into the ridge, forty-pound cratering charges were prepared for detonation and then pushed into the holes. This gave a very suboptimal crater. In general, the process had to be repeated with the shaped charges and somewhat smaller cratering charges, all supplemented by a good deal of sweaty pick and shovel work. The sun came up before they were finished, which required the engineers and sappers to lay off and blend back into the ever-so-blessed rain forest until evening. That whole next day the infantry concentrated on making the defenders' lives miserable.

Morgenthaler heard a low and pitiful moan, coming from down the slope. Without asking for permission—he really wasn't that kind of soldier—he went to investigate.

What he found was a body in a camouflage uniform, half covered with dirt and rocks, and with the legs bent at

an angle that made him nauseous. He wasn't at all sure
the body was even alive until he heard the moaning again.
He walked around and began brushing rocks and dirt
away from the head.

One eye opened up and said something in Italian. It
was one word every speaker of a romance language was
likely to be able to understand from any other.
Morgenthaler took out his canteen and tried to place it to
the victim's mouth, but the angle was all wrong, letting
the water dribble wastefully to the ground. He tried a
different tack, which was to pour some into his cupped
palm and hold that out by the poor crippled bastard's
mouth. It was demeaning, he supposed, but it worked.

The next three words were also easily translatable.
"*Grazi . . . molto dolore . . . aiutami.*"

"The accent's funny, friend," said Morgenthaler, "but
I understand." He handed over his canteen, saying,
"Here, take this and do your best with it while I go for
help."

"*Grazi . . . grazi.*"

Patting the Tuscan reassuringly, Morgenthaler set off
in search of the company medics. They weren't quite sure
what to do. Evacuation was next to impossible from this
place and they had their hands full with their own
wounded. Moreover, they were part-time citizen soldiers,
militia, not all that well schooled in what might be called
"the niceties of the law of war." They could, after all, just
ignore the man and let him die in his own time.

"Fuck that shit," said Tribune Chacón, who *was* better
versed in those niceties. "He's just a regular guy, from a
regular formation, doing a job not a lot different from us.

Go get him. If he dies it won't be because we failed in our duties as either soldiers or human beings."

The niceties of the laws of war did not require that an enemy be allowed to escape to fight again. Once the mountain gun platoon was dug in near Glacier Mountain, and another platoon similarly dug in on Cerro Irbet, they commenced a bombardment of the defenses around Cerro Noroeste, which was, despite the name, actually almost due north of Cerro Presinger. At the same time, under that covering fire, the one previously uncommitted maniple began its ascent up the north side of Cerro Noroeste, even while the mortars began to drop rounds to the south of the peak. The mortars let up after a time, the objective was to show that they could block retreat at will.

The Tuscans here were not wimps. Chacón sauntered over to watch the fun. The mountain guns didn't fire fast and the procedure was, to the tribune's eye, a little odd. He asked about it.

"It's because we're firing direct lay and haven't laid in a parallel sheaf, sir," said one of the gun crews between shots. "Ordinarily, artillerymen estimate the range and then set their elevation and charge. Oh, and deflection, too, of course. It works because, with the same data, all the guns at pointing at the same point on the ground only offset for their position within the battery.

"Doesn't work for us when we're set up like this. Oh, sure, we estimate the range and set our sights for that. But range estimation in this kind of terrain is tricky. And our laser range finder's been on order for, like, *years*. So, when we fire with our 'base gun,' it's called, it's almost meaningless to the other guns. So, we aim the sight at the burst—first round's usually a miss—and then move the gun so the sights are back on target. Then we fire again. Sometimes takes two or three shots, you know, sir?

"Once we have a hit, we don't do anything but level the sight. Then we look at the elevation, and get the right range and charge from the charts that have that. We give that range to the other guns, and then we all have target practice.

"Figure it must be pure hell in the receiving end."

"Yeah, I figure," agreed Chacon. He watched the guns do their thing for a couple of bunkers: "Fire!" Boom. Rattle. Boom. "Adjust the sight . . . reload . . . fire!" Boom . . . rattle . . . boom. "Target!"

Kinda pretty, really, thought Chacón, watching the point of impact transform into a black, red, and orange flower. *Course, not so pretty on the receiving end.*

A well-built fighting position could take a lot. It couldn't take four seventy-five-millimeter guns pounding, pounding, pounding until a shell burst through. Chacon figured one must have gotten through, because the roof lifted and fire and smoke shot from the firing ports.

Good men, never even tried to surrender or pull out. On the other hand, I wonder if, by the time their position's almost wrecked, they aren't so stunned silly they can't even think, let alone think about surrender or retreat.

In any case, the Tuscan Ligurini held on well past normal human endurance. Finally, with more than half their men down and well over half their fighting positions smashed, with machine guns ripping air and ground all around them, with the Balboans reaching grenade throwing distance—because another nice feature of direct lay was that it was very safe to maneuver friendly troops very close to it—with their barbed wire chopped up and scattered, only then did their company commander, from what amounted to his deathbed, give the order to surrender.

Perhaps they'd had to spend a day or so fighting off guerillas around their base, but it was only then that the first Tauran aircraft came in. They circled for a while, dodging a couple of missiles thrown their way. They never did attack.

Chacón theorized, aloud, "They can't go after the guns, because though at the edge of the rainforest that means they're still in the rainforest. They can't attack the men on top of Cerro Noroeste because they're probably not sure who owns it, in the first place, but have to figure there are prisoners there, if we own it, in the second. And there aren't any other good targets around."

He added, finally. "The blessed fucking rain forest; if those dumb shits had to live in it, fight it back every day to eke out a living, I wonder if they'd be so enthusiastic to keep it untouched. Not that I'm exactly bitching, mind you."

"Who do I pull out of the line to block this hole?" asked Marciano. "I already know I don't have enough to counterattack to re-establish the line where it was."

Rall, the Sachsen colonel, shook his head. "There's nobody, sir. The two regiments we were already dealing with are pressing hard all along the front. Yes, they're paying a higher price in blood than we are, but there's a reason for that, a reason they're willing to pay that."

"In two days," said del Collea, "or three at the outside, that regiment—let's not pretend it's anything but the Balboan Fifth Mountain—or a goodly chunk of it, acting under official orders—is going to pop out of the jungle and cut our road to the capital. They'll be dropping mortars on our head a day before that."

Marciano pursed his lips, looked at the map, looked down, then back at the map. He cocked his head and raised one quizzical eyebrow.

"Ever read Xenophon, gentlemen? The *Anabasis*?"

"Yes, sir," said Rall.

"You assigned it to me when I was a lieutenant," said del Collea, with a genuine grin.

"Good," said Marciano. "I hope the lessons took."

"Sir?"

"We've done all we can here. We're bugging out; there's no place left for us to make a stand in front of the capital. We cannot make a stand *at* the capital. But there *is* still a place we can make a stand, maybe even save something from this goat fuck. We'll take the government with us as we go, along with any civilians or police who want to join us as well. But we're going to the last place we can make a stand." Marciano leaned over and tapped the map at the place where the Mar Furioso and Santa Josefina's border with Córdoba joined to form a narrow place, maybe fifteen miles across, with a huge lake to anchor one flank, a huge ocean for the other, a small but adequate bay for shipping, and adequate road net, and heavily settled and farmed enough that the rain forest would not impose much in the way of restrictive fire measures.

"Something we've always had, gentlemen, but have rarely been able to make much use of, is the ability to move faster than the enemy. But this time tomorrow I want the entire task force on the road or in the air, and legging it trippingly for that."

"We'll have to give up any semblance of our own air force," Rall observed.

Marciano disagreed. "Not exactly. We'll have to give up some responsiveness, but we'll also give up the need to secure their bases when we send them to Cienfuegos."

"Good point, sir."

"Okay," said Marciano, "enough chatting. I want to brief orders this evening just after dark. Make it happen."

CHAPTER TWENTY-THREE

"If there is one attitude more dangerous than to
assume that a future war will be just like the last one,
it is to imagine that it will be so utterly different we
can afford to ignore all the lessons of the last one."
—John C. Slessor, *Air Power and Armies*

**Tauran Union Expeditionary Force Headquarters,
Academia Sergento Juan Malvegui (Under New
Management), Puerto Lindo, Balboa**

The old Balboan military academy, overlooking the port,
besides serving as a headquarters for Janier's
expeditionary force, also served as a casualty collection
point cum medical clearing station, as well as a convenient
spot to evacuate the badly wounded to the hospital ship
thirty or so miles out to sea.

Down the coastal road, in a plainly marked ambulance,
Werner Verboom was carried in a state of pain barely held
in check by the drugs he'd been given. Besides having lost
quite a bit of blood, the bones in his heel and leg were in

a bad enough state that a just-this-side of uncontrollable infection was possible. If the infection wasn't contained and defeated, that leg, below the knee, would have to come off. And no one would listen to him when he said, "If it gets that bad, just kill me."

The road on which Verboom's ambulance rattled, the road from Cristobal to Puerto Lindo, had, over the centuries, gone from a mule trail to widened dirt to gravel to cobblestoned to corruption-afflicted asphalt to potholes interspersed with bumps and boulders to, finally, under the legions, a fairly decent two-lane highway. It had taken some damage in the fighting and been subject to considerable wear in the logistic effort, but, precisely because it was so important, Janier's engineers had kept it in pretty fair order, even making a few improvements here and there.

On the whole, the road wasn't considered safe to drive without escort. Indios from the deep jungle to the west, formed into Carrera's Forty-fourth Tercio, regularly ambushed logistic columns and lone couriers. The Indians, descended from and still calling themselves "Chocoes," had little but rifles and some machine guns, and those of older, simpler design. They wore not much but loincloths in legionary pattern camouflage or, sometimes a shirt. Rank was painted on as often as not. But not once had a patrol trying to clear the road found the Indios unless they'd wanted to be found. Not once had they been made to pay the price of an ambush if they'd had so much as twenty seconds to blend into the jungle.

Corporal Moya—no first name, no surname, just

"Moya"—wearing just a loincloth and the temporary tattoos called "jagua," and carrying a Volgan rifle, watched the ambulance pass by. He vaguely remembered that the big red crosses weren't supposed to be attacked, that it was, as the *Cazador* team that had come to train the men and older boys of Moya's village told them, extremely bad magic to do so. From the bushes in which he and his men hid, Moya raised two fingers. Immediately, blowguns and rifle butts were lowered, as the men relaxed again, waiting for their next opportunity. The Cazadors had originally offered regular pay for regular work, as regulars, but the Chocoes really weren't interested in that. What had brought them over were the twin promises of rifles better than any they had, and payment—and in real silver coins, no less—for Tauran heads. *That* was something the Indios understood.

Unfortunately, as the first platoon pursuing an Indio-initiated ambush had discovered, the Chocoes *owned* the jungle. You couldn't see them, you couldn't hear them, and if they wanted you dead, a small poisoned dart from a blowgun worked about as well as anything else in jungle range. The platoon had learned that, albeit the hard way, and had never been able to pass the lesson on as men need heads to speak with and they'd lost all theirs.

Moya and his men frowned. A head, was after all, a head, but they didn't want to risk the evil magic. They heard a sound then, one which had become familiar. It was, they'd smiled as they saw it, another truck, one without the forbidden markings, coming down the road.

The medevac helicopter that would bring the stretcher-bound Verboom to the ship for extensive surgery and possible return to Haarlem disgorged some other people as it touched down on the old fort's parade ground. Most of these were Tauran troops, previously lightly wounded, being returned to duty. One, however, was Sergeant Juan Sais, being returned to a prisoner of war camp. Sais still had his protective mask, and his helmet—those belonged to the soldier carrying them, even if he was captured—and still wore regular legionary battle dress, which had been cleaned and repaired for him on the hospital ship where his wounds had been treated.

While a stretcher team, assisted by the helicopter's crew chief, worked to buckle Verboom into one of the racks in the bird, a two-man military police team had shown up to take charge of Sais and bring him to the POW camp. This was actually not all that far away, straight line, at maybe twenty miles. Going by road, largely because a helicopter was too important to risk on a mere POW, was a little longer.

The MPs put flexicuffs on Sais before helping him into their vehicle. "Nothing personal," said the Anglian MP, "but you gents have proven a little difficult in the past." Sais understood, actually. *Given half a chance I'd be off this son of a bitch and into the jungle in no time.*

Still, he took the whole trip philosophically, right up until the jeep came to a place where the two highways across the isthmus came close together. A substantial increment of construction equipment was in the area, busily digging trenches and later holes for bunkers. There weren't any concrete mixers to be seen, but off in the distance, he could hear a number of chain saws in operation. Sais had a sort of sinking feeling at seeing all this, for a couple of reasons. Then they turned to the right and toward a former housing area for legionary officers and senior noncoms.

Sais expressed his feeling on that *sotto voce*, "Oh, fuck!"

Janier barely noticed the lone MP vehicle following the asphalt road toward the small POW camp near the former housing area. It wasn't an especially important place, anyway, what with fewer than five hundred prisoners being held there for now. The buildings were useful for interrogators and the staff of the corps responsible for this area, neither of whom, after all, were used to roughing it.

He wasn't especially concerned about the siting of the defenses being dug in this area. He *was* concerned with their strength.

Janier jumped up and down on the earthen overhead cover on a section of trench. It bounced. Stopping, he began to turn until he caught sight of a senior noncom.

"Get me your company commander!" shouted the general. "And while you're at it, get the word I want to see your battalion and brigade commanders, too. And fast!"

As the noncom trotted to find his commanding officer, Janier folded his arms and put on a fierce mien. The expression gave no clue to his inner thoughts.

I've made so many mistakes, the Gaul thought, *I cannot be sure I am not making one, by standing fast, now. But I see no other choice. It's taken months to get everyone ashore that we have, very nearly the entire deployable military force of every state in the Tauran Union. I'd be lucky beyond my desserts if I could get a quarter of them out—and that without their equipment—without Carrera finding out and launching on us immediately. And the three-quarters that would still be stuck here would be out of positions and probably panic-stricken. And I wouldn't blame them a bit.*

Our only chance is to stand here together. He's only got one bolt to shoot at us, after all, assuming the information my lovely Major Campbell was given and analyzed was correct, and that's the way to bet it. He can hit us with a massive barrage for several hours, enough to have destroyed us in the open several times over, but probably not enough to do so if we're dug in. Well . . . I hope it's not enough. And if we can survive, we can beat off the attack that will follow on the barrage. And if we can do that, his bolt is shot and we can march into the capital as victors.

But what did the Spartans say to Philip? Ah, yes, I remember; "If."

Janier noticed then a captain standing off to one side. "Are you the company commander, son?"

"Yes, sir; Captain Bengliu, Dacian Gendarmerie."

Janier stepped off the overhead cover he'd been bouncing atop, then ordered, "Jump up and down on that a few times."

"I will, sir," said the Dacian, "but it's really not necessary; I know it's shit. But what can I do? The court has ordered no destruction of the rain forest because of the treaties . . ."

Janier stepped forward, and put a sympathetic, even fraternal, arm around the Dacian's shoulders. "Ah, I see the problem. They didn't, you know, Captain."

"But, sir, my government said . . ."

"Fuck them," Janier interrupted, amiably, "and fuck the court, too, at least in principle. What that never sufficiently to be damned court did was to forbid the bombing by air or artillery. Their ruling seems to have missed chain saws entirely. Now, shall I call the engineers and have them loan you a few?"

"Oh, General, the *tuica*'s on me for life if you would."

"Consider it done," said the broadly smiling Gaul, adding, with a wink, "and I'll hold you to that booze, after we win."

Hide Position Sierra Two-Nine, Cristobal Province, Balboa

Flores hauled Sergeant Rojas in through the narrow entrance, then both of them pulled in Domingo. With him inside, Flores closed the light barrier and turned on their backup light, a crank-driven piece.

The sergeant and the soldier—technically and by title, the *cazador*—had been topside for one of the not especially frequent patrols launched from their hide. It was vibrations felt through the sodden ground that had sent them topside. Both were breathing fairly heavily, causing Flores to ask, "What happened? Did you get spotted? Are they on your tail?"

"None . . . of . . . the . . . above," Rojas got out, with some effort, words interspersed with heavy breathing. "But . . . we do have . . . guests. There's a company of . . . something—heavy machinery or tanks, based on the sounds—maybe three hundred meters . . . from here, digging in like crazy. Domingo and I . . . heard the sounds and got as close as we could to investigate. We'd have . . . gone closer but"—Rojas held up one hand to show several black spikes sticking in it—"we ran into this crap. They probably, and sensibly, cut it down . . . to get it out of the way, but where they left it I crawled right onto the shit. We couldn't get through."

"Okay. Radio Balboa put out several radio messages while you were gone, Sarge." Flores pulled from his pocket a small notebook, removed it from a plastic bag, and read off. "'Yvette has a monstrous dildo,' was one. 'It is a time of great sorrow,' was the second. And 'there was a fire at the steamship company.' Important?"

"Yeah," said Rojas. "The second one means maximum reconnaissance of all areas of operation; report by most secure means available. We did tonight's, so far. The first one isn't for us or the deep stay behinds in this area, as far as I know. I don't know who it is for. The third one means 'counterattack in three days.'"

"No shit, huh."

"No shit. This merits a pigeon. You get one ready; I'll prepare the message."

Headquarters, Tercio Amazona, deep in the jungle

"But I do *not* have a monstrous dildo!" insisted the radio operator, indignantly. "I *don't!*"

"It's all right, Yvette," answered her tercio commander, like his partner and the tercio exec, seconded to the Amazons from the Tercio Gorgidas. "I'm sure someone here does if you need one. In the interim, we need to get the word out to the maniples to go ahead with their attacks."

Ramirez's Battery, "Log Base Alpha"

The battery commander and his command group, plus the chief of the fire direction center, all sat around the radio listening. The FDC chief wrote frantically as the latest meteorological message came through: "Line 00 follows: direction . . . 26 . . . speed . . . 18 . . . Temp . . . 00 . . . density . . . 946 . . . line 01 . . . direction . . ."

Blue-eyed Rodriguez's guitar was laid aside for the time being. Instead, he looked through the sight of his light artillery piece, aligned for the nonce with the tube of the gun. In his sight, engineers, hanging from straps in the trees, were clearing away lower branches or wiring the upper ones, or the trees themselves, for demolition on command. The engineers on the ground were connected to the individual guns by field telephone lest radio traffic give the game away. From there, they directed the men in the trees on what to cut and what to prepare for demolitions based on guidance from the gunners themselves. They didn't try to be perfectly thorough for at least two reasons. One was precisely to avoid tipping off the Taurans. The other was that they didn't have to; the guns could do a degree of clearance themselves with their first couple of salvos.

"Right," said Rodriguez to his engineer liaison, "that

big branch to the right of . . . mmm . . . yeah, that one. It needs to go before we open up. Right, demo will work."

Centurion Avilar stuck his head into the opening through which the cannon protruded. "Any problems, Rodriguez?" he asked.

"No, Centurion," Blue-Eyes answered, without taking his eye from the sight. "It's going to reduce the effectiveness of our fire, though, when we have to blast our way through a layer of the jungle before the shells can fly free."

"You would think so," Avilar agreed, "but that's more important for surprise fire and time on target. When you're simply going to rearrange a chunk of the planet it matters less."

"Fair enough," the gunner agreed, then said into the field phone, "Right . . . okay, now that set of vines about fifty meters past that trunk . . . yeah, those . . . can we take them down?"

Avilar tapped the open door of the shipping container to indicate he was finished, then walked to the next gun.

Headquarters, 10th Artillery Legion, "Terremoto," Ciudad Balboa

There were twenty-four artillery tercios in the legion—one of which was manned by sailors from the *classis* and fired land-based torpedoes—as well as enough separate batteries and cohorts to make up at least another ten tercios. There was, however, only one artillery legion, the Tenth "Terremoto," or "Earthquake." The Tenth, like the others, was an outgrowth and expansion of the old Eighth

Cohort, which first saw action in the invasion of Sumer. It had grown a great bloody deal since then.

Five of the twenty-four tercios were under the Tenth's normal and direct command. It also had the wherewithal, in terms of command, control, communication, and coordination to take charge of the efforts of all the rest, plus infantry mortars. In this case, it was somewhat undertasked, since Fourth Corps, around Cristobal, would take care of its own problems, while the Twelfth Brigade of Artillery, oriented to the defense of and—for the most part stationed on—the Isla Real, couldn't range.

"Undertasked," however, was something of a relative concept. In Tenth Legion Headquarters, currently set up in a thickly walled shelter under a parking garage in the city, nobody felt remotely undertasked as they distributed the fire-support plan, supervised the preparations for its implementation, or made the sometimes large but sometimes rather minute changes required of an unfolding situation. These showed up on a map, of sorts, projected against a screen almost five meters on a side.

The map had areas of impact, color coded for the density of fires to be directed against them, called "Density One," which showed as green for "go," red for "Density Two," "Density Three," which was blue, and "Density Four," which was yellow. Some eleven spots, quite circular, and, in scale, about seven hundred meters across, were in deep black. Others were squares and ovals in various shades and colors. Black meant that no one was expected to survive in the impact area or that it was a no-fire area, for a period of time. Green indicated a serious level of casualties, but more shocked than dead. The various colors darkened as pixels, representing shells and shell weight over a given period of time, were added. Five deep lines were carved in green into the Tauran depth, one of those being the road to Cristobal, along which were also nine of those black circles. Date-time groups written next to the circles and connected by lines to them indicated the periods for which they were to be no fire areas.

Screens to the left and right of the main one showed committed and uncommitted batteries by time.

One area, surprisingly close to a swamp, showed an undetermined but heavy Tauran unit. No fire had been planned for it, initially, as it hadn't been there, initially. The commander of the Tenth, Legate Pablo Carrasco, looked at the hole in the plan, graphically portrayed, then looked left at what was unassigned. He made a best guess of what was in range, and said, "Assign a battery of one-eighties to it, if they range."

A non-com, one of a dozen on the work stations updating the fire-support plan, typed in a few numbers and used a mouse to paint the area as a square. "They range, but not enough power, Legate," he judged.

"Reason?" asked Carrasco.

"Sir, it's reported to be a heavy target," said the sergeant. "Might be engineering equipment but also might be self-propelled guns or tanks or infantry fighting vehicles. We just don't know. The norms we inherited from the Volgans demand a heavier weight of fire, and some kind of anti-armor round, for that kind of target."

"Any three-hundred-millimeter rocket launchers uncommitted? I don't see any, but . . ."

"There are two batteries being held in reserve after the

initial volleys, under the direction of the counterbattery radar, sir. You could use one of those for one mission, if you're willing . . ."

"To accept the risk," Carrasco finished. "No, we'll need the counterbatt. Give me something else."

The sergeant scrolled through his spreadsheets, looking for someone underemployed. "The heavies that are doing the Volcano mission are also supposed to go to counterbatt, if they survive. We could put them on it."

"No . . . no," said Carrasco, after a moment's consideration. "They need to go silent to preserve the illusion as long as possible."

"The Aviation Legion has got a couple of dozen Condors with fuel-air-explosive cargos, if you want to deal with the air folks, sir."

Carrasco nodded, then shouted out, "Get me a call in to Lanza with the *Alae*. Let's see if he can fill our gap."

Joint Headquarters, 16th Aviation Legion/18th Air Defense Legion, Ciudad Balboa, Balboa, Terra Nova

It could have been considered rather advanced thinking for Balboa to have formed a joint headquarters, under the command of their air force, the Sixteenth Aviation Legion (which had *alae*, Latin for wings, instead of tercios), to control their own air space. For his part, if asked, Carrera would likely have said there was really "No other way to make it work. Somebody had to be in charge. They're both just different methods of doing the same thing. I could have flipped a coin, I suppose, or I could have promoted somebody into the job and created a whole headquarters around him. But, in the first place, I don't have that many hypertalented senior officers to spare and, in the second place, since they only had to act two or three times, it wasn't really necessary to do so."

So far it had worked, not only to humiliate the Taurans but to force them to stop using a very efficient "conveyor belt" method of aerial attack and go to assembling much less efficient large strike packages. This was not only hard on the ground crews, but it wasted fuel, as strike packages were assembled in the air, which also meant it reduced ordnance, and generally provided Balboa with a day where their skies were clear more often than not.

And the director of the effort, when the effort had to be made, was one Miguel Lanza.

"Lanza, here . . . one FAE Condor? Yeah, we can do that. I'm saving them mostly for something else but I can spare one . . . yeah, I could probably spare more than one but let's not get ambitious or greedy, Pablo; you may just find something else you need hit . . . yeah, sure . . . I'll give the order, just have your people send the request over . . . Yeah, you're welcome." Lanza hung up.

Carrera was sitting in his office at the time. "What did Pablo want? Rather, I gather what he wants but why did he need it?"

"He's got a target, a new one, unplanned, that he doesn't have a good way to take out with his own assets, so he asked for an FAE from me."

"How the hell is that going to survive the trip over during the prep?" Carrera asked.

"It won't. We'll send it a couple of hours early and let it ditch in the trees, then go off on a timer."

"Fair enough. Now how are we on recapturing our airspace for a day or so?"

"A lot depends on whether Sixth Corps, which is to say, Fifth Mountain and Thirty-sixth Amazona, plus the citizen guerillas, can force a major air effort from the Taurans. And that, because of the ban on bombing, is an open question."

Carrera smiled, slyly. "You're not rebuking me, are you?"

"No, Duque, I am not. But I am wondering how we guarantee the Tauran air forces will put in a max effort."

"Oh ye of little faith. Tsk. Double tsk. The short version is that when Fifth Mountain attacks the ports of Capitano and Armados, and the Amazons and guerillas go after the bases in their area, none of it is actually jungle . . . okay . . . not none, but so little as not to matter. So, yes, their air forces will put a major effort into saving their gains and their troops. Which should be of effect . . ."

"In about three days," Lanza finished. "But if they've been so scrupulous about not bombing the rain forest, how do you know they will go all out when we begin our attack?"

"Because survival cancels programming."

Parilla Line, Stollen Number One-Twenty-Six

A *"stollen,"* so-called for its resemblance to a Sachsen Christmas cake, was a very thick and very strong concrete

bunker, big enough to serve as an assembly area for large
numbers of men, even up to cohort sized, in a few cases.
This one, formed in years past into the cut-out slope of
the ridge that formed the spine of the Parilla Line, then
covered and camouflaged with fast-growing trees, was
about thirteen meters by twenty-four, and of only one
floor. In other words, it was big enough to shelter an
infantry maniple, to provide for them adequate room to
sleep, in triple bunks, mostly against the walls, plus twelve
stalls for toilets and ten urinals, and with minimal facilities
to heat rations. There were chemical septic tanks under
the stollen for the waste. Tunnels connected the six stollen
assigned to the second cohort, three for the infantry
maniples, one for combat support, and two slightly smaller
ones for the headquarters, those being for the field trains
and the combat trains and tactical operations center,
together. More tunnels, none larger than required for a
short man to walk upright, connected the headquarters of
the cohort with tercio HQ.

A four-wheel-drive vehicle pulled into a small, C-
shaped and gravel-layered cut in the jungle, then stopped
briefly. From it Sergeant Major Ricardo Cruz rotated his
legs over the side and straightened up to stand with his
feet on the gravel. Cruz winced as he did; he was barely
out of the hospital. His wounds had been severe, his loss
of blood considerable, and the almost inevitable infection
a touch and go thing for weeks. Even now he still sported
bandages and could, under some forms of movement, set
blood to oozing again.

*But I wouldn't miss this one for the world. And it's only
oozing, after all, not gushing.*

Other than his cohort commander, now Legate Velasquez, and the tercio sergeant major, "Scarface" Arredondo, he hadn't seen a familiar-looking face since Centurion Ramirez's brother, just before he'd passed out. And they'd only been allowed to visit him in hospital for a brief period of time. Cara, his wife, could not come, of course. It had been a miserably lonely time, there in the hospital. Even though he'd never been here before, Cruz felt like he was going home.

A young private from the cohort's personnel office, or II-shop, met the sergeant major just off the cut. He carried a shotgun over his shoulder. Cruz glanced around and saw the remains of a couple of blasted antaniae not far from the road. The area was notorious for the noxious little bastards, so he was unsurprised. The ruined bodies were covered with ants and reeked, to boot.

The boy stood to attention and said, "Sergeant Major Cruz, Private Arredondo, to lead you to the cohort."

"You Scarface's boy?" Cruz asked. There was some degree of family resemblance.

The private shook his head. "No, Sergeant Major; I'm his nephew by an older brother."

"Good enough. Lead on."

Cruz noticed that there was surprisingly little sign that the stollen even existed. Following Private Arredondo, he asked about it.

"Well, Sergeant Major," said the boy, "when we first holed up here we did cause wear on the ground. You'll get that when a couple of hundred men pass by in single file in a short period of time. After that, though, the tunnels—"

"Wait, we've got tunnels?"

"Yes, Sergeant Major; they connect the maniples and headquarters to tercio headquarters. There aren't any, as far as I know, to connect tercio with legion. Anyway, for most purposes the tunnels allow sufficient intercommunication that essentially no one in the cohort, or, indeed, the entire Second Tercio, absolutely *has* to go topside. So, once we took over the position, the jungle, and grass where there was no jungle, came back very quickly.

"Note, though, that the tunnels are narrow and a bitch for two men to pass going in opposite directions."

Cool, thought Cruz, weaving through the trees behind the boy. *Cool, narrow or not.*

At length they came to a concrete facing, pierced by what looked to be one heavy door and that flanked by two ball-type firing ports with periscopic vision blocks. The firing ports looked real and the vision blocks looked as if salvaged from an obsolete or wrecked armored vehicle. *Hell, they probably are real; wouldn't cost much and they would provide some sense of security.*

Young Arredondo reached over and pulled a little cord, then stepped out of the way. The door opened. Cruz walked in to find. . . .

"Welcome home, Cruz, you malingering ass!"

That was Scarface's melodious voice, melodious for the nonce, in any case. Cruz knew in his bones that, yes, he was home at long last.

CHAPTER TWENTY-FOUR

"Wounds my heart with a monotonous languor."
—Radio Londres message announcing D-Day

Port of Capitano, El Toro Province, Balboa

The terrain leading to the port was odd, being a series of widely separately but remarkably steep parallel ridges running from the mountains, in the southeast, to either side of the port itself, to the northwest. In the valleys between the ridges, various hides and caches had been long prepared against the day of a counterattack. Between the jungle cover, the heat, and the clouds and general humidity, it was believed that even the Peace Fleet, orbiting overhead, would be hard-pressed to identify the troops' movement.

Because of the caches, which included food, ammunition, sundry other supplies, and even a battery of eighty-five-millimeter guns, with auxiliary propulsion, the troops could move light and fast, and with only a comparative few donkeys for outsize loads. Moreover, because they'd established the caches themselves and left local guerillas to secure them and the routes to them, they could move safely, with only minimal attention to security. In short, the two cohorts ordered by Carrera to take the town could arrive long before they were suspected of having left their mountain base.

As much was true of the other two cohorts, aiming for the port of Armados, though the terrain, physical and human, both, was different.

The port itself was small but well equipped, outfitted to export a huge quantity of bananas for consumption and tranzitree fruit for rendering into wax and candles. Indeed, it had been well equipped before the Taurans showed up. Now, with a large company of stevedores and cranes, it was better than it had ever been. The bay to the south and east of the port was enormous, protected by large islands further out into the Shimmering Sea. Indeed, the total protected water area exceeded sixty square miles. This was sometimes taken to mean that either God or the Noahs had a sense of humor, since the area was *never* wracked by a storm of any significance and never had been since the day of founding.

Currently, the town and port were held by a battalion of Gallic Gendarmerie, a supply battalion and a transportation battalion, which included the stevedores, a detachment of engineers, a battery of mortars, manned by reservists, as well as a small squadron to service the planes that brought supplies landed at Capitano to the main Tauran force investing Cristobal. Shipping by sea would have been more efficient, and not necessarily all that much slower, once loading time was accounted for, but the fear of Balboan Meg Class submarines, never actually seen but confidently believed to be lurking in some of the many inlets along the Shimmering Sea coast, ruled that out.

As it was, the port was *just* worth having, allowing stockpiling of supplies of some importance, and easier and faster transshipment of those than would have been possible from Cienfuegos. In a different world, had it been deemed cost effective to fight the half division or so of mountain troops based—and well dug in—around Hephaestos, and to clear and keep clear the highways over the country's central spine to the city of Cervantes, and from there to the capital, it could have been a war winner. Unfortunately, none of those things seemed possible: The Fifth would have fallen back to the jungle and come out at times and places of its own choosing, the highway could never have been kept clear, and Carrera's human minefield of a refugee center meant that the more logistics sent that way, the more the refugees would soak up; the International Community of the Ever So Caring and Sensitive would see to that.

Worse, the Taurans would have had to coordinate as peers with the Zhong, a prospect utterly distasteful to both parties.

It had been a very different war here from the beginning. The population density was, for one thing, quite low, with maybe one hundred and thirty thousand people across the province. The Taurans held the port, plus the town on the other side of the bay, on the island of Colombo. In theory, those held perhaps twenty or twenty-one thousand Balboans between them.

Every other town in the province was firmly held by Carrera's Sixth Corps, the partisan corps, with a mix of discharged veterans, legionary retirees, cadets, and sundry well-wishers and new volunteers. After a few weeks of more or less continuous sniping, of mines and booby traps, of ambushes executed with surprising skill and ferocity, to say nothing of daily mortaring of their positions in the town of Capitano, the Tauran commander had decided, perhaps wisely, "Enough is enough. Let them keep the bananas and the tranzitrees. If they'll leave us alone, we'll leave them alone."

To emphasize the point the Gallic commander put a series of thick barriers of mixed concertina and single strand-based barbed wire fences around the town, with a berm behind that to protect his men from direct fire, and anti-personnel boobytraps—no mines being officially available—between the two.

It was, perhaps, not insignificant that the gendarmerie commander answered, ultimately, to a very different chain of command from Janier's. It was also possibly significant that, although the locals took the hint and ceased their mortaring of the port, they never officially agreed to any permanent halt or cession of the port to the Taurans.

There were a number of towns outside of the port, mostly owned by fruit companies. Those fruit companies had once been based overseas but, since the ascension of the legions to power, they had for the most part been nationalized. Unusually enough, the nationalization had been with full compensation, rather than simple government-sponsored theft. Moreover, after nationalization, the land and other facilities had been neither socialized nor distributed among the workers, but continued to operate as they always had, only with new, in some ways harsher, management.

That management was harsher because military, there being essentially full integration between the fruit companies and one cohort, plus some support, of the Fifth Mountain. Thus, when that cohort came down from Hephaestos, in little packets of a squad here and a platoon there, they simply fell in on the houses and families they had left behind. A careful headcount could probably have determined there had been an unaccountable increase in population. However, the Gallic commander wasn't well positioned to take that headcount, while the people who were, notably the UEPF and the various Tauran air forces, never really thought about it.

"It's going to be a hell of a surprise for the motherfuckers," said the cohort commander, Legate Durham. Durham was tall, skinny, and blacker than sin. For all that he was native-born Balboan, he spoke an odd English dialect, with roots in Elizabethan England, on Old Earth, more than he did Spanish. He spoke Spanish now, though, for the benefit of the allied mountain battalion that was placed under his own for this attack.

"Probably," half agreed the other commander, lieutenant colonel and honorary legate Ugarte.

"You don't like the plan, do you?" Durham asked.

"I don't see a good choice," Ugarte said. "Mixing troops, or attacking side by side, given the terrain, seems to me problematic. Not just that, but your boys' Spanish and my boys' Spanish don't have all that much in common."

"Precisely. This way we fix them all around their perimeter, and when I make them weakest in the south, I turn over command of that maniple to you and you push through them."

There was, in fact, a good road that would have served as a dividing line but for three things. One was that the road itself was divided into two parallel ones, with a wide and heavily built-upon strip in the middle. This could have been overcome by assigning that strip to one cohort or the other. It might have been confusing amidst the smoke, fire, and soiled underwear, but it was doable.

The other problems could not be so easily overcome. One was that, to the north, the actual port, a fifty-meter-wide, nonfordable inlet from the sea, ran perpendicular to the road. That would have left whatever cohort had the northern side stumped and frustrated before they got fairly into the town. The other problem was also water based, in that the dividing road, itself, then split further, and had yet another very lengthy, also unfordable, inlet between the lengths of road. Thus, there was a quarter of the town—and that the most important quarter—that was protected by major water obstacles with only a narrow gap of about two hundred and fifty meters that was not blocked off by water.

"The trick," continued Durham, "is to get them to commit entirely for the perimeter of the town, then to keep pushing hard on their flanks until they weaken the center. They'll do it; my boys are good and brave and know the place well. We'll *make* them do it."

Sergeant Paul Cheatham and his squad had bunkered

down with his parents, on the floor of the living room. They had an allied fire team with them, but it would stay temporarily at the house when Cheatham and his boys moved out. Neither of Paul's parents were veterans, though his grandfather, who also lived in the house, had joined Tercio Socrates some years prior, and was still not discharged. The old man kept his rifle—not an up to date F-26 but an older one that used brass-cased cartridges—in the thatch of a *bohio*, taking it out only to snipe from time to time.

Paul was rather proud of the old guy, really. *Good thing he's farsighted, though, rather than nearsighted, since the rifle has only iron sights to it.*

Cheatham consulted his wristwatch, an old-fashioned, wind-up issue item, green, robust, with a mildly radioactive dial. His stomach lurched, just a little bit. *About that time.*

"Let's go," he said to the squad, flipping his monocular down over his eye. "After all, we don't want third squad to get first pick of the girls."

The squad, eleven men, made a few last-minute adjustments to their armor, mostly of the open every louvre available sort of adjustment, then went in single file out the back door, the one away from the town. Overhead, the moons Bellona and Eris shone down, each at about forty percent. A cloud obscured the *Leaping Maiden*, for the nonce, though not the *Smilodon* that stalked her. The Beer Galaxy and The Tap hadn't arisen, yet, although *The Dragon* constellation hadn't yet set.

The point man, Cheatham's B Team leader, Clarke, turned around and physically pushed his four men into a wedge, then made a brief trot to take the lead. He had a monocular, too, as did the other team leader, but the rank and file did not.

Ahead, their platoon leader, Centurion Lee, came out of a nearby house and gave two red-filtered flashes. Clarke aimed straight for those. Lee had the weapons squad around him, as well as his optio. Clarke and Cheatham both sensed nearby company. Looking left and right they saw the other two squads, first and third, angling in toward Lee. Those two squads stopped short and took a knee about one hundred meters to Lee's left and right. Cheatham could see long tubular projection over some of the men's shoulders, bangalore torpedo sections to get through the wire and what informers assured them were either mines or booby traps. A bangalore could generally clear at least a three-meter-wide path through wire and a meter-wide footpath through mines, though it was still at least a little chancy. Against Volgan concertina it was nearly useless, but the Taurans weren't using that.

Clarke, on point, passed Lee, who told him, "No changes." Cheatham got exactly the same message, which he acknowledged with a nod. Since Lee didn't ask for more he figured the centurion had either seen it or figured Cheatham knew it, since Lee hadn't said that there *were* any changes.

Cheatham's squad moved past Lee and Weapons to take point. Another glance left and right showed that first and third were on their feet again, but waiting for second to make some progress. After a few minutes' careful advance, Cheatham turned around to see the whole platoon in a diamond shape, moving quietly ahead. Here and there Cheatham also caught glimpses of the other platoons of the maniple, and possibly even of another maniple.

His eyes sought the light he'd have expected to come from the town, as in former days of peace. There was a little bit of ambient, reflecting upward, but with the country's electrical system mostly out of order, what little light there was came strictly from candles, kerosene lamps, wood fires, and the buildings the Taurans had wired to their own generators for their own convenience.

Even those disappeared as the maniple moved to interpose a block of trees and a low, perhaps sixty-meter, hill mass between itself and the town.

Cheatham couldn't see it or hear it, but it was about that time that the mortar section of the maniple weapons platoon cut left to go around and then ascend the far slope of an amazingly regular oblong ridge to the left. The anti-tank section, meanwhile, cut right to ascend the lesser hill mass. From there it could enfilade a large piece of the Tauran berm with its Volgan *Impaler* rocket launchers.

The *Impaler* was an odd piece, and arguments raged regularly over whether it was better classified as a rocket launcher or a recoilless musket, since it was smoothbore *but* burned out its rocket before the warhead ever left the tube. What couldn't be argued was that it wasn't quite as effective as the Tuscan equivalent that the Legion had also considered and rejected over costs. Still, with its tripod and competent, albeit not "brilliant," sight, the *Impaler* could range with considerable accuracy out as far as eight hundred meters and do more damage at that range than the Tuscan piece could. Moreover, though the official maximum effective range was eight hundred meters, with a touch of elevation on the tube the round would sail considerably further than that and make a most satisfying boom at the far end of its flight; it just wasn't that accurate at maximum range. On the other hand, four of them, firing thermobaric rounds at a section of trench, even at fifteen hundred meters, were still likely to make anyone in that section hightail it for safer pastures.

Cheatham caught sight of a light again, off to his right, as the platoon cleared the lesser hill mass. They went about two hundred meters past it, in fact, before Lee directed him to turn ninety degrees to his right, heading straight for the town about six hundred meters to the northeast.

Cheatham found himself surprisingly calm, considering this would be only the second real battle of his life. He attributed it to, *Well, it isn't like we haven't been rehearsing this attack for months, after all.*

That calm disappeared in an instant when a machine gun somewhere off to the left sent a blizzard of brightly burning tracers—*boomboomboomboombomboomboom, crackcrackcrackcrackcrackcrackcrack*—through the general area of Lee's platoon.

Okay, okay . . . calm down . . . nobody screaming . . . not even for a medic . . . so nobody hit . . . okay, okay . . . maybe somebody hit, but if so, unconscious or dead. Now what?

The whole platoon went to ground, suddenly leaving every man alone with his own terrors.

Cheatham heard Centurion Lee shouting to the weapons squad. Pretty quickly, return fire lashed out at the Gauls' machine gun. Next thing Paul knew, Lee was hauling him up by his combat harness, shouting, "Get you and your men off your asses and maneuver to the wire, goddammit! Base of fire for the bangalore bearers. Now go, go, go!"

Off in the distance, Cheatham heard the faint pops of his own maniple's mortars, as well as the more distant but more authoritative *clang* of the two cohorts' dozen one-twenties, further back. From behind—*Shit, I forgot about those for a minute*—the double whammy of the Impalers kicked in, with a concussive blast behind and a larger one to the front.

Nothing like some friendly fire support to brighten your day.

"What the fuck are you waiting for, Cheatham, a gilded and engraved invitation from the *Duque* himself?"

"No, Centurion. Sorry, Centurion. Second squad, off your bellies and race to the wire!"

There's a place to move slowly, by individual and team bounds. There's also a place to move as fast as you can with whatever you can. In this case, that latter was the best choice, to move and gain the most advantage that could be squeezed out of what surprise there was. Second squad fairly bolted to the outer wire that surrounded the Gaul-held town. On the way, Cheatham heard one scream that sounded altogether too much like the leader of his A team. And then he was at the wire.

It's just protective wire, Cheatham thought, *not tactical at all.*

That was a huge relief, since it meant the men would not be lying down in some machine gun's preregistered beaten zone, as would have been implied by wire jutting out at angles from the berm.

"Clark, left, suppressive fire. A team, come to me, right. Same deal. And get some smoke on the berm,"

In a few moments, cylindrical grenades arced out, trailing dense but narrow streamers of smoke. They either reached the berm or got very near it, where the smoke that poured from them began to obscure the berm from his soldiers, *And hopefully my boys from the Gauls.*

Someone apparently called for illumination from the heavy mortars. With an odd pop, then a rattle accompanied by an eerie *whoosh,* a bright light suddenly hung high over the town. Three more followed, in quick succession.

Close call, thought Cheatham, *using illumination, but doctrine says that when they have more night vision than you do, fight in the light.*

In a moment, he was joined by Lee, who said, "So you can move when you want to, after all."

The centurion then ignored him as the first of the bangalore bearers reached the wire. That mountaineer dropped to prone, dropping from his shoulder two tubes, one of which bounced when it hit the ground.

"Just like in the rehearsals, numbnuts," said Lee, in what passed for encouragement among the centurion class. The soldier duly stuck the other tube into the one that had bounced, or, rather, into a smaller cylinder which held them together. These he fed, empty and bouncy one first, under the wire.

"Okay, get the fuck out of here. Next!"

Huffing and puffing, another soldier slammed himself

down next to the centurion. He attached first one and then another tubular section to the first assembly, and pushed them forward.

Thought Centurion Lee, *It can give one a warm and fuzzy feeling, when doing this shit, to know that if the hollow-front piece hits a mine or booby trap it won't send a sympathetic hundred-pound detonation down to your hands and next to your head.*

Taurans now manning the berm—it must have been entrenched and probably revetted, with an entrance on the town side—returned fire blindly through the smoke. There were screams coming from both sides now, even as bullets whipped back and forth, though whether they were screams of anger or pain or fear none but the individual screamer could really say.

"Next!"

A charging soldier, Lee wasn't sure who it was, suddenly spun like a top and sank to the ground. His shoulder-borne tubes went flying. Lee raced for them, even as he called out, "Next!" Then the two of them, Lee and the next bearer, got in each other's way while trying desperately to fit two at once.

"For fuck's sake, Private, back off and wait!"

"But, Centurion, you said—"

"Just wait, goddammit!"

By the time twelve-meter-and-a-half-long sections had been joined, plus the dummy on the front, no further progress was possible; the thing was just too heavy for two men to move against its weight and friction. At that point Lee gave the order to clear out—more specifically, "Fire in the hole! Fire in the hole! Fire in the hole!" even though there was no hole—and pulled the ring on the friction igniter before joining the men scurrying for such safety as a little distance might give. The explosion that followed was awe-inspiring, picking the men up and slamming their chests to the ground with almost stunning force. The force increased with sympathetic detonations from the booby traps. Little bits of wire and other metal pattered down from the sky, generally without enough mass or velocity to hurt anyone. A few larger pieces might have caused injuries, but fortunately landed on open ground out to the flanks. At about the same time, there were further explosions all around the town's perimeter as other platoons blasted their way through the wire and booby traps.

The second thrust into the wire was worse than the first. For one thing, the Gauls were fully alert now, and pouring fire as best they could into the smoke concealing the breaches. Roughly a third of the men trying to reach Lee with bangalore sections didn't make it unscathed. Lee himself was safe enough; he was so deep into the enemy obstacle that the angle of the top of the berm—essentially parallel to the ground—meant that any Gauls foolhardy or brave enough to venture out to try to pick off a target past the protective wire were easy meat for the machine guns on the closer in hills, the riflemen and light machine gunners on the ground, and the *Impalers* and mountain guns firing from the ridges.

Even with those in support, prayers floated heavenward, sometimes aloud but more often silent. Cheatham thought, over and over, *Jesus, this is Hell; Jesus this is Hell; Jesus this is Hell* . . . even as he swept the edge of the berm with his F-26.

In time, though, enough beavers gnawing will work their way through the stoutest trees. Lee pulled a small ring and stood. Running to the south he screamed, "Fire in the hole! Fire in the . . ." At that point a Gaul, very brave or very lucky or, more probably, both, stitched the centurion up his right side, from calf to hip to lower right side of his torso. Stifling a scream, Lee fell forward, plowing the bullet-swept ground with his nose and chin. Arms and legs flailed, still trying to move away.

Cheatham saw his leader fall. Ordering his squad to bugger off, he raced through tracers and menacing-sounding cracks to the downed centurion. Cheatham passed the first gap in the wire, then crouched very low to let the fire pass overhead. Lee was still struggling, however feebly, when the sergeant reached him. Without a word, Cheatham passed his rifle to his left hand and with his right grabbed the back strap of Lee's harness. He didn't try to lift him far, but rather used him like a kind of sled, holding his flopping head and shoulders up while dragging the lower torso and legs across the explosively packed ground. Back through the gap in the wire they went. A machine gun behind and to their left churned the dirt around them, sending little earthen geysers spouting upward. Paul thought something tugged at his leg but kept on dragging.

"Get down!" Lee shouted, as best he could. "Get down before—!"

Cheatham dropped the load and flopped down ahead of the centurion. It wasn't quite in time. The explosion, about two hundred pounds of a mixture of TNT and RDX, with a trace of paraffin, was at this range just shy of deadly. The two men were not just picked up and slammed to the ground. Rather, they were effectively clubbed over every square inch of their bodies. Prone, Lee was pushed a few meters away. Not quite prone, Cheatham was flung end over end for about twenty meters.

On the plus side, Cheatham was perfectly relaxed when he hit the ground, largely because he was totally unconscious. He was also, of course, oblivious to Clarke screaming like a banshee and taking the lead until the Optio could get forward. Neither did he see the rest of the platoon, such as still stood, charge through the new gap to ascend the berm, drop into the Gallic trench, and hammer, beat, stab, and slash their way forward. He was still there, oblivious and hovering between life and death, when the allied battalion under Ugarte stormed through the weakened spot in the Gallic perimeter, and forced their way into the main part of the town.

He also didn't know about it when the first Tauran air support showed up.

Since the outlying areas of the country, the occupied areas, didn't have the air defense umbrella or vertical launch fighters to make using the conveyor system an exercise in humiliation, the aircraft carriers and the fields for the land-based aircraft in Cienfuegos had been able to respond without wasteful and time-consuming aerial assembly of large strike packages. Asked for twenty-four sorties *here*, they could get those sorties in the air in a matter of minutes. Asked for a bombing mission *there*, they could have the aircraft over that part of Balboa in anything from ten minutes, for a carrier-based strike, to an hour and ten from Cienfuegos.

Those requests, and others just like them, had been coming in with panic-stricken regularity since the previous evening. It was, no doubt, a measure of the Balboans' inability to coordinate the series of attacks to take place at the same time that allowed the packages to be sent out so efficiently, though, it had to be admitted, the Court's rulings made that theoretical efficiency considerably less useful than it might have been over most of the country.

It was early morning, with just the hint of the sun peeking over the horizon. Half the town below was swathed in smoke and flame. A goodly chunk of the rest had already been burned to a cinder.

Squadron Commander Richard Halpence was in the air, just outside of light missile range, circling over the town and fuming at his impotence. Below, the Gauls still holed up in one corner of the town begged for help as the Balboans closed in around them. They were, Halpence gathered, a somewhat motley crew of gendarmes, engineers, mortarmen, supply and transport weasels, and God alone knew what else. What those men asking for help didn't understand, and Halpence could only surmise, was that not only was the town still fairly full of civilians, but that something like a thousand prisoners were now in Balboan hands. Under the circumstances, they were surely not very far yet from the men who had captured them, which was also to say not very far from where the huddling Gauls wanted bombs dropped and rockets fired.

"And I can't," Halpence told the men below though a

relay. "I'm sorry, but I can't." *And that you're too panic-stricken to give me proper coordinates doesn't help, either.*

There were hundreds of sorties in the air, a panicked response to what appeared to be a do-or-die offensive all across the occupied parts of the country. Certainly, reports from the ground were that the Balboans were attacking without regard to losses, and had found success at at least a substantial number, maybe even a majority, of their objectives. There were even reports of them using their women in places and in large numbers, though Halpence discounted most of that. *Who wastes perfectly functional women, after all? Madmen? Queers? Rich feminists who know it won't be their daughters slaughtered?*

Halpence was constrained by the courts. The Zhong, in their area, suffered no such restrictions. They lashed at their tormentors mercilessly. They also had few enough aircraft that the lashing they could deliver was highly limited. The squadron commander suspected that some Tauran aircraft had used the excuse of the Zhong to drop their loads on the enemy, even in the rainforest. He couldn't prove that, however, and had no interest in gathering evidence.

And I'll drop mine, too, if I get the slightest excuse and opening. In the interim, at least while I'm here there are limits on the fire support they can use.

CHAPTER TWENTY-FIVE

"Amateurs study tactics. Amateurs also study logistics. But war is that art and science that subsumes all other arts and sciences, hence *real* professionals study *everything*."

—Some Hack Science Fiction Writer,
Early 21st century

Cayuga Field, Cienfuegos

A few aircraft had been lost—at least one to an *extremely* surprised pilot's ejection seat malfunction—but only a few. The Balboans had certainly tried to do more, but anyplace very far outside of their dense air defense umbrella between the capital and the Parilla Line, they just couldn't.

Still, over a period of about twenty-four hours, the Tauran air forces based at sea and on Cienfuegos had sent out about fifteen hundred sorties, lasting an average of just under four hours each. That roughly fifty-nine hundred hours was bad enough, representing a bit over one hundred thousand extra maintenance hours among already overstretched crews. At least that was the optimistic estimate. Cynical crew chiefs often doubled and trebled those figures, partly based on cynicism and partly on the knowledge that not all repairs can happen simultaneously, that sometimes, even often, there had to be a linear sequence of repairs that slowed things down considerably. Moreover, getting planes back into the air required a certain, and rarely small, number of maintenance man-hours, as well, both for pre-flight checks and repairs that the pre-flights often showed being needed.

Worse; the supply of spares immediately on hand wasn't quite up to the demand. Still worse was that facilities available for maintenance, from shelter from the rain to engine test sets, were also badly overtasked, and that among a group of senior officers who answered to more than a dozen different chains of command, were in the main egomaniacs, all terribly skillful as bureaucratic infighters, and generally disinclined to cooperate.

Moreover, even at sea, the Gallic and Anglian aircraft carriers were undercrewed by design, and gave barely enough hull space to spares and fuels for much less intensive operations than they'd just conducted.

Most of this, the various air chiefs were willing to admit to Janier, when he flew to a muggy and hot combined meeting at Cayuga Field to explain to them that simple soldierly morality demanded that they ignore the Court's order in the difficult days soon to be coming.

An enlisted man, basically responsible for making and passing out the coffee, overheard this and resolved to let the media know the Expeditionary Force commander was inciting illegal action.

"It's very simple, gentlemen," the Gaul said; "I am facing a counterattack in our area of operations that will, I believe, drench us in fire at essentially nuclear levels. My own guns are not, and will not soon be—indeed, most of them cannot be—adequately dug in. Theirs are. I do not have enough artillery ammunition ashore now, and may never have, to win the counterbattery battle my gunners will have to fight. I am outnumbered about three or four to one in guns"—this was something of an exaggeration, as he was counting Balboan mortars but not his own—"and more than that in throw weight. My only chance is if you ignore the ruling from the Global Court of Justice and bomb the ever-loving shit out of the rain forest."

Janier gave a smile both cynical and wicked. "Now, of course, we all know that your governments are firmly committed to upholding the rule of law, which is to say the rules that human rights, environmentalist, and cosmopolitan progressive lawyers think we ought to follow. Let me suggest to you, however, my very dear friends, that if your countrymen under my command in Balboa are obliterated, your governments will not stand for long, and you—yes, each of you, personally—will be held accountable for both the loss of life and the defeat.

"Understand, then, that when I call for an attack, in whatever density I demand, and against any target I say, most especially to include the just ever-so-fucking-blessed rain forest, and all the cute little animals therein, that I expect you to do just what I demand."

Janier took a proffered styrofoam cup of coffee from some Anglian enlisted man with "Bateman" on his chest. He absently nodded his thanks.

"Do I have any dissenters at this point in time?"

Only the Gallic air commander, le Gloan, had the balls to raise an objecting hand.

"Yes, old comrade?"

"One problem," he said. "I am sure you are aware of it, Bertrand, but I'll mention it just for the record. The Balboans are holding many thousands of our men prisoners of war, inside the fortress of sorts they've drawn around their capital. Those men are in small camps, above ground, and only *just* outside the blast radius of our smallest bombs, were those bombs to hit a legitimate enemy target. We're not even sure which are POW camps, which are enemy medical facilities, and which are just places they don't want us to bomb. I can accept, though, that probably most of the places they announced as off limits really are supposed to be off limits.

"None of this would necessarily be all that great a problem, were two things true. One is were we to have a very large, to the point of unlimited, supply of precision guidance packages. We do not. The other is if the Balboans had not found a way to utterly befuddle the Global Location System, which they have. In other words, when we bomb in that area, we *will* hit our own men, and will probably kill them in great numbers."

Janier nodded, soberly. "It is, as you say, a problem. Indeed, it is a moral and a practical and a political problem, all three. But the enemy holds fewer than twenty thousand men. More than ten times that are at risk in our lodgment area. What would you do? What would you have me do?"

"Nothing beyond what you plan and what you will demand," le Gloan replied. "Yet it had to be said."

Prisoner of War Camp 42 (noncommissioned), South of Ciudad Balboa

Marqueli Mendoza showed up at the gate with two dozen mostly elderly guards. One of the Anglian noncoms in the camp shouted out, "Hey, boys, it's Mrs. Mendoza, our teacher!" There followed an immediate rush to the gate, partly based on Marqueli's absolutely magnetic personality and looks, but as much on a degree of genuine affection and respect the men had acquired for the enemy who had done her very best to educate them, and with such a degree of tact, understanding, and sympathy. Indeed, she'd done well enough that the education in *Historia y Filosofia Moral* had continued in the camp, with a strong additional element of "death to the TU and to the lampposts with the Kosmos."

The guards opened the gate to allow Marqueli in, the foreign troops automatically backing away to clear a path for her.

"Gentlemen," she shouted, "gentlemen, my little lungs aren't big enough . . ."

Immediately about two hundred of them called out, "Not so little as all that, Ma'am!"

She laughed; it was an old joke between and among them. "Okay, but be quiet for a bit anyway, will you?"

A sergeant majorly voice called out, "All members of the mess, and you fucking subhuman corporals, will shut the fuck up for the lady."

Marqueli nodded her thanks. "I don't have much

time," she said. "I have a dozen more camps to visit in the next half day. The short version, which is all I can give you, is that you have to leave here and very soon. The only safe place for you is the airport, Herrera International. This area"—she swept her arm to indicate that she meant the very expansive version of area—"is going to become a battleground within a day or two. Those guards"—she inclined her head toward the gate—"aren't here to prevent you from escaping or to protect you from anyone with a bad case of the stupids so much as they are to give you an excuse not to try to escape. You don't want to try; there's no good you'll be able to do commensurate with the value of your lives. Sergeant Major?"

"Here, Ma'am," he said, striding out from the crowd.

She handed him a map, though it was devoid of much in the way of useful information. It showed, however, a route to be taken and stops along the way for water and meals.

"Just follow this," she told him. "The guards can help if you run into a language problem or some officious fucking asshole . . ."

"Ma'am!" said the sergeant major, utterly shocked.

"Well, what did you expect after understudying you people for months now?"

"Good point, Mrs. Mendoza. Okay, we'll follow the map. I can't say none of the boys will try to escape, guards or no."

"Sergeant Major, this whole area is likely to be blasted in ways that haven't been seen since the great battles of the Great Global War. I understand even nuclear weapons are not off the table. Please do your best to convince them that their best route to safety is the one I gave you and their best chance of survival is at the airport where they can be seen and not attacked."

He nodded. "I'll try, Ma'am. And from all of us, thank you for everything you've tried to do for us."

"It was my job," she answered. "Do you have any sick or wounded?"

"None we can't carry, Ma'am."

"Then in the name of God, and with God, go."

"Yes, Ma'am," he said softly. Then, after turning about, in his best parade ground bellow the sergeant major shouted out, "Attention! Camp Forty-two will be fallen in and prepared to leave this place, quite possibly forever, in one hour. More instructions then. Now fall out! Oh; except for Sergeant Major Hendryksen; Kris, we need to have a chat about rear guard and straggler control."

East of Arnold Air Base, Balboa

Tribune Juan Ordoñez hadn't slept well the night before. His sleeping mind had kept dreaming back to the last national fighter race day. He'd been a participant, as had about forty-five other pilots.

But winding in and out of the valleys of the Cordillera Central, *between wires hung from balloons, and between the capital's high rises at only a couple of hundred feet above street level? I'm not sorry I did it, except for the nightmares, but I'll never volunteer to do it again.*

Now, instead of winding through sheer mountain passes, the tribune wound his way through the trees that shielded his flight of Mosaic-Ds, obsolete fighters that had proven still capable of taking on and killing the best the enemy had, albeit at usually a less-than-ideal exchange rate. They sat on rails that could be elevated to as much as eighty degrees. The rails, in turn, were attached to turntables that were mounted on trucks. As a general rule, launching close to vertically wasn't a good thing for the trucks, as the planes also had slung underneath them rockets for a very quick, and usually somewhat painful, launch.

We still need airfields to get the planes back, of course, thought Ordoñez, *but they needn't be much and, if they're not available, what the hell, the planes are cheap.*

"Cheap" hardly covered it. At about twenty- to twenty-five thousand drachmae for a depot rebuild, in very good shape, and another seventy- to eighty-thousand in modifications, the planes cost less—*much* less—than most of the missiles that were used to shoot them down. Moreover, as dogfighters, if they could get to knife fighting range, they were at least as good as the best their enemy had and, given the pilots' training, with its typically rather philosophical approach to training casualties, quite possibly better.

Ordoñez stopped at the next position. It was a log-and-earth-built structure, with radar-scattering nets over it and trees draped with long strips of foil over that. The position could be sensed from the air or from space, either magnetically or by heat, the tribune was certain. What couldn't be sensed was any difference between it and fifty others of the same design and with roughly the metallic mass of a Mosaic D and scrapped truck or just scrap metal. It was another case of the bombs needed to destroy the shelters costing more than the planes, and, worse, having only about a twelve percent chance of achieving a hit. And even that was assuming they could somehow lay it on exactly the right place in the absence of reliable guidance. That, in turn, depending on the Taurans being able to take out the many and redundant directional and omnidirectional antennae that served to spoof all three global locating systems.

Ordoñez had six planes and six pilots. He'd lost two of each, previously, but another flight had lost four, including its commander, so the survivors had been assigned to Ordoñez's crew. Moreover, he had an increased increment of ground crew now, because a portion of those from the butchered flight had been sent to him, while others went to make up losses another flight had suffered to aerial attack on their base.

Camouflage and deception will sometimes only carry you so far.

This shelter's plane was his own, though he'd never had it personalized. He tapped the truck that cradled it affectionately with an open palm, as if patting a child's back. *Day after tomorrow, my old friend*, he thought, *the day after tomorrow.*

Broadly smiling, he turned to the six pilots and several dozen ground crew gathered around in the shelter. "Day after tomorrow," he said. "We drive the enemy from our land the day after tomorrow."

Not far from Ordoñez, indeed close enough that he thought about stopping by for a visit, Carrera watched a tethered balloon being filled. Many hundreds more balloons, all across the area around the capital, were likewise being filled, but this one, and a few score of its sisters, were special. The others, the *hundreds* of others, would lift anti-aircraft cables and the anti-aircraft mines that were based around the Volgans' man-portable air-defense missiles.

This one, though, and that few score mentioned, lifted unmanned Condors carrying—except for three—either fuel-air-explosive bombs or a hefty load of scatterable mines, but mostly the former. The three exceptional ones were presents for Cienfuegos' *Presidente* for life. These were mixed explosive and incendiary, matches for the one that had taken the life of the Tauran Defense Agency's incompetent chief, Lady Ashworth. Unlike hers, though, these were devoid of the five-minute warning. No warning would be given because Carrera wanted both the president, whom he and Balboa considered to be a traitor to their culture, and as many of his followers as possible to die, and didn't really care about losses to their families. They were merely stationery.

Lanza, who had been nearby, at another launch point, pulled up in his vehicle. "I'm letting them go as they're able to lift," he said, "except that I want the second wave, with the mines, to reach target half an hour after the last FAE goes off there. I saw off the three for the presidential palace first, though."

"Works for me. Are you ready to shield the attack?"

"Oh, I'm just shivering with anticipation," Lanza said. He sounded perfectly sincere.

Carrera consulted his watch. "Right at thirty-six hours. I need to go make a call."

"You're really going to call them?"

"Short of nukes, there's nothing they can do in the next thirty-six hours that will make any difference. And they won't use nukes for obvious reasons . . . well . . . obvious to some."

"It's true, then? You never admitted it but . . ."

"Yes, we have a small number," Carrera answered, "both tactical and city busters. And they know now that we can hit their cities with more than enough precision at more than enough range. That's half the reason I need to talk to him, to sense if he and the Tauran Union understand the rather dire consequences of escalation beyond conventional arms. But also . . ."

"You're hoping he'll surrender? Pretty forlorn hope, I think. He's made his mistakes but he's no wimp for all that."

"I know."

Hide Position X-Ray, Rio Calebora, Balboa's Shimmering Sea coast

One of the tricks, so to speak, to hiding the country's coastal defense submarines, their *Megalodon* Class SSKs, was that they were hidden, some of them, up estuaries that were non-navigable except at high tide. This meant that for most of any given day, the subs sank into the mud, with only their upper half exposed, and floated free when the tide came in and their sheltering streams backed up. It also suggested to the Taurans that no such river could hold a submarine.

Up one such estuary, the *Meg*, the original, the killer of Gallic warships and tracker of Zhong submarines, arose gently with the incoming tide.

Meg had been stationed at different times on both the northern and southern coasts. Her skipper, Captain Chu, had brought it through the transit way sometime between the defeat of the Zhong landing on the Isla Real and the beginnings of the Tauran attack on the town, port, and fortress of Cristobal. It had come through, then headed many miles out to sea before turning back to Balboa. Once in sight of shore a shore party had guided it into its current berth by flashlight and flag.

That shore party remained ashore, unseen in the jungle's dark. They and the crew lived in tents and cots, though they all took at least one meal a day inside, where the cooking would not present a heat signature. One hot meal was all they got. The rest came canned or pouched and cold.

It was high tide now. Captain Conrad Chu looked upward at the thickly intertwined branches and vines, themselves over a huge assembly of radar-scattering camouflage nets, hung from the trunks of the trees. There wasn't much to see, really, since the moons had not at the moment risen very high.

Darker than three feet up a well-digger's ass at midnight, thought Chu, with some satisfaction. *We'll only be vulnerable from when we come out from under the trees until when we have enough depth under our keel to sink.* He corrected that thought. *Well, we'll only be vulnerable on the surface until then. It's always possible they'll find some way to track us underwater. They've got to know by now that the clicker is just a trick.*

The "clicker" had served the Megs well for some time and in several actions. It was a simulator that gave off a distinct set of clicks, different for each submarine, as if the submarine's main gears were mechanically cut, hence slightly off. It could be used to convince a hunting enemy that the submarine was in the last place it had been heard before the clicker was turned off, even though the boat was long gone or even in a position to donate the hunter a torpedo.

"Huerta?" said Chu into the intercom.

"Yes, Skipper?"

"For my peace of mind, tell me the clicker is off."

"It's off, Skipper; I checked it five minutes ago and locked it in 'off.'"

"Are we ready?" It was a moral more than a mechanical question.

"We're ready, Skipper."

"Very good, ahead slow."

Estado Mayor, Sub camp C, Ciudad Balboa, Balboa

A parlementaire, under flag of truce, had gone forward at daybreak to deliver an invitation to the Tauran commander to meet, via radio. There was a hint inside the meeting that only Janier would understand, that, in his discretion, the message could be three way, and include the High Admiral, via the communicators Carrera was "quite certain we all share." For reasons of his own, Janier declined that, but did agree to converse at two that afternoon, via radio.

Sundry signalmen and a number of women, on both sides, worked to set that up. It was only a little late when one of Carrera's people could stand away from a desk and say, "We're on with the Tauran commander, *Duque*."

Carrera sat and took the handset. Unseen, a small machine was recording this for posterity. "General Janier? Bertrand?"

"Yes, Patricio, *c'est moi*. What can I help you with?"

"Not to seem pushy or demanding, old friend, but I need you to surrender your command."

Apparently, the Tauran was not using a normal microphone but something sound activated. His laughter came through loud and clear. Carrera just smiled, perhaps a touch sadly.

"What are you going to tell me, Patricio; that your more than three thousand guns, mortars, and multiple rocket launchers stand ready to pound my army to pulp? No need; I know you have them and believe you *intend* to do just that. You will fail. The attack that will follow on will fail. I stand, on the other hand, fully ready to accept your surrender and to allow you and your close subordinates to escape to a country of your choosing with whatever you care to take with you. Volga is a bit cold, this time of year, I understand, but there are other places without extradition treaties to the Tauran Union or the Global Court of *Justice*."

The way Janier said that last, with a verbal sneer amounting to palpable contempt, was a bit of information Carrera didn't have before. *He's convinced his air forces to ignore the court order. Good for him and good for them. And he thinks it will make a difference or that I was*

counting on them restraining his air power.
Unfortunately, I can't tell him any different. Hmmm . . .
what can I say that might convince him? Ah, I know.

"I'm no more concerned with the Court than I am
with yesterday's long disposed of breakfast, Bertrand.
But I don't think you understand what you're facing.
Every one of your soldiers is going to be at least shocked,
battered, and frightened every fifteen seconds for
several hundred minutes. What's that going to do to their
morale and ability to resist? They're going to be within
the lethal burst radius of something explosive at least
once every minute for that same length of time. Even if
they're better dug in than I have reason to believe you've
had the chance to get them, they're going to be nervous,
trembling wrecks before they have a chance to fight.
Something between fifty and a hundred times, over the
course of that time, every one of them is going to have a
shell come in close enough to do damage, to ear drums,
if nothing else.

"Their positions are going to be collapsed upon them,
Bertrand. Their calls for medical help will go unheeded,
since unlike you I haven't the first clue where your
medical units and facilities are, so they'll get blasted. Their
ammunition supply points—and I seriously doubt you've
had a chance to dig *those* in—are going up in smoke and
fire. Same for your fuel. Same for every other class of
supply you've managed to stockpile.

"My wire communications are dug in and secure. I
doubt yours are. And I doubt a single radio antenna will
survive what's going to be thrown at you.

"Your army is going to be destroyed, Bertrand, and

with sickening casualties. The prospect sickens me, at least, and should be even worse for you. And it's totally unnecessary, too. All your men can go home, healthy and sane; all you need to do is give up. What is your personal shame, old friend, compared to the lives of your soldiers?

"Worst of all, the people you are fighting for do not deserve to be defended, and their septic tank of a political system is best buried forever."

The answer was a long moment in coming. Finally, that French-accented voice returned. "All that you say could be true, Patricio. But it still would be only a half truth. The other half is that my men still gave their oaths to support their countries' decisions by force and with their lives, that I have given my oath to command them, and that I have a duty not to give them up while they still have the means to resist.

"So you go ahead and do your worst, and we shall do our very best, and then we shall see who should have surrendered to whom."

Carrera couldn't quite keep that little touch of pride out of his voice. "Good luck to you then, you frog bastard; you're going to need it. By the way, someone is going to suggest nukes . . ."

"We won't use nuclear weapons, Patricio."

"Good. Oh, and one last thing, we're moving your POWs out to the north and assembling them near and on Herrera Airport. I'm not going to use the airport for anything, nothing at all, except for prisoners and medical, so there's no need for you to bomb or shell it. Carrera, out."

Academia *Sergento* Juan Malvegui, Puerto Lindo, Cristobal Province, Balboa

Carrera hadn't been the only one with an interest in recording the conversation. As soon as Carrera broke the connection, Janier ordered, "Get me a call through to Major Campbell."

That took no time at all. As soon as Jan answered, Janier said, "Listen to this and tell me what you think."

She recognized the voice immediately. When she heard, "Carrera, out." She answered as immediately. "He, at least, believes he can do what he says, General. Is that what you wanted to know?"

"That, but more importantly, what do you think, my dear and lovely *ecossaise*?"

She dropped to English and to her native accent. In sorrow, she answered, "Ah dinna ken."

CHAPTER TWENTY-SIX

"Renown awaits the commander who first restores artillery to its prime importance on the battlefield."
—Winston Churchill

Isla Colombo, El Toro Province, Balboa

A couple of days before, Hauptmann Nadja Felton, Sachsen *Luftstreitkräfte*, had railed and fumed, screamed and did everything but cry, to try to get rocket pods affixed to the two underwing hardpoints of her Hacienda-121 to help to defend the port of Capitano, across the broad bay. Nothing had worked. Her commander had refused, and none too politely, explaining that there were people and places to do that kind of thing that were better suited to it, that her cargo-carrying capacity was more important that her limited strike capability, and that the never-sufficiently-to-be-damned Balboans weren't presenting any engageable targets anyway.

Her cargo-carrying capacity hadn't meant much of anything in the next day and a half or so. She'd come in from Cienfuegos with about five minutes' worth of fuel left in her tanks. They'd loaded her here with about two tons of medical supplies. She was supposed to fully refuel here, plus pick up some packaged POL—motor oil—in theory for medical vehicles, and bring the two to the newly constructed airstrip southwest of Puerto Lindo. In practice, the fuel just hadn't been allocated because no one had yet worked out what to do about the loss of the port.

Instead of moving on, however, she'd sat while the powers that be tried to decide if it would be better to drain her tanks to refuel a Gallic C-31, and transfer her cargo. While the committee that ran the base and, as far as she could tell from her lowly perch, the war, argued, she either slept in a tent or sat with her co-pilot and load master on the rear ramp, drinking whatever was available and legal. In this case, that meant coffee for her while her co-pilot indulged in a single local beer, which was basically piss.

"Like making love in a canoe," the loadmaster observed, after a sip. At her inquisitively raised eyebrow, he amended, "Fucking close to water, *Hauptmann.*"

The thought was enough, still, to give her a mild case of the giggles, *"fucking close to water"* . . . *speaking of which, I miss my husband. I miss the spark of . . . What the . . . ?*

Nadja noticed a bright flash across the bay, in enemy occupied—or liberated, depending on point of view—territory. The spark reflected strongly off the low hanging clouds. *Relax, girl, it could be anything. It could be . . .*

Then roughly a pound and a half's worth of explosion went off, with a slightly brighter flash than that seen a minute earlier. This was followed by the rattle of incoming. The two left her in no doubt what that first spark had been.

"They have guns," she said, dully, "and they can range."

Both her co-pilot and her load master turned their eyes to her. "What . . . ?"

She said, "Let's get out of here."

"We don't have fuel to get back to Cienfuegos."

"No, matter, we can get to Puerto Lindo."

"But . . ."

The previous explosion had been four or five hundred meters away. The next one was not only closer, but it impacted on a plane only about two hundred meters away. That plane was parked among a dozen others whose crews waited for some kind of direction or mission. The shell passed completely through the plane before exploding on the tarmac below. The spine held, the explosion wasn't really all that big, but pieces of the aircraft flew off, anyway. One or more fragments must have hit a tire, or perhaps the landing strut had been hit and broken or bent. In any case, the plane suddenly fell on one side, though not enough for the wing to break on the tarmac.

Within maybe fifteen seconds of that single hit, Nadja saw what looked to be five or six or seven more sparks from the area of the first. She caught a slight whiff of fuel in the air.

"Get in the goddamned plane! Get in the goddamned plane! We're getting out of here!"

Then it was scramble and push and use anything that would touch a fixed surface for her and her co-pilot to get to their seats.

By the time they were a quarter of the way through their preflight checklist, and with shells coming in on that aircraft parking area at what sounded like a couple of hundred per minute, Felton said, "To Hell with this; we leave now or we die."

She flicked the engines to life, first port and then starboard, released the brake, and gave them just enough juice to begin rolling to the runway from the apron. A roar came from behind her, punctuated by a huge blossom of fire that lit up the entire airfield and the town beyond. The shock of that caused her to let the plane go a little further than she planned, all the way over to the left side of the runway. Turning it was a sheer bitch.

Then, in the light from the burning aircraft behind her, Felton saw a sudden angry cloud of black smoke ahead. It was not a matter of chance; the next shell had landed to the left, and closer. *Oh, crap; they're adjusting on* me, *the dirty bastards. Time to gamble a bit, I think.*

Their last adjustment that I saw was maybe three hundred meters. I don't know it's so but maybe they can only adjust their fire, or are, at least, most comfortable adjusting their fire, for that distance . . . okay . . . so that last one was five hundred meters to my front . . . in a minute it will be only two hundred if I stop here . . . screw that.

She reduced the gas to her starboard side engine and fed it to her port, applying partial brakes on starboard as she did so. She still had some forward momentum, enough that when the next shell came it was only one hundred meters in front and to the left. She thought she felt some light fragments hitting her hull.

Releasing the brake, she fed gas back to the starboard

engine, driving it a little faster to straighten up on the runway. In her mind she began to count down from fifteen.

The plane shuddered as if in a stiff breeze. Her loadmaster, looking out the gap over the rear ramp shouted through the intercom, "Crap, that was close, Hauptmann. Six or eight shells no more than fifty meters behind us. Get us the hell out of here!"

She didn't need the encouragement. Pushing the twin throttles forward and feeding the engines all they'd take, she began to race down the runway. At about four hundred and fifty meters from where the loadmaster reported that battery's worth of impacts, she felt the wheels lift from the strip.

"You'll never catch me now, coppers," she whispered to herself as she put a more than adjustable difference between her aircraft and the runway.

Run or stick around until the shooting stops? she asked herself, as soon as she was airborne. Yes, her first thought had been that there would be safety at Puerto Lindo. *But what if they need me here?*

She'd circled then, for a few minutes, watching the enemy artillery firing from the mainland turn the airfield into an inferno. *Must make the decision now, there's just enough fuel. Do I stay here in case it clears enough to land or go to Puerto Lindo where I know it's safe? It may not ever be safe enough to land here, and if not, I lose my plane.*

Even so, she called the field and asked, getting a major who was obviously ducking some incoming. "Go," he

ordered. "No telling when or even if you can come back
here. I think they've got someone on the island adjusting
fire for them; they're turning this place into a graveyard."

With an acknowledgement, she turned west for Puerto
Lindo.

Watching her fuel gauges nervously, Nadja went for
the most economical speed she could find. She gave some
serious thought to jettisoning the cargo. *If it were
ammunition or a supply of condoms, I would, but two tons
of medical supplies are not to be tossed away lightly.*

Glancing out to her port at the sea, below, Nadja saw
the two glowing sides of a triangle that indicated a vessel
passing through bioluminescent waters. The triangle
abruptly disappeared, but whether this was because a
fishing boat had stopped or a submarine dived she had no
idea. She called in the sighting, anyway, as a possible
submarine.

SdL-1, *Megalodon*, Shimmering Sea.

Chu cursed not himself but fate. He'd had to come up,
and would have to come up again, to get the message on
the locations of the enemy carriers. He'd just been
receiving when that plane, presumptively Tauran, had
passed by and driven him below, message uncompleted.

There will be another chance in twelve hours, he
consoled himself, *if nothing else comes up. I'd really like
to get a carrier I should sink to make up for the one I
probably shouldn't have.*

I wonder if the others we hid—Orca II, Baiji, or Monk

Seal, *managed to get the full message. They all should be coming out for the party now.*

HMAS *Indomitable*, Shimmering Sea

The ship's exec brought the dire news to her lord and master, Captain Allingham, who was said to have a taste for whiskey and wild women. The captain's day cabin fairly reeked of cigarette smoke.

"There's very little doubt, sir," said the exec, after announcing himself and gaining admittance. "We had two intercepted partial messages believed to have been from two of their *Megalodon* Class SSKs. A Special Boat Service team, returning from a mission to put a little fear of God into the headhunters the enemy has been using, spotted one leaving an estuary to the west of Cristobal. And now we have reports of a wake where there was no ship or boat to be seen. They're coming out and they're coming out looking for us and the Frogs."

"What do the Frogs say?" asked the captain.

"*Charlemagne* and *Charles Martel* and their battle groups are all pulling back, sir. Makes sense, really; we've both been on station pretty close to the action. Good chance the enemy knows where we are but will lose us if we pull back to just inside maximum combat radius."

Allingham looked grim. "Problem is that the bloody Frogs' *Tourmantes* outrange our Sea Hurricanes. Their combat radius is nearly twice ours. If we follow them—disgusting idea, no, us following the bloody Gauls?—we'll be useless for the battle."

"Then what, sir? We have no good answer to their SSKs yet."

"Tell me about it." Allingham thought for a moment, then said, "We can hide by running away. We can hide by going someplace useless. I wonder if we cannot also hide by being considerably gutsier than the enemy has any reason to expect."

"Sir?" The exec didn't like the sound of that. With something akin to genuine terror in his voice he asked, "Captain?"

"Bring us to within fifty miles of Puerto Lindo. Let's see if they think to look for us there."

"Sir . . ."

"Just do it. It will not be said that *Indomitable* shirked her part in the greatest battle in three generations."

Estado Mayor, Sub camp C, Ciudad Balboa, Balboa

Soult passed around the glasses—well, small paper cups—while Carrera poured the legionary rum himself. The clock showed half an hour before the liberation began. It was just enough time for a short speech and a toast. The speech was over.

Parilla walked in, looking shaky and strained. "Patricio," he asked, "Have you no rum for an old friend?"

Carrera put down his can of rum and raced to the old man's side. He put his own forearm under one of Parilla's and, beginning to lead him to one of the few genuine chairs in the command post, asked, "Should you be walking? I've spoken to the doctors . . ."

"Fuck them, you insubordinate son of a bitch," Parilla whispered. "And don't pretend it's anything but the merest truth."

"Yeah, but my dog likes me," Carrera rebutted.

"You don't have a dog."

"Well . . . I can always get one."

"No self-respecting dog would have you. Why Lourdes puts up with you is beyond me. Why *I've* put up with you all these years . . ."

"Because, while I *am* an insubordinate son of a bitch, I am *your* insubordinate son of the bitch."

."Fair enough. Now get me that rum."

"Jamey, a glass—yes, a real glass—for the president, if you please."

Easing the president down to the chair, Carrera asked, rhetorically, and loud enough for everyone to hear, "There's something I can't figure out: When a counterbattery radar sees something like sixteen thousand shells per minute, does the radar's computer have a nervous breakdown first, or will it be the operator?"

After the laugh one of the radio-telephone operators, acting *sua sponte*, struck up the song, "*O, Campo, Campo Mio.*" Everyone, including Carrera and the President, joined in.

Ramirez's Battery, "Log Base Alpha"

The gun chief opened a can of legionary rum and poured some into the canteen cup of every man in his crew. "May we and our own balls still be attached, each to the other, this time tomorrow," he said. The crew raised their cups and answered "hear, hear," before downing theirs, each in a gulp. The shit was strong, one hundred and sixty proof, for weight and cube savings, and burned its way down every throat. It was normally meant to be cut with something, water or coffee or fruit juice, but, for certain occasions, raw and straight was called for.

Outside, in trenches, tunnels, bunkers, and containers, the rest of the battery did likewise. The two great-*great*-granddaughters of Digna Miranda hesitated when a sergeant brought them theirs. Digna raised her nose slightly, looking down into the paper cups to make sure the sergeant hadn't shortchanged her girls. The girls hesitated, not sure what granny might say if they drank.

What she said was, "Maybe last chance, niñas; drink up." They did, and both choked and gagged. Somehow, though, the old woman managed to down hers without so much as a wince. "Don't be weak," she said. "Think of it as a kind of communion." *And besides, fair chance that you're going to miss another kind of communion, that you're not necessarily too young for now, so take what you can get.*

Not far away, toast done with, sweating crews worked or waited in all eight gun-filled shipping containers, the containers having been buried on their sides and at a slight angle along their long axis. Besides the containers with guns, others had been sunk into the earth and covered to serve for fire direction, communications, ammunition, medical, and mess. The latter were utterly empty now, as even the replacement cooks, old Mrs. Miranda and her girls, reinforced by all the ash and trash from cohort and tercio, stood by to carry more rounds to the guns as needed.

A portion of the battery's ammunition likewise waited in shipping containers. The rest was in bunkers dug into the ground. Only a few hundred rounds per gun, perhaps twenty minutes worth of firing, waited in ready racks. On command, the doors were raised and propped up. They opened parallel to the ground, exposing a nearly five-meter-long barrel topped by a multi-baffled muzzle brake.

Inside the container holding the gun bearing serial number 12543, Blue-eyed Rodriguez gunning, Rodriguez and his mates heaved to push the gun forward, to get the barrel and especially the muzzle as far out as possible. Once they had it there, they went to work chaining the axle to a large piece of wooden reinforcement to the forward wall, even as others hammered more wood into position to hold the spades. This was all overkill, really, but enlisted and non-commissioned artilleryman liked preparing for eventualities beyond the expected. If their officers expected too much to go right? Well, a good part of that was the junior ranks making sure it did . . . as was right and proper.

One of the crew cursed when he hit his head on the spare barrel, hanging from the roof. Yet another tripped over the shallow, water-filled trough that would receive an overheating barrel to cool it down completely after the bore had been sponged out.

Outside, a wet tarp had been laid over the earth to keep down dust.

Each man assumed his position around the gun as his tasks were completed.

There was a field phone, connecting the whole unit by wire in what was called a "hot loop." Standing by the phone, with the handset pressed to his head, the gun chief received the fire command. It came with the proviso "at my command"—from the fire direction center. He shouted it out with the crew repeating it. Rodriguez set the data on the sight then adjusted the gun by its elevating and traversing cranks to bring it on line with the stakes. Other, more powerful guns used infinity reference collimators for aiming, but the lightweight regimental guns, much like their junior cousins, the mortars, kept it cheap and simple.

An assistant slammed a round, shell plus the brass-washed steel casing for the propellant, into the breach then stepped out of the way.

The gun chief turned and flicked a switch. Suddenly a very powerful fan began to suck air from outside the container, pull it through a filter, and then release it inside. This created a mild overpressure that forced old and somewhat stale air out the front. It would soon be more than a convenience, as it pushed out the toxic fumes of burnt propellant.

From the direction of the front, to the south, there came a sound of explosions, some smaller, others larger, together with the cries of some very unamused monkeys, birds, and trixies. That was the commander of the battery—rather the commanders and leaders of every battery and mortar platoon, blowing the remnants of the jungle canopy that still stood between their guns and their targets. Ahead there was a veritable blizzard of falling branches and vines. From overhead it looked like holes appearing in the jungle cover.

"Incoming," the gun chief heard in his earpiece. He repeated it to the men.

"Why are they shooting now, Sarge?" asked Rodriquez.

"'Counterprep,' it's called," replied the sergeant. "Counterpreparatory barrage. The purpose—their purpose—is to catch us in assembly areas or wherever we're concentrated and vulnerable, to try to fuck up our attack. It's a good technique, but not that useful against infantry or guns dug in as well as—"

The sergeant's little lecture was silenced by the sound of many, many explosions going off overhead and all around. Shell fragments and bits of wood pattered like rain from the raised door over the gun's barrel. Others hit almost silently upon the heavily sandbagged and wood-reinforced roof.

"And the price you pay for a counterprep . . ." The sky was full of the symphony of very large cannon shell, one-eighties, and rockets, three-hundreds, storming overhead.

"They revealed their positions, and for not much gain, if you ask me . . . stand to the gun . . . stand to the gun . . . five . . . four . . . three . . . two . . . FIRE! FIRE! Continuous fire!"

On the first "FIRE!" crewman number three gave the lanyard a yank. The gun's barrel leapt back, even as the carriage strained against its restraining chains and wooden blocks. The expended casing was flung out the back with enough force to hit the rear of the shipping container and bounce. Number seven picked it up and shoved it out a small hole covered with the hinged metal flap. Before the flap had clanged shut the next round was spinning down range.

In that first minute, Ramirez' battery put out about two hundred rounds. A few of these served only to clear away any remaining obstacles in the jungle canopy. The rest went on to make the day of someone to the south very miserable indeed.

Inside his gun bunker, Blue-eyed Rodriguez finally got the inspiration to finish the song he'd been working on for months. He sang, loud enough to be heard, at least by those whose ears were able to tune out the muzzle blast, as artillerymen generally could.

"We are the cannon of death
Under our feet you are roaches.
Ten thousand shells a minute
Are what we shall throw at you."

He sucked in a great chestful of air for the chorus:

"And we will fuck you up."

The rest of the crew knew where it was going from there. They joined in, *sua sponte*, while feeding the ravenous appetite of their gun.

"WE WILL FUCK YOU UP
WE WILL FUCK YOU UP
THIS IS YOUR LAST DAY."

Fan or not, the fumes were getting bad. Some of the men had put on their protective masks, though Rodriguez kept his off in order to serve the gun better. They switched position, occasionally, to give gunners' eyes a rest and ammo haulers' backs and hands the same. After putting out about four hundred and fifty rounds, the gun chief ordered Rodriguez and the loader to switch positions.

After ramming one shell up the spout, and turning to get another, Rodriguez was surprised to take one from the next ammo hauler in line, the old woman who had come with her granddaughters to cook for the battery.

"*Gracias*, Madame," he said, taking the one shell she bore and ramming it in. He didn't hear the returning, "*De nada.*" He turned again and this time it was one of the younger girls, fifteen or sixteen, he thought, and really very cute. She had two shells, one over each shoulder. Rodriquez relieved her of one, then decided, *Why not?*

"What's your name?" he shouted, since everyone was more than half deafened at this point.

"Martina," the girl shouted back. "*Llame me*; I'll get you my number."

Parilla Line, Stollen Number One-Twenty-Six

Ricardo Cruz, sergeant major of Second Cohort, Second Tercio, figured that his position had only a couple of uses, neither of which involved excessive concentration on police call and haircuts. One of these was as a directed telescope, someone who could go out and gather information for the commander and *know* what it was he was seeing or, in this case, seeing *and* hearing.

He was surprised, but only a little, at the counterprep.

Yeah, we must have given off enough signals for them to know we were coming. I wonder what it was that was the decisive signal.

Some of the counterpreparatory bombardment was oriented at the Parilla Line, but not much. Most of it he could hear, and occasionally even see, in the dark, impacting on "Log Base Alpha" which, *I am pretty sure is no longer fooling anybody. I hope Carrera evacuated the prisoners and wounded before this.*

Cruz saw a few flashes through the night, which he assumed was counterbattery fire going out. Certainly, it was nothing like the volume he'd been expecting. There were more and then still more such flashes, as the fire direction people received targeting information from the radar. Still, it was nothing like what he thought it should be, not for the kind of do or die offensive they were about to engage. He looked at his watch; *Ah, a little too early for that, anyway.*

Not that we won't at least try, no matter the artillery preparation, but we're not going to win unless . . .

And then he saw it, beginning off in the distance, an incoming tide of light, flashing, flashing . . . burning . . . rising to the sky. Some of the flashes were obvious, so close together and clawing the same path upward to the sky that he knew what they were: *Multiple rocket launchers, and they're not playing.*

Whether those were the lighter versions, the one-twenty-two jobs, or the heavies, he couldn't really say. It was useless, too, to try to count the rising pillars of fire to identify what was what. A battery of launchers simply threw out a lot more rockets than could be counted, even though the smaller ones fired forty and the larger fired fourteen. It all got lost amidst the hundred or more from any given firing position.

The huge one-eighties weren't hard to discern; they belched forth a flame completely different from the ones the rockets left behind them. Shorter ranged, nearer to the Parilla Line, and still firing quite heavy shells, the one-fifty-twos kicked in. They weren't the most common piece in the artillery park. Cruz remembered, vaguely, from a briefing he received at one time, *maybe at Centurion Candidate School,* that there were two cohorts in each legionary artillery tercio. *Maybe four or five hundred one-five-twos? That's about consistent with God's own strobe light.*

The volume picked up as the tide of light came closer. *That would be the one-two-two cannon, I suppose. Not that many of those in the inventory, under one hundred and fifty, I seem to recall, and all with the First and Sixth Armored Legions. Well, no matter, every little bit helps.*

Though one could try to describe the barrage episodically, that wasn't how Cruz was seeing it. There was no noticeable gap between one kind of gun firing and the next commencing to fire. It was all, he was sure, driven by time of flight to the target.

And then the wave of sound hit, a palpable force, palpitating his inner organs. Cruz couldn't say what he heard or felt first, all he knew what that he was suddenly inside a storm of a magnitude he'd never even imagined before.

All our live firing, all our demolitions training; nothing could prepare us or anyone for this. And on the receiving end? Those poor bastards.

The mortars, some of which were very close, kicked in then.

Twelve Miles south of Cristobal, Balboa, at Eight Thousand Feet

Hauptmann Felton still kept one eye glued to her fuel gauge, but she and the plane had come far enough, and were close enough, that she felt she could relax, if only a little. Three things then happened at once: she felt something like a slight wind buffet her plane, just slightly. It was hardly enough to adjust her controls or altitude for. She heard a rumbling the like of which she'd never heard before. She imagined a volcano could sound like that. Finally, she saw some lights, like fireflies, play across the glass in front of her and above her head.

She looked out her window and gasped. Across a band that had to have been fifty miles deep—it ran from one sea to the other—and at least fifteen across, there was nothing to be seen but flashes. She tried to count and couldn't. She tried to identify a discrete area and count the flashes from inside that. She couldn't.

There seemed to be more of them coming from the side of the Shimmering Sea, which heartened her slightly. Then she realized that some of those were pouring from Cristobal, and most of the rest had to be incoming.

"Those poor men," she whispered.

"Poor them, yes," agreed her copilot, who had, apparently, heard her. "But poor us, too, because we have to land and the airfield at Puerto Lindo seems to be under fire, too."

The copilot flicked a switch so she could hear the radio from Puerto Lindo. It was all disaster, the control tower allegedly down and people being killed right and left.

"And the runway is cratered," said ground control, too.

She made a decision she'd been putting off. Calling her loadmaster on the intercom she said, "I'm dropping the ramp. Push the cargo out the ass and let it fall into the sea."

To her copilot she said, "We're going to try for the airstrip at El Futuro. Maybe we'll make it."

CHAPTER TWENTY-SEVEN

> You can't describe the moral lift,
> When in the fight your spirit weary
> Hears above the hostile fire,
> Your own Artillery.
> Shells score the air like wavy hair
> From a forward battery.
> As regimental cannon crack;
> While from positions further back,
> In bitter sweet song overhead,
> Crashing discordantly,
> Division's pounding joins the attack;
> Mother-like she belches shell;
> Glorious it flies, and well, as,
> With a hissing screaming squall,
> A roaring furnace, giving all,
> She sears a path for the infantry.
> —Alexandr Tvardovsky, *Vasili Tyorkin*

Vicinity Volcano Number Nine

However the Taurans might have behaved amongst other company and in other places, here, Sergeant Sais had to admit, they'd been pretty civilized. Oh, sure, they'd left the possibility of a more rigorous interrogation in the air, but who didn't? Fear of that was part and parcel of any hostile interrogation, to include by the most civilized and restrained police: "Talk to us now and save us the trouble and I'll have a word with the prosecutor about a reduced sentence."

The principle of the thing was no different than showing someone a dental chair and saying, "And this is where we drill your teeth without Novocain." More civilized? Yes, it was. Different in principle? Not a bit; reduced pain or no pain for cooperation.

It didn't work on Sais at all because he knew, and they hadn't, that they were all under a death sentence anyway, unless the Taurans withdrew them. *Maybe even if they do. My team was one of how many? I never knew. This whole corner of the country could be wired for the biggest non-nuclear, man-made explosions possible. Maybe there is no safe spot.*

Of course, they'd probably pull me out, me and the others, if I show them where the Volcano is. But I can't, no matter what, I can't. These things are important to the counterattack when it comes. When? If? No, Sais, permit yourself no doubts; it is when, not if. My life, five or so hundred other lives, against the country we swore to defend? Patria wins; so, no, I'll keep quiet.

And, no, I won't even think about putting it to a vote.

Sais did what he could, making a small scrape hole for himself inside the camp and encouraging others to do the same. It was tough, frankly; most of the Balboan prisoners were so demoralized by capture that they tended toward indifference. The chain of command in the camp . . . well, there really wasn't much of one.

When one of the guards asked about it he answered, with feigned innocence, "Well, I saw the others digging in like furies back toward the road when I came here, and thought there was probably a reason for that."

"There's a reason," the guard said. "Don't see any reason you shouldn't know; your side's supposed to be putting in a counterattack, a big one. There was also supposed to be a convoy to take you lot and ourselves out of here a few days ago. What happened to it I don't know. I do know that the Indians that raid the road have been very active, so . . ."

"Yeah," Sais agreed, "they can be mean little bastards. As for us, I think—I'm quite sure, actually—that we'd be willing to walk out," Sais said. "Even give our parole, under the circumstances. If you could pass that on to your commander."

"That idiot?" said the guard. "Fat chance. You cannot imagine what it's like to get a thought past that thick skull that didn't originate there."

"Every army has a few of those," Sais commiserated, "but they really do need to . . . oh, never mind."

Sais' eyes were fixed in the horizon, the horizon that was suddenly lit up like all the Christmases that ever had been or would be.

The guard turned and looked. "Fuck," was all he could say.

"Don't know about you," Sais said, "but I'm going to my hole. Save everyone the trouble of burying me, don't you know?"

As it turned out, Sais needn't have hurried to his shelter. He doubted anyone else this side of the Parilla Line knew why. *No need to bomb us, the Volcano is going to kill everyone within about four or maybe five hundred meters . . . and it will do so without churning up the ground.*

Near Hide Position Sierra Two-Nine, Cristobal Province, Balboa

The heavy equipment engineer company never really knew what hit it. Rather, they'd known something was there, some kind of aircraft stuck in the trees forty meters overhead, but died too quickly to make the connection. One minute the thing was there, with some curious reservists looking up at it with flashlights, the next— *WHAMMO!* The world lit up as a five-hundred-pound thermobaric warhead first exploded to dispense a mix of propane gas and other things, then let off another small explosion to torch off the propane. The resultant blast obliterated them, both the men, and a few women below the cloud, mixing them as raw—rather somewhat cooked—chemicals with the mud below. Outside of that blast radius the shock wave battered flesh and tossed people about like a spoiled child's toys, smashing them into trees and rocks or, in some cases, smashing trees and rocks into them. The returning shockwave, basically rushing into the vacuum, almost tore lungs from bodies. And if anybody somehow managed to survive all that? There was no oxygen to breathe, and wouldn't be for a while, long enough to suffocate.

Even buried as their hide was, the blast still shook Ramos, Flores, and Domingo.

"We should go out and look," said the latter. "They may need a report."

"No, son," said Ramos, who had a pretty good idea of the class of the explosion, if not its precise delivery mechanism. "What we should do is break out the old potash gas masks and put them on. I think we may need the oxygen and very soon. We'll stick our heads up in maybe half an hour."

Battle Position H-14, South of the Parilla Line

In legion doctrine, there were four densities of shelling, which also tied in to the scheme of maneuver. In the present case, Density One included—along with headquarters, communications nodes, and artillery and mortar positions, as well as known and strongly suspected defensive positions that might impede the advance—the five axes of advance into the Tauran depths. These got a double dose of fire, except in those areas where the Volcanos were expected to give an effectively infinite dose of fire. Density two was almost everything else not expressly identified as a Density One target area. Density Three, in this case, were the areas outside of density one, which the pieces firing into Density One would shift to as the troops passed up the corridors smashed by Density One fires. Density Four was everything else, the once over lightly. From the point of view of those in Density Four, it wasn't all that light, really.

***

Private den Haag was of 14th Commando Troop, with which group Thirteenth Troop had, owing to casualties between them, been consolidated into a somewhat above-normal strength company. Sharing a fighting position with the disreputable and despicable coward, van der Wege, den Haag had the misfortune of being in a unit along one of the five corridors through which the legions intended to pass, and that about two kilometers from the enemy's so-called Parilla Line.

He knew about the Parilla Line, but didn't know about Density One. Indeed, he had no real frame of reference outside his own, once the barrage commenced.

It commenced with what seemed to be a mix of one-twenty mortars and eighty-ones or eighty-twos. *Bigger than sixties, anyway, but not as big as a one-twenty.* The first shells went off overhead, amid the trees. Blowing down shredded leaves, branches, and twigs.

Den Haag was not, initially, all that impressed. His position, after all, was built to standard and then some. He had good overhead cover, due to the general's commendable interpretation of the Global Court of Justice's rain forest injunction; that, and liberal use of his own shovel. *It will pass soon enough.*

But it didn't pass. Every fifteen seconds, it seemed— and den Haag consulted his watch once to check it—*yes, four times in this last minute*—a shell came in close enough that he could feel it, felt it as at least a slap against his face.

That was tolerable, if not to be enjoyed, but then one landed—so he guessed—four or five meters away. The limits of the firing ports to the fighting position attenuated or deflected the blast, to a degree, but *damn*, that hurt.

It didn't get bad though until van der Wege folded his arms around himself, and began to rock back and forth, weeping like a raped woman, while sitting down in the muck of the hole. That began right after one probably heavier shell—a one-twenty, and likely on a delay fuse—sank itself into the dirt, rock, and sandbags overhead before detonating. The shell's three pounds of high explosive mostly cleared off the overhead cover, except for the logs. However, partially tamped by the dirt and rocks, it managed to crack a couple of those, though not enough to drive them into the hole.

Den Haag could hear van der Wege's little girl scream even over the blast and even through the hands he'd cupped over his ears.

And it wouldn't end. *My God will it never end*? With each new shell, and they still kept coming in close enough to frighten four or five times a minute, van der Wege set up a new and improved form of keening.

After a period of time—he could not even guess how long it was, so much had time been dilated by terror—den Haag noticed his own hands had begun to shake uncontrollably. With one of those shaking hands, he took the flashlight from his combat harness and turned the trembling light on to van der Wege, who had unaccountably gone silent. The light shone on eyes wide open and filled with terror and madness. Van der Wege had his own rifle's muzzle in his mouth, but his hands kept going to the trigger and falling away.

A coward, just like always, den Haag sneered.

Steeling himself to a determined calm, for a moment at least, den Haag reached over, put his own finger on the trigger, and depressed it, saying. "Good riddance, you cowardly motherfucker!"

But still the barrage went on. The trembling picked up again, quickly, as well.

Forward Command Post, Fourth Corps, Cristobal, Balboa

Jimenez, Samsonov—"Who is getting too old for this shit!"—and Qabaash, accompanied, as always, by the faithful Sarita Asilo, on radio, wound their way through trenches and tunnels. Sound was all around them, for now, finally, "at last," Jimenez authorized his corps and legionary artillery to open up without regard to anything but pounding the Taurans. The city was—rather, its ruins were—lit up with tongues of flame reaching for the clouds, even as impacts all around, except out to sea, cast a flickering light over the ruins. The effect, was, on the whole, bizarre to the point of sickening.

Asilo looked a little ill but, brave girl, hid how she felt pretty well. This was her hometown and, while it wasn't much, so many memories were tied up in it . . .

I just want to cry. But I won't.

At the covered and camouflaged post—camouflaged, as what else but another ruin? This camouflage job had been done by the Taurans to Balboan benefit—Jimenez pointed out what he wanted done to Qabaash and Samsonov. Pointing toward the wrecks of Campo de los Sapos and Magdalena, he repeated what had been thoroughly briefed in an order, days before.

"Achmed," he said to the Sumeri, while pointing to show what he meant, "I want you and the Forty-third"— the Forty-third Tercio was also a brigade in the Sumeri Presidential Guard, on loan, so to speak—"to liberate both towns and then dig in and prepare for relief from the armored corps."

Qabaash nodded his head, deeply and seriously. Then smiling, he added, "It will be good to see Sancho Panzer again."

"Especially good this day, old friend, especially good for all of us. Now, Samsonov; Arturo Killum's tercio, over by Fort Tecumseh, is probably about at the breaking point by now. They've been on their own and pressed hard since this invasion began. Facing the better part of a division of Anglians and Sachsens for as long as they have . . . well . . . I am not surprised. Relieve them. Drive the Taurans back."

"With one regiment?" Samsonov had voiced his doubts before.

"Not just one regiment, not *just* one tercio," Jimenez corrected. "Attack with the Red Tsar's Three-fifty-first Guards. I am sure they can do the job."

Samsonov, too, smiled; it was a nice touch from Jimenez, to have remembered, even though the tercio was more Balboan than anything now.

"Well . . . maybe," he said. "It would help if . . ."

"You will have absolute control over the Seventy-sixth Artillery and Sixty-fourth Heavy Mortar Tercios, as soon as you are ready to cross the line of departure. And, gentlemen, you attack at dawn. To your regiments."

Saluting, the Russian and the Arab went back the way

they'd come, to the cellars and tunnels, the sangars and bunkers, and the crumbling ruins where they'd left their units.

Once they were gone, Sarita Asilo, still under her radio, admitted, "Sir, you told me the *Duque* would come for us; that he wouldn't forget us just because we were poor and black. I doubted it. I doubted him and I doubted you for believing in him, both. I was wrong and I am so sorry."

"Tell you the truth, Sarita, I was beginning to believe the rumors about him breaking down, so I had my doubts, too. And I was wrong. If I ever have the chance to apologize to him, I'll be sure to add your name to the list of people who doubted."

Her eyes went wide as her hand flew to her mouth. "You wouldn't tell him . . ."

"Yes, yes; I surely will, and, now that I think about it, a good time to do so would be when I arrange for him and Lourdes to invite us over for dinner."

"Us?" she asked, incredulously.

"Well . . . once the war's over—and we *are* going to win big—I'm planning on retiring; maybe go into politics. So we can at least discuss a possible us, no?"

To that she had no words. Glancing around to make sure there was no one else nearby, she threw her arms around Jimenez and buried a tear-covered face against his lorica.

"I'll take that as a yes," he said, reaching to stroke her hair.

She nodded, then sniffed. "Once the war's over . . . because . . . you know . . . it just . . . wouldn't be . . . appropriate . . ."

Academia *Sergento* Juan Malvegui,
Puerto Lindo, Cristobal Province, Balboa

It was death to go above. Even so, Janier went as far as a
loggia that looked out upon the parade field and the
smoking remnants of two batteries of self-propelled one-
five-fives. The guns burned merrily. Since a good deal of
the armor was aluminum, quite a bit of it had caught fire,
too. The bright spark from burning aluminum was painful
to look at, partly because of its own intensity and partly
for the scene of horror it illuminated.

Ambulances and medics scurried about under fire,
looking for wounded. Artillery, though, was no respecter
of a red cross; in Janier's view a rocket landed atop a
tracked ambulance and simply disintegrated it and its
crew. Screaming was everywhere, both from incoming
rockets and people burnt or bleeding or simply scared out
of their wits.

He saw what he thought was a girl—the soldier was
small, in any case—trying to drag a big artilleryman to safety.
They were caught in a storm of the improved conventional
munitions that amounted to so many sixty-millimeter mortar
shells mixed in with a much larger number of much smaller
ones similar to those of the TU. When the smoke cleared,
Janier couldn't make out the bodies.

He shook his head and let his chin fall to his chest.
*There will never be enough historians and citation writers
to do justice to my soldiers.*

He forced himself to something like his normal

arrogant carriage, then strode into the depth of the building that served as his headquarters.

"What is wrong with us?" he demanded of his chief gunner, Lavalle.

"We are simply outclassed," said that general, shoulders slumping. "We are also—I am also—outthought and outfought."

Janier shook the man by those slumped shoulders. "You don't get off that easily, you son of a bitch. Tell me what is happening and why!"

"Their guns are well dug in; ours are not dug in as well, for the most part, and could not be. They've got so many they can generally afford to put in even overhead cover for theirs and still cover everything. But to fight the counterbattery battle, having many fewer guns, we had to be able to traverse widely. No overhead cover for any of ours but some of the self-propelled we're saving for the attack. They have some equipment better than ours; we have nothing to match their three-hundred-millimeter rocket launchers and we have no cannon greater than one-five-five. They have numbers, massive numbers."

As Janier let the man's shoulders go, he slumped again, a complete and utter failure and disgrace in his own heart.

Another artilleryman in the headquarters, a lieutenant colonel, piped in in defense of his own general, "Sir, our counterbattery radar simply cannot make out a valid target grid with all the sheer shit flying around."

"*They* were able to!" Janier shouted. "Why could they, with their two-generation' old equipment, find our guns and ourselves not find theirs with the best and most modern in the world?"

"It was," answered Lavalle, "that we only threw out a comparative few shells in the counterpreparatory bombardment, a couple of thousand over six or seven minutes. They saw those; those few were not enough to overwhelm their radars. Then they did the calculations and fired. When they fired, though, within minutes they were firing everything and we, our systems, were overwhelmed."

"Sir, there *is* something interesting," said the artillery colonel, desperate to relieve the crushing moral pressure on his chief. "When we figured we could not get useful targeting data we started looking for useful data on the ground. Let me show you on the map."

Janier walked to the display the colonel indicated.

The colonel picked up a laser pointer and began to paint a picture. Circling a long tendril, one of six, he said, "We tracked the impacts on the ground. We can't tell much about shell weight, except for the longest ranged ones where we can make an educated guess. But we are seeing approximately twice the effort along these six corridors," the laser bounced from one to the other. "Left to a guess, I think those represent points they intend to break through and follow through on."

"I don't see another reason for it, no," Janier agreed.

"We've also tabulated that against units that have gone completely dark; no one is answering or, rather, no one is answering who isn't also gibbering. The correlation is very close."

"What kind of shape is our own artillery in?" Janier asked.

"We've lost almost everything we've used in the counterprep," the colonel replied. "That's about forty percent of our artillery train. A lot of it isn't destruction but neutralization; the crews are scared silly, certain key equipment was destroyed of damaged, key positions are temporarily unfilled. Give it a couple of days, maybe even a day, and three quarters of it will be back in business."

Janier shuddered. He had been counting on using superior gunners and systems to gain an edge on Carrera. *So much for that fucking theory.*

"Should we move the rest?" he asked the colonel.

Lavalle answered, from behind. "No point, other than those corridors that are getting hit especially hard, they're pounding everything pretty much equally. The guns are safer in their holes than they would be behind trucks in the open. And besides, the fuckers have used scatterable mines on the roads."

Janier sneered. "And we, of course, don't have any of those because our masters think they're too icky."

"It's 'for the children,'" the colonel said, joining Janier's sneer.

Biting his lower lip, Janier nodded twice, then shook his head slowly from side to side, while keeping his eyes on the map.

"You know," he observed, "of those six corridors, four go through the jungle. The other two are really the same, the two parallel highways from the capital to Cristobal. Even if they manage to stun silly every rifleman and machine gunner in those corridors, they're also turning the ground soft, knocking branches down . . . their progress isn't going to be quick; ten kilometers a day, maybe twenty if they really push it and take risks."

"I think we can count on that," said the colonel.

Janier agreed, then added, "So even if they begin their attack at dawn, it's tomorrow evening before they reach the sea."

"By those jungle routes, yes," said Lavalle. "But the highways . . ."

"They're going to move fast and be up our asses on those highways."

"We need to drop the bridges over the river north of the Parilla Line," said Lavalle. "I have no good way to do it. Honestly, I have *no* way to do it."

"The bridges and the highways . . ." Janier called for his operations officer. When he arrived, the general asked, "First off, how is that Sachsen armored brigade doing under the shelling?"

"They're in good shape, actually," Ops reported. "The shelters we built for their vehicles have pretty much stymied the enemy artillery. They've lost less than ten percent in men and equipment, in any case, and some of that will return to duty within twenty-four hours."

So, I have the means. With Panzers and Panzer Grenadiers, I'll match the Sachsen against anyone. So where . . .

Janier had been around long enough to have a pretty good eye for terrain. His finger tapped the map five times by the twin highways, Janier saying at each tap, "This is key . . . this is key . . . this is key . . . this is key . . . and this is key. Prepare the orders; I want the Sachsens to occupy this terrain and defend it to the death. They can expect two armored divisions, if Major Campbell is to be believed. Still they must hold. Add to them"—Janier cocked his head, thinking—"add to them the entire

Thirty-first demi-brigade of *our* legion. Those cutthroats
are half Sachsen anyway; I am sure they'll work fine
together. Got it?"

"Yes, sir."

"Now, Lavalle?"

The artillery general stiffened, sure that the next words
would mean his dismissal and disgrace. Thus, he was
surprised when Janier said, "We've made mistakes, both
of us. I have less excuse than you because the enemy has
already humiliated me at least twice. Let's say no more
about that and get on with the job ahead."

Lavalle almost wilted with relief, thinking, *Now here is
a commander a man can follow.*

"Yes, sir."

"Job one, therefore, is to get our losses made good. Job
two is to preserve what we have for our own
counterattack." Here Janier raised his voice so the entire
staff could hear. "The enemy is shooting his last arrow.
After this he has no more in his quiver. And then, my
friends, we kick his little brown ass.

"Now, as for those bridges—Air, get over here!"

Another officer trotted over, this one an Anglian air
marshal, the equivalent of a ground forces major
general.

"These bridges," Janier flicked his finger at the map
twice, "here and here; they need to come down."

"We've dropped them each at least twice over the
course of the campaign," said the Anglian. "The Balboans
just fixed them again each time. And the cost of getting
through was very high."

Janier sighed; *There are some things it is very hard to*

get through the skull of some pilots. He asked, gently enough, "Did the Balboans fix them instantly?"

"Well, no, it took them a couple of days, each time."

Still gentle, "A couple of days is all I need."

"But the cost?"

At that Janier bid his cool farewell. He grabbed the flyboy by the collar, shouting into his face, "You fucking simpleton; you moral cripple, you total fucking imbecile; the cost to the ground forces if you do not drop those bridges is destruction! Maybe in your warped technocratic view, a couple of hundred pilots are of greater value than a couple of hundred thousand soldiers and marines, BUT THEY FUCKING ARE NOT!"

Janier let go the collar and reached for the pistol hanging from his belt. Lavalle and his colonel moved in to stop him, in case he was serious, which they thought he just might be. "Those bridges come down or I will fucking shoot you myself for dereliction of duty. Clear?"

The Anglian turned a ghastly pale and answered, meekly, "Yes, sir, we'll do our best . . . bu' . . . bu' . . . but there's something you need to know."

"What's that?"

"The enemy killed the president of Cienfuegos, along with his entire family, and many of his key followers. Also, they have attacked all six of our bases there, mining the runways and blasting a good deal of the infrastructure, along with quite a few parked aircraft. I have about one hundred and fifty planes coming in, about half and half air superiority—including radar and command and control—and ground attack. I can put them on the bridges but they're going to be *it* for a while."

CHAPTER TWENTY-EIGHT

"In any envelope except nose down and full throttle, the F-100 was inferior to the F-86H."
—Colonel Les Waltman, Maryland ANG

Cayuga Field, Cienfuegos

High in the post-midnight air, Squadron Commander Halpence circled the field, waiting for the rest of his strike package to take off and form up. It was a small package that would join up with several others from the other five bases enroute to the target. The waste of fuel, therefore, was minimal. There were, on the other hand, some serious prices paid for that efficiency in the form of mixed ground crews on the bases, along with incompatible ordnance and spare parts.

But what can we do? If we assign bases by nationality, it would take so long for one airstrip to get a strike package in the air that it would cut into ordnance.

Yawing a bit left Halpence thought he caught sight of something, a quick glimpse of something slow and even a bit birdlike. It was only for the barest millisecond, before the thing disappeared into a cloud.

Maybe it was a . . .

Whatever it was, Halpence forgot about naming it instantly, as a tent city near the airfield was briefly lit up as bright as day. He couldn't see much from this altitude, of course, but he did happen to know where the ground crews were billeted, in relation to the field. That whatever-it-had-been was right over the section of tentage containing his own ground crews evacuated from Santa Josefina as everything went south there.

"My God," he said aloud. "All the work they put into . . . What the fuck happened?"

There was no answer by voice. A second huge fireball erupted, this time over a peace-symbol shaped parking and dispersal area northwest of the field. There were more than a few secondary explosions and fireballs from that, as ruptured fuel tanks spilled their contents to the continuing explosion, the fuel then feeding the blast and blaze.

A third fireball erupted, and then a fourth, though Halpence wasn't sure precisely what was under those blasts. There were two smaller eruptions over the airfield itself, but those weren't even noticed by the pilot amidst the other blasts. On the ground, for someone lucky enough to have found him- or herself not under a thermobaric bomb, the last two looked a bit like a fuse for demolitions, a linear sparking thing tracing a track across the sky.

Senior Aircraftman Bateman was sometimes called by his peers, "Esquire," for his penchant for commenting on laws about which he was utterly ignorant, likewise incompetent, by both training and intellect, to comment. He thought firearms were icky, hence, he had left his rifle behind when he left his tent and went off to masturbate in the bushes a hundred and fifty or so meters from ground zero for the first bomb. He was also incredibly turned on by any kind of notoriety, such as he hoped to gain by reporting on Janier's meeting with the air commanders. That, too, tended to explain his current activity.

However, at the range he was from ground zero, Bateman was not one of the lucky ones, the ones killed more or less instantly. He saw a small flash, followed within a couple of seconds by a larger one. The heat from that was intense enough to flash fry his eyeballs and cook the skin of his face and uncovered arms. There was no hair to burn away, since Bateman was as bald as a billiard ball (and approximately as intelligent), but his formerly shiny dome of skull erupted in blisters and charring.

The blast wave entered his open mouth, ripping his lungs from the inside. From the outside the overpressure wrought considerable damage to his other organs. The damage done to the exposed head of his penis was unspeakable.

Clothing afire, Bateman was picked up by the blast wave and tossed, trailing fire and smoke, before he was impaled on the sharp branch of a tranzitree, breaking off the bulk of a small branch as he did so. The worst part of the initial injuries was that they were insufficiently serious to prevent him from feeling himself abdominally raped by a tree.

There he hung, writhing like a worm on a hook, for seconds that seemed eternal, until the blast reached its ultimate extent and, rapidly cooling, turned into vacuum. At that point, the hook analogy became altogether too accurate. The vacuum not only ripped Bateman's lungs half out his throat, while explosively pulling out his eardrums, but it also pulled him from the tranzitree, dragging him back to ground zero. The tree's small branch, however, the one that Bateman's body had knocked the end off during his impalement, had become a large hook thereby. His intestines caught on this newmade hook, and were pulled out his back as he flew.

After a dozen feet his intestinal limit was reached. The small intestine tore at the point where the hook had caught it. Thereafter Bateman flew with what appeared to be a flapping tail. He landed on the tarmac of the runway and skidded for fifty or sixty feet. That abraded off the bulk of the charred skin of his face, leaving the bone exposed.

Only then—not weeping only because he lacked eyes with which to weep—did Bateman finally begin to die.

Halpence had about half his group assembled when the next aircraft to try to take off exploded as it turned into the wind on the runway. The message from the tower—it had survived, surprisingly—was that the enemy had mined the runways and that he should expect no more planes until they were cleared. His radio then spoke up in the voice of another pilot, "Same story at Santa Julio, Santa Clarita, and La Paloma, friend; they've all been hit hard and none are going to be operating soon."

At that point, Halpence signaled his force, what there was of it, "We have to go; we don't have to come back. Assume heading three-five-zero."

Halpence knew better than to ask why the Balboans could hit accurately and the Tauran forces couldn't, *GLS is useless over the central part of Balboa but functioning just fine everywhere else. Bastards.*

Enroute to Trans Balboa Highway Bridge, *Rio* Gamboa, North of the "Parilla Line," Balboa

Halpence had had a bit over an hour to think about the problem, winging it for Balboa and the bridges. *In the first place, the artillery, firing at that density and rate of fire, pretty much refutes the "small bullet-big sky" theory. At that rate, the sky isn't so big and, if many of those shells are proximity fused, they might as well be an anti-aircraft barrage.*

The balloons? Well, they're only low to south, to give room to the artillery. But if I try to go in that way they're denser than a convention of Eastminster whores waiting for the theaters to get out. That would suck like that very same convention on a payday. In fact, every side of the area has a thick barrage of balloons and you apparently can't tell where the wire is from the position of the balloon because a lot of them are double and triple wired.

That means take my chances going through or go high and over them. But high and over them means exposing myself and the rest to their air-defense umbrella, not least their fucking lasers.

Okay, I make our best chance—not a great chance but the best one—to come in low from the flank, try to dodge the balloons' wires, follow the river valley and lay the bombs at point-blank range. No time for anything fancy and no room either.

But, then, shit; small arms fire alone, going up that river, is going to collanderize our planes.

Hmmm . . . .the wires are invisible but the balloons are not. The wires might be two or three per balloon, spreading out as they descend, but right up at the balloon they'll be underneath.

Okay, then, we come in front the flank, try to skip from balloon to balloon, and then dive down once we're past them, lay our bombs, and try to do the same thing on the other side to get away.

"You've got to be shitting me," said one of the pilots of his package. "Seriously?"

"Best chance we've got," Halpence replied.

"Right. Well, I will be *most* happy to follow you."

"Yeah, I intended to go first anyway."

Halpence descended to almost sea level, pulling back on his stick just in time to rise above the tree line. The central *cordillera*, the mountain range that was the spine for two continents, arose ahead of him, dark and forbidding. He had as good a night vision and radar capability as money could buy, so skimming the trees wasn't all that hard or dangerous. Even so, he improved his chances by getting in a river valley outside the battle area and following it to the north. A quick pull on the stick, which pressed him down into his seat, was followed by a push and a rapid descent which saw his harness as the only thing keeping him from hitting the canopy with his helmet. Past the mountain range and down, he banked hard right, then waited two minutes before sending, "Everybody still with me?"

A chorus of "rogers" came back. *Whew; didn't lose anyone I started with.*

With the *cordillera* to his right and the main highway, the Trans-Colombian Highway, to his left, Halpence began scanning for the balloons. It was made easier by the steady flashing of the masses of cannon firing ahead.

Though heat contrasts between the ambient air and the balloons and the steel cables holding them up showed pretty plainly in his display, the cables intermeshed in every which direction, making it impossible to tell which ones held which balloons. He thought the density of balloons was not less than ten per kilometer, which meant anything from ten to thirty wires.

An average of maybe fifty meters between wires. Sounds like a lot until you realize that your aircraft has a fourteen-meter wingspan and you just might have misjudged a space.

Halpence felt something pass by his aircraft. He imagined it as a battery of large guns, spitting shells that he almost coincided with.

Hmmmm . . . try to knock down the balloons with cannon fire to make a path for the rest? No, they'd have to wait while one or two of us tried and . . .

A radar warning alarm sounded in Halpence's ears. He started to dive to try to lose it when he realized, *No, I'm already too low for a missile. But if we try to stick around while we down balloons, we* will *be on the receiving end of cannon fire.* He aimed for the left side of what he thought was the nearest balloon. Passing it, easily, he nosed down slightly, aiming for the right side of the next one. Then came a frantic call followed by a scream that cut off abruptly. He sensed rather than saw a fireball in the night.

"Fucking balloon just shot at us!" someone exclaimed.

"Aerial mines?" asked another. "Now that is just fucking unfair."

"How do you *do* that?" someone asked.

"What difference, at this point, how or who or why?" Halpence asked. He turned his plane on its side, passing close enough to a balloon that the shock wave actually broke it, causing it to burst, to release its gas, and to begin a graceful, fluttering fall. "Just follow me; we're almost through. Who did we lose?"

"It was the ECM bird."

"Shit."

Halpence pushed his stick forward into the narrow river valley just, and only *just*, in time. Behind and above him, twin arcs of fist-sized tracers ripped up from either side. His radar warning became a continuous shriek in his ears. Like lightning, his fingers input targeting data for both banks as he pulled the stick back to shoot skyward. The guns below tried to track him, but he was too fast for them or their radar. He felt a sudden pain in his eyes. *Lasers. Motherfucking lasers. But they must have been trying for someone else or I'd be blind rather than just in pain.* He blinked repeatedly to try to clear away the spots.

Near apogee he felt the plane shudder as it released a

pair of cluster bombs. Those continued upward for a space, as he, stick still pulled to his gut, completed his loop. He pushed forward, toward the first of the bridges, as twin bursts of firecrackers behind him said that, if nothing else, his bombs had managed to hit the ground. *I'll be happy if they'll just shake the gunners a bit.*

"There's some secondaries down below, south side of the river. I'd say you got at least one, Squadron Commander."

No time for self-congratulations. Halpence could see the bridge ahead in his display. Push-click-push-click-push-click-push-click: He selected the target, then a pair of thousand-kilo bombs, and the engagement method, which was lob. The plane showed him a window on his display and an airspeed he had to match for a perfect toss. He gave the Hurricane a little more throttle, and was rewarded with a change in image and a sort of "well-done-happy" tone.

Halpence pulled back once again on his stick, which pushed him down into his seat. The plane, itself, announced "bombs away," at the same time as he got another radar warning. He broke hard left and dove before righting himself at an eye-popping closeness to the ground. Then he forced the plane to climb again, because the amount of small-arms fire in the form of tracers he saw rising to meet him was nothing short of ridiculous. *Gentlemen, really, I appreciate the honour, but I'm not that important. Save your ammo for the ones coming behind me.*

He was just beginning to feel a small touch of confidence that he might make it back to Cayuga in one

piece when two things happened. The first was that the
sun shone on the top balloons ahead of him. That was no
problem; if anything, it made steering a safe course easier.
The second was that, in the still darkened area below, he
saw half a dozen very bright rockets that cut out
suspiciously soon.

*Oh, shit; I was hoping to avoid those. On the plus side,
the lasers cease fire when their own planes are in the air.*

Santa Cruz, East of Arnold Air Base, Balboa

"Two . . . one . . ."

Oh, shit, thought Tribune Ordoñez, as the rocket
kicked in, propelling him and his Mosaic D fighter
outward at about a forty-five-degree angle. Others,
depending on the configuration of their launch positions,
went almost straight upward. He counted down from
there, silently, *one . . . two . . . three . . . four; it's not
supposed to take fucking four!*

Fortunately, the jet did kick in, continuing his climb
skyward. Unfortunately, two of his pilots' jets did not start.
One continued trying to start his on his own, mixing
prayer with still more devout cursing all the way down
until he crashed. He never even screamed into his radio.
The other didn't try, but pulled his eject lever as soon as
he realized the jet hadn't started.

"Report," Ordoñez ordered. The result of that was,
Fuck; my own wingman rode his in. There was thus one
standard pair and two singletons, counting Ordoñez,
himself.

"Number Three, you're on me."

"Roger. Shame about Ignacio."

"We'll do our crying over a beer, later."

"Roger."

Some woman—her voice fairly dripped sex appeal—at ground control at Sixteenth Legion Headquarters reported, on the general frequency, "Half a dozen to eight enemy fighter-bombers, trying to escape the defended area after dropping their bombs. Look to the east of the balloons. Take them out or we'll probably see them again."

"Ordoñez and three more Mosaics on it," he said. Several other flights piped in with similar reports. Ordoñez counted, mentally, and came up with twenty-three Mosaics moving to intercept the Taurans.

If drachma were combat power, we'd be fucked. As is, I make it as a slight edge to us.

"Roger," continued ground control. "Be advised, the lasers are back on weapons tight except on the arc southwest to southeast."

"Is that all that's tight?" asked someone from some other flight.

The woman at ground control replied, still sweetly but with an edge to her voice, "I can loosen up the lasers, again, if you like."

The answer to that sounded most chastened, "Oh, no, no thank you, madam. Sorry, ma'am."

More flights of Mosaics reported in and were given instructions by ground control. Ordoñez tallied up, *Jesus, about two hundred and fifty of us in the air. Maybe one hundred of them or fewer. We're going to take this round.*

Ordoñez stopped his climb and turned the Mosaic over to scan the skies by the edge of the balloon barrage. He spotted them and announced, "Bandit, bandit, three-one-five, level, intercepting."

His new wingman acknowledged and conformed, loosely, to the flight commander's attack path. "A Hurricane, is it? I'll go for the one after."

"Yeah . . . missile lock . . . firing . . . shot . . ."

Another air-to-air missile shot past on a slightly different vector from his own. The target aircraft began to weave, more or less violently, while dispensing flares. Sadly, this missile was on active radar guidance, not heat seeking. It exploded in front of its target, sending out a pattern of seven continuous rods. These expanded, into somewhat irregular metal circles. The target aircraft must have passed through at least one of them, for when it emerged from behind the dense black cloud it was missing part of one wing, half the tail, and was spinning like a top.

The sudden change from forward motion at high speed to spinning uncontrollably while moving in the same direction at equally high speed pinned Halpence's left arm just that little bit too far from the eject lever. His right hand was still firmly fixed on the stick, but the spin pulled that hand and stick so far off that it was worse than useless for controlling the aircraft. Halpence played with the foot pedals, trying to use what remained of his control surfaces to adjust the plane's altitude so that when he released his hand from the stick, centrifugal force would drive it to the other eject lever. It was only ever a guess, and if it had any hope, it was a slim one. He did release the stick but his hand flew to the side of his leg. From there it was a finger crawl to the lever, as his spinning plane descended lower and lower and . . .

The wingman announced, "I confirm that one."

"Thanks, but no matter," said Ordoñez. "What matters is clearing our skies for the infantry and armor. Come on; we're going through the barrage; rather, through *both* barrages."

"Wooohooo, just like the national air races!"

"Nah; way worse than that."

Still flying low, down where the Taurans' superior radar was unlikely to pick him up for all the trees, Ordoñez put his Mosaic over on its side. *I have to see it, to see the counterattack going in.*

He wasn't disappointed. Just a couple of hundred meters below his plane, a mixed line of tanks and infantry fighting vehicles, "Ocelots," in legionary lingo, seemed to roll on water as they moved across the river. Other Ocelots entered the water from concrete boat ramps, while those who had done so before them sputtered across at about six miles an hour under the drive of their water jets. He thought he saw a wrecker on the far side, maybe intended to help the vehicles get out of the water, if needed.

Ahead, a bridge was down, or rather, damaged enough that it would take no vehicular traffic. Notwithstanding this, a dual line of infantry crossed, helping themselves and each other across the ruins of the bridge with the aid of ropes rapidly strung and beams roped to the still extant pylons. Just past the ruined bridge, crawling with those dangerous vermin, another underwater bridge, composed of concrete culverts placed in the water long before, and open into and from the direction of flow, upheld the point of another armored formation as it strove to get to the action.

The guns to Ordoñez's right were still firing, though with the rising sun the flashes had become mostly invisible. Still, they put out enough smoke and kicked up enough dust that there was no doubt but that the artillery was still searing a path for the infantry. With a nudge of the stick the pilot rolled right.

And speaking of artillery, there's a battalion moving up. I wonder if they'll even need to cross the river to get a useful firing position. Not my subject matter, I'm afraid.

Ordoñez was down to three planes now, including his own. What had happened to the third one his wingman hadn't been able to say. But with those three he took advantage of the Mosaic's tremendously tight turn radius to fly a racetrack under the still flying shells of the artillery.

God bless the National Air Races.

Cayuga Field, Cienfuegos

The planes staggered back by twos and threes, their pilots exhausted and, in more than a few cases, scared positively witless and white.

"I hope you've enough fuel to make it to Dos Rios International," said the control tower, which at the moment was more of a control scraping with a few weary men and women, a large semi-portable antenna, and a couple of radios. "We're still mined and, at the moment, haven't a damned thing to clear the mines with. We've asked the locals to help but, with the death of their president and a good deal of his cabinet, nobody's willing to commit to much of anything.

"And if you don't believe that you shouldn't try to test the mines, you can see the remnants on the field of the last one to try."

"And what do we do at Dos Rios?" more than one returning pilot asked.

"I'm just a chief technician filling in for somebody; what do I know? Still, higher command has its skills and responsibilities, and I have mine. I certainly can't make decisions for them, at least until their bodies are positively identified.

"Even so, I note that you can get refueled at Dos Rios and fly to one of the other bases. On the other hand, if you have enough fuel to make it there, I understand La Paloma claims that all their mines went off like a string of firecrackers, about fifteen minutes after they were deposited. Sometimes, you know, quality control at the factory isn't everything it might be.

"In the alternative, eventually I am sure we can start trucking ordnance to you at Dos Rios, though that promises to be neither neat nor quick.

"If you don't like any of these alternatives, gentlemen, I have a civilian here who observes that you can also point your planes to sea and eject. This, to me, seems altogether too permanent."

HAMS *Indomitable*, Shimmering Sea, near Cristobal

The commander of the air wing briefed the ship's captain in his day cabin. "The news, sir, is not good. We launched twenty-nine combat sorties, all we were capable of this morning. The following pilots have not returned: Baird, believed to have run into the cable anchoring one of their barrage balloons; Gorbin, believed blinded by a laser and crashed; Dixon, shot down by four or five of their Mosaics, ganging up on him; Danks, air defense fire; Gibbs, unknown . . ."

"Just the short version, Air; I can deal with names later."

"Fine, Captain; the short version is that we sent out twenty-nine and got seventeen back. We can't even claim it as a Pyrrhic victory; another half day like this and we are done. I am sure we took a great many down with us, but when a pissant peripheral country like Balboa can replace her losses and we cannot replace ours . . ."

"Never mind that; echelons above both you and me. How about the Frogs?" the captain asked.

"They're not talking. When a frog isn't crowing about his successes you can be pretty sure he's taken a pretty nasty defeat."

"Spares?"

"We can knock together four more Sea Hurricanes, but that will not happen all that soon."

"Do it. We're also pulling back to Cienfuegos to establish a screen line to prevent them being hit again by those nasty damned stealthy gliders."

CHAPTER TWENTY-NINE

> "Sancho, my armor!"
> —Don Quixote, from *Man of La Mancha*
> —Patricio Carrera,
>   during the liberation of Sumer and after

Battle Position H-14, South of the Parilla Line

Den Haag didn't know anymore how many times the fire had lifted off before coming back with redoubled fury. The first three times—*or was it four?*—he'd dutifully manned the firing port of his fighting position. He'd waited and waited—he thought the breaks in fire had ranged from five minutes to fifteen—watching out for enemy attack, before seeing, instead, a storm of shells, fire, smoke, and flying steel shards. After the third—*or maybe the fourth; I can't seem to remember anymore*—he'd just stayed down, praying alternately for a shell to put him out of his misery or for the storm to end.

Occasionally, he thought he saw van der Wege's ghastly corpse grinning at him or even laughing around the muzzle still stuck in his mouth. Den Haag really didn't know anymore what was impossible and what was not. Before this morning, he'd have said that the kind of barrage he'd endured was impossible. Now he couldn't really say much of anything; it all came out as "gahgahgahgah."

His left hand was locked so tightly to his rifle that he couldn't pry it away. The right hand shook like a leaf in the wind. He was nauseated, but whether that was from concussion or fear he didn't know. His vision swam in and out of focus, without any obvious pattern.

He still could feel—hearing was not going to happen any time soon—the shells falling. They felt to him like they were falling some distance away, three or four hundred meters, maybe. But they'd fooled him before; he wasn't coming out of his hole just because they teased him or tried to fool him. It wasn't safe anywhere but in the very bottom of his position.

South of Stollen Number One Twenty-Six

Cruz and his cohort commander, Velasquez, weren't the first ones into the early morning light. By the time they left their concrete shelter, the tercio's *Cazador* maniple was already spread out on the south slope. There was a bunker also at the military crest, from which they could watch the bombardment and judge the timing and effects. The bunker was—*mirabile dictu*—connected by buried wire to the stollen, but, more wondrous still, the wire was intact. Even so, Velasquez had taken two radio bearers with him.

Before the party, shells still fell at the rate of about fifteen thousand per minute. Behind, audible over the shelling only because closer, the armored mass of First Corps rumbled to and across the crossing points. There were also planes roaring through their dogfights overhead, but neither Cruz nor his boss had an eye or an ear for those. Their job was on the ground; let the air take care of the air unless they needed some air defense suppressed.

Cruz had never seen nor thought to see anything so horrible in his life, and he had seen plenty of horror across a good part of the planet. The jungle to the south was eviscerated, brutalized, raped. And still the shells fell. What had been green was now all brown and black, shattered and splintered. A thick veil of smoke covered the ground, though it was beginning to swirl and ascend as the sun warmed it and such ground as could be touched.

He took scant comfort from the knowledge that it would grow back surprisingly quickly. It was an obscenity now.

None of the sounds changed all that much, but the rumble of shells flying overhead shifted outward. Before their eyes, the shells ceased to fall over an area of about four or five hundred meters across and, though they couldn't see it they knew it from studying the fire-support plan, about one and a half kilometers to the south. For that one and a half kilometers, control of their own supporting fires had been returned to the leading cohort commanders. The tercio guns, the eighty-five-millimeter jobs, would not return to tercio control until that three-kilometer limit had been breached. Instead, the eighty-fives pounded the flanks of this corridor and the others, as did the mortars of those cohorts and maniples not in the leading thrusts.

Down below, the *Cazador* maniple stood almost as one man and, again, with as near to unity as might be hoped for, began a fast march, sometimes a trot, into the gap that had been opened up for them,

"Top," said Velasquez, "I'm going to leave one radio with you and take one with me. I'm also going to get on the ass end of the *Cazadores*, and not lose sight of them. Start bringing the maniples up now and push them towards me. The boys are going to be a little nervous about going up that gap with artillery coming in to both sides. Can't say I blame them, but talk it up to them. Remind them it's not, in principle, different from their training. While I'm at the point, you take the ass for straggler control."

"Wilco, sir," Cruz replied. "If I don't see you before then, I'll see you at the Shimmering Sea."

"*Thalassa! Thalassa!*" quoth Velasquez, with a wicked smile.

Ahead, the first fusillades of small arms fire sounded, and, from the sound, it was almost all friendly.

I suppose, thought Cruz, *that they've just had the fight simply beaten out of them.*

UEPF *Spirit of Peace*, in orbit over Terra Nova

Much as the Balboan Condors existed and thrived in one

environment, the environment of the very slow and relatively weak and small, where high performance jets could not function, the still smaller and slower recon skimmers of the United Earth Peace Fleet operated where Mosaics couldn't target them well, lasers were fairly useless, and the radar of the self-propelled cannon was unlikely to notice them, even though they generally noticed and made short work of Tauran drones. Usually, this was true, anyway; they had gotten lucky with a skimmer a few times in the past.

From her day cabin, Marguerite watched the skimmer-sent image on her screen. It was of a mass of tanks and other armored vehicles crossing the river pretty much unimpeded. Pale at the final stake into the heart of her plans to ultimately secure her home world from these barbarians and to save it from the decadent Class Ones who had ruined it, she pressed a button to call Janier.

"Bertrand," she said, when he answered, her own voice quivering, "I don't know if you can see it with your own resources, but the Balboans are coming at you in force. The bridges are down but they're not using bridges. I understand that their lighter armored vehicles can swim, but how do they make tanks swim? I can *see* them, crossing the river like it's not even there."

Janier was silent for a long moment, then he answered, "Underwater bridge, I suppose. They're hard to spot and comparatively hard to destroy. That will be his heavy corps, First Corps, I think it is. I'm rolling my armor to meet him along the highways."

"What have you got to deal with it?" Wallenstein asked.

"One brigade, though it's a large one and rather good;

Sachsens, you know. It was all the heavy force we could support through Puerto Lindo. I'm also moving in two very good infantry battalions, plus support, by truck."

"Where are you now?" Marguerite asked.

"At my headquarters, but I'll be going with the Sachsens to stop Carrera."

"Don't," she said. "Please . . . just . . . don't."

"I must."

"Bertrand, has he ever not predicted us, you and me, both? I mean about anything important? There will be something waiting for you and the Sachsens."

"Like what?"

"I don't know. But there will be something." Marguerite drew in a long slow breath. She didn't want to admit this but, "Your people have to have suspected it, but I doubt you knew. Well I *do* know. He got a number of nuclear weapons from my predecessor, Bertrand. Who knows, maybe he has others, too. Do you think for a minute he won't use them?"

"And you're just telling me this now?"

"I was hoping never to have to tell you at all, frankly. But please don't accompany the Sachsens."

"I must. Janier, out."

Vicinity Volcano Number Nine

Sergeant Sais had pretty much been able to sit out the bombardment in his hole, well-sheltered enough from the occasional long or short that landed in the general area. The worst and most frequent had been the one-twenty-two—

or so he supposed—rockets. They packed an amazing amount of explosive—over fourteen pounds—for what wasn't even a five-inch shell. Indeed, the standard five-inch shell had less than half that explosive weight.

Still, none came close enough to make Sais more than lay back in his trench. Sometimes he didn't even bother since, after all, *What difference if killed by a short round or killed by an inferno next door?*

Does my side know we're here? Sais wondered. *I'm almost surprised none of the shells that hit near us set off the Volcano. I suppose a very near miss with thirty-three pounds of buried explosive is enough, where half that, twice as far away, and above the surface is not enough. Still, only a matter of . . . uh, oh, what's this?*

"This" was a mixed column of tanks and infantry fighting vehicles, maybe thirty of each, though Sais had the sense of some outliers, both to the north and south. *Mortars and scouts, I suppose. Well, the more the merrier. I wonder; will I get credit in the hereafter for getting this many Taurans, personally?*

As the tanks and IFVs pulled into hasty positions, another column showed up, this one about forty trucks carrying an ethnic kaleidoscope of infantry, though all in the same uniform. A light vehicle showed up after that, and raced to the head of the column of trucks. Stopping in a cloud of dust, a tall and slender officer stepped out— *Oh, a general I suppose he must be from the way he acts*—and began issuing orders to a group that clustered around him after dismounting from the trucks.

That group dispersed explosively on the presumptive general's order, returning to their men and leading them to Sais didn't know where, except that they seemed to be orienting themselves on the Sachsen companies.

That general took a look at the little compound holding Sais and the others, then began to stride toward the gate purposefully. Reaching the gate, he shouted for the officer in charge. When that pudgy worthy came out, Sais was shocked to see the general punch him in such a way that his feet flew out from under him, before delivering a swift kick to his midsection. Then the gate opened and a senior sergeant came in and called the prisoners to muster around him.

When they'd all formed roughly on the sergeant, the tall Gaul—*Definitely what the manuals say is the uniform of Gaul, anyway*—strode over and began to speak.

"I am Janier," the Gaul said. "You have . . . heard of me? Ma Spanish bad. Like ma English. Try not to speak. Embarrassing, *tu sabes*? You not supposed to be here. Gave orders take away. You go now, for safety. These men . . . escort you. Apology for not getting away with safe. Try get message your side. Maybe work."

He turned then and bellowed "Malcoeur!" At which point a rather tubby mid-grade officer came out of the vehicle, too. Janier said some things to Malcoeur that set the latter to violent disagreement. Sais didn't know what it was. He didn't understand the other things Janier said, either, but something must have been very sad, for the tubby officer began softly to weep.

The sergeant translated what was going on, after Janier turned and left. "The general—yes, that's really Janier, the Tauran Union commander—has, shall we say, 'relieved' the former commandant of this camp." His finger pointed at the body writhing on the ground. Inclining his head, he continued, "Major Malcoeur, in whom the general reposes the greatest trust, has been placed in charge. He and we are going to try to get you away to safety. There's going to be fighting here, and soon. There is, as you can hear, still artillery falling all over creation, so we may not make it. The general thinks we have a better chance if we try than if we remain.

"So grab a canteen and a ration if you have one; we leave in five minutes."

That Frog general, thought Sais, *is a brave man. If I make it, I am going to put him in for the Cruz de Coraje.* Though he'd been prepared to die rather than reveal the secret, on the whole Sais was happy enough to have a chance at life.

Battle Position H-14, South of the Parilla Line

The *Cazadores* had bypassed everything they could possibly bypass, this battle position included. It was up to Velasquez's and Cruz's Second Cohort to clear the resistance bypassed. Already the other two cohorts had committed to clearing out the shoulders of the corridor; there was extensive firing from behind, though most of it, to Cruz, sounded like it came from an F- or M-26. The corridor had also been opened another two kilometers into the Tauran rear, while the eighty-five-millimeter guns had, for the most part, ceased fire, backed out of their shipping containers, after some shoveling and sandbag tossing, and were displacing forward. There was still plenty of steel going overhead, but the bulk of it was heavier stuff, striking further back.

One of the maniples of Second Cohort assaulted across the battle position, mostly walking while firing from the hip. The return fire . . . *Well*, Cruz thought, *it's just ineffective, flying high, badly aimed, something. And there's not much of it.*

A few white flags appeared, which caused the cohort's fire to slacken. From the moonscape the artillery had made of the ground, emerged pale shadows of trembling, twitching, simulacra of human beings. They held their hands out, some of them, as if begging. A few, Cruz saw, just shook their heads. One man screamed, for no obvious and timely reason, which set half a dozen more to screaming.

One kept repeating over and over, "den Haag . . . den Haag . . . den Haag."

Sergeant Major Cruz looked up and thought, *You know, God; I am ashamed. You really shouldn't let us do things like this to human beings.*

Some of the Taurans spoke a language surprisingly similar sounding to English, which Cruz more or less understood. It wasn't English, though, and he could only make out the faintly scented trail of a word here and there, something that seemed familiar but lacked context and meaning.

Then he noticed one of the Taurans trying to treat another's wounds. *This, at least, I know how to deal with.* Radioing Velasquez he said, "Sir, we've got a bunch of prisoners and a lot of Tauran wounded. We need to start evacuating the ones who can move and treating the ones who can't."

"Yeah," answered the legate, "it's not much different further ahead. Men can only take so much, and these poor bastards got more than their share. You're authorized to detach from that maniple one squad as guards and to tell the cohort medical platoon to meet you and get to work. Velasquez, out."

Between the Parilla Line and Madrigal, Balboa

Aaron Brown was a diminutive black tanker, originally from the Federated States Army but for decades now a part of the Legion del Cid. He'd trained and commanded the heavy battalion during the invasion of Sumer. He'd led what amounted to a heavy legion in Pashtia.

Now he had a corps, composed of his own former command of First Armored Legion, plus Sitnikov's Sixth Cadet Armored, composed of a sprinkling of officers from the military schools, plus a goodly chunk of the schools' cadet bodies, as well, along with Young Scouts, retirees, and a number of secondments from other units. The average age of the Sixth was under sixteen, and really closer to fifteen. There were combatants in the legions as young as twelve, as young as nine if one counted part-time guerillas. That's part of how a country with a population of about three million mobilized an army of almost four hundred thousand, the other parts being extensive use of women and old folks, and the disabled, plus the addition of several divisions' worth of foreign auxiliaries, and complete shutdown of the economy for the period of the campaign, coupled with stockpiling of all necessities beforehand.

And that four hundred thousand, nearabouts, also didn't include perhaps as many as a couple of hundred thousand part-time guerillas, making life miserable for the Zhong.

Though without doubt it set Cosmopolitan Progressives, or Kosmos, running for their fainting couches on a global scale, in fact, during the previous invasion, the cadets had more than shown their worth. As a military force not anticipated hence not accounted for on Tauran Union orders of battle for the legions, they had been instrumental in defeating the invasion by a combination of ambush, surprise attack, and simply buying time for the adult reserve forces to mobilize. The Taurans still lacked a good understanding of the cadet component of the legions, since there was also a massive cadet organization outside of the military schools.

Brown's corps also normally contained the Tenth Artillery legion, which was now fighting the battle more or less independently but would partially revert to corps control soon, and the Twenty-first Combat Support Brigade, containing tercios of armored cavalry (Twenty-fourth), engineers (Ninety-first), and air defense (One hundred and first).

Carrera had long since dubbed the commander of the legions' armor contingent, whatever size that might be, "Sancho Panzer." Brown had held the title continuously since and, indeed, answered the radio and signed official correspondence as "Sancho Panzer."

To this, Carrera responded, "Sancho! My armor!"

Brown answered, "I've got a tercio and a half to two tercios of each legion across the river, plus some few maniples from the Twenty-first Combat Support Brigade. The rest, and all the artillery, is on the other side waiting for their chance. Shall I attack?"

There was no hesitation on Carrera's part. "Yes, shortly. I'm going to order the *special* prep, and when you see that go, go in. Let me know if and when you meet serious resistance; sometimes we may be able to fix that for you. Otherwise, Tenth Legion, minus a bit, is back under your corps' control."

"A bit?" Brown queried.

"I'm keeping the heavy rocket launchers and a single battalion of one-eighties, plus the two-o-threes. The rest is yours, again. Break through to the sea."

"Roger, waiting for the special prep."

Brown knew his Jaguar IIs and Pumas—Volgan tanks renamed by the legions, with a few modifications from *Obras Zorilleras* and Zion—were outmatched, tank for tank, by the Taurans.

But, Hell, I'm not facing more than one hundred—max one hundred and fifty—Tauran tanks, while my corps can field better than five hundred Jaguars, plus a hundred or more SPATHAs of our own. And then there are a couple of hundred more SPATHAs in the infantry legions, and we both have a swarm of Ocelots. And then the boss suggests he has a trick for the Taurans. I suspect it's going to be a doozy.

In any case, I like our chances just fine.

The SPATHAs, Self Propelled, Anti-Tank, Heavy Armor, were former obsolescent tanks, the turrets of which had been removed and emplaced atop fixed concrete positions, mostly on the *Isla Real* in the *Mar Furioso*, though a number also faced to the northeast, where the plain raised up to the mountains. The hulls had then had a casemate built up on them, with a worn out one-hundred-and-fifty-millimeter gun mounted, the gun having been bored out to one hundred and sixty. They also had enough composite armor slapped on the front to stop even the Tauran tank cannon from penetrating.

The gun fired charges weighing forty pounds. These were plastic explosive, sometimes called "HESH." They had surprising accuracy up to a range of about twelve hundred meters.

The effect of that much plastic explosive, in close contact with and self-conforming to a target tank, tended toward the near catastrophic, with turrets being deranged, main guns bent or even blown off, optics smashed beyond hope of repair, radio antennas disintegrated, and even machine guns detached and launched into their own tanks at great velocity and with terrible effects on the crew. They were pretty much a brute force solution to a brute force problem.

The other thing about the SPATHA was that, while Jaguars, with their one-twenty-fives of fifty-one calibers, often had trouble maneuvering between the trees, the SPATHA's stubby little gun offered no such problem.

Vicinity Volcano Number Nine

Past the lightly hit area, down the hill where the barrage had been fierce, there were a number of light vehicles and a few trucks that still flickered and smoked from the barrage. There were bodies, more than a few, scattered on the ground or half incinerated behind drivers' wheels.

"We need to hurry," Sais told the senior sergeant in charge. "Don't ask me any questions but we, all of us, need to hurry. The barrage is lifting, that means we can find shelter *almost* anywhere, but we *need* to fucking *hurry!*"

"You'll just want to escape," the Tauran sergeant insisted.

"I want to escape something, goddammit, but not you. Look, let me ask the prisoners for their parole."

That was problematic for the Tauran sergeant, too, but the Balboan seemed so sincere. He clearly wanted to get away from *something*.

"Major Malcoeur," the sergeant shouted, "could you come here please? Quickly, please, sir?"

"I understand Spanish," the Tauran said. "If you tell them to escape I'll shoot you where you stand."

"Fair enough. But no time to wait. Now . . . let me see . . . I'll stand on that wreck there." Sais pointed at a four-passenger light vehicle, the tires blown out and four bodies inside, slumped over in death, still oozing blood from multiple jagged tears and punctures.

Jumping atop the back, he did his best to keep his feet from inflicting a sacrilege on the Tauran dead. "Listen to me," he shouted to the prisoners. "Listen to me and gather around. Hurry, there isn't much time." He waiting until the troops formed a loose three-quarter ring of maybe as many as five hundred. "Okay, quiet. There is a huge bomb, a kind of mine, about to go off on that hill. The destructive radius will be immense, almost nuclear."

He looked to see if the Tauran really did understand. The wide-eyed, gap-mouthed, shocked expression on his face said he did. "We need to give our parole to the sergeant here that we will not try to escape. Repeat after me, 'I give my parole.'"

He waited a couple of seconds while the men muttered this, some with obvious reluctance. After they'd finished, the Tauran sergeant gave some orders in a language Sais didn't understand, and began to run back whence they'd come.

"What are you doing?" Sais called after the Tauran.

Over his shoulder the sergeant answered, "You have your duty; I have mine. I have to warn our men atop that hill. My man knows what's going on. He'll inform the major. Form your men up and start to run."

"What's your name?" Sais asked.

"Constantinescu, Alexander. Why?"

"Just to remember." *So I can put you in for a CC, too.*

Constaninescu met Janier about halfway back up the slope. Breathlessly, the sergeant cried out, "General, for the love of God, run. There's a bomb . . ."

Janier directed his driver to take him to the sergeant. "What was that?" he asked.

"No . . . time . . . Balboan . . . warned me . . . bomb . . . really big fucking *bomb* . . ." He pointed up toward the now empty housing area and POW camp.

"So *that* was the next trick," Janier muttered. "Of course, that son of a bitch can read a map, too." To Constantinescu he said, "Look, you go take charge of those prisoners again, I'll warn . . ."

Before he could finish the sentence, they heard an incredible roar, an unparalleled blast coming from the south. It was accompanied by a bright flash, itself followed by a massive rising mushroom cloud. Mesmerized by the rising cloud, they were stunned by a much larger and more powerful, but only because closer, blast. The flash from that left spots on their eyes.

"Take cover," the general shouted. The sergeant did so instantly, but the driver was still stunned. Janier jumped over the man and physically hauled him from the driver's seat. The vehicle began to drift forward on its own, unattended, while the general threw the young driver to the ground before joining him. Then they, all three, heard the freight train rattle of an incoming heavy shell. It stood out particularly in the lull of the bombardment.

"A bomb?" Janier wondered, "Or was it the nukes Wallenstein warned me about after all?"

CHAPTER THIRTY

"The blast kill mechanism against living targets is unique—and unpleasant . . . What kills is the pressure wave, and more importantly, the subsequent rarefaction vacuum, which ruptures the lungs . . . If the fuel deflagrates but does not detonate, victims will be severely burned and will probably also inhale the burning fuel. Since the most common FAE fuels, ethylene oxide and propylene oxide, are highly toxic, undetonated FAE should prove as lethal to personnel caught within the cloud as most chemical agents."

—Defense Intelligence Agency,
*Fuel Air and Enhanced Blast Explosive
Technology, Foreign*
(Quoted by Human Rights Watch, February 1, 2000)

Volcano Number Nine

There were thirteen Volcanos emplaced between the Parilla Line and Cristobal. Five of these were at four of the termini of the especially heavily blasted corridors, such as the one Cruz, Velazquez, and Second of the Second moved along. The other eight were emplaced in extremely likely battle positions along and between the twin highways that led from *Ciudad* Balboa to Cristobal.

The Volcanos, themselves, were nothing more than ridiculously large thermobaric bombs. Indeed, they were several times larger, although not several times more effective, as any ever dropped by an aircraft either on Terra Nova or on Old Earth. They could be larger, since they didn't need to fit inside of, nor be light enough to be carried by an aircraft.

Apart from size, the differences were mostly a matter of taste. There was, for example, a fairly large component of powdered magnesium, both for the flash and to ensure more complete detonation. Moreover, while thermobarics derived a lot of their efficiency from using the oxygen in the area where they detonated, in the case of a Volcano there was so *much* fuel that the oxygen in the air would have been exhausted before—long before—detonation was complete. Hence, they also had internal oxygen tanks, rigged to be split by shaped explosives, to help feed the blast.

The real problems were always timely detonation and avoidance of discovery. For the latter, they were put in underground, generally as part of a building project and always empty of fuel. The fueling had taken place in the lull between the two Tauran invasions and always in the context of some other, nearby operation.

Detonation was the bigger problem. Radio required antennas, which the Volcanos had, generally at some distance from the mines and connected by buried wire.

These, however, were somewhat unlikely to survive the preliminary bombardment Carrera had been planning since Pashtia. A time fuse would have demanded precision of time in the execution of the counteroffensive, when circumstances could never be predicted with that kind of accuracy.

The solution *Obras Zorilleras* had come up with was rather ingenious. There would be, and were, timers, but they were only set to turn on and sensitize seismic detectors, and only for short periods of time every other day. A near miss would not set off the mines at any other time, and even a near miss would have to be within a certain distance, have the fuse set on delay, which multiplied the power of the blast by effectively tamping it with the earth it had dug through, and carry a certain amount of high explosive. This was all somewhat variable, as a larger delayed blast, further away, could set off the bomb. But even that was only if the bomb's seismic detector was activated, which was only the case for about one half of one percent of the time, roughly fifteen minutes every two days.

At those times, forty pounds of TNT, buried within sixty meters, was enough for detonation.

There were only twelve two-hundred-and-three-millimeter guns in legionary service. These were self-propelled Volgan pieces that had been ensured to have new, rigidly tested and carefully registered barrels. The twelve were part of the special bombardment maniple of Tenth Legion. They had specially trained and selected crews, and were issued ammunition carefully made, weighed, and measured to have the minimum possible Circular Error Probable, or CEP. Those twelve had not taken part in the preparatory bombardment, lest Tauran counterbattery been able to get through. They were too important to risk on that.

As the main bombardment ended, and with considerable confidence that neither Tauran air nor counterbattery were going to find them, the crews had set to driving the guns out of their shelters, settling them into their emplacements, and then setting them on the correct deflections and elevations, which measures had long since been calculated and updated for the morning's meteorological message.

After that, it was just waiting for the command, "Fire!"

Artillery shells, so far at least, have not yet been proven to be capable of pride. Had this one been capable, it would have practically burst its fuse out of the fuse well and split the steel of its sides with sheer pride. Not only was it a special shell, super carefully manufactured, but it was on a mission to save its country, and the crew that had cared for it since being taken from the womb of the ammo bunker.

Even so, the shell had waited patiently; if incapable of pride, artillery shells are still perfectly capable of patience. It had waited and waited and waited. Then, finally, it had been fed into the breech of its one true love, the gun, and followed up with bagged charges. Again, had an artillery shell been capable of excitement, this one would have said, "Ohboyohboyohboy!" But, of course, being a shell, it said not a word.

A loud alarm sounded for about five seconds, sending the crew and anyone else nearby scurrying for shelter from the organ ripping, brain ping-ponging blast. And then the gun spoke.

Down the tube the shell flew, kicked in the ass by a preposterously large propellant charge. Engaging the rifling, it began to spin. Spinning for the roughly forty feet of the barrel's length, it emerged past the pepperpot muzzle brake and into the open air.

Through the air it flew, kilometer after kilometer, rising and rising until, beginning to be overcome by gravity, it began its descent. Descending, the shell also slowed, thus making the arc of its fall steeper than that of its rise. It was still at a fairly steep angle, though, when it struck the earth near Volcano number nine and buried itself several meters deep. At that point the shell exploded, instantly excavating a large hole and sending a considerable shock wave through the ground.

Magdalena, Balboa

On a hill overlooking the town, and also high enough to see over the jungle, a single Tauran counterbattery radar detachment came back to life as the crew finished repairing the damage taken since the enemy barrage had opened up.

The radar set owed its continued existence to being closer to Cristobal and Fourth Corps than the Parilla Line and the preparatory bombardment south of it. It had, in any case, proven quite useless at backtracking incoming shells to firing batteries, owing to a volume of flying shell its onboard computer was simply unable to deal with.

Now that the bulk of the shelling had stopped, though, the battery could make out both some specific firing batteries as well as the probable target grids. They couldn't exactly tell shell weight or caliber, but the range and track of a shell could often suggest a type of system, which amounted to the same thing.

"That's a long-range bitch, isn't it?" commented the sergeant in charge, watching one shell, in particular, trace across the screen.

"Only thing it matches is a Volgan two-o-three," judged the operator. "I didn't know the enemy had . . . ooops . . . there's another . . . then another. Another . . . another . . . shit . . . thirteen of them, all from separate locations."

"What's that suggest to you?" asked the sergeant. Both men's eyes grew very wide. There was only one type of attack for which that made sense.

"Fuck. Nukes. Get the warning out! Nukes!"

Volcano Number Nine

The fuse package had turned the seismic detector on a scant few minutes before. This sensed the nearby underground blast, determined that it was sufficient for its detonation parameters, and sent a strong electrical charge down the wire. The charge did three things. Firstly, it set off the elevation charge under the Volcano. This fairly well destroyed the outer casing in the course of pushing it up through the ground, but that didn't matter at this point. Secondly—though, in fact, simultaneously—it blew apart the tanks holding the liquid oxygen. Thirdly, after a very short delay, it set off the central explosive charge. This, itself, also did three things; it began the dispersal of the fuel, set off the sparklers that would begin the reaction, and, with the fuel, dispersed the magnesium dust that would add brightness to the flash.

Janier reached over and ground the driver's upraised head to the dirt, then ducked his own and covered his eyes as best he could in the crook of one arm. What happened then, those seven events from impact to flash, were too close together for the human brain to tell the difference. There was a flash, a blast, a roar, a fireball, and a rising mushroom cloud. It was, under the circumstances, indistinguishable from a nuclear explosion both for those similarities and because no living human being in the universe had ever been close enough to one to be able to tell the difference, anyway.

Janier felt heat on his shoulders, back, and arms. It was less than he might have expected, if he'd been in a position to expect anything but death. He had the impression of being picked up by an invisible hand and tossed a goodly distance. Somewhere in there his eyes opened up and he saw the driver, arms and legs outstretched, sailing and spinning like a top through the air. He thought, but couldn't be sure, that he saw his staff car likewise rolling end over end across the ground, trailing smoke and flame. Of the brave sergeant who had run toward the blast to try to warn the Sachsens up there, there was no sign. He also saw that his own uniform had caught fire. He couldn't feel the flames though, which he found odd.

If I live, that's really going to hurt. Of course, the odds of that are exceptionally poor, so . . .

Janier was on the edge of the blast wave. When the blast collapsed and air began to rush in to fill the vacuum, it was relatively mild where he was. Instead of detaching his lungs, it blew out the flames of his uniform. It also twisted his upper body toward the blast, while not actually stopping, or even much slowing, his flight. That was just another form of death, too, of course, because when he hit the ground, his body was going to be pulverized . . .

Except for that lake and the angle of his flight. He hit water, feet first but at a very shallow angle, then more or less skipped across the water like a stone, except that stones don't scream anymore than artillery shells feel pride.

When he reached the other side of the narrow lake, the ground also was fairly smooth. Oh, it still broke both legs, one of them in three places, partially collapsed one vertebra, and gave him a miserable concussion, but, at least for the moment, General Bertrand Janier lived. Lifting his head and looking toward the hill, the slope of which he'd just been blasted off of, he saw a fuzzy, shimmering, shaking steel rain descend on the armor there. The raindrops hit with black expanding splashes.

"Why," he wondered aloud, "would they need to drench the thing in DPICM if they've just used a nuke? Wasteful . . . wasteful. I shall make a negative comment on Carrera's annual efficiency report, when I have Malcoeur draft it . . ."

★★★

The infantry that had been dispatched to flank the hill disappeared into a draw shaded by some dense smoke.

Sancho Panzer's own tank was in defilade as he watched three of his SPATHAs duke it out with a pair of Sachsen tanks. He saw one of the SPATHAs take a hit, the front of the hull more or less exploding with a mix of smallish steel hexagons, ceramic plates, polyurethane mesh, and other odd bits and pieces. The tank's projectile apparently failed to penetrate, since the SPATHA, a half a second later, fired its stubby gun at the Tauran. At these ranges armor and numbers were all. Nobody was missing who kept his cool and had a target.

There was a great explosion on the front of the Sachsen tank, temporarily hiding it behind a sudden cloud of dense smoke.

The other tank took a shot and this time the projectile was enough to get through. The SPATHA simply blew apart from its own internally stowed ammunition.

Setting off the propellant is one thing, thought Brown. *Setting off more than half a ton of plastic explosive in a small place is something else entirely.*

The Sachsen didn't last long, though. The two remaining SPATHAs of that section each hit it with a HEP round within a few seconds of each other. It went dead and silent then, though like the other one now being revealed behind the dissipating smoke cloud, it didn't burn.

Brown wasn't following the internal communications nets of his subordinate tercios and cohorts, though he did keep lines open and one ear focused on his three legions. Thus, he didn't actually hear the chat between the

SPATHAs, their commander, or the infantry Brown had seen trying for the flank. But then, suddenly, the infantry were on the hill, shooting very little but jumping up and down with glee while beckoning the entire force forward.

Above the distinctive smell of solvent that went along with most plastic explosives, the air around the tank was thick with the coppery smell of blood, spilled in copious quantities.

Brown climbed aboard the second of the Tauran tanks he'd seen hit, the one that had taken two forty-pound charges of plastic explosive. On this tank, the gun was noticeably bent and the turret deranged. Still, it wasn't burning, so he thought it safe enough to climb aboard.

The crew seemed most sincerely dead, the driver having had his head more or less pulverized by the blast, while the tank commander, probably fighting unbuttoned, as was Sachsen doctrine, simply didn't have a head anymore.

Must have blown it clean off. Well. At least it was quick.

The interesting one was the gunner. He had had the tank's coaxial machine gun blown out of its cradle and driven, butt-first, through his chest. The gunner, though dead, had his hands rigidly fixed to the machine gun, indicating that he, unfortunately, had not been as lucky as his chief.

Poor bastard.

Assuming the loader hadn't had any better chance than the other three crew members, Sancho Panzer turned to jump off the tank and continue to follow the attack as closely as he could without actually getting in the way.

far enemy air has not been able to cut the runways again so we're bringing them in to refuel and rearm."

"Roger, in broad terms, what have the Sixteenth's losses been like?"

Lanza hesitated a moment, before answering, "Really bad, above forty percent lost or damaged enough to need repair, though the exchange rate has been better than we expected."

"Roger, keep me posted."

"Wilco."

When Carrera re-emerged into the sunlight, the first thing he saw was a large column of disarmed, dirty, shuffling men in foreign uniforms. They were being guarded, albeit a bit loosely, by a mix of Balboan support troops and walking wounded. He made a guess that there were about two thousand of them.

"Pull over there, Jamey," he told Soult through the intercom.

"The prisoners?" Soult asked.

"That's what I suppose they are."

As the Ocelot moved closer, more detail could be made out. There were men blinded and without bandages being led by the hand by men limping on blood-oozing legs. Others were carried on stretchers, a few with a mix of Taurans and Balboans straining on the poles or straps.

Still, for all the wounded, most of the Taurans, Balboans too, for that matter, looked simply exhausted, helpless, hopeless, and defeated.

Reaching down to flip the switch on the intercom system to talk to his staff, Carrera keyed his boom mike and said, "I want three things. I want the medical brigade

And then he heard a low moan, followed by a few words that sounded vaguely familiar.

Taking a flashlight from his combat harness, Brown shone it down into the tank, scanning for the loader. He found the man, prone on the floor amidst some of the detritus of war, as found in a wrecked tank. There was another moan and then an arm arose and waved as if searching for something by feel.

"Son, relax. I'll try to get you some aid."

Standing up on the tank's hull, Brown cupped his hands and shouted, "Get me a medical team over here! Now!"

Not all that far from Brown, riding his personal Ocelot and followed by a representative crew from the staff, Carrera paralleled the westernmost of the two highways, keeping low in the valleys and draws between the mostly scoured of life hills.

Brown had five radios in his command vehicle; Carrera had nine, all squawking more or less continuously. It was something one learned, over time, the ability to have all that chatter going on and still be able to key on what was important: "India Three Five . . . Past Phase Line One . . . Romeo Two Seven . . . break . . . Resistance continuing, intermediate objective two . . . request . . . never mind, lower reports they've broken in and the enemy are folding . . . Duck, this is Hussar Six, weapons free, weapons free . . . all ours are down . . ."

That last caused Carrera to duck down into the passenger compartment and break into the conversation. "Define 'down.'"

"Just refueling, *Duque*," answered Miguel Lanza. "So

to start displacing forward along the highways as quickly as possible. Tell them to be prepared for a humanitarian crisis like they've never seen. Second, have the MPs call for volunteers from the Tauran POW collection at Herrera International for volunteer stretcher bearers and for any medical personnel, generally. Have the MPs explain the situation and get the Taurans' parole. The MPs can also draw from any assets they can pin down for trucks. Thirdly, get the news and diplomatic people—yes, I know diplomacy isn't your job. So?—to start transmitting to the Taurans that we are going to be evacuating their prisoners, in fairly ridiculous numbers, a couple of hundred meters to either side of the highways. Bombing and loss to their own is on them. Carrera, out."

Switching the mike to pure intercom, he told Soult, "Jamey, pull us right up in front of that column and turn as if to bar the way."

"Roger."

The column recoiled as Soult pulled a flashy turn directly in front of it. Without being told, one way or the other, he dropped the ramp so Carrera could exit like a gentleman in front of these foreigners. This Carrera did, pulling off and tossing his helmet on the side bench, then running his hand through sweaty hair.

"Does anyone speak English or Spanish?" he asked aloud. "German, maybe?"

"We are Sachsens, yes?" replied one of the lead men in the prisoner column, a tall and slender sort, with blue eyes and brown hair. He had an accent though he spoke in English. "Well, mostly Sachsens. There are a couple of hundred each Dacians and Gauls."

"Who's senior?" Carrera asked.

"Among the healthy?" asked Sachsen, "I am. *Oberst* Kausch, sir."

"Very good, Kausch. I'll give the chief of your guards instructions in Spanish. Here's what I want. Have your medical people triage those who will probably die if they move much further. They stay here. Leave with them enough medical and non-medical personnel to keep as many of them alive as possible. You can leave your less . . . what's that term? The people you expect to . . . oh, that's it . . . leave your less expectant non-walking wounded here, too. The rest move forward to Herrera Airport."

Kausch nodded his understanding but then added, "Sir, we haven't had any . . ."

"Food and water since the bombardment started? I'm sure. I'll issue the orders." He thought on that briefly, then asked, "Will there be a problem if the rations include a decent increment of high-proof rum?"

Kausch, very briefly, looked as if he could cry. "God, no, sir. I could use a drink. We all could."

"Standard legionary, then," Carrera said. "It might be a little off to you but it's all wholesome fuel. And booze. Oh, and cigarettes."

"Cigarettes? *Cigarettes*? Dear God, there's an army that still understands that soldiers are only human and so still issues *cigarettes*?"

"Well," Carrera replied, "less than a pack per man per day. Most of my soldiers don't smoke, actually."

The Sachsen asked, "*Your* soldiers, sir?"

"Oh," Carrera asked, shamefacedly, "didn't I introduce myself? I'm Carrera."

"Ah," Kausch said. "Then, sir, there's something, someone, you ought to see, a little further back in the column."

Janier, lying on a stretcher on the ground, was a ghastly pale. The Gaul was obviously in tremendous pain, so much so he could barely speak and with his eyelids scrunched together.

"Can't you give him something?" Carrera asked Kausch.

"He refused and said to give it, if we had it, to the men."

Janier forced his eyes open. "Is that you, Patricio? I keep seeing and hearing things that are not there."

Carrera took one knee by the stretcher. "It's me, Bertrand. To prove it, didn't that Scot captain you had for an aide de camp have a disconcertingly fine rack?"

The tiniest trace of a smile came to the Gaul's lips. "She did, didn't she?" The Gaul was interrupted by a vicious bout of coughing, which can't have done any good to his roughly set broken legs. "I think maybe a little pneumonia coming on. Tell me, Patricio, how bad is it?"

"Well, your legs look . . ."

"No, not me! My army. How fares my army?"

"Crushed," Carrera said. "There's no other word. I'd tell you I'm sorry but, of course, I am really not. The legions are advancing essentially as quickly as the terrain allows. You've been almost split in two at the town of Magdalena. Linkup between my Fourth Corps and First Corps will happen within a few hours. The Anglians, what there is of them, are falling back to the east through the jungle, and away from Fort Tecumseh. We are nipping around the edges of Puerto Lindo. Your infantry formations—no shame to them, mine would not have withstood that barrage any better—are surrendering en masse. And a lot of them are running in sheer panic, thinking they've taken a massive dose of radiation from nuclear weapons."

"Not nuclear?" Janier asked.

"No, just big FAEs. Really big."

"So, it really is over then?" Janier asked. "Your word of honor?"

"It's over, here. I still have to round up the Anglians and drive the Zhong into the sea, but there isn't much left of the Tauran Expeditionary Force."

"Can you get me to a radio or maybe a radio to me?"

"Yes, surely, but why?"

"I wish to order my forces to surrender."

Northeast of Puerto Lindo

The artillery fire had dwindled to almost nothing. This did not, however, mean there was any shortage of ear-splitting booms. Nearby, for one thing, Sancho Panzer was privileged to see something he wasn't sure had ever happened before.

At least on this planet.

To his front, out in the Shimmering Sea, a Tauran destroyer rode low in the water, barely making headway, and firing with guns not entirely suitable to the purpose.

That purpose should have been to fight off the tanks

now forming on the high ground above the beach and the beach itself, to smash any Tauran attempt at relief of the town or evacuation of its defenders.

To his right, a Jaguar fired its one-twenty-five. The flash on the ship came about a second later and seemed to be right at the water line. That meant three things. One was that, as the ship settled down further, the ingress would be another leak. It also meant that there was very likely a new jagged tear or two on the other side, now gushing water, where a projectile, or its parts, having gone unstable, ripped the hull from the inside out. The third matter was that, in between those two events, any Tauran crewman unfortunate enough to be caught was going to be something between hurt and homogenized, if not even pasteurized.

How do they even control flooding when they've got that many rips through the hull? Brown wondered.

Two more hits and then another three and the destroyer simply turned over. In his field glasses, Brown saw very few heads pop to the surface after that.

Down below, Sancho Panzer's communications sergeant began elbowing him frantically on the thigh. "What is it, Escovar?"

"Sir! Sir! General call from headquarters, all bands, both clear and encrypted! The Taurans have surrendered! We've won, sir, we've won! All our forces are ordered to defend themselves if attacked, but otherwise to cease offensive action and to take charge of the Taurans and render them all reasonable aid in caring for their wounded. Jesus, fuck, sir, we *won*!"

EPILOGUE

I

World League, First Landing, Federated States of Columbia

Lourdes Carrera, five-eight, slender, and all-around sexy, with eyes the size of moons, was dressed for business. She wore only a minimum of jewelry, and bore what appeared to be—but wasn't—about five minutes' worth of hair and makeup. Thus, she strode to the rostrum of the League Assembly. Her heels clicked like a tocsin of despair and doom. Once there, she smiled wickedly at the bank of shocked and distressed Tauran diplomats.

Diplomacy, in the nicer sense, was not actually one of Lourdes's personal strengths.

She spoke directly to them. "Point the first: Now that the armies, navies, and air forces that you sent against us are no longer *necessary* obstacles to our peaceful reconciliation, we may perhaps begin anew our peace negotiations. I tell you with all sincerity that you had best hurry, for a calamity is about to befall you all, a calamity that you either willfully blinded yourself to or lied to your own people about. We did not create this calamity, but we have done our best, as you have been doing your worst, to enhance it. You will admit, at this point, I am sure, that we have proven most adept at creating and enhancing calamities for you. You're going to want to do your best, this time, in mitigating this one.

"By the way, you fish-faced enemies of the people; time is running out for your entire rotten and corrupt class. Soon, very soon, you shall hear the people sing."

At that she went silent while the other representatives of Colombia del Norte and Colombia Central stood as one and sang a somewhat out of key rendition of, "Fuck the Tauran Union." They'd had their place in the victory, too, and knew it. It was not impossible that those delegations had been drinking.

When the singing was over, and the laughing Latins sat back down, Lourdes again turned her gaze back to the assembly, and then to the official observer from United Earth. "And, Point the second: As for you swine, after having seen your long and filthy list of depredations against us, the Senate of Balboa, a legal quorum having met, directs me to inform you that a state of war shall exist between the Timocratic Republic of Balboa and United Earth as of this morning, at eleven hundred hours, our time.

"You Earthpig filth are going to lose just as stinking as the Taurans, too. My husband comes for you. My son comes for you. Our people come for you. In fire and lightning, they come for you. With blood in their eyes, they come for you. In tempest and thunder, they come for you. Like vengeful gods and avenging angels, they come for you.

"Tremble for your fate; you cannot avoid it."

In silence, unable even to comprehend what she had just declared, so far from sanity did it seem to them, virtually the entire non-Spanish speaking assembly of the World League of Terra Nova sat shocked and stunned. The doom she promised to Old Earth, and the doom just visited by her country on the Tauran Union, was, they sensed, their doom as well.

II

National Assembly Aserri, Santa Josefina

Most of the assembly wore battle dress now, though a few score, longtime friends of the revolution, wore their usual business attire. Other members of the assembly were either in flight with the rump of Marciano's brigade, or at large, or in prison, or joining the rapidly growing piles of rapidly cooling bodies in a fly-swarming ditch by that prison.

The soldiers had taken over the legislature, as seemed only fit, having won it by force of arms. They would, they had resolved, relinquish power as soon as fighters could be demobilized, qualified citizen rolls organized, and elections run.

Lagazpi was nowhere to be seen. In fact, he was having a drink with his staff in a nearby bar.

The country's interim president, Legate Salas, read off

the proposal under consideration: "Be it resolved then, that a state of war shall exist between the newly formed Timocratic Republic of Santa Josefina and both the Tauran Union and the Empire of the Zhong. All in favor?"

The massive hall shook with a resounding "Aye."

"Opposed?"

There was not a single nay even whispered.

"So is it resolved. Ladies and gentleman, we are at war. Our next item of business: Be it resolved that Santa Josefina shall extend to our Balboan brothers an offer of full alliance, under their command. In favor?"

"AYE!"

III

BdL Dos Lindas, Puerto Bruselas

Across the bay, the heavy cruiser *Tadeo Kurita* poured steam from her stacks as her nuclear power plant, long unstrained, suddenly was prodded into full life. Other, lesser ships, non-nuclear, poured forth clouds of thick white smoke. Like the Kurita, the *dos Lindas* gave off steam. She also gave off the sounds of a warship readying for action.

On the carrier's deck, both fore and aft, elevators rose and fell, lifting and depositing above the ship's complement of strike aircraft.

"Slow they may be," Fosa said, "but in the kingdom of the blind the one-eyed shall be king."

From behind, the ship's senior non-com, Sergeant

Major Ramirez, asked, "Son of a bitch planned this all along, didn't he, Skipper?"

"He did, Sergeant Major," Fosa answered, without turning. "He said this fleet must remain intact and that the only way of making it so was to intern it. He also said the internment would end in good time. I had, I confess, my doubts."

"When's the internment officially over?" Ramirez asked.

"It was over the second the Santa Josefinans declared war on our enemies."

"Son of a bitch."

"Yeah, but he's our son of a bitch."

IV

Barco de La Legion ALTA
(*Armada Legionario Transporte de Assalto*),
Mar Furioso

The speakers on the bridge sounded off with, "Terra Nova, Terra Nova, this is Radio Balboa calling to our friends around the world. We have the following notifications and messages: Austin's wheelchair is very cheap. I repeat, Austin's wheelchair is very cheap. Gary the welcher has only middling intelligence. I say again, Gary the welcher has only middling intelligence. Lourdes has a magnificent ass. Need I say again? Lourdes has a magnificent ass. And now a riddle: What is gray, has long ears, and eats grass? I ask again . . ."

"She's my mother," Ham said. "I really never noticed, though I think my dad would agree."

"She's got more than a shapely butt, Ham," Terry Johnson said. He passed over to the boy a message received earlier that morning.

The boy read it, smiled, and said, "You know, for all her sweet exterior and her big, soulful eyes, my mom is really a cast-iron bitch."

"Yeah, but she's your dad's bitch."

Johnson told the captain of the ship, "Launch the Condors. Unmask air defense. Unmask long range missiles. Prepare to bring the helicopters on deck. Prepare the hovercraft for launch. Order the landing force to the assembly decks. Make heading and full speed for our launch and assault position."

"Aye, Legate."

V

Oppenheim, Sachsen

Khalid watched as, from the Oppenheimer Mosque, in groups of ten, or twenty, or fifty, or one hundred, young men quasi-uniformed but fully armed poured forth into the streets and began the hunt for their quarry. For the most part, this involved the police and such reserve armories as were to be found in the city. They also had lists, prepared by their imam, of those he considered the most depraved of Sachsen citizens in the town. This included large numbers of atheists, Tsarist-Marxists, and

Kosmos, to the extent those categories differed. From the point of view of the iman and his minions, their fighters would merely be purging this world of the very people condemned in Allah's Own Voice, in the Quran. From the point of view of Khalid, Fernandez, and Carrera, on the other hand, they would be purging those most responsible for the existence of the Tauran Union, as well as those most likely to object to the Union's abject surrender to Balboan demands.

Sometimes, thought Khalid, *even devout enemies can find common ground.*

VI

Isla Real, Balboa

I am going to hang that treasonous bitch by her heels, thought former High Admiral Robinson, in contemplation of his revenge on Marguerite Wallenstein. He'd had years, many years and hard ones, to perfect his revenge. *Then I am going to slit her belly open, and pull her guts out with my own hands. I'll burn them before her eyes. Then we'll shoot her up with antibiotics so infection doesn't kill her before I am ready to let her go.*

His gaze shifted so that he could look upon the two crosses set up outside his holding cell and the Marchioness of Amnesty's. His smile was positively beatific as he thought. *Then it will be the nails, but on a low gravity part of the ship . . . I'll move my own quarters down there so I can hear her scream for days or maybe even weeks. I wonder how long someone could last on the cross on the hangar deck. Wouldn't that be nice?*

Robinson's reveries were interrupted when his cell door opened, followed by the entrance of his chief keeper, his physical training instructor, and the tailor.

"Time to get dressed, High Admiral," said the former. "We have places to go and people to kill."

GLOSSARY

AdC: Aide de Camp, an assistant to a senior officer.

Adourgnac: A Gallic Brandy, alleged to have considerable medicinal value, produced from ten different kinds of grapes, of which the four principal ones are Maurice Baco, Cubzadais, Canut, and Trebbiano. There is an illegal digestif produced from the brandy that includes a highly dilute extract from the fruit of the Tranzitree, qv.

Ala: Plural: Alae. Latin: Wing, as in wing of cavalry. Air Wing in the legion. Similar to Tercio, qv.

ALTA, MV: A ship, owned by the Legions. The title is an acronym for "Armada Legionario, Transporte de Assalto."

Amid: Arabic: brigadier general.

Antania: Plural: Antaniae, septic-mouthed
                          winged reptilians, possibly genengi-
                          neered by the Noahs, AKA Moonbats.

ARE-12P: A Gallic Infantry Fighting Vehicle

Artem-Mikhail-
23-465 Aurochs: An obsolescent jet fighter, though
                          much updated.

Artem-Mikhail 82:   Aka "Mosaic D," an obsolete jet
                          fighter, product improved in Balboan
                          hands to be merely obsolescent.

ASW: Anti-Submarine Warfare.

BdL: Barco de la legion, ship of the legion.

Bellona: Moon of Terra Nova.

Bolshiberry: A fruit-bearing vine, believed to have
                          been genengineered by the Noahs.
                          The fruit is intensely poisonous to
                          intelligent life.

Caltrop: A four-pointed jack with sharp,
                          barbed ends. Thirty-eight per meter
                          of front give defensive capability
                          roughly equivalent to triple standard
                          concertina.

Caltrop Projector: A drum filled with caltrops, a linear shaped charge, and low explosive booster, to scatter caltrops over a wide area on command.

Cazador: Spanish: Hunter. Similar to Chasseur, Jaeger and Ranger. Light Infantry, especially selected and trained. Also a combat leader selection course within the *Legion del Cid*.

Chorley: A grain of Terra Nova, apparently not native to Old Earth.

Classis: Latin: Fleet or Naval Squadron.

Cohort: Battalion, though in the legion these are large battalions.

Conex: Metal shipping container, generally 8' × 8' × 20' or 40'.

Consensus: When capitalized, the governing council of Old Earth, formerly the United Nations Security Council.

Corona Civilis: Latin: Civic Crown. One of approximately thirty-seven awards available in the legion for specific and noteworthy events. The Civic Crown is given for saving the life of a soldier on the battlefield at risk of one's own.

Cricket: A very short take-off and landing aircraft used, by the legion, for some purposes, in place of more expensive helicopters.

Diana: A small magnet or flat metal plate intended to hide partially metal anti-personnel landmines by making everything give back the signature of a metal anti-personnel landmine.

Dustoff: Medical evacuation, typically by air.

Eris: Moon of Terra Nova.

Escopeta: Spanish: Shotgun.

Estado Mayor: Spanish: General Staff and, by extension, the building which houses it.

F-26:   The legion's standard assault rifle, in 6.5mm.

FMB: Five-Minute Bomb.

FMB-I: Five-Minute Bomb-Incendiary.

FMTIB: Five-Minute Thermobaric and Incendiary Bomb.

FSD: Federated States Drachma. Unit of money equivalent in value to 4.2 grams of silver.

GPR: Ground Penetrating Radar.

Hecate: Moon of Terra Nova.

Hieros: Shrine or temple.

Huánuco: A plant of Terra Nova from which an alkaloid substance is refined.

I: Roman number one. Chief Operations Officer, his office, and his staff section.

Ia: Operations officer dealing mostly with fire and maneuver, his office and his section, S- or G-3.

Ib: Logistics officer, his office and his section, S- or G-4.

Ic: Intelligence officer, his office and his section, S- or G-2.

II: Adjutant, Personnel officer, his office and his section, S- or G-1.

IM-71:   A medium lift cargo and troop carrying helicopter.

Ikhwan: Arabic: Brotherhood.

Jaguar: Volgan-built tank in legionary service.

Jaguar II: Improved Jaguar.

Jizyah: Special tax levied against non-Moslems living in Moslem lands.

Karez: Underground aqueduct system.

Keffiyeh: Folded cloth Arab headdress.

Klick: Kilometer. Note: Democracy ends where the metric system begins.

Kosmo: Cosmopolitan Progressive. Similar to Tranzi on Old Earth.

Liwa: Arabic: Major General.

Lorica: Lightweight silk and liquid metal torso armor used by the legion.

LOTS: Logistics Over The Shore, which is to say without port facilities.

LZ: Landing Zone, a place where helicopters drop off troops and equipment.

Maniple: Company.

Makkah al Jedidah: Arabic: New Mecca.

Mañana sera major: Spanish: Balboan politico-military song "Tomorrow will be better."

MB: Money Bomb.

MRL: Multiple Rocket Launcher.

Mujahadin: Arabic: Holy Warriors (singular: mujahad).

Mukhabarat: Arabic: Secret Police.

Mullah: Holy man, sometimes holy, sometimes not.

Na'ib 'Dabit: Arabic: sergeant major.

Naik: Corporal.

Naquib: Arabic: Captain.

NGO: NonGovernmental Organization.

Noahs: Aliens that seeded Terra Nova with life, some from Old Earth, some possibly from other planets, some possibly genetically engineered, in the dim mists of prehistory. No definitive trace of them has ever been found.

Ocelot: Volgan-built light armored vehicle mounting a 100mm gun and capable of carrying a squad of infantry in the back.

Meg: Coastal Defense Submarine employed by the legion, also the shark, Carcharodon Megalodon, from which the submarine class draws its name.

M-26: A heavy-barreled version of the F-26, serving as the Legion's standard light machine gun.

PMC: Precious Metal Certificate. High denomination legionary investment vehicle.

Progressivine: A fruit-bearing vine found on Terra Nova. Believed to have been genengineered by the Noahs. The fruit is intensely poisonous to intelligent life.

Puma: A much improved Balboan tank, built in Volga and modified in Zion and Balboa.

Push: As in "tactical push." Radio frequency or frequency hopping sequence, so-called from the action of pushing the button that activates the transmitter.

PZ: Pickup Zone. A place where helicopters pick up troops, equipment, and supplies to move them somewhere else.

RGL: Rocket Grenade Launcher.

Roland: A Gallic Main Battle Tank, or MBT.

RTO:　　　　Radio-Telephone Operator.

Satan Triumphant:　　A hot pepper of Terra Nova, generally unfit for human consumption, though sometimes used in food preservation and refinable into a blister agent for chemical warfare.

Sayyidi:　　Arabic form of respectful address, "Sir."

SCIB:　　Shaped Charge Incendiary Bomb.

Sergeyevich-83:　Or Serg-83, a Volgan-designed, Zhong-built naval fighter-bomber, capable of vertical take-off and landing, and of carrying an ordnance load of about two tons.

SHEBSA:　*Servicio Helicoptores Balboenses, S.A. Balboan Helicopter Service, part of the hidden reserve.*

Sochaux S4:　A Gallic four wheel drive light truck.

SPATHA:　Self-Propelled Anti-Tank Heavy Armor. A legionary tank destroyer, under development.

SPLAD:　Self-Propelled Laser Air Defense. A developed legionary antiaircraft system.

Subadar: In ordinary use a major or tribune III equivalent.

Surah: A chapter in the Koran, of which there are 114.

Tercio: Spanish: Regiment.

Tranzitree: A fruit-bearing tree, believed to have been genengineered by the Noahs. The fruit is intensely poisonous to intelligent life.

Trixie: A species of archaeopteryx brought to Terra Nova by the Noahs.

TUSF-B: Tauran Union Security Force-Balboa.

UEPF: United Earth Peace Fleet, the military arm of the Consensus in space.

Volcano: A very large thermobaric bomb, set off primarily by a seismic fuse.

Yakamov: A type of helicopter produced in Volga. It has no tail rotor.

LEGIONARY RANK EQUIVALENTS

Dux, Duque: Indefinite rank, depending on position it can indicate anything from a major general to a field marshall. Duque usually indicates the senior commander on the field.

Legate III: Brigadier general or major general. Per the contract between the *Legion del Cid* and the Federated States of Columbia, a Legate III, when his unit is in service to the Federated States, is entitled to the standing and courtesies of a lieutenant general. Typically commands a deployed legion, when a separate legion is deployed, the air *ala* or the naval *classis*, or serves as an executive for a deployed corps.

Legate II: Colonel, typically commands a tercio in the rear or serves on staff if deployed.

Legate I: Lieutenant colonel, typically commands a cohort or serves on staff.

Tribune III: Major, serves on staff or sometimes, if permitted to continue in command, commands a maniple.

Tribune II: Captain, typically commands a maniple.

Tribune I: First Lieutenant, typically serves as second in command of a maniple, commands a specialty platoon within the cohort's combat support maniple, or serves on staff.

Signifer: Second lieutenant or ensign, leads a platoon. Signifer is a temporary rank, and signifers are not considered part of the officer corps of the legions except as a matter of courtesy.

Sergeant Major: Sergeant major, with no necessary indication of level.

First Centurion: Senior noncommissioned officer of a maniple.

Senior Centurion: Master sergeant, but almost always the senior man within a platoon.

**Centurion,
J.G.:**   Sergeant   First   Class,   sometimes
                   commands a platoon but is usually the
                   second in command.

Optio: Staff sergeant, typically the second in
                   command of a platoon.

Sergeant: Typically leads a squad.

Corporal: Typically leads a team or crew or serves as
                   second in command of a squad.

Legionario,
or **Legionary**,
or **Legionnaire:**   Private through specialist.

★★★

Note that, in addition, under legion regulations adopted
in the Anno Condita 471, a soldier may elect to take what
is called "Triarius Status." This locks the soldier into
whatever rank he may be, but allows pay raises for
longevity to continue. It is one way the legion has used to
flatten the rank pyramid in the interests of reducing
careerism. Thus, one may sometimes hear or read of a
"Triarius Tribune III," typically a major-equivalent who
has decided, with legion accord, that his highest and best
use is in a particular staff slot or commanding a particular
maniple. Given that the legion—with fewer than three
percent officers, including signifers—has the smallest
officer corps of any significant military formation on Terra

Nova, and a very flat promotion pyramid, the Triarius system seems, perhaps, overkill. Since adoption, regulations permit but do not require Triarius status legionaries to be promoted one rank upon retirement.

RING OF FIRE SERIES
(with Eric Flint)

1635: The Papal Stakes
978-1-4516-3920-9 • $7.99

Up to their necks in papal assassins, power politics, murder, and mayhem, the uptimers need help and they need it quickly.

1636: Commander Cantrell in the West Indies
978-1-4767-8060-3 • $8.99

Oil. The Americas have it. The United States of Europe needs it. Enter Lieutenant-Commander Eddie Cantrell.

1636: The Vatican Sanction
978-1-4814-8386-5 • $7.99

Pope Urban has fled the Vatican and the traitor, Borja. But assassins have followed him to France—and not only assassins! The Pope and his allies have fled right into the clutches of the vile Pedro Dolor.

STARFIRE SERIES
(with Steve White)

Extremis
978-1-4516-3814-1 • $7.99

They have traveled for centuries, slower than light, and now they have arrived at the planet they intend to make their new home: Earth. The fact that humanity is already living there is only a minor inconvenience.

Imperative
978-1-4814-8243-1 • $7.99

A resurrected star navy hero attempts to keep a fragile interstellar alliance together while battling and implacable alien adversary.

Oblivion
978-1-4814-8401-5 • $7.99

It's time to take a stand! For Earth! For Humanity! For the Pan-Sentient Union!

When Diplomacy Fails (PB) 978-1-4516-3911-7 • $7.99
High-tech mercenaries Ripple Creek Security must protect
an obnoxious world government minister from the enemies
who want her dead—and killed in the worst possible way.

Angeleyes (PB) 978-1-4814-8295-0 • $7.99
Angie Kaneshiro never planned to be a spy; she was free
and that's the way she liked it. Then the war with Earth
started. . . .

Forged in Blood (HC) 978-1-4814-8270-7 • $25.00
Those who wield the sword show uncommon courage and
a warrior's spirit; these are their tales. Stories by Tom
Kratman, Kacey Ezell, Larry Correia, and more.

OTHER NOVELS BY WILLIAMSON

A Long Time Until Now
(PB) 978-1-4767-8172-3 • $7.99
Ten U.S. soldiers find themselves in Paleolithic Asia and
they are not the only time-travelers there. Groups from
throughout history have been gathered—but by whom and
to what purpose?

Tour of Duty (PB) 978-1-4767-8172-3 • $7.99
It's a tough universe out there. This hard-hitting collection of
Williamson's best fiction also offers a generous helping of
nonfiction truth-telling.

Tide of Battle (TPB) 978-1-4814-8336-0 • $16.00
(PB) 978-1-4814-8419-0 • $7.99
This collection of stories, essays, and provocations is sure
to entertain, thrill—and scandalize!